Summary Justice

S. J. Michaels has worked for the Inland Revenue, has run her own catering business, and at present is an Appeals and Public Relations Officer in the Voluntary Sector.

She lives in Belfast with her husband and three daughters.

Summary Justice is her first novel.

S. J. Michaels

SUMMARY JUSTICE

Pan Books
London, Sydney and Auckland

First published in 1988 by Frederick Muller,
an imprint of Century Hutchinson Ltd
This edition published 1989 by Pan Books Ltd,
Cavaye Place, London SW10 9PG
9 8 7 6 5 4 3 2 1
© S. J. Michaels 1988
ISBN 0 330 30570 0
Printed and bound in Great Britain by
Richard Clay Ltd, Bungay, Suffolk

To Ettie Brown

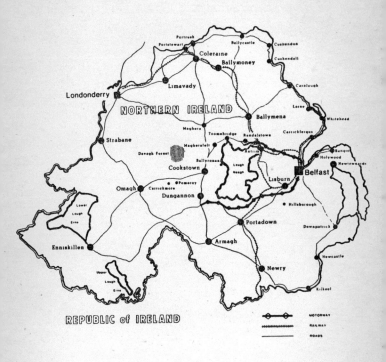

Introduction

Sometimes things happen in Northern Ireland which never make the headlines; in fact, they may never make the news at all.

This may be one such story. It is the story of a man who disappeared; his body was never found. Some said he was driven by the tragic circumstances which had engulfed him, others that the complete affair had far more sinister undertones. Whatever the explanation, it is up to you, the reader, to decide.

This book is an explanation as to what may have happened. All the characters have fictitious names to help protect many of those involved, but one fact does remain. For a short time during 1982, the joint Republican terror offensive in the North came to a standstill; perhaps this is why.

Policemen the world over have a saying for handing out their own punishment in the streets. It has a legal meaning which should be completely disregarded. They call it simply SUMMARY JUSTICE.

1980 – St James's area, Falls Road, Belfast

In the squalid little kitchen, two young boys sat nervously on simple wood chairs tucked tightly beside the old gas cooker. A third, much older youth stood at the locked outside door which led to the enclosed backyard. He lolled in the opening which had once held a door, but now gave open access into the cramped living room. He smirked at the two boys and, as if mesmerised by his constant stare, they watched his every movement, especially when he menacingly patted the large bulge in the waistband of his jeans. Concealed by his cheap green parka jacket lay the Colt .45 revolver, already warm against his body.

There was a rap on the yard door, and the older youth immediately pulled back the single bolt. Two men entered, both in their twenties. The taller, with black curly hair, remained silent as the other – the elder of the two – moved into the centre of the kitchen directly facing the two boys. He was Michael Reilly, insignificant in appearance, only five feet two; with his light, unkempt hair he had received the nickname 'Mousey' well before doing 'time' in St Patrick's Training School for the wayward youths of West Belfast. But that nickname was far from the thoughts of the boys as they stared back at him with the reverence of children at first communion when facing the priest. 'Mousey' had come a long way in his twenty-nine years. A wife- and child-beater to his young family of six, he had risen steadily in the ranks of the Provisionals, having quelled the unrest in the rank and file after the split which produced the INLA. He liked arranging things, as many young men and boys had found out to their detriment, but most of all he enjoyed making people squirm. Now he looked at the elder of the two boys: Francis Moran, 'Francy' to his mates and widowed mother. Seventeen years old, he came from a similar Turf Lodge background to Reilly. The only difference between them was that, on leaving St Pat's, he continued stealing cars instead of killing and maiming the so-called enemies of nationalism. A lesser evil perhaps in most minds, but not to the disciplinary arm of the Provos.

'You called Moran?' Reilly snapped.

'Yeah,' replied the boy in a half whisper.

Mousey looked over at the young lad. 'And you, you're Tommy Murray?'

The fourteen-year-old nodded, his mouth too dry to reply. He had enjoyed the exhilaration of helping Francy nick the cars, but now that was all past. How was he to know that in taking the Ford Fiesta for that last 'joy-ride', as the press put it, they had taken just one car too many, especially as it was owned by Mousey himself? How was he to know? He was from the Lower Falls, not Turf Lodge, and Francy was so high on glue he couldn't drive the frigging thing. It wasn't Tommy's fault he had crashed his first 'ride' into the traffic island at Kennedy Way. God, they were both lucky to have escaped, but now it seemed unfortunate they had even lived.

'It's been decided by the court that youse two are to be capped for yer anti-social behaviour,' said Mousey. He normally didn't say as much to his intended victims, but these two youngsters were going nowhere and could give him no bother. He glared at Francy. 'You, Moran . . . for yer anti-social behaviour in leadin' this boy here astray' – he pointed towards Tommy – 'you're ta be shot in both kneecaps.'

Francy tried to get up. It was a futile attempt to run,

and the left hook from Mousey landed squarely on his face, sending him reeling into the stacked pots and dirty dishes on the side table. He collapsed on the grubby lino, unable to move. Tommy was petrified but couldn't speak. He closed his eyes tight shut.

'Now you, young Murray . . .'

Tommy looked up at Mousey, opening his eyes in a squint and wiping the tears away.

'The court's been lenient with ya. You're to be capped in one leg only.' Mousey then turned, pushing past the black-haired young man and out into the yard. Almost immediately two more youths came in and grabbed Francy. The youth with the green jacket reached for Tommy and bundled him out of the kitchen into the dark, rainy night. The yard led into an alleyway where they both were made to lie face-down on the wet concrete, each boy held in position by a heavy 'Doc Martin' boot on each shoulder-blade. The third youth in the green jacket stood behind them, Colt .45 in hand. He checked the 'scouts' positioned at each end of the high-walled alley and both gave a 'thumbs-up' signal on recognition of his whistle. 'All right, give it ta me.' He held out his right hand to the youth in the green jacket.

'Mousey says I'm doin' it,' growled the youth.

'I don't give a fuck about Mousey – or you for that matter! Give me the gun.' The black-haired man moved forward and this time he spoke quietly, almost in a whisper: 'You've two seconds to give me the gun or I'll break both yer arms after I tear yer balls off . . .' The youth still hesitated, then he heard the click of a switch-blade and felt the sharp jag of the point as it gently prodded into his jeans, just two inches below his genitals. 'Just give me the gun, son . . .' He let the words penetrate further than the knife. 'Yer day'll come, I promise ya . . . now give us it here.'

Slowly, the youth handed over the .45, barrel first.

'Thanks, I'll not forget this.' The man turned quickly to the two youths holding the boys. 'Hold them firm, lads.' He placed his left foot on Francy's left leg, just above the ankle. Before the boy could react, an explosion echoed around the enclosed space. He quickly replaced his foot on Francy's right ankle and repeated the performance. The shock had nullified Francy's nervous system and he felt no pain. But after a few seconds he began to scream, more with tension and fear, ignoring his broken and swollen nose. The two big bullets had shattered Francy's kneecaps and the concrete did nothing to cushion the impact. He was still screaming as the man trod firmly on Tommy's left ankle. Tommy was unaware of it, but he too was now screaming and crying and the youth in the green jacket had to help hold him still. The black-haired man took careful aim at the knee and then raised his aim high. The bullet entered Tommy's leg, breaking the femur; the two youths were unaware of the deliberate mis-aim as they continued to hold the struggling boy. 'Let's get the hell out of here!' snapped the man. Immediately the youths ran off, the one in the green jacket pausing to take back the gun. The black-haired man stooped over Tommy. 'An ambulance is already on the way . . . just lie still and you'll be OK.'

With five minutes the ambulance was there. By then both boys were being comforted by nosy neighbours who had ventured into the alley. The casualty doctor later told Tommy he had been lucky; with a clean break in the bone he would be playing football for Celtic within six months, unlike his friend who would remain a cripple for the rest of his days – according to the orthopaedic surgeons, even plastic kneecaps had their limits.

The man with the black hair walked slowly across the

car park of the Greenan Lodge Hotel and stopped at the open window of the red Cortina car.

'Hello, Seamus.' The little middle-aged man with the bald crown smiled.

Seamus Doyle nodded in return as he leant against the side of the car.

'I've been on the phone. Tommy's been taken to the Royal. How did it go?'

'He'll walk all right, even run in another while; he was lucky this time, damned lucky.'

'Here's the money, Seamus, just as I said.' He proffered the brown envelope through the window.

Doyle stared at it for a few seconds and looked back at the man's face. 'Keep it, Desi, the boy'll need a few things to occupy him in hospital. Just make sure he doesn't do it again, it mightn't be as easy the next time.'

'No, I insist. I offered you the two hundred quid to get him off light, fair's fair.'

'You offered, but if you remember I never accepted . . . Now you might have a lot of pull in the Republican movement, Mr Murray, but none with me . . . Yes, I'll want something in return some day, but not yer money . . . Just remember that!'

Before he could respond, Doyle was walking away from the car. Desmond Murray sat for some time in the Cortina thinking about what the young man had said. He knew him as Seamus Doyle from Kenard Avenue, Andersonstown. He was an intelligent one; he had made it through the ghetto atmosphere to the Christian Brothers Grammar School and then on to Queen's University in Belfast, where he had got a first-class honours degree in psychology, whatever that meant. But by that time Seamus had already qualified as an impressive activist in the Provisional IRA, not only targeting potential victims at the University but helping organise the jobs, on more than one occasion

5

taking the major role. Seamus Doyle was now well-known in the higher echelons of the Provisionals as the man to get things done and intellectual to boot – whatever intellect was worth, puzzled Murray. Yes this was a young man to be reckoned with and Murray knew that some day he might be required to pay, and on that day he would. As he drove out of the car park his thoughts turned to his brother and sister-in-law at the Royal Victoria Hospital, crying over their little boy as he went through emergency surgery. Little did they know that Desmond Murray had sanctioned Mousey Reilly's action. He hoped his guilt wouldn't show when he went into that hospital waiting-room.

2

Tuesday 18 May 1982 – Andersonstown, Belfast

The red Cortina pulled up at the 'Busy Bee' shopping complex off the Andersonstown Road; it was typical of the West Belfast area, dilapidated and dotted with nationalist slogans. It was raining as the little bald-headed fat man hurriedly parked the car next to the overpacked builder's skip beside the small bookshop. From the outside one could easily have been forgiven for failing to recognise its existence behind the wire grille permanently fixed into position across the shop frontage. He ran to the doorway, head hunched into his chest against the downpour.

'Good morning, girls!' smiled Murray. 'Is he in?'

'Hi ya, Desi!' The smaller girl beamed. 'The Da's in the back room . . . drinkin' his tay as usual!'

Murray made no reply, but waved his left arm as he passed by the crammed bookshelves and tables to the small back-room store. He heard the noise of a radio from within and rattled the opaque glass panel as he went through the door.

'Well, Paddy, get the brew up!' The words were out before he realised that Patrick Hagan, Brigade Commander of the Provisional IRA in Belfast, was not alone; he immediately recognised the young man in the corner of the dimly lit room. Seamus Doyle had come a long way since 1980. Murray had not seen him since that awful night almost two years before and Doyle had changed since then. He had cultivated a full beard, neatly trimmed, which made him look much older especially with the shorter hairstyle. Murray was suddenly wary of his debt to the young man and his growing reputation, or what he had heard of it. The IRA Council had sent him south in the winter of 1980, where he had helped produce Sinn Fein's latest publication, *Iris*, in early 1981. He had put his mark on the magazine, getting a lengthy interview with Sinn Fein's president, Ruairi O'Bradaigh. Some said he wrote the answers for O'Bradaigh himself, since the man hadn't the ability to formulate his own opinions.

Although he could have stayed in Dublin in a healthier climate, Doyle had chosen to return to the streets of Belfast, and had even gone to England on one operation that Murray knew about – and he knew a hell of a lot. After all, hadn't he got young Doyle his Dublin job in the first place! He certainly had no love for Seamus Doyle, but a debt was a debt, even if the young man was unaware of his benefactor. Murray nodded at Doyle in embarrassed acknowledgement of his presence.

'Come on in, Desi, plant yer seat here!' Paddy smiled, patting an orange box behind the small table in the centre of the room. Tea was poured from a steaming pot on the portable Beldray on the corner shelf. Murray took the chipped mug and quickly swallowed the first mouthful of the sweet, stewed liquid. The radio continued to broadcast the 11.30 a.m. special bulletin on the Falklands, and Paddy leaned across and switched it off. 'Well, Desi, you've something to tell us, ya say?'

Murray's eyes flashed momentarily at Doyle and this did not go unnoticed by the commander. 'Ye can speak freely in front of Seamus. He was asked here personally,' Hagan snapped.

'I received a call from our . . . benefactors.' Murray paused, pulling a cigarette from the packet placed in front of him by Doyle. 'Thanks, son.' He winked at the young man and continued. 'The peeler who gave us all

8

the trouble with our financial operations in Belfast last year is still talking, and has mentioned names. He seems to know a hell of a lot about us.' He paused again to accept a light from Doyle's disposable lighter.

Doyle took advantage of the break in the conversation. 'I thought that bastard was taken care of. He was promoted or transferred away to some other area, wasn't he?'

Doyle's knowledge surprised Murray, but then he had obviously become Hagan's right-hand man. He cleared his lungs of the smoke before continuing. 'That's right . . . he was, but apparently he's still kept up his interest, even though we were told that the case had been taken over by another and would die a natural death.'

The stream of conversation was interrupted by a knock at the glass door. Philomena Hagan, a thin sickly-looking sixteen-year-old, pushed her head around the door. 'Da, the Brits are sniffin' round Desi's car.'

'That's fine, love, keep an eye on them', replied Hagan.

The door closed and Desi Murray continued. 'Well, as I was sayin', Paddy, the bastard's kept some records or somethin'! Probably copies of the books he seized on the various raids, and we think he'll come up with some more. It's only a matter of time.'

'I thought he was taken care of. You told me personally that he'd be dead meat!' said Paddy.

'I did. But what we didn't know was that some of yer stupid runners were keeping records of their takings and proceeds in strict contrast with the so-called "real books", and for some reason the peeler's still making waves and askin' his own headquarters what action's been taken by them since!' Murray was annoyed. He did not want to reveal too much in front of Doyle, and began drawing deeply on the cigarette.

Paddy Hagan eased back against the pile of packing cases.

'Jasus . . . that's all we need, especially now.'

'Well, listen, it's OK! It's OK!' exclaimed Murray. 'He's bein' fixed good and proper. It's already on the slips to frame him for some pay-offs; just think of the adverse publicity on the RUC! He'll be suspended, probably dismissed, but he'll be well offside in any case. Our benefactors are takin' a personal interest, and I will take care of it myself.'

'There's only one way to take care of a black bastard!' said Doyle.

There was another knock at the door, and Philomena came into the store-room. 'Da, they want the driver outside, it's the usual. They want ta check out Desi's car.'

'OK, luv, he's on his way out, tell them,' replied her father. The door was left ajar, and Hagan could see the tall squaddie standing just outside the covered entrance into the small shop. He couldn't decide if the soldier was trying to see into the rear of the shop or to avoid the now heavy rainfall. Murray rose to leave.

'Just who's fixin' him, Desi?' enquired Hagan in a quieter tone than usual.

'Williams himself. I just thought you should know in case between now and the time he's sorted, the cops start another investigation on the strength of his comments.'

'Don't worry, Desi, we'll see to it that the Belfast operation is absolutely airtight. We'll say nothin' more on the matter. See you at the club tomorrow night after mass.' As Hagan stood, he picked up three books tied with a piece of cord and handed them to Murray. 'Just in case they want ta know why yer here. Give me them back tomorrow and keep yer grandkid's sticky fingers aff them!' He began to laugh.

Murray took the books, noting the title on top: *The Science of Society: An Introduction to Sociology* by Stephen Cotgrove. 'Hell's gates, they'll think I'm some schoolteacher!' They all laughed, but beneath Murray's smile he wondered what the young man really thought of him. Accepting the books, he left for the rain and the usual Brit questions and rehearsed replies.

Hagan opened the metal-plated rear door, easing the bottom latch bolt with his foot. He turned to Doyle. 'You're right, of course. There's only one way ta take care of a black bastard and you're the boyo to do it. See us at the club tonight. I've got some calls ta make.'

'No problem, Paddy . . . Have gun, will travel.' Doyle smiled as he passed through the door out on to the gravel pathway.

The door was quickly shut again, and Paddy returned to his chair and lukewarm tea and thought of the policeman who had caused all the headaches in the previous year. They had had to reorganise their entire Belfast set-up. It had even affected other parts of the six counties and Dublin was not amused. He tried to recollect the bastard's name. Sommers . . . no, that was not it. Then he remembered: the bastard was called Somerville!

Patrick Hagan made several calls from his storeroom and home that day. One concerned taking a party of Catholic schoolchildren to the American Folk Museum near Omagh. It was received by the local Sinn Fein office, in the town; Sally Dines was excited by the caller's voice. 'Yes, Uncle Paddy, that's fine. I'll arrange some tea and a picnic for the kids and expect them at three o'clock on Sunday afternoon. Give my love to Auntie Mary – bye-bye now.'

The line went dead. The tape recorder clicked off

automatically five seconds later. The tape would be placed on to transcript later that day.

Desmond Murray telephoned twice that evening. Each time the female with the English accent answered, and each time he hung up without comment. He knew her to be Julia Williams, the young wife of Geoffrey Williams – architect, builder, businessman and 'some-time dealer in artefacts' as Murray often described him. Usually, however, he enjoyed the term 'benefactor' because of his work for the organisation.

Sitting back in his dingy windowless office, Murray reflected on Williams and his type. He remembered the father, Sir Frederick Williams, and the time when Geoffrey had come into his inheritance following his father's tragic death back in 1972. 'Old Fred', as Murray had known him, had given up a commission in the British Army following his own father's death. Using the residue of the family's estate, diminished considerably by excessive death duties, Williams put his brilliant management skills to use, and the small building firm he established expanded to become one of the largest development concerns in Ulster. A natural entrepreneur, Fred Williams soon monopolised the Stormont government's local housing programme and seemed set to carve his name in future history books. Desmond Murray first met him during this period. There had been an acute labour problem on a north Belfast housing project and Williams, undaunted by his site manager's remarks, had taken the bull by the horns, marching on to the site and sacking the entire work-force including the site manager and foreman. Then the pickets had started and no new work-force had been permitted to recommence building work. Desmond Murray made his first approach to Williams and within two days took up appointment as site manager, after which a new work-force had resumed

12

work and the pickets had been dissipated by fear and intimidation. The new site manager was a force to be reckoned with. In Desmond Murray, Fred Williams saw a kindred spirit, hungry and with that sharpened edge which spelt survival. From that time on Murray, with the approval of his IRA godfathers, was to become trouble-shooter on many further development projects, during which time he watched young Geoffrey grow into a man – always paying visits to the various sites, always eager to learn, but always aloof, as if there was something unclean in dealing directly with Murray and his kind. Shortly after Fred Williams' knighthood and the tragic accident, young Geoffrey found himself the sole heir to Ulster's largest builders and developers. During that honeymoon period of adjustment, Murray found that contact with Geoffrey became less and less frequent. Then he picked up on the young man's acquaintance – Sir Ralph Hawthorne, a banker of considerable influence. He had reported back on the matter to his own people and was told to do nothing. Eventually, several months later, he was surprised to learn that they wanted him to leave the firm which was about to amalgamate. But Desmond Murray knew better than to question orders. He was given enough money to front and form a new company to be called Murray Developments Ltd. In turn he went into the leisure industry, opening up a number of gaming establishments specialising in bingo and one-armed bandits. During the next year he had little contact with the firm of Williams and Briggs, and was busily laundering money on colossal proportions, buying into hotels and pubs as well as forming additional companies with front men all supplied by the organisation.

Then one day he received fresh instructions from the Provisionals' Army Council in Dublin: he was to expect a visitor and take details. As ordered he rented a room at a city centre hotel and was bewildered when Geoffrey

Williams walked through the door. It was the first of many such meetings. Meticulously he took down all the information and photographs of the armaments and went personally to Dublin to report. Williams had set up in the arms business – obviously not by himself, but that was all Murray knew at that time. The Provisionals had carried out their own investigation before arranging the meeting. Murray did not need to know any more, and from then on Williams and his associates became the main suppliers for the IRA. Of course, the Provisionals were aware that the same group was supplying the Protestant paramilitaries, but what did that matter? Sure, they had supplied the UVF themselves in the past!

Murray's contacts with Williams were infrequent and always in a different place. It was not until 1980, when the organisation had decided to put pressure on their suppliers for the procurement of surface-to-air heat-seeking missile systems, that he had arranged the meeting between members of the Army Council and their suppliers to thrash out the intricate details of such a phenomenal purchase. Only then, through a close associate in Dublin, did he confirm his suspicions on the identities of the persons involved. For the first time in his life he was in the position to influence the opinions of his own people on the likes of Ralph Hawthorne, Geoffrey Williams and his business partner, Roland Briggs. About the fourth member, Mark Taylor, there was little to be said. Murray did not know him; he appeared, in every respect, to be superfluous to the entire episode.

Desmond Murray placed the recollections to the rear of his mind as he dialled the Holywood number again. The telephone rang several times before being answered.

This time he struck lucky. Murray recognised the

voice immediately. 'It's meself, could we arrange ta meet right away?'

There was a pause on the line. 'I told you never to ring me here! How did you get this number?' Geoffrey Williams was furious.

'I'm indeed sorry, Mr Williams, but you're the only one that can help. It's ta do with that wee job we talked about before and it's real important.'

'Was it you who disturbed my wife twice earlier?' asked Williams.

'Yes, I'm sorry. I didn't want to leave any message, ya see.'

'This had better be important!' snapped Williams. 'All right. I'll see you at the same place as last time. At ten o'clock.'

'Thank you, Mr Williams. I'll see ya then.'

There was no reply as Geoffrey Williams banged down the receiver.

In the car park of the Crawfordsburn Country Park, only a few miles from Williams' home, the pair met. Having parked his Mercedes convertible, Geoffrey Williams strode over to the red Cortina, opened the front passenger door and sat down beside the bald-headed little man.

'Get to the point,' he said curtly. 'I've only a few minutes, and we've already used this place before.'

'It's this Somerville. Your police contact was ta have fixed him for us before. Well, in short, he's raisin' a lot of eyebrows, this fella, and we want him outa the way. So, can yer man get him silenced before he sticks his nose further inta things?'

'Look, I got him transferred, didn't I? What else do you think I can do? Don't you have your own means to keep him quiet?' snapped Williams.

'If you mean give him the chop, yes. If you mean ta put an end ta any further investigations into our busi-

15

ness, which'll lead ta yours eventually, then I gotta do a bit more. Ya know what I mean?' Murray stared ahead into the surrounding blackness. Rain was beginning to fall again on the windscreen.

Williams was frightened. 'Yes! Yes!' he said. 'You said that last week. It can be arranged as discussed. I'll see my people, but remember this, I want no more direct contact. Understand?' He prodded Murray on the left shoulder.

'Keep yer hands ta yerself, Mr Williams!' Murray let the words sink in before turning towards him and continuing, 'I can leave it with ya then. We'll look forward to an early completion, say this comin' Monday at the latest.'

Geoffrey Williams smirked. 'The police will be calling on you some time tomorrow. I do hope you're a good actor, Murray!' He stepped out of the car and slammed the door shut. He detested having to deal with the little man and was only too aware of the vulnerability of his role as go-between. But Murray was right. Everything was in jeopardy while the policeman still pressed for a further investigation.

Williams failed to return home directly, but instead he travelled to his city centre office block, and from his private office line dialled two numbers. The first call was to a bank manager called Geddis. The other was to Eastleigh House, the country residence of Sir Ralph Hawthorne. Hawthorne had qualified in law from Oxford University and had been called to the Northern Irish Bar in 1956 after a short military and government service. As a Queen's Counsel of considerable standing, he was deemed to be a pillar of the old guard. Like Geoffrey Williams' father, he too had been a member of the Stormont parliament. Of course, the Northern Irish Bar Council had rules governing the outside interests of its members, but then Ralph Hawthorne was no ordinary barrister and the rules had ceased to apply to

16

him long ago. His hands could reach deeply into many dark corners, as his close friends and colleagues had often remarked. He had even turned down the opportunity to become a High Court Judge. Not all could understand why he declined the accolade, but then not everyone understood the man's true aspirations.

Later that night Geoffrey Williams stopped off at the exclusive Union Club in Belfast's city centre. He sat in the readers' lounge, where in half an hour he was sipping his third whisky. Even the old head waiter had noticed the man's jittery behaviour. He had bitten his head off on several occasions and kept glancing at the eighteenth-century clock on the tall Adam fireplace.

The Club's membership was by invitation only. Established in 1925, shortly after the formation of Ulster, invitations to join first went to some of Ulster's new Unionist MPs in the Stormont parliament. In fact most members came from outside the political world, tending to belong to aristocracy and the highest echelons of the Province's business community. Geoffrey had virtually inherited his membership after the death of his father, or so it seemed at the time. Membership was not hereditary, but in his case he had received the invitation to join a month after his father's untimely death in a yachting accident off the County Down coast.

The General Purposes Committee of the Union Club had quickly approved the recommendation of its chairman to open its doors to Williams, then only qualified in architecture and fresh from Queen's University, Belfast. It was important to establish continuity, especially when one – so young – became the overnight heir to Ulster's largest building corporation. No one imagined that the heir could possibly refuse, but he did. It was not until his Corporation's chief banker and his father's old associate, Sir Ralph Hawthorne, explained the importance of membership

17

that the young man began to take an interest. Conversation over lunch that day had been particularly dull. Sir Ralph had attempted to explain to young Geoffrey the importance of the balance of power, and how it could be maintained only by the closest union with the financial world. But Geoffrey was not impressed. He had explained at length what he wanted to achieve artistically, and how he wished to develop and improve the working class's standard of living and housing.

However, his declaration of intent was brought to a sudden stop. 'My boy, we all need each other, never forget that!' Initially, he had not understood what Sir Ralph meant, but then the financial stability of his business empire was discussed in brief. It had been explained to him in no uncertain terms, and indeed demonstrated over the following weeks with the sudden demise of one of Geoffrey's minor companies, how necessary it was for him to have a stable base upon which to operate his business. After the collapse of the apparently healthy company, he was again invited to the Club for lunch. This time the chairman of the General Purposes Committee had no difficulty in obtaining his agreement to join.

The young man soon realised that he was not independently based. He was quickly caught up in the web of power and money. True, the financial columnists all raved at Geoffrey's increasing wealth and success, noting that he had truly carried on the tradition set by his father so long ago, but Geoffrey was no longer a free thinker. His every action and decision was predetermined by Sir Ralph Hawthorne. He was aware of only a few forced decisions; the remainder were manipulated behind closed doors and without his knowledge. He had not minded. His lifestyle and that of his socialite English wife, Julia, were second to none. He had even achieved some success with his intention to improve the standard of working-class housing.

Then came Ralph Hawthorne's decision to enter the arms trade. At first Geoffrey had taken it all as a bad joke, but true to Sir Ralph's prediction he had fallen for the high financial return of such a venture. So had his business partner, Roland Briggs, and associate Mark Taylor.

When Sir Ralph Hawthorne finally arrived that evening, a long discussion began. After a few large brandies on top of the earlier whiskies, Williams loosened up to reveal his considerable anxiety about what he had been asked to do.

'It's got to be Monday at the latest.'

Sir Ralph smiled. 'I'll see Roland and Mark Taylor. They can sort it out. Meantime, just continue as usual.' He stood up, emptying the Hennessey down his throat before setting the glass on the tall mantelpiece. 'Sorry, Geoffrey, must dash. Give me a ring before the board meeting on Thursday. I'm sure I shall have some news for you.'

Then he was gone, leaving Geoffrey Williams to ponder over the imponderable.

It was not until Saturday the 22nd that Seamus Doyle got his clearance to do what he enjoyed best. That night, when Seamus went to meet the chief, he was shown into the snooker room of the prefabricated social club at Ballymurphy. The smoke-filled room stank of bodies and spilled beer. Doyle took in the four people already in the room as the door closed behind him; they were all known to him and he to them. This was a Brigade Staff Council meeting.

He walked into the centre of the room past the plastic chairs and side tables until he was directly in front of the full-size snooker table, where he drew his feet together slowly to come to a relaxed state of attention.

Hagan sat almost facing the centre of the table, two

men to his left and the fourth to his far right. 'Stand easy.' His command was quickly complied with.

'The job's on, Doyle. As ya have guessed, the target has been approved. Ye're instructed ta go to Tyrone as discussed, and there you'll meet the local Brigade Commander. You'll be under his orders at all times, of course.'

Doyle nodded.

'The target's details will be awaiting ya. Make yer preparations carefully, but have the job done by Friday of the comin' week.' He paused, removing his spectacles, then looked hard at Doyle. 'The usual arrangements will apply for yer supplies. You choose the method and Tyrone Brigade will approve it.' He began to smile. 'Yer gun will not travel on this occasion.'

Doyle smiled back. 'Yes, I understand, I have the details and contacts.'

There was no sign of amusement on the faces of the other three. The oldest of the group, Joe McNulty, terminated the meeting.

'This is a serious matter, Doyle. Much rests on yer success, and this movement does not tolerate failure well.'

'The job will be completed, I can assure you, sir,' replied Doyle, his smile now faded completely.

The old man met the piercing black eyes of the twenty-six-year-old and could only see contempt there.

The Brigade Commander interrupted. 'Listen carefully. I can tell ya this . . . the Army Council itself is very concerned that this must be seen ta be a local action, so you should arrange several other incidents for the day of yer hit. It'll make it look like a general upsurge in the area.'

'Yes, sir.' Doyle came to attention again.

'That will be all for now, Staff Officer Doyle. Long live the Democratic Socialist Republic. Long live Free Ireland!'

'Long live Free Ireland!' returned Doyle, but without Hagan's genuine dedication.

The atmosphere was more relaxed for Paddy Hagan and Seamus Doyle when they sat over a couple of pints later the same night.

'A lot of people will be watching yer mission with great interest. Ye could do well outa this for sure.' Hagan patted Doyle on the arm.

'I'll not let ya down, Paddy, I can promise that.'

It was not policy to send soldiers into other areas for specific missions. The reorganisation of the movement into small Active Service Units had reduced touting to the Security Forces, especially since the super-grasses had raised their dirty heads. But to send one man seemed either a last-ditch effort or a great compliment. Doyle chose the later assumption, and was excited by the Army Council's interest. 'Christ, it must be important,' he mumbled. The remark was not heard by the chief, now busy shouting for two more pints of Harp.

Saturday 22 May – Omagh, County Tyrone

The parade room was packed to capacity. The crews were sitting in separate groups, some drinking coffee, others tea, from plastic cups. They were all young policemen, but with the additional bond that they were members of the RUC's crack Headquarters Mobile Support Unit – trained by the SAS to refine the ingredients of speed, aggression and firepower so necessary to their task and so aptly described by the press.

A general quiet fell over the gathering as Barney Somerville and two sergeants entered the room. One of the more cocky young constables in the front row boomed out, 'Hope we're going to get some action this time, Inspector!'

Somerville looked at the constable, but did not acknowledge the comment.

'Settle down and listen carefully.' He paused to ensure the group's fullest attention. 'Gentlemen, further to your briefing at 1800 hours, we have the green light from Special Branch. You will now all be briefed in exact detail. But beforehand, I've a few points I want to stress. Firstly, no individual heroics; secondly, the area you're entering is border country and it's therefore important that at all times you know precisely where you are. We do not want needless border incursions and if the situation demands pursuit you take direction from me. The objective is to intercept a van bomb we know is coming across from Ballybofey. We assume that it will cross from Lifford and is destined for Strabane town centre. It may be the case that PIRA will use an indirect route across the border and we, gentlemen, will be well stretched to get them if that's the case. But intelligence indicates the direct route and we'll bank on that. No doubt PIRA will have the route all scouted and it looks as though up to eight players will accompany the bomb, which is estimated to be between one and two thousand pounds. It will be brought over in a blue Sherpa van, registration number not known, but probably with an Ulster plate. We know that they can only use one of four routes. E4A's not in on this one, and at this stage we cannot get additional support from military or local police. Therefore, you will be scattered in your various teams but with a concentration on the Lifford-Strabane crossing. You will be spaced over a large area, which will mean tight coordination by Section Sergeants. Red Section will operate as our forward observation group and be dressed in civilian clothes in unmarked cars and under my personal control. The remainder – Blue, Green, Purple and Orange – will be detailed for the four routes. We can't put a time on the PIRA move, but indications are for around 2 a.m. So on that note, gentlemen, I shall leave you to your hurried specifics . . . All crews to be ready to move out in precisely 45 minutes.' Somerville nodded to the two sergeants and one began handing out the intelligence briefs as the other, Billy Martin, switched the slide projector into action. A map depicting the craggy line separating the Republic from Northern Ireland filled the screen on the small dais. The briefing had commenced in earnest.

Barney Somerville commanded a respect that was not easily earned. Not only had he led his men into many difficult situations since taking command of the Unit, but he had led from the front and that did not go unnoticed. He was thirty-seven years old and still able to match – or if he had wanted, to embarrass – the Unit's best. Men over thirty-five years are precluded from entry into the HMSUs, but Somerville was different and his superiors knew it. He was transferred on promotion from CID at what he deemed to be a crucial stage in racketeering investigations. He had protested strongly to his Assistant Chief Constable in Crime Branch, although his appeal got nowhere with the man. 'No one is indispensable,' he had said on more than one occasion during that interview. 'Take my advice and settle down in your new role. Someone else will clear up this case.'

Barney Somerville had accepted the position reluctantly and had moved house from Belfast to Omagh. He had thrown himself into the new job, relishing the hard and lengthy training which was reminiscent of his old Army days. Somerville was a perfectionist in every sense and it showed, though hiding his enthusiasm from the SAS instructors proved difficult at times.

It was not until his return to Northern Ireland some months later that Somerville found out his old investigation had been temporarily shelved. The excuse was 'an overload of work in other fields, more pressing', though he was assured this was only 'temporarily set back'. There was even a hint of his being returned to CID for continued enquiries. He had long since become frustrated with the rubber wall of indecision and had gone on paper to that effect several times without having received a single reply. As he walked the length of the annexe to his office, he tried to clear these thoughts from his mind. He sat down in a worn armchair and poured a cup of coffee from the newly purchased percolator. It was his only comfort in the place: ground coffee always stimulated his senses. As he filled the beaker the door swung open and when Somerville looked up, his eyes caught a hand moving around the jamb. He recognised the distinctive gold and onyx zodiac ring on the index finger immediately; it belonged to Detective Chief Inspector Winston Black of E4A, the RUC's Surveillance Branch.

'Hello, Barney, long time no see!' The Special Branch officer grinned as he peered round the door and fixed his small brown eyes on Somerville, who remained impassive. He had half expected the tall figure; he knew Black to be an opportunist. The fact that something was going on down in the insignificant far west of the Province was enough to ensure Black's presence. Somerville eyed the man carefully, noting the paunch that had come with forty-two years and a relaxed office lifestyle. Barney detested his kind of headquarters stereotype. He slowly gestured towards him with the full coffee mug, in mock salute.

'I thought you should know,' said Black, 'that Detective Chief Superintendent Grange came down from headquarters with me. He's personally taken charge of this one. He's already with the Divisional Commander in the joint operations room at the station.'

'Thanks, Winston. While I get my feet wet, it's nice to know I've got such high-powered support to stand on my hands if I foul up out there!' Somerville tried not to look too surprised.

Detective Chief Inspector Black was not amused. 'Look, Barney, I know you don't like the man, but he's already said he wants to see you before you go out . . . just thought I'd warn you. See you later.'

The door slammed shut before Somerville could reply – not that it was necessary. His feelings for Grange went back to the time when he was a junior sergeant and Grange his local chief inspector. He remembered how Grange had failed to warn him or his men of an imminent terrorist attack in the Markets area of Belfast. He remembered the face of the young policeman lying more dead than alive with his left leg blown off, after the front door of the little terrace house splintered out to meet him when he had pressed the door-bell. He had completed a simple 'bell-push' circuit which was wired up to an electric detonator stuck into one pound of commercial explosives placed in the middle of a plastic bucket, which contained an assortment of rusty nails, nuts and bolts. The bucket had been set on a chair placed tight against the door. The young man took the full blast of the explosion on his left thigh and flak jacket as he stood angled in the doorway, having reached for the buzzer with his left hand. That very action had saved his life. Had it not been for his resting the Sterling SMG in his bent right arm he would have faced the doorway squarely, and his groin would have been reduced to pulp. Grange had come down heavy after that, saying he had placed the area out of bounds only one hour beforehand and using Somerville as the scapegoat. It had been no use his denying the lies. Grange had even produced a piece of paper dated and timed, indicating he had passed the information directly to Somerville well before police left Musgrave Street Station that same evening. Barney Somerville was duly transferred to another part of the city, but not before he had told Frank Grange a few home truths. It was providence that saved Grange from a broken face.

Somerville had found it hard to put the pieces together after that. And it was only after a tenacious effort that he eventually left beat and patrol duties for detective work. He had been lucky. Someone, somewhere shared his view – not only of the incident, but of Frank Grange.

Somerville stood in the vehicle compound. All around him men hurried to vehicles, laden down with guns and equipment. He pressed the hand switch to his throat microphone, easily concealed under the black polo-neck sweater.

'Blue, Green, Purple and Orange call signs from Red India, report status.'

The ear-piece receiver crackled in response. 'Blue ready over . . . Green ready over . . . Purple ready over . . . Orange ready over . . .'

'Roger, move out. I repeat move out,' instructed Somerville.

The cars roared away, headlights flashing as they streamed past him. With the noise and static emitting from the ear-piece he did not hear the approach of the two men to his rear, not until they were within six feet of him.

'Well, Inspector – all set, are we?'

Somerville turned. Within punching distance stood Detective Chief Superintendent Frank Grange. He was tempted . . . for a single second he was tempted. He did not reply to the question and stared back; Grange knew exactly what it meant.

'I see you're incognito tonight, Inspector.' Grange ran his eyes over Somerville's six-foot frame dressed in grubby combat jacket, black pullover, faded jeans and desert boots, combined with a blue woollen hat pulled down over his thick blond hair.

'As you see,' replied Somerville.

'Sorry I couldn't make your briefing. I assume you and your men know their task?' continued Grange.

'Yes.' Somerville's face was deadpan.

'Along with the Detective Chief Inspector here, I've personally placed your area of operation OOB to all military and police until further notice. We wouldn't want any own-goals, would we, eh?' Grange affected a smile. It reminded Somerville of the rows of yellow teeth he had seen in *Jaws*.

'You're quite adept at putting areas out of bounds, I just hope you managed to pick the right one . . . sir.' It was out, and Barney found it hard to avoid a small smile. 'Of course, it'll make all the difference having your support!'

Grange's face drooped, his pretence at being pleasant over.

'Just do your job, Inspector, and remember I'll be monitoring your every movement!'

Somerville continued to smile. 'I always do my job and we don't take unnecessary chances in the HMSU.'

At that a beige Citroën car pulled up and the front passenger door was flung open. The driver, Sergeant Billy Martin, leaned over the seat and shouted out, 'Come on, sir, we've fifteen minutes to make our first point!'

Somerville nodded and looked at Grange. 'Excuse me . . . sir.'

Not waiting for a reply, he jumped into the car which raced out of the courtyard.

Grange stood still in the drizzling rain, watching the disappearing brake lights as the car screeched round the corner of the encompassing buildings and out of sight. Detective Chief Inspector Black tried to avoid smiling.

*

The Provos were taking no chances either. They had clearly scouted their route into Northern Ireland, taking an unmarked and unmanned border crossing six miles south of Strabane. They brought the blue van across in a convoy of two other cars and did not see the beige Citroën parked thirty yards up the laneway as they streamed past towards the main Strabane road.

'Red India to all call signs, Code Green, Yankee Plan.'

Somerville then turned to Sergeant Martin. 'Let's go. Keep your distance behind. And let's hope the others make the RV points in time.' The two men moved off in the unlit car, always keeping the rear lights of the IRA cavalcade in their view.

The Black Section crews set up their roadblock four miles ahead of the IRA vehicles and were swiftly joined by the Orange crews. As the first IRA car turned the bend in the road, the driver slammed on the brakes at the sight of the four police vehicles blocking his path. He reacted so quickly that his single passenger hit his head on the front windscreen, temporarily stunning himself. The blue van careered to a halt some ten yards behind and the driver, having the advantage of a few seconds, jumped out and made a run for the hedgerow. Before he could reach it the Shermulley flares lit up the sky, casting long shadows on the road and surrounding fields. The driver realised the hopelessness of escape as he stared into the face of the uniformed policeman taking cover behind the hedgerow. He could also clearly see the Hecker and Koch rifle trained on his head. Immediately, he put his hands in the air and on command lay flat on the roadway. The leading Renault 16 had stalled on coming to rest, and before the startled driver or stunned passenger could react, both doors were flung open and they were dragged unceremoniously from the car. Both men were placed in handcuffs before they could utter a word.

The remaining vehicle, a Mazda hatchback, completed a three-point turn and raced back down the road leaving the mêlée. As the driver glared desperately around for any sign of a cut-off action, it was becoming apparent that the police trap had been a quickly sprung affair. Then he saw it two hundred yards ahead: another VCP of two cars end to end blocking his path completely. But the police had not reckoned on the driver's intricate knowledge of the area. Thirty yards from the line of vehicles the silver Mazda swerved right into a bumpy laneway and sped uphill and away into the night. The car carried four men. In the rear was Fergus Sloan, a twenty-two-year-old terrorist, on the run and living in safety in the Republic. He was a native of Pomeroy and had gone OTR after being wounded during a shoot-out with the British Army in Carrickmore during 1979. He had been shot through the left shoulder by a 7.62mm round. A clean wound – the bullet had passed through him – but he had required urgent medical treatment. His comrades had taken him to a remote farmhouse where their make-shift facilities had furnished his first aid. It had been enough to stop the bleeding and the morphine jab had given him temporary relief. For almost thirty-six hours they were unable to move him, and then it took three hours to transport him to Monaghan Hospital in the back of the cattle truck. Of course he had been questioned by the Garda 'dicks' after he had come round from the emergency operation and his fever had abated, but he had said nothing. He did not need to. They knew the full story from the RUC, but the joke was that they could not do a thing with him – no bullet, no evidence to connect Sloan with the shoot-out, just the suspicion on their part – and his PIRA-appointed solicitor was quick to point that out to the Garda. He never returned to the North after that unless it was on

a job; it suited his purpose and it suited the organisation too.

He had become a bit of a folk hero back in Pomeroy
and some schoolgirls had even written a bloody song
about him and his Armalite. He was really chuffed
about that.

Fergus Sloan was inwardly cursing as his mind raced
over the details of the present operation and how the
police must have been tipped off. But finding the traitor
was irrelevant now. They had to get away and fast.
The driver knew it too, and just where he was going.
The laneway led through the deserted farmhouse yard
and past the ruins of what were once labourers'
cottages. He estimated another half-mile to the
unmanned border crossing – a half-blown-up bridge
over the river – and then into the Republic. They
couldn't drive across, they would have to leg it until
they got themselves another vehicle on the other side.
But that was no big deal. It would take the unprepared
Garda up to an hour to get organised and by then they
would be drinking tea in a safe house. The driver got
the shock of his life when he saw the laneway blocked
by the Citroën. He slowed up, seeing the unlit vehicle
more clearly in the fullness of the headlights, and
looked around to Fergus Sloan for inspiration.

Sloan was quick to reply. 'Get fuckin' out! Take to
the fields!'

The four men bailed out, two to each side of the
Mazda, and bolted away from the car, clambering over
barbed-wire fencing on one side and a dry stone wall
on the other.

'Stop! Police! Put your hands up and stand still!'

Immediately Sloan pulled out the 9mm Star pistol
and fired in the direction of the voice ahead of them.
Sergeant Martin dived to one side and rolled over,
simultaneously applying pressure to the trigger of the
9mm Ingram SMG. The driver, who had already prod-

uced a .38 revolver, ran in front of Sloan in a sudden surge of heroics. 'Run! Run!' he screamed and pointed his revolver at the policeman. He fell back, hit three times in head and face by the Ingram's bullets. Then the policeman made the mistake of rising to his knees and Sloan emptied his remaining bullets at the Sergeant. A lucky shot caught the policeman in the shoulder just as he brought the Ingram to bear on the terrorist and he spun backwards into a water-filled ditch, losing his grip on the SMG. Fergus Sloan ran to the ditch and pointed his pistol at the policeman's head. Billy Martin looked up at the gun barrel, not recognising the face behind it.

The unmistakable cracking of the Heckler and Koch made Sloan hesitate. He heard two quick bursts followed closely by two single shots. He could also hear someone running on to the laneway behind him, only yards away. He dropped his aim and jumped over the policeman, escaping into the darkness and across the shallow river into the Republic of Ireland.

Barney Somerville surveyed the scene, with the Heckler and Koch rifle at the ready. It was clear. Within thirty seconds he was pulling Billy Martin out of the mud and water.

'One's got away . . . behind me, right over the Shuck!' croaked Martin.

'And into the South, Sergeant. How the hell did they get the upper hand on you, anyway?'

'Easy, I gave them a chance, didn't I?' He winced with pain. 'Gave a warning and all . . .'

Just then Somerville heard a further clatter of gunfire and he threw himself to the ground. It came from across the river, he estimated 150 to 200 metres off. Automatic small-arms fire. The closed-net receiver crackled in his ear.

'Red India from Red two, that was friendly fire,

repeat friendly fire. We are approaching your location now, over.'

Somerville squeezed the hand-switch dangling from his wrist.

'Red two from India, Roger, approach now, out.'

In no time the two policemen were jumping over the fence and ditch.

'Got him. It was Fergus Sloan all right.' The smaller policeman was slightly out of breath as he pulled the black balaclava off his head and eased the zip on the combat jacket. Stuffing the balaclava into the jacket, he continued, 'We left his gun beside him.'

'Who did the shooting?' growled Somerville.

'I did,' replied the same man.

'I told you strictly no border crossings unless I said so, you bollocks!'

'Sorry, sir. We just thought – ' The young man was cut off in mid-stream.

'*Thought?* You're not paid to think in this team! Just do as you're told. Now listen, you two, just remember in your debriefing that you acted on my verbal directions to cross over the border in pursuit when required. Make sure you stick to it!' Somerville's anger was clear, but both men appreciated his detached assessment of their situation.

'Thanks, Barney,' said the young policeman.

'How far away had he got?'

'About a hundred metres over the river, no more – he was hiding in a clump of bushes. He just came out at us shooting and I'd no choice. Couldn't even give him a warning.'

'You say his gun is beside him?'

'Yeah. He had it in his hand, cocked, one up the spout from the look of it.' The young man turned to his partner, who nodded in agreement as he fought to control his breathing.

'Fine. We'll let the Garda worry about the sudden

death file on him,' said Somerville. 'All right, let's get back to the vehicles. You two pass on the information to the Incident Room. I want local police and necessary services to this place right away, and make sure the area around that van bomb is well cleared.'

'Right.' The pair of them ran off towards the Citroën.

Somerville turned to Billy Martin and smiled. 'You'll never learn.'

'What about the other two bastards back there?' Billy bit his lip to control the increasing pain.

'Well, I don't give out invitations like you.'

The euphoria back at Omagh was dampened by the injury to Sergeant Martin. True, he would live, but they all knew his injury would keep him out of the HMSU. The second dampener for Somerville was Grange's assessment of the operation. He conceded the 1500-lb bomb and five recovered firearms. He accepted that three PIRA volunteers were behind bars and three more dead on Ulster soil. But a policeman had almost been killed and a top terrorist had escaped, only to be shot dead in the South.

'So much for the HMSU taking no chances . . . that's what you said, wasn't it, Inspector?' snapped Grange.

'It's something to do with all that lead in the air,' said Somerville. 'Something you know nothing about, obviously.' He turned on his heel and walked away.

'That's the last time you'll ever turn your back on me, Somerville, remember that! The ACC's on his way here right now!'

Somerville stopped in his tracks, half-way across the open yard.

Grange continued, 'According to the Garda superintendent in Letterkenny, this man Sloan was riddled with bullets.'

Somerville remained silent.

'The officers involved in the shooting say they acted

under your orders, Somerville. There'll be a full investigation of course. I'll have your pips for this, I promise you!'

Somerville turned to face Grange, standing twenty feet away.

'You seem to have forgotten something,' he shouted. 'Sloan wasn't a man. He was a murdering son of a bitch! A bomber! In Derry he didn't give the women and children and unfortunate peelers who arrived on the scene any warning either . . . Ten people, ten fucking people died when that car bomb blew up! And if you ever took the time to check your source reports, which I doubt, you'd see he's responsible for at least another seven or eight killings, never mind the maimings.' He walked back towards Grange until he was within five feet. 'I think we did the courts a favour, don't you? If the bastard had been caught in the South, all he would have done is time for possession, that is if they'd been able to catch him with the gun!'

Grange failed to reply. Shaking with rage he turned and walked away closely followed by a perturbed Winston Black who wasn't sure which side to take.

Somerville did not get home until five-thirty that morning. The usual debrief and series of statements were more protracted because of the presence of the Assistant Chief Constable and his entourage from Complaints and Discipline Branch, who appeared determined for a kill. Somerville was reminded of the words of an old friend in RUC Headquarters. 'When the hunting party leaves the lodge, they don't like to come back empty-handed.' But the hunting party was unsuccessful. The only aspect they could pursue was the border incursion, and that would have to wait until a formal complaint from the Irish government.

Somerville relished the hot shower, reviving senses he had almost forgotten. Easing himself into bed, he

34

found the weight of the night's work had taken its toll. He quickly drifted into a deep slumber beside his wife and he did not even stir when Janet Somerville awakened to the noise of the children as they pounded each other in a pillow fight in the next bedroom of the bungalow. She looked tenderly at her husband. The tiredness on his face betrayed him; she would let him sleep until lunchtime and awaken him after their return from church. It was a good afternoon and the sun filled the car with a sticky warmth as they drove on to Benone beach. Thank God they could stop and enjoy the sea air, thought Janet. The children were quickly in the water and dad was urged to join them. After a few minutes, he escaped from their clutches and returned shivering to the Cavalier, leaving seven-year-old Maria fighting with her five-year-old brother, Thomas, for control of the plastic airbed. Janet had already put out the rugs and picnic basket. She laughed at his gooseflesh and reached over a thick towel. He quickly rubbed himself dry, and sat down beside her.

'God, it's cold in there!'

'You're getting too old for it,' she replied. He looked up at her, smiling, already half-way through a cucumber sandwich. 'I heard the lunchtime news. Do you want to talk about it?' Janet was now serious.

'You know I can't, love.' Barney pulled the towel round his shoulders.

'I know . . . but it's beginning to tell on you. You're thirty-seven years old, a family man. You . . . we, deserve more than this.'

'I know, love. And before you say any more I'm seeing the boss tomorrow. I've already decided.'

'But will they give you the transfer?'

'They've no choice. If I refuse to involve myself they have to remove me immediately. Fair enough, we might not stay in Omagh, but I'd be sent out of the HMSU.' He smiled reassuringly.

'Talking about moving,' said Janet, 'would you like to remove yourself to the water and referee between your son and daughter before they drown each other?'

He looked round to see Thomas kicking water into the screaming face of Maria, who was then engulfed by a large breaker. Throwing off the towel, Barney jumped to his feet. 'Once more into the breach – or is it beach? – dear friends'.

'By the by, Superman, when you've sorted out your offspring perhaps you could rescue the lilo!' Janet shouted after him, pointing to the far right of the children. The current had taken the abandoned air-bed some hundred yards down the beach and off-shore. She heard her husband echo her laughter as he ran into the waves.

The journey home was too much for the children. The picnic had lain heavily in their stomachs and sleep overtook them well before they reached Omagh. Janet, too, had dozed off in the front passenger seat. Barney found himself suddenly roused by the sight of her legs when her front-buttoned beach skirt parted company at the bottom three buttons. He switched on the radio, and as the soothing music of Phil Coulter's orchestra filled his mind, he reflected on what a lucky man he was. He owed it to them all to get out of his present situation.

Seamus Doyle was not much impressed that Sunday afternoon. He had driven the minibus the length of the M1 Motorway with ten screaming children. Even his companion, trainee school-teacher Susan White, was no consolation, despite being what he would have readily described as a 'cracker'. He didn't get much chance to chat her up and he supposed there was not much point. After all, he would not be returning to Belfast from the American Folk Museum and he had no means of knowing just when he would be back.

There was no way that he was going to get his leg over. He had felt all the right vibrations, and there was even a dance that night in the INF hall on the Falls Road. An impressive turn-out in his brother's Toyota, a few vodkas and she might really loosen up, might drop her pseudo-intellectual pretence, might even drop her pants.

He had been taken by her arrogant contempt for the police at the VCP, when all traffic was turned off the Motorway at the Craigavon roundabout. Yet she had carefully avoided upsetting the policewoman who did the body search and that impressed him. The full search of the bus, inspection of papers and meticulous logging of all the passengers, young and old, had taken all of fifteen minutes. He noticed how Susan had even helped the policeman search the bus by pulling back seat-covers, lifting out the little baggage they carried and generally being polite, but always retaining an underlying but unexceptionable contempt.

The road from Dungannon to Omagh was at least more scenic than that of the dreary Motorway. Susan wasn't much surprised when he said goodbye at the Folk Park and handed over the bus keys to a young man with curly red hair. Seamus was collected from the car park in a Mini Clubman driven by a slightly-built girl with short brown hair and glasses. He knew her to be Sally Dines, Paddy's niece. Nineteen and unemployed, she helped run the local Sinn Fein advice centre and by the end of the journey he was convinced that her head was filled with utter nonsense. Doyle reckoned the girl had worked too long with the movement's propaganda to recognise reality as distinct from the illusions they tried to create in the mind of the Catholic population.

'Have you ever been in Castlereagh?'

'Do you think women have enough to do in the struggle?'

'I think *Iris* is super. Did you do it all yourself?'

'What's it like to speak to the Commander-in-Chief?'

'I can't ask you what you're to do up here, but if I can help, will you let me?'

He wouldn't have permitted such loud-mouthed talk from anyone else. Perhaps she thought she could get away with it, being Paddy's niece and all, but that last question cut to the bone and she knew it from his sudden glare.

'Listen, you stupid wee girl. You've got a big mouth – shut it or I'll fuckin' shut it for ya! Do ya fuckin' understand, I'm none of yer business. Now just take me to wherever I'm going and keep yer mind on the road.'

Sally Dines was not easily put off and after a few minutes she tried to restore the situation.

'See the bastards killed four of the boys this mornin'.' She glanced at him for a reaction, but there was none. She continued, 'Murdered them in cold blood, so they did. Did ya know Fergus Sloan was among the dead?'

'As a matter of fact I did. Now shut up, and keep driving!'

That ended Sally Dines' attempt at conversation. They arrived at the farmhouse at 5 o'clock; it was a small building, single-storey, with a corrugated iron roof red with rust. Although only a short distance off the main Omagh to Cookstown road, the farmhouse and outbuildings were completely hidden from passing traffic by the overgrown hedge and bushes. Sally turned the car in a tight circle on the gravel area and pulled up outside the green front door.

'The house belongs to Mrs Devlin, a widow. She's expecting ya. Now I'll collect ya later, about seven. You've some people to see.'

He nodded and climbed out of the little car. The Mini sped off, wheels spinning, churning some gravel on to his cord trousers. That wee bitch needs a lesson, he thought. The green door opened as he approached and an old woman stood half behind it. She was small, five feet tall he supposed, aged about seventy. Her grey hair was tied back in a rough bun and she was wearing a black dress and dirty white apron. As he stepped past her, he noticed her wrinkled surgical stockings and worn carpet slippers. She reminded him of his own granny.

'Yer expected. Sit yerself down by the fire there. The tay's near ready.'

Doyle nodded to the old woman, walked through the little porch into the living room and hesitantly went over to the rocking-chair, sitting down on the neatly embroidered cushion. It was an interesting little room, lived in yet neat. The high fireplace was made of a wooden veneer and the inset was of cream-coloured tiles, most of which were cracked and discoloured with age. The fire glowed and the smell of burning peat was overwhelming. The fire seemed the only bit of life in the place. The walls were a faded grey colour and he could only just make out the pattern of the old wall-paper which was almost lost with age and damp. All the other furniture was old. The only recent addition to the room, it seemed, was the carved mahogany harp on the middle of the fireplace. He stood up to examine it more closely. The harp had been made in the Kesh, he reckoned; it stood eleven inches high and sat on a bevelled mahogany base about six inches wide and three inches deep. Resting at an angle of 45 degrees was a small three-inch-square brass plate. Doyle had to squint in the poor light to read the inscription:

LEST WE FORGET — VOLUNTEER FRANCIS HUGHES —
HE DIED FOR A FREE IRELAND AND JUSTICE FOR
ALL NATIONALISTS AND THEIR REAL ASPIRATIONS

The hunger strike was still fresh in the minds of the nationalist population. It was one of the reasons why

Doyle had wanted to get out of Dublin; the place stifled him.

'Do ya like it?'

The old woman's voice startled Doyle; he hadn't heard her shuffle into the room from the kitchen. She was carrying a steaming pot with some obvious difficulty.

'Let me help ya, missus.' Doyle took the pot and gingerly placed it on the plastic mat in the centre of the small oval dining table.

'Sit yerself down.' She went back into the kitchen, returning quickly with a single dish and spoon.

'Did ye know him, then?' asked Doyle.

'Know who?' The old woman's face was expressionless.

'Francis Hughes'.

'No, can't say I did now. Just terra the way he died.' She muttered and began to ladle the food on to his plate. 'Stew, nice and hot, just help yerself.' She turned and walked out of the room, closing the kitchen door. She had no intention of eating with him, but her behaviour didn't puzzle him. People didn't want to know too much, which was for the best. Familiarity was a weakness, Paddy Hagan had always taught him that. After he had finished she showed him where he was to sleep: a small box-room, the only other bedroom in the house apart from her own. It was damp and slightly smelly, or maybe it was stuffy due to the twisted metal window being jammed closed by rust. He would look at that later. In the corner sat a canvas camp-bed. Three blankets and two sheets lay folded on top; to one end lay a stained pillow, no pillow-case in sight.

'You didn't bring any luggage, did ye?'

The old woman studied him.

'No, I didn't,' he replied, trying to hide his embarrassment at having left his holdall in the Mini. She

40

handed him two old collarless shirts, clean but well-worn.

'These belonged to my old man, God rest him. Ye may have them now, son.' She smiled at him and nodded slightly and Seamus Doyle reckoned he had made a friend after all. He would amend his own rules with this old woman, at least slightly.

He met the local Commandant later that evening in a smart housing estate on the outskirts of Omagh. The OC was called Kevin McNamara, and it was obvious from the outset that the man was hostile.

'I'd better make one thing clear,' he said. 'I don't like strangers in my area. I got orders ta help ya, but I don't have to like it. Do ya get me, Doyle?'

'Loud and clear.'

'You'll have young Jamsie Sloan here ta help ya; anything ya want, he'll get. If ya want to get in touch, he does it, OK?' The OC was unrelenting. 'Another thing, when you're ready I'll sanction the hit. You tell me the plan in every detail, OK?'

'Whatever you say.' Doyle tried to subdue his anger, which could get him into trouble here.

After the room cleared and McNamara and his heavies left, Doyle sat at the table with Jamsie Sloan.

'You know where the bastard lives, do ya?' asked Doyle. He was summing up the seventeen-year-old youth, who didn't seem too dependable.

'Know where he lives? We know everything about him. They think he got our boys shot last night!'

'Aye, we heard about it. It was a bad show, I thought maybe it would hold things up here – well, at least until the funerals,' said Doyle in a more mellow tone.

'Funerals don't hold us up, mister.'

'Well, when do we start?'

'Tomorrow, tomorrow mornin' early. I'll collect ya

41

at the farm about seven. I'll be on a motorbike; I'll get ya a crash hat.'

Doyle stood up and went towards the door. 'Well, that's it then, until tomorrow.'

'Just one thing, mister, I've a wake ta go ta. It'll be tomorrow night and I've a funeral the next mornin', but I'll only be away a short time. Ye should manage without me for a while, like.'

'That's all right. Is it someone in yer family that's died?' responded Doyle, out of inquisitiveness more than politeness.

'Fergus Sloan was me brother, mister.' The youth showed no emotion. Suddenly Doyle felt guilty about his attitude. Jamsie spoke up again. 'It's like this, mister, the bastard we're sizin' up could be the one who murdered me brother. That's the way I think of it, anyway.'

Seamus Doyle was beginning to think this youngster could be pretty useful after all.

'We'll get him all right, ye can bet on it,' he said.

'Oh, we'll get him, mister. He's goin' ta be fixed good and proper.' Doyle wasn't sure if he saw a tear in the corner of the youth's right eye, but Jamsie Sloan quickly wiped his face with the sleeve of his pullover as he turned and left the room.

3

At 9.30 a.m. Barney Somerville telephoned the Chief Superintendent's office.

'I'm sorry, Barney, the Chief's engaged at the moment, but I think he'll be wanting to see you later on this morning.' The response took him by surprise. The staff officer continued, 'In fact you saved me a phone call; he said to tell you to keep yourself available. I assume you'll be in your office until lunch?'

'Yes, George, I'm here when he's free. Thanks.' Somerville put down the receiver. Something in George's voice alarmed him.

The door of the Divisional Commander's office was closed behind Somerville by the staff officer. He was in full uniform and came to attention in front of the executive knee-hole desk. Chief Superintendent Morrow was seated, head down, signing papers. He was fifty-three years of age and had been in the RUC since he was twenty-one. A tall man, slimly built, he could have easily passed for someone in their mid-forties, except that his white hair – brushed over a barren area from just above the left ear – betrayed him. He removed his black-rimmed glasses and looked directly at Somerville, who responded with a salute. Without speaking he motioned Somerville to sit in the side chair. Barney complied and removed his cap, running a hand through his thick blond hair.

'Inspector, I shall come directly to the point. I have this morning received a communication from the Chief Constable's office. A full investigation has been directed into your activities while you served in Belfast, specifically into your own financial background.' Somerville had expected some trouble over his men's actions at Strabane, but this was preposterous.

'What are you talking about exactly?' he asked.

'Specific allegations have been made to the Chief Constable about your involvement in the illegal gaming and racketeering investigations in Belfast last year. A number of officers have been implicated, and you in particular.'

'I'd like to hear the details of these so-called allegations. This thing's ridiculous, sir!'

The Chief Superintendent pressed an intercom on the side table. 'Have the Superintendent come in, please, and see we're not disturbed until further notice.' He flicked the switch off, not waiting for any reply.

Seconds later the door opened to reveal a man in a smart lounge suit. Somerville immediately recognised him as Superintendent Percy Johnston from the RUC's Complaints and Discipline Branch, an ex-detective from one of the Crime Squads. He didn't much like the man.

'I believe you know Superintendent Johnston here,' said the Commander.

'Yes, sir.'

'I will let the Superintendent outline the allegations.' Johnston moved across to the Commander's desk, opened the black briefcase and removed a manila folder, pulling out some papers.

'Is your full name Inspector Edward John Somerville, Registered Number 9846?'

'You know it is.'

'Inspector, while a Detective Sergeant serving with C1 Branch in Belfast you investigated a number of illegal gaming establishments during the early and middle part of 1981.'

'That is correct.'

'Did you investigate the "Golden Nugget" Amusement Arcade owned by Murray Developments?'

'Yes, I believe I did.'

The reaction of the Superintendent was slow and deliberate as he handed Barney two sheets of paper. They were photocopies – the first being the cover of a bank deposit book from the Allied Irish Bank. It was marked clearly in the name of Edward John Somerville, with the address of his old house in Belfast and his new Omagh address superimposed in black ink. The second sheet depicted an account ledger, or part of it, showing monthly deposits, always on the fourth or fifth day over the last twelve months and up to 4 May 1982. Each was for the same amount of £1,000: a grand total of £12,000, with a withdrawal of £700 in January 1982.

'Is that your account, Inspector?' snapped the Superintendent.

'I wish it was.' Somerville smiled as he handed back the sheets.

'This is no joking matter, Inspector!'

'No, that is most definitely not my account.'

The Superintendent handed Somerville some further papers.

'I now show you the statement obtained from Mr Desmond Murray, managing director of Murray Developments Limited. Take your time to read it.'

When Somerville had finished, he gave the typed copy back to the Superintendent.

'Furthermore, we have another statement from the bank manager with whom you opened the account. He – and indeed one of his members of staff, a cashier – can identify you as having opened the account and calling in each month to deposit the money.' The Superintendent paused. 'We naturally reserve those statements for the moment, Inspector.'

'Well, it's obviously not a mistake, Superintendent,'

45

said Somerville. 'Someone has the knife out for me. I made a lot of enemies in Belfast.'

The Superintendent appeared to ignore Somerville's words. 'The Deputy Chief Constable has been consulted. He has instructed that pending a full investigation into this matter you are hereby suspended from duty on full pay.'

The words echoed in Somerville's ears and it appeared that Johnston was actually enjoying the moment. He was then handed two more pieces of paper. One outlined the allegations, and the other was formal notice from the Chief Constable of his suspension from duty and an explanation of his new status. The Divisional Commander pressed the button on his intercom again and then quickly switched it off.

Somerville did not reply to the Superintendent's caution. He stood up slowly, but felt like punching a wall. At that moment the staff officer re-entered the room.

'I'll be in contact with you next week. Be available,' said Johnston. As Somerville was being escorted from the room, the Superintendent fired a parting shot. 'Just one more thing, Inspector, your bank account is frozen. I've a court order in my possession.'

Somerville was met in the hallway by a Chief Inspector hurriedly summoned from the local station. On returning to his office, he changed out of uniform and quickly accounted for all of his equipment and clothing to this man. He was sympathetic. 'Look, Barney,' he said, 'just leave things as they are. I'll take care of the documentation and make sure the place is left secure. I'll have one of the SB boys take over the paperwork in your absence.'

'Thanks. I don't think I've the stomach to speak to anybody right now.' Somerville's mouth and throat were sore and dry. All he wanted was a drink.

'There's just one thing, Barney,' continued the Chief

Inspector. 'You know you'll have to be issued with a firearms certificate for your service revolver now you're suspended from duty.'

'Yes,' replied Somerville, pulling on his leather jacket over the maroon sweatshirt.

'Look, I'll arrange that for you.' The Chief Inspector almost apologised. 'Hold on to the gun and ammunition in the meantime.'

'You'll be needing this,' Barney hissed, tossing his warrant card on the desk top where it clicked sharply against the veneer surface. A crop-haired, convict-like photograph of a much younger Somerville stared innocently at the ceiling through the blur of the plastic cover. When Somerville flashed that card he was known not as a person, not as Mr Edward Somerville, but as Inspector Somerville, a policeman. It brought respect, awe, entrance to pubs, clubs, society. It was better than the 'old school tie', membership of the bankers' club or a Masonic handshake! It was part of him. Now he felt stripped . . . empty . . . personless. The sense of loss overwhelmed his anger.

The telephone burred into life in a second-floor office in RUC Headquarters, Brooklyn, at Belfast. It was answered after the second ring.

'It's Johnston. He's suspended with effect from this morning.'

'Thank you, Percy . . . Perhaps you would join me for lunch some day next week. Give me a shout nearer the time.'

'I will, thank you. Cheerio.' The line went dead. Detective Chief Superintendent Grange returned to the array of files which covered his desk.

When he got home, he found Janet had taken the youngest child to the doctor's. He'd caught a chill after refusing to come out of the water at Benone beach.

Relieved to be alone, Barney flicked on the kettle and switched on the radio. The latest news from the Falklands was gloomy – another ship sunk, numerous Argentine aircraft destroyed. Momentarily, he imagined himself in the thick of the San Carlos landing . . . But he had no patience for the news and he switched off the radio and, leaving the kettle to stop automatically, he headed for the bathroom.

Standing under the shower he turned the handle to cold, but even the chill of the water couldn't make him stop thinking about what had happened.

His head began to clear afterwards, and his embarrassment gave way to anger – anger at whoever had done this to him. He decided to go for a long walk with Boots, the family's black labrador; he could always think better outdoors.

The afternoon he spent at the bedside of Billy Martin, whom he found to be improving rapidly.

'Tell me it isn't true, Barney?'

'Do I need to?'

'What the hell's it all about?'

'Simple, someone wants me off the force . . . and by the looks of it they've done a fine job. OK, I'd plenty of opportunity to take bribes and I always suspected there were those who had, but the fact is that I didn't. I'd even made several requests to the ACC, Crime, for my original investigation to be taken off the shelf it had so conveniently been placed upon.'

'Well, surely even the Chief Constable can see that it's them just trying to get their own back.' Billy wriggled himself into a more upright position.

'What can I do?' said Somerville. 'Officially I'm not permitted even to approach my accusers.'

'Typical, bloody typical.' Billy Martin gritted his teeth. Somerville forced a smile.

'Enough about me, Billy. You're tired. Get some rest and I'll see you at the weekend.'

'I might be getting out soon. The doctors say the bullet went almost clean through, no bones broken, just a bit of muscle and nerve ends damaged . . . I'll be up and around in a couple of days. You'd better get a bottle ready to celebrate the homecoming. The wife says now she'll get all that decorating she wanted, but only after I promise to take her to Majorca!' Billy managed a painful laugh.

'That's a date, old son. We'll have a hell of a party.' Somerville smiled back. He left the hospital grounds quickly – at that moment Barney Somerville needed a drink more than breath itself.

It was late when Janet returned. She was laden down with shopping, and it took Barney several trips to the Cavalier to clear the boot completely. Thomas and Maria were engrossed in their orange lollipops. Afterwards Barney made little conversation and sat in the lounge watching a children's television programme. He was quickly joined by the youngsters and partook of a small piece of each ice. Janet hadn't asked any questions, even as to why he was home from work early. He decided to leave the issue until later, after the children were tucked up in bed.

He had made the right decision. Janet was extremely upset, at one stage almost hysterical. He believed she was even half convinced of the allegations when she said there was no smoke without fire. Bitterly, he realised he had anticipated as much. The next day was little better. Word soon got round town, and Janet did not react well to the mock concern of the other police wives, nosy neighbours and even shopkeepers.

Wednesday 26 May – A housing estate at Omagh
Doyle had studied his prey at close range and noted the man seldom left the white-walled detached bungalow. He assumed the other business mentioned

by Murray had taken place, but that would not stop his particular plans for the bastard.

The meeting with McNamara was more than he had expected. The Commandant was not alone. As well as the heavies, who had disappeared into the hallway, another man stayed in the room. McNamara placed both hands on the table facing Doyle.

'This here is Brian Magee. He'll help decide yer plan.'

The men talked for over an hour, and when the door finally opened again Doyle could be in no doubt about one thing.

'I never wanted ya here from the start,' said McNamara. 'You'd better be fuckin' sure of yer plans.'

Doyle left in the Mini driven by Sally Dines. She had accepted his silence, but never gave up. 'Want to go for a drink, Seamus?'

'Why not!' The reply startled her.

Kevin McNamara left the house an hour later with Brian Magee.

'What do ya think of him, then?' McNamara asked as they drove away.

'Can't see why Dublin wants the hit by him. We've plenty just as good, maybe better.' Magee shifted the Escort into top gear.

'Think he'll do the job all right?'

'Or I'll kick his fuckin' guts out!' Magee laughed.

'Can ya set up the other actions for Friday morning, then?'

'I could have taken in that black bastard as well, if they'd liked!' said Magee, glancing at the Chief.

'Make it good, will ya? After buryin' them four yesterday, I want them to remember Friday. I want that real bad.'

Kevin McNamara was forty and, although the OC in Tyrone, leant heavily on his thirty-one-year-old deputy. Magee was the product of Long Kesh, the

Maze Prison. He had been sentenced for his minor part in the planting of explosives at Ballygawley. The prosecution lawyers had dropped the 'possession with intent' bit and he had quietly accepted 'possession', receiving the clemency of the court and resultant five years' imprisonment. He had already served one and a quarter years on remand and, with the government practice of releasing offenders on licence after they had completed half their sentence, he had only endured another fifteen months. In 'H' Block, he learnt much about the theory and principles of terrorism: how to arm and fire an RPG rocket-launcher, how to make improvised explosive devices from everyday kitchen items and fertiliser, even the theories of Marx and Lenin. He preferred the first two lessons to the latter. He lost some weight in prison, not as a result of hunger strike, just from aversion to the place. And then some do-gooder social worker argued with the prison authorities that life behind the wire was prejudicial to his health, and that there was no reason why Magee should not return to society and use the experience he had gained from the prison tool-shop. There was even the offer of a job in a local light engineering works outside Cookstown. The naïve social worker had no inkling that the job had been arranged by the Provos to enhance Magee's chances of freedom. And that what he had learnt in the tool-shop was, basically, how to construct home-made mortars, make their warheads and build their firing platforms.

So it was that Brian Magee, aged twenty-five, standing five feet eight inches tall and weighing only nine and a half stone, was released from prison. During the next six years he had been lifted regularly by the police and Army. He paid visits to the Holding Centres at Gough Barracks and Castlereagh on a regular basis, but said nothing every time. He wouldn't tell them his name, ask to go to the toilet, or walk from his cell to the interview room or back again. He would refuse to eat while he was in their custody, and it soon became a well-known fact that 'the animal' Magee would quite often urinate on to the table in the interview room or literally drop his trousers and squat on the floor. His behaviour had incurred many beatings, but even the detectives from the Crime Squads squirmed when their names were picked to interrogate him. Interrogating Magee was akin to talking to yourself for four hours non-stop. In the end the interviewer went mad.

His behaviour was well noted by his own side. Not only was he deeply involved in the development of the Mark IV mortars, but he now took personal charge of debriefing all the boys lucky enough to get out of the Holding Centres. They appointed him Intelligence Officer for the area, number two to McNamara, and he didn't take kindly to any city slicker coming to his area, even if he was a good Provo.

Doyle had ruled out a gun attack; he had decided on explosives and knew his technique. Over the last four days he had observed one important weak link in the armour of his victim. Somerville took his children to school each morning, and there was a short time that he spent in the car alone, when he was taking it out of the garage.

Across the kitchen table of the old woman's house, he examined the pieces Jamsie Sloan had procured for him – the timer power unit which had been adapted for physical ignition and the fishing line he had selected in place of the mercury tilt switch. He estimated the full impact of the explosion would be better in the confined space of the brick garage, and that made his task easier. He didn't care what the children saw of their father afterwards, but his war was not against kids. They always remained in the house until he got the car out of the driveway. He completed the device with 5lbs of Frangex commercial explosive and attached the electric detonator that he had carefully removed from its cotton-wool wrapping. The fresh battery was placed inside the TPU and for the moment the wires leaving the box remained unattached to the explosive. He bonded their ends with insulating tape as a safeguard.

Thursday 27 May – Blackhill Park, Omagh
Somerville had not conversed with Janet that evening. She finally went to bed at around ten o'clock and he heard their bedroom door slam shut. She didn't care for his drinking and had told him to stop feeling sorry for himself. She had even voiced her suspicions again, and that he couldn't take. The telephone rang in the kitchen, but he didn't answer it. He turned up the volume on the stereo unit and reached for the whisky bottle. The more questions he asked himself, the more confused he became. By 3 a.m. his head was pounding. On the radio, the Falklands campaign still dominated the news headlines, interrupting the dreary dance-band show. But by then Barney had at last fallen back on to the sofa and was asleep. He didn't hear the radio show draw to a close or the ensuing static from the twin speakers. Nor did he hear gloved fingers tampering with the garage door. Neither did Boots, already dying in his kennel, overcome by poisoned meat.

The garage door was of the 'up and over' variety, constructed in lightweight metal. Doyle had done his homework well and had practised on the same type of door at another unfinished bungalow on the adjoining building site. He slipped the five-inch-bladed knife down the left-hand side until it came into contact with the horizontal holding bar. A little careful manipulation induced the bolt to move from the wood– and metal-lined door frame and a further adjustment eased the bolt well into the open position. The door was eased slowly open by Jamsie Sloan. It gave a slight rattle and Jamsie stopped for a moment, but kept the door up to give Doyle the additional benefit of the strong moonlight.

When Doyle turned to the youth and took the haversack, Sloan was trembling and visibly sweating. Doyle smirked and set the haversack down gently beside the driver's side of the Cavalier. Jamsie Sloan turned and kept an eye out for unwelcome visitors. Doyle gently cleaned the road dirt from the underside of the car, directly under the driver's seat. After clearing the small area, he blew the dried mud over the garage floor to the far side and began unbuckling the haversack. The TPU was a wooden box, nine inches long by four inches wide and two inches deep; it had a swivel lid which he eased to one side, and then primed the watch safety mechanism. Attached to the box by two-inch-wide adhesive tape were two powerful magnets. After a few seconds the box clunked gently against the body of the car, and Doyle connected the protruding wires on the near side of the TPU to the detonator and explosives which he stuck alongside. The wires were taped to avoid their hanging down, and he placed a further piece of tape across the Frangex to make sure it remained in position. The clothes-peg sat just proud of the one-inch hole in the side of the TPU.

He tied the nylon fishing line to the peg and attached the other end around the front axle of the car. The watch mechanism had given Doyle five clear minutes to arm the device, but it was done in less than three. All that was keeping the circuit from completion was the interruption of the clothes peg between the two tiny metal plates. The four feet of fishing line had a ten-ounce breaking strain, just sufficient to pull the peg from its nest but not enough to pull the TPU from its position. He made an adjustment to ensure the line was taut.

Doyle left the garage as quietly as he had entered. The small haversack was once again slung over Jamsie Sloan's shoulder. The only noise was heard by Freddie, the neighbour's cat, as the garage door was shut – a soft, metallic resonance as the sprung bar snapped into the home position. The journey over the garden fence and into the adjacent parkland went unnoticed, and Doyle could breathe again. There was no pleasure in fiddling with explosives. He returned to the old woman's farmhouse at 5 a.m. She had left the door on the latch for him. He went straight to bed and lay down, his body aching with the expulsion of all that nervous energy. It would be the last night he would stay in that poky room, and he was already tasting the pint of Harp that awaited him in Belfast.

Janet Somerville stirred to the sound of the alarm clock and rolled over in the empty bed to turn it off. Barney's side was cold. She made her way into the bathroom and, after showering, wrapped herself in a towelling robe and went into the kitchen. She saw the empty whisky bottle and imagined her husband sprawled on the lounge floor.

Janet knew perfectly well that he had to get the matter out of his system. She could have been more understanding and sympathetic ... not that deep within her she didn't feel those emotions. She loved Barney; she recognised his love for his job, and had always known that was the way it was. Once upon a time she had naïvely thought that she could accept second best. But like the parasite it was, the more love grew, the more of him she wanted. For years now she had wanted all of him – body, mind and soul. And yet she had to contend for him with this mistress. Yes, she was jealous, jealous of the time, energy and commitment he gave to work.

But she hated those who were now trying to hurt

him. She experienced his pain, knew his hurt, felt sick from the injustice of it all. After all, wasn't she an expert on the feelings of injustice! And maybe that was why – to get rid of her anger, her loneliness, her hatred of her husband's mistress – she had hit out at the man she loved. She couldn't quite touch the mainspring of his emotions, nor grasp the precise motives of those who were making this country such an agonising place, so she vented her distress on Barney himself. Even when she wanted to run and hold him to her, the defence mechanisms took over and her anger hit back. It was time to change. She knew he needed her more than ever now and she had to make an effort before they tore each other apart. Today, when the kids were at school they would talk in peace and, God, she promised she would try.

The kettle whistled before automatically switching off. Before getting the children, Janet took a blanket from the airing cupboard and went into the lounge. Barney was in quite a comfortable position, she thought, sprawled out on the three-seater settee, snoring quite loudly. She saw the second empty bottle on the coffee table and put it away before placing the blanket over him. He didn't stir. The warm feeling of her love rose from the pit of her stomach and, once more, she resolved her promise.

It was 8.45 a.m. before Janet Somerville got the children out of the house. It was pointless to disturb him; he would probably sleep until lunchtime. She looked long at her husband before closing the door. Outside she heard Julie Bennett, her neighbour, shout over, 'What! No Barney today? He's getting as bad as my Andrew!'

Janet kept a brave face and forced a smile. 'He's got a migraine this morning ... Afraid I'm caught with the job!' She waved the car keys at her neighbour and unlocked the garage door from a smaller key on the same ring.

The Cavalier would have to be reversed out and she could waste no more time. 'Come on, will you!' she cried to the two children, who bundled quickly into the rear passenger door. She jumped into the driver's seat, slamming the door shut. The car shook, the fishing line held taut.

'Damn him!' she thought, throwing her grey leather handbag on the front passenger's seat. He'll have to pull himself together, and with my help he will. She thought of waking him up after all, and dousing his drunkenness with black coffee when she returned from school. Her anger abated.

The 1798cc fuel-injected engine roared to a start with the over-use of the choke and Janet's foot. Reverse gear was always a problem to her, but on this occasion finding the gear position the first time reduced her life by another few seconds. The Cavalier had hardly moved from its position when the explosion occurred. Janet Somerville knew nothing of it. Nor did Maria or young Thomas. They only experienced the blinding white flash, the searing heat that entered their lungs, the nothingness.

The roar of the explosion echoed throughout the suburbs of Omagh town that morning. The first to know of it was Barney Somerville as the bay window and its mahogany frame crashed into the lounge, flinging the drawn curtains on to the centre of the floor. Barney sensed what had happened immediately, but refused to believe it. Rushing quickly to the hallway over broken glass, wood, and masonry dust, he was met by the sight of the front door blown open and hanging limply on its hinges. He tore out into the debris and black suffocating smoke, where he found the burning remnants of the Vauxhall surrounded by the ruins of the lean-to garage. The car roof was shoved high in the air, half detached from the body like an open sardine can. Janet's torso was sprawled on the front passenger seat, both legs severed at the groin, her face bloated and grey from the force of the blast which had ruptured lungs and blood vessels alike. He found Maria in the rear of the car. She was lying in the boot area of the hatchback, her neck obviously broken, covered in masonry and glass. Thomas. Oh, Thomas! he thought. Where was he? His heart raced, he cried out, 'Son, where are you!' He began to feel the tears well up, and the sickness in his stomach rose to the tightness of his chest. *He was standing on him!* Or at least one little arm. The rest of him was outside the car, partly splattered against the rubble and partly under it. He was in pieces.

Barney staggered out of the rubble, half running up the driveway. He had seen it so many times, but now he had lost all self-control. He stumbled and fell on to his knees. People began to gather at the scene, but he didn't see them; he looked into the sky, spread his arms outwards and shouted. The sound he emitted was unrecognisable, a war-cry, a scream of despair.

By 9.30 a.m. police, Army and other relief workers had taken control at Blackhill Park. Ambulances had taken Julie Bennett and her young daughter to the local hospital, both slightly cut by flying glass and suffering from shock. They had also removed three other neighbours, one an old man who had since suffered a heart attack. He was later to become the fourth victim of Seamus Doyle – not that anyone seemed to care, except for his family who said openly to the newspapers, 'That's what you get when you live beside a policeman.'

Barney Somerville was sitting on the wet grass at the bottom of the garden. He stared blankly at the parkland beyond, towards the tracks in the long grass where the two terrorists had made their entrance and escape. When Constable John Ross found him, he stood up automatically and walked towards the house. He paused for a moment to look at Boots lying dead in his pen, his face distorted and swollen tongue protruding between his teeth. Barney did not react. He felt no pain. He walked on towards the back door.

The news of the explosion travelled fast. But it was heard fastest and most accurately from the commercial station, 'Downtown Radio', which is one of the main means the Provisionals have to quickly confirm their own success or failure. Doyle was awakened at 10 a.m. when the first report was being broadcast.

'C'mon quick!' shouted Jamsie Sloan.

Doyle stirred in the camp-bed and began rubbing his eyes.

'You're to get up. The Chief wants ya. He's in the livin' room!'

'OK, OK, I'm comin',' muttered Doyle, coughing and sniffing as he stood up from the unsteady bed.

'C'mon, townie!' shouted Jamsie Sloan.

Doyle wiped the sleep away and attempted to focus on the obvious insult. 'Who da'ya say wants me?'

'The Commandant. Get inta the other room now!' Doyle thought for a moment that young Sloan was going to try a swing at him.

On entering the living room Doyle saw Kevin McNamara with legs astride by the fire. Beside him stood Brian Magee.

'What's up?' He sensed the hostility in the air, and took in a third man, his explosives supplier and quartermaster for West Tyrone, Peter Walsh.

'From the news, it appears ya've fucked up. Ya've killed a complete family – all that is except, of course, the fuckin' target himself!' shouted McNamara. 'Ya've really fucked it up, ya bastard!'

Doyle made no reply. His mind raced, going over the plan point by point, trying to assess how the miscalculation had come about. He wasn't prone to mistakes. The fate of the family was irrelevant to the effect on his pride.

'I've stopped our other action. We're not coverin' for the likes of you!' McNamara was still shouting at the top of his voice. 'I don't intend to reduce this Brigade's standing any further! I want ya out of here now! So pack yer fuckin' bag and piss aff before I change ma mind . . . Understand?' McNamara stepped away from the fireplace, and for the first time in ages Doyle felt frightened. As the Commandant moved, Magee took his clenched hands out of his pockets as if preparing to back up his chief's words with force.

'All right! All right!' said Doyle. 'Whatever ya say.'

Sally Dines was waiting for him when the others left the farmhouse. The old woman stood in silence as he passed through the doorway. She watched the Mini pull away from the small house and gave no reaction to Doyle's wave as they sped off.

On arriving at the Ulster bus depot he sat in the car with Sally until the 11.15 a.m. was ready to board. 'Will I see ya again, Seamus?' She tried to make him relax.

Doyle was tapping his right foot on the floor of the Mini, a nervous reaction to his failure and dressing-down by McNamara. 'Aye, I suppose so. If yer ever in Belfast seeing yer uncle, give us a call.'

'I'd like ta see ya again. If ya want us to, that is?'

Doyle thought of that Wednesday night when he had taken advantage of the wee girl and got himself drunk, mainly on her money. The drink had got the better of him when she parked the Mini outside the farmhouse, and her kissing had quickly aroused him. She had asked him many questions:

'Do ya have a regular girl, then?'

'Where do ya go drinking in Belfast?'

'Uncle Paddy says ya could have stayed workin' for

the magazine down in Dublin. Ya must have brains ta burn.'

He politely responded to her excited interrogation, but clammed up at the mention of Dublin. Work never combined with pleasure, but Doyle didn't mind really. He was amazed by her sexual expertise.

'Yeah, I'd like that,' he said. For the first time in the conversation he looked at her face. 'You're a hell of a wee girl, d'ya know that?'

She smiled and kissed him on the cheek. 'There's yer bus now. You'd better hurry.'

He opened the car door and lifted the small bag from the rear seat.

'I'll see ya, then.' He nodded at the girl and closed the door.

11.30 a.m. – Royal Courts of Justice, Belfast
Sir Ralph Hawthorne was called to the telephone at the Bar Library, situated in the heart of the Royal Courts of Justice at Chichester Street. He had been briefing several of his newly-appointed junior counsels on the pitfalls of a forthcoming murder trial involving a young IRA activist from Londonderry, and had only consented to leave the meeting after the second interruption from the elderly porter. On being shown to the telephone amidst the table-top array of legal journals and magazines, he picked up the receiver.

'I'm telling you, Ralph, they are bloody dead!' cried Williams.

'Control yourself man!' Sir Ralph turned round, glaring across the room, but no one was within earshot. 'Just keep calm and listen . . . I do not want to discuss this subject now. I will be in touch when I get more information. Don't contact me like this again, do you understand?'

'I'll be at home this evening,' replied Williams, the

61

panic still apparent in his voice. 'Maybe you'd give me a call or meet me at the Club.'

'I'll be in touch.' Sir Ralph replaced the receiver without waiting for a reply. As he walked back across the great hall that segmented the ground-floor court-rooms, he reminded himself to keep a closer eye on young Geoffrey in future. There was no room for mistakes, and there was a limit to his capacity to tolerate fools.

Doyle's journey to Belfast was not a direct one. The bus travelled to Coleraine eventually. Then, as he had been told by the girl, he waited before getting the train to Belfast and did not arrive at York Street Station until 7.15 p.m. that evening. He was tired of the journey and glad to be back, but also apprehensive about the inevitable reaction of his superiors and timid of the waiting reception. He remembered Joe McNulty's words and shivered.

Sunday 30 May – Omagh Town

The funeral was not from Blackhill Park, but from the funeral parlour at the High Street. The church was bulging with tightly squeezed bodies amidst the press and television reporters, the interior bathed in the brightness of powerful arc-lamps. Extra speakers had been placed outside in the church grounds, where the remainder of the gathering stood in silence. The church service ended at 11.50 a.m. and the interment at the cemetery was completed by 1.15 p.m.

Barney Somerville stood at the side of the hole staring at the three coffins below. At his insistence they had been placed one on top of the other. Firstly Janet, followed by Maria and then finally the little box containing what they could find of Thomas. He stood grim-faced as the minister recited the seventy-third psalm, but the loving words and message were lost on him. He reacted with automatic acknowledgement to the offering of condolences. By the end of that afternoon he imagined he must have shaken the bones of his right hand out of position. The sympathy extended by senior police officers, politicians and local dignitaries was accepted in silence. Everyone remarked on his coolness and fortitude, everyone except Billy Martin. Billy approached Barney at the graveside as part of the long queue of mourners.

'Sorry I can't shake your hand, mate,' said Martin timidly.

Somerville emerged from his mesmeric state momentarily to catch sight of Martin's right arm in a white sling underneath the flapping jacket, as the wind rose up yet again that showery day.

'Billy . . . I didn't know you were out . . . you're looking good.'

'I'll catch you later, Barney. I'll call at the house.'

Then he was gone in the continuing line of people as if shunted along in a railway siding.

Billy Martin called at 9 p.m., let in through the replacement front door by the duty constable. The police had placed a guard on the house until after the funeral, and to Chief Superintendent Morrow's great displeasure Somerville had refused to move out, stating, 'I'll go when I'm good and ready.' Billy found his friend in the kitchen ε .ting at the breakfast bar paging through a photograph album.

'Can I join you?'

'Billy . . . come in. I knew you'd come.'

'What does that mean? Telepathy?' Billy smiled.

'We've been in some tight fixes and survived. You know my mind better than me at times.' Barney closed the album.

'I do, that's what's worrying me . . . I could see something today that frightened me.'

Barney looked at him coldly. 'So what are you going to do about it?'

'Nothing . . . if it's what you want. I can't say anyone would blame you.' Billy turned away. 'I'd join you myself if – '

'No!' Barney stood up. 'I'll pay for your silence though. Let's have that drink.' He went to the high-level kitchen cupboard and produced a bottle of 'Cream of the Barley'.

'Now you're talking,' Billy grinned.

Both men drank deep. Billy referred to it as the 'Last Supper', and Barney quickly reminded him of what happened to Judas.

That night he lay alone in the south wing of the bungalow; the remainder was sealed off by sheets of hardboard and polythene. He ignored the constant police guard that kept changing every 90 minutes, and the clatter of their feet and muffled conversation which only emphasised the emptiness. He had already decided what had to be done, and he slept a dreamless sleep.

The local police didn't take the triple killing lying down. The death of the pensioner from coronary thrombosis – his final attack attributed to the explosion – only enhanced their determination to apprehend the perpetrators. Special Branch, and the Crime Squad detectives drafted into the area, had decided to pick up ten of the best-known Provisionals in the region. Amongst those arrested under Section 12 of the Prevention of Terrorism (Temporary Provisions) Act (N.I.) 1976, was Kevin McNamara. It meant that he would spend forty-eight hours in Gough Barracks at the Holding Centre and then the Secretary of State would have to extend his detention for another five days or they would have to release him.

*

Somerville's day and night routine continued uninterrupted until the following Saturday, the fifth of June, when he put his plans into irreversible action. He had left the house on foot, running over the parkland to the Rover Saloon situated in the large council car park.

The guard at the main gate to the police complex even forgot that Inspector Somerville was no longer permitted to travel freely round the establishment. The murder of a man's family overrules the rules.

'Hello, sir. My condolences. I'm sorry, I couldn't get to the funeral,' blurted Constable Glasgow.

'Thanks, George,' said Barney, as he drove slowly through the gateway. He didn't look back; he couldn't afford to. When he estimated no one was about, he left the car in the rear yard and entered the separate annexe. Once in the hallway, he used the combination door lock and went into the office area. Gathering up what little he required from his office, he placed the items in a canvas bag and proceeded to the armoury. Each HMSU had its own separate armoury, which avoided unnecessary questions by inquisitive local police with big mouths. Somerville knew exactly what he required and took it.

At 10.30 that same night Kevin McNamara was released and finally arrived home at his house in the Killybann Estate. He had spent a full seven days in Gough Barracks at the pleasure of the Secretary of State and of course Special Branch, but they couldn't make him talk. The system was against them anyway. He was surrounded by closed-circuit TV cameras and uniformed guards. The only thing he had to do was say nothing. 'Say fuck all. That way the bastards can't twist anything.' The words of Magee rang in his head the whole time. Yes, the bastards were good at twisting things around, but they weren't good enough to get the Commandant. They would get fed up talking to the wall before he would tire looking at it. It was a waiting game and he had decided the ground rules a long time ago. The PIRA solicitor had already telephoned to say he was on his way to Omagh, courtesy of the RUC.

He was delighted to be home. The youngest of his kids were kept up especially to see him. He ate the Ulster fry quickly, washing it down with a mug of hot coffee. The kids were climbing all over him, but he didn't care. He had been on his own and nobody cared. Nobody cares when you're inside, faced with the prospect of years of prison life – at least, not unless you decide to 'grass' in lieu of your mistakes. He went to bed happy that night and, as he lay between the stale-smelling sheets, he held his wife closely, just glad he was still there. He had beaten the Holding Centre for the seventeenth time in four years, but each time it was becoming harder, and others knew it just as he did. That was his biggest danger.

4

Kevin McNamara slept poorly. He hadn't enjoyed
making love that night; she had tugged and pulled at
him like some wild beast. Perhaps it was her way of
welcoming him home, or maybe she really was frustrated. He lay there and let her do the work. She jerked
off his underpants and was quickly straddling him,
guiding him inside and bouncing up and down. She
had pulled off her nightdress and bent over him,
rubbing her large breasts in his face. He had put on a
show that night; his testicles hurt from her downward
thrusting, but he played the game until after she
climaxed, shaking and shuddering. He had lain there
beside her sweating body, unable to relax again, but
finally drifted into the twilight zone between sleep and
consciousness.

He was aware of the single kick to the back door as
wood and glass burst from the door-frame. The figure
raced through the house at speed. A single light was
turned on from above. McNamara stood at the top of
the staircase, half expecting the Brits in yet another
late-night search. But this was too early, even for them.
What he did not expect was the nightmare awaiting
him at the bottom of the stairs. From the small landing
he could see the figure clearly, green woollen balaclava
helmet covering the face except for eye-holes and
mouthpiece. The camouflaged man stood squarely
behind a folded Luigi Franchi Spas 12 military
shotgun. The first magnum-loaded cartridge erupted
towards McNamara, taking him in the chest. Blood
splashed over the walls and staircase, combining with

wooden splinters from the balustrade. The force threw McNamara two feet back into the mezzanine wall and, as if hitting rubber, he rebounded forwards in slow motion, slithering to an eventual stop at the bottom of the stairs. He couldn't feel the pain, but he knew he was finished. He hadn't taken in air since being blown open and was even too weak to choke on the blood now entering his throat and mouth. McNamara could just about focus on the black size-10 boot as it dug into his shoulder, kicking him back against the wall. He got a better look at his killer and saw the eyes, emanating hate. Then the muzzle also came into vision, barely twelve inches from his eyes. His mind never recorded the flash from the blast.

The assassin exited through the back door. As he reached the car he heard the screaming. He jumped in and threw the Spas 12 on to the seat beside him, pushed the automatic gearstick into neutral and twisted the ignition key. The car spluttered, indicating an overdue service. It took all of twenty seconds to fire into life, which was enough time for Moira McNamara, in blood-stained nightdress, to reach the partly open door. Pulling it wide open, still screaming at the top of her voice, she grabbed for his right shoulder. His war was not with her and he gave her that benefit, until he saw the ten-inch kitchen knife poised in her right hand. He feinted on the tug and then, lashing upward with his taut left hand, he struck the woman on the throat. Choking, she toppled backwards on to the tarmac-adam, the knife slipping from her grip. As he glanced back, pulling the door shut, he saw the figure of a young boy – probably Gerard, the thirteen-year-old son. The boy quickly closed on the car, but not quickly enough to catch it as it pulled out of the estate.

Barney Somerville had made one miscalculation – his blow on Moira McNamara was more powerful than intended. He had crushed her windpipe and she died three and a half minutes after the blow landed.

The investigation of his mother's and father's murders did not concern young Gerard. He certainly was not going to help any black bastard of a detective find the angel of death.

It was not until that afternoon that Gerard had a chance to speak to the new Commandant in Tyrone. Brian Magee was greeted with respect when he arrived at the house and reacted, as they all wanted, to the family's cries for vengeance. He asked many questions about that night and the stranger in combat outfit:

'Was it the SAS?'

'Did he speak?'

'Did the cops seem surprised at the killing?'

'Was he alone?'

'How did he leave?'

He had almost given up getting anywhere. He had ruled out a feud with the INLA; it was not their style. He was concerned not so much by the professionalism of the shoot, but by the death blow inflicted on Moira. A shiver went up his spine. He was just leaving the sitting-room, gazing at the dried bloodstains in the hallway, when he heard young Gerard stir from his enclosed world of shock. The boy spoke in a whisper.

'There's one thing . . . I got the number . . .'

'*What* did ya say?' Magee moved back into the room, shutting the door and excluding the remainder of the family from the conversation.

'The car used was a blue Rover . . . the number was TOI 4322.'

He still only whispered; the injection and tablets from Doctor McKinley were taking effect.

'Are ya sure of that number?' asked Magee, shaking the boy by the shoulders to keep him awake.

'Yeah . . . I writ it down on the phone book in the hall.'

Sure enough Magee found the number scrawled almost illegibly on the front cover: 'TOI 4233'. He returned to the sitting room.

'Have ya told anyone about the number, son?'

'No . . . nobody,' whispered Gerard as he drifted off to sleep in the armchair. Magee left the house, assuring relations crowded in the kitchen and dining room of the Provos' actions, promising to be back for the wake and announcing that the double funeral would be with full paramilitary trappings. None of them argued. They knew better.

The police made little headway that day. McNamara's family were aggressive and distant, which was consistent with the attitude that peelers endured in the nationalist areas. They were even accused of the murders by the local Sinn Fein representative; there was nothing new in that either.

It was 4 p.m. when the local PIRA council of war met. The meeting was short and swift and Magee gave his first briefing and directions. He outlined the incident and dampened their speculation by repeating the car number TOI 4233 – a stolen car perhaps, false number plates probably. Johnny Montague undertook to check his contacts in the motor trade that same afternoon and they all agreed to meet again at 7 p.m. that night.

What Johnny Montague found was more than even he had banked on. The local garage of Phillips and Maxwell had actually sold the same car four days previously and the name of the purchaser bounced his heart almost from his chest: '*E. J. Somerville, 42 Blackhill Park, Omagh.*'

'Yes, that's him!' said Montague, tightening his grip on the telephone.

The garage man continued, 'He paid cash. Say, wasn't that the fella that lost his wife and kids in the bomb?'

The 7 p.m. meeting was at Magee's cousin's farm and the room was crowded. Not only were eight members of the PIRA present, but an additional three from the local INLA. Magee stood up. 'I've taken the liberty of asking our INLA comrades here,' he said. 'The murder of our esteemed comrade and leader earlier this mornin' is widely condemned throughout Republican circles, and we've asked the INLA to help us track down the murderer. Information is that the car used belongs to a fuckin' RUC inspector!' He stopped, looking around the room. 'It's Somerville!'

For a moment there was silence, then someone muttered, 'I fuckin' told ya so.'

Magee continued. 'Ya all know his wife and kids were killed last week and no responsibility's been claimed.' All murmuring ceased. 'We've two considerations. Either this attack was carried out by Somerville and his mates in retaliation for the bombin' or else we've got a "renegade". In any case, no nationalist family is goin' to be safe until he's got. That's why it's been decided to work with the INLA to track the bastard down. The info is being passed on to the South Derry Brigade in case he moves north and I've got an assurance from the INLA that their people will do the same.'

Brendan Tully, commanding the INLA in West Tyrone, nodded his approval.

'I have here some copies of newspaper pictures taken at last week's funeral and I've circled the bastard in red ink.' Magee handed out the photographs, which showed Barney Somerville as one of his wife's pallbearers.

Brendan Tully spoke up for the first time. 'May I

71

say that on behalf of the INLA we'll stop at nothin' to get the bastard.'

Magee acknowledged this declaration. Their petty differences were once again set aside as they united against the common enemy. The meeting drew to a close and Tully took Magee to one side. 'There's just one thing. I agreed in principle that we'd stop any offensive action until this cunt's caught, but there's something ya should know.'

'And what's that?' responded Magee, eyeing Tully warily. The settlement of their differences could never be permanent and at a later time he might be required to kill this man.

'We've a wee job set up in Pomeroy for Tuesday lunchtime: the Post Office. I suppose we'll have this bastard by then, but just in case we don't, I thought ya should know – wouldn't do if ya thought we were goin' behind yer back, like. It's important and it's been set up for some time. It would be a shame to lose out on choppin' a couple of black bastards.'

'No problem. We'll have the cunt by then all right.' Magee patted Tully on the back. 'C'mon, I'll see ya to the door.'

The meeting was over, and Magee and his two cronies sat drinking from the crate of Guinness left on the table by his cousin's wife. The young woman left the room again, shutting the door.

'How long's her hubby go ta do in the Crum?' asked Peter Walsh, referring to the woman's husband serving a prison sentence in H.M. Prison, Crumlin Road, Belfast.

'Another two at least.' Magee belched aloud from the gas in the bottled Guinness. He raised his left hand in front of him, fist clenched symbolically. 'Not fuckin' enough time to satisfy that wee girl in there!'

They all laughed, each indicating in turn just what they could do for her. It was now 10.30 p.m. and

Magee went on his own to speak to the young woman. After ten minutes he emerged from the front door accompanied by the other two men. Peter Walsh climbed into the driver's seat of the yellow Escort four-door saloon and they sped off through the driving rain, leaving the woman standing at the open door. The lane was about 400 yards long and was interrupted at intervals by additional side lanes, leading to adjoining fields and outhouses. It was at one of these junctions that the empty hay trailer had been rolled into position, but in the heavy rain Walsh didn't see the obstacle until it was too late. He jammed on the brakes and slid to one side, hitting the thorn hedgerow with the rear offside wing. The vehicle halted within inches of the trailer and the trio remained stunned for a moment, but Magee took control quickly.

'Reverse, fuck it! Quick!' he cried.

Walsh had already thrown the gears into reverse before Magee had finished speaking. As it moved slowly back through the mud tracks, the Escort halted momentarily in the side drain. Their hearts raced as the car then continued to move backwards. Visibility through the rear window was non-existent and the darkness of the night engulfed everything.

'Stick yer fuckin' head out!' shouted Magee and Walsh hurriedly rolled down the window and tried to get a better view from the side. They travelled thus for another twenty yards, it seemed, until they rounded a bend in the lane. Suddenly their path was lit up by headlights on full main beam, helped by two additional spotlamps on the front bumper of Somerville's Rover. The car came to a halt; it was then that Peter Walsh lost his head when the magnum cartridge ripped off his skull. The body shuddered with the nerve-ends interreacting, and began to shake uncontrollably, arms and legs thrashing, blood spurting on to the roof lining. The engine stalled, and Magee took the opportunity to escape by the rear near-side door. He dived into the thorn hedge and attempted to scramble over, ignoring the thorns and barbed wire as he hauled himself towards the other side of the five-foot-high obstacle. The pain was nothing to the paralysing blow on his back as his spine was snapped by the force of a metal shotgun stock. He lay half-way over the hedge, helpless in mid-air.

The other front-seat passenger had finally untangled himself from Walsh's writhing body and was half-way out of the car when he paused at the sight of Magee. Scrambling round the open door, he slipped in the mud and water and his escape bid ended six feet in front of the Escort. Bathed in the headlights of the stricken vehicle, his arched body catapulted forward with an increased velocity that could only come from the Spas 12. Like a juggler's object, he was hurled to the right by a second almost simultaneous blast which exploded his left buttock and kidneys in a translucent splash. He collapsed dead on the laneway.

Those moments seemed like for ever to Magee and he almost convinced himself, in the midst of his pain, that he'd been forgotten. He didn't feel the powerful grip of the hands on his legs as he was torn from the hedge and dumped face down on the road. A black boot rolled him over, and his eyes fixed on the sight which had so chilled his dead companion. He couldn't speak for shock as the black figure pulled him by the anorak hood and dragged him to the Rover. He was finally tumbled into the rear and through the crippling pain, he managed to push a few words from his throat.

'Why me?' The anger welled up inside him. 'Yer dead, ya bastard!'

The balaclava-helmeted figure leaned over and hit him with a haymaker on the chin. Brian Magee melted into oblivion.

*

At 11 p.m. the conference room at RUC Headquarters at Belfast burst into action. The meeting proper got under way at 11.15 p.m. on the arrival of the Chief Constable. Elements were present from Command Secretariat, Crime Branch, Force Control and of course Special Branch in the form of Detective Chief Superintendent Grange.

'Well gentlemen, shall we begin?' The Chief Constable looked at those seated around the top end of the long table.

'I have requested this emergency meeting of COG after careful consideration of information received from Tyrone. Mr Grange, perhaps you will lead off, please.'

'Yes, sir.' Grange slowly eyed the remaining officers at the table. 'Last month, on the 28 May to be precise, the family of Inspector Somerville was murdered by PIRA.' He paused, removing his reading glasses. 'The murders were never officially acknowledged by the terrorists because of the obvious embarrassment of failing in their real objective. Furthermore, the widespread condemnation from all sides has been, to say the least, ferocious . . . Today, as you are aware, a leading figure in the Provisionals, namely Kevin McNamara and also his wife Moira, were killed by a single man. Needless to say, the family were quite uncooperative with the police and not even a description has been given to the officers investigating.' He paused again, turning over the papers before him. 'However, our intelligence sources have revealed that the murderer was dressed completely in combat outfit and wearing a mask of some sort. Further, he had the ability to kill with a single blow. The deputy state pathologist's initial findings are that the woman died as a result of a karate chop, if you like, on the throat. It was delivered in such a way that the windpipe was crushed completely – the work of an expert.' He stopped and lifted another page, focusing his eyes through hand-held spectacles. 'The final aspect of this case is the use of a semi-automatic shotgun, using a magnum load of Winchester Super X. The make of gun has not yet been determined by our forensic people, but they seem to think – from the markings left by the ejector and striations on the spent case – it was a military shotgun produced by Franchi Arms. Our source further indicated that PIRA have started a hunt for a car, a blue Rover TOI 4233, which was seen leaving the scene.

'And now to the reason for this meeting. The vehicle in question was purchased last week in Omagh by Inspector Somerville, who, according to local police in the town, disappeared from home at some time during the last twenty-four hours. He was last seen at Five-miletown, when he purchased 100 shotgun cartridges of heavy magnum type, the same as that used on McNamara.'

The hush was broken by the Assistant Chief Constable responsible for Crime. 'I don't believe it. I know the man, he was in one of my Crime Squads until last year. He wouldn't take the law into his own hands like this!'

'Maybe, but what we have to accept is that we have a very dangerous man at large!' replied Grange. 'Everything points to him having killed these two people in direct retaliation for the deaths of his own family.'

The telephone on the side cabinet began to ring and was answered by the Chief Constable's staff officer while the discussion continued. Having replaced the receiver, he turned towards the Chief Constable, bending over him to whisper a message.

Grange was finalising his report. 'What we now have to decide is what action we take to stop him before the matter gets further out of hand.'

'It's already out of hand!' interrupted the Chief Constable. 'I have just received a message from Chief

76

Superintendent Morrow in Omagh with early reports of a double murder. Two sourced members of the Provisionals. A shotgun was used . . . it looks like our man again!' Grange stared at the table in front of him. 'A killing machine.'

'What did you say, Frank?' asked the Chief Constable.

'We, through the training we've given him – and of course PIRA, by their atrocious actions – have created a killing machine. Without emotion, nothing to live for except the destruction of his enemies – and I'm afraid that probably includes us!'

The Chief Constable looked over at Chief Superintendent Rankin. 'Bill, I think it's now appropriate for you to return immediately to Force Control and give me an operational order showing our coordinated efforts to catch this man without delay.' He turned to Grange. 'Frank, it's up to your people to get a fix on his whereabouts.' He glanced quickly at the remaining officers. 'I suggest we all adjourn, consider our options and meet again at 10 a.m. tomorrow. In the interim I want hourly reports throughout the night from you, Frank. And, Bill, I want the operational order on my desk within the hour.' Rankin paused at the door as the Chief Constable continued, 'This is an all-out effort, non-stop until he's in custody. There will be absolutely no press release at this stage, and the Force should be informed by MSX that Somerville is missing, believed to be mentally disturbed, possibly suicidal after the loss of his family. Are there any questions?' There were none. 'Thank you gentlemen, that will be all until tomorrow.' The first meeting of the Chief Officers' Group was over.

The room emptied quickly and the Chief Constable stood gazing out into the black void from the bullet-proofed window. Only his staff officer remained. The Chief Constable spoke in a whisper. 'You know, Frank

Grange is quite right; Somerville is a killing machine.'
He continued staring, not expecting a reply and
receiving none.

Monday 7 June – Davagh Forest, north of Dunamore, County
Tyrone

It was 12.30 a.m. by the time the Rover entered the
outskirts of the forest. The rain gusted hard against the
windscreen and visibility was difficult, even using the
full glare of the headlights. Somerville didn't see the
Volkswagen Beetle parked in the small lay-by at the
side of the road as he pulled into the track leading into
the centre of the forest; he was too busy keeping the
car on the narrow track. Driving rain obscured the
pothole and there was a sudden crack as the engine
sump hit rough stone and the car lurched to a halt.

In the Volkswagen, the teenage boy extricated
himself from his girl-friend's hot embrace and peered
out of the passenger window, rubbing the steamed-up
glass with the sleeve of his blue shirt. He caught a
distorted view of the Rover's tail-lights and stared as
he heard the engine running and the car door bang
shut. Then the vehicle disappeared down the lane into
the forest.

'What was it, Richard?' enquired the girl.

'Oh, nothing, just some fella looking for a place to
screw!'

'Don't be so crude!' She giggled. They fell back on
to the seat and continued kissing.

Barney Somerville had expected the sump to be
cracked and oil to be spilling out and his suspicions
proved correct. Within 300 yards the oil warning light
began to flash; by the time he got to the wooden barrier
it was showing a constant red. He quickly alighted
from the car and examined the barrier, which was still
held in position by a rusty nail. He kicked it open and
drove through, then closed the gate behind him. He

did not concern himself with the tyre-marks on the muddy laneway. Who would guess he was two miles inside the forest maze? He pulled up at a workman's timber hut next to a large concrete storage bunker.

The rusty lock on the hut door had been replaced with a new one which snapped open with ease. The room was damp and very cold. Lighting the Tilley lamp and turning up the wick, he surveyed the room. Everything was as he had left it. He quickly returned to the Rover and removed the Spas 12 along with the rucksack. Then having deposited them in the corner of the hut, he returned to the car with a flashlight. Magee was still alive but unconscious; he lifted him carefully from the car, carried him to the hut and laid him out on an unrolled sleeping bag in the far corner. Somerville checked his pulse; it was strong. Camouflaging the car took twenty minutes; cut wood and branches provided adequate cover from ground level, but from the air it could be discovered after a few seconds' prying. He banked on no helicopters being in the area.

Back inside, he sat on the floor and poured a cup of black coffee from the thermos flask he had removed from the rucksack. It was still quite warm. He drank slowly, thinking of 'the animal' lying on the sleeping bag – how he wanted to finish him, yet how much he needed him. He dozed off, still clutching the flask-top.

Somerville was awakened from the shallow comfort by 'the animal' stirring. He shook the tiredness from his head and crossed the wooden floor. Magee had opened his eyes and Barney burned the flashlight into his face.

'Good morning.'

Magee's eyes squeezed tight against the brightness of the light. His head ached and he felt peculiar. 'Give us a drink, will ya?' he croaked.

Somerville lifted his shoulders and gave him a sip of

the now cold coffee. Magee shook his head in a vain attempt to clear the pain and began to speak.

'What do ya want, Somerville? It is Somerville, isn't it?'

'I want answers to a lot of questions.'

Magee nodded. 'Why can't I move my body, what's happened?'

'I've broken your spine. You'll be dead soon unless I get you to hospital.'

'Ah, Jasus, no! No!' Tears formed in Magee's eyes.

'If I decide to leave you here, you're dead. Do you understand?'

'Yes, yes, for fuck's sake give us a chance!'

'Who killed my wife and children?'

'He was an outsider!'

'What do you mean "outsider"?'

'He was sent from Belfast.'

'What's his name? Who is he?'

Magee hesitated before answering. 'Doyle . . . Seamus Doyle. He comes from Andytown . . . that's all I know, I swear!' He was sobbing now.

'Why was he sent for me?'

'I don't know . . . but we'd to disguise his attack on ya by doin' other jobs.'

A strong hand closed on his throat and Magee felt the air in his chest well up as the fingers tightened. 'I'm going to ask you that again! Now think this time!' said Barney. He released his grip and Magee gasped new air into his lungs.

'I swear I don't know . . .' Magee gulped. 'He was sent, special, by Dublin and had to do the job by the end of that week. He was only with us for five days.' His eyes pleaded.

'Now tell me about your organisation in this area. Tell me where you got the explosives from. Tell all you know!'

The questioning continued for half an hour. Twice

80

Magee drifted into unconsciousness, only to be smacked sharply round the face until he was fit to continue.

'Who have you got looking for me?'

'All our Tyrone and Derry people and the INLA . . . Help me, please!'

'An unholy alliance, my friend,' said Somerville, unmoved. 'Who's in charge of the local INLA?'

'Tully,' Magee groaned.

'Brendan Tully?'

'Yeah.'

'He's come up in the world. What's he planning this weather?'

'Y'know better than that. The INLA tell us nothing!'

But Somerville detected something in Magee's face. 'He's planning something.' He shook the wounded man brutally. 'What? You haven't much time, you bastard!'

'Pomeroy Post Office on Tuesday. They're goin' ta take it when the money van arrives. Now please, for God's sake, help me!'

Somerville grabbed him by the throat for the second time and the squeezing continued for thirty seconds – not enough to crush the vital airpipe, but adequate to restrict its supply. Finally he released his grip and gave Magee ten seconds to recover.

'What was your part in the affair? Think carefully before you answer!' Somerville got to his feet.

'I told ya, ya killed the main one when ya killed McNamara. The others were just volunteers, helpers for Doyle.'

'I know that already. I asked you what your part in the affair was?'

'I had some knowledge; I was just asked what I thought about it after it was set up, honest.'

'The word "just" seems to belittle your involvement. I hope that wasn't your meaning?' Somerville began to pace the floor. 'One more thing.' He stopped. 'You don't have any kids, do you?'

'Naw.' Magee was watching Barney's every movement, a new fear creeping into his heart.

'Well, you'll find it a hard job now with that bust back.'

'Bastard!' cried Magee, the anger burning in him again. 'Kill me, damn you! Kill me! If you've the fuckin' guts!'

Somerville yanked Magee to his feet. Before he could say another word, a strong hand gripped his head by its thick hair. The second hand clasped his jaw and his head was twisted slightly to one side and then sharply to the other, and the jaw pulled upwards. Somerville heard the bone snap. 'The animal' was dead.

It was 4 a.m. by the time the young couple stopped at the vehicle checkpoint on the road back to Cookstown. The operational order had already taken effect. The policeman who spoke to them was well-known to the young man and they chatted for a few minutes. As he prepared to drive off, the officer in charge came over and bent down to the window.

'Just before you go, son, have you seen a blue-coloured Rover car at all tonight?'

'No, Sergeant, I can't say I have.' Richard looked embarrassed.

'Have you seen anything unusual up in the hills?' continued the officer.

'No,' Richard replied.

'What about the car at Darvagh?' interrupted his girl-friend.

Richard had forgotten about the incident. 'Oh yes, that's right. I saw a car when we were parked beside the forest. Come to think of it, it was a Rover!'

'What colour?' asked the sergeant.

'I couldn't be sure, but it was dark anyway.'

'How do you know it was a Rover?'

'I'd know the rear lights of a Rover anywhere. I'm a mechanic; it's my job to know.'

It was not long before Richard was pointing out the exact location on an Ordnance Survey map. He was sorry he had spoken, and that the girl had opened her mouth. They were held up at the VCP until well after 5 a.m.

It was 6.30 a.m. when Somerville heard the faint sound of a helicopter. His senses put him on full alert; it couldn't be a normal patrol at that time of the morning and in that area. How could they know his position? Nevertheless, there it was circling to the east. For three long minutes the four-seater Gazelle hovered overhead. The tyre-marks at the entrance to the clearing were spotted through self-focusing binoculars, but that was all. The discovery was reported to the Army commander on the ground.

'Hello, Sunray, this is Eagle 415. Have sighted tracks, grid reference 7124–8560. Over.'

The reply was immediate. 'Hello, Eagle 415, this is Sunray. Roger on your last, any sign of the vehicle? Over.'

'Hello, Sunray. Negative, I repeat negative. Over.'

'Hello, Eagle 415. Roger on your last, carry on a sweep to the north-west of the forest. Over.'

'Hello, Sunray, this is Eagle 415. Wilco and out.'

The Gazelle finally soared away and Somerville made his preparations. The roads would be blocked and he couldn't be certain that the helicopter had not spotted the car. He emptied the rucksack of all non-essential contents, then placed the blue package in the bottom, followed by the Zyconn FM 9000 U hand-held transceiver. With the additional crystals he had fitted into the radio, he could easily pick up both police and Army networks, using a combination of the 999 channels. The first-aid box was followed by ten rifle magazines each containing twenty-eight rounds, then the Ruger revolver wrapped in a leather shoulder holster and an accompanying box of twenty-four rounds of .357 magnum. The Spas 12 was completely dismantled and slid down the sides, along with the boxes of Winchester Super X.

Finally, Somerville checked the IWS night-sight he had removed from the Ruger rifle in the armoury. He switched it on to test the battery strength before wrapping it in the black jacket and tucking it into the side pocket alongside the hand-held Shermulley flares. Barney placed the smaller haversack on top of the other items in the rucksack, briefly counting its contents. Finally he checked the OS map of Tyrone and the smaller AA road-map of Ireland before zipping them into the top flap pocket. When the packet of sandwiches and carton of milk had been placed in the final pocket, he covered the bulky rucksack in a camouflage netting stretch cover. He chose to leave the fresh change of clothes behind. Checking the compass set, he looped it around his neck with a thong of leather; then, having zipped up the combat jacket, he put on the webbing belt, checking first that the small pouch was secure. A leather sheath was pulled on to his left forearm; into it Somerville slipped a six-inch double-edged Sykes-Fairbairn knife and secured it by an elastic strap. Placing an extra MI magazine in the calf pocket of his camouflage trousers, he pulled down the elasticated trouser bottoms well over the boot-tops. Then he tied a net scarf loosely around his neck and pulled on the rolled balaclava over his head. The broken-down version of the MI carbine was closely examined. He had chosen it because of its compactness; since the introduction of the Heckler and Koch weapons, the gun's disappearance from the armoury would go unde-tected that much longer. Not that it really mattered any more. He loaded the two long magazines taped together by black insulating tape; the second magazine was taped to the first with the open end facing the bottom, and a further piece of tape placed across the open end to keep the rounds in position. Each magazine contained twenty-eight rounds and two further magazines were placed inside the two jacket breast-pockets.

Finally Somerville set the charge on the home-made explosive device. It consisted of petrol in a gallon can, taped to a metal-cased charge with batteries, electric detonator and circuit. Making sure the clock hands were set at 8.30, he checked a second similar device and set its clock for 8.35. On leaving the hut he went over to the pile of wood and, removing three pieces, pushed the bomb in under the petrol tank of the Rover. Having replaced the wood he ran back to the hut, pulling on his rucksack and grabbing the MI carbine. He didn't even glance at the dead Magee.

Stepping outside the hut, Somerville locked the door and threw away the keys. The rain fell steadily as he moved through the thick spruce and pine and on to the dry bracken of the forest floor. He had just entered the cover when he heard the helicopter for the second time; dashing across another small clearing he stopped as it roared overhead. He could feel the downdraught on his head; they had spotted him. To Somerville's amazement the observer opened up with a GPMG from an opening in the side door. He dived for cover in the trees as the bullets danced around him. The helicopter's observer was cursing as the craft swayed in the increasing wind, causing his aim to be wide. Somerville cleared the open ground quickly, although bullets still rained into the spruce trees above and around him. It was all over in ten seconds, but they knew his position. He hadn't realised their determination to kill him; they would definitely be heading for his lair. For a few moments he lay still, assessing his proposed direction and tactics.

The corporal from the Ulster Defence Regiment found the wooden barrier at the track. He could see where the rusty nail had been removed and repositioned in the side post. This discovery was radioed to the Incident Control Point. The cordon around the forest was well planned by the local police inspector; the inner cordon consisted of police, with UDR and tracker dogs. The outer was made up of UDR checkpoints on all the approach roads. The first police search team to reach the clearing found the tyre-marks as they had been told. The forward search party, consisting of two constables and tracker dogs, was within a hundred yards of the hut when it exploded, sheets of flame pouring from the building. They dropped immediately to the ground, but the Alsatian which had approached within twenty feet of the hut was killed instantly.

The two constables approached the burning shell after a few minutes, then Constable Robert Bell decided to take cover behind the thick concrete bunker wall and pile of wood. Nervously he lit his first cigarette for two hours. As the wall caved in with the force of the second blast, he was killed outright when the concrete blocks collapsed on top of him.

It took some time for the confusion of the searchers to meld into organized reaction, and a further forty minutes for fire-brigade and ambulance services to arrive. The time was now 9.15 a.m. The outer cordon of police and Army was strengthened to double its original number. At the ICP, the inspector was questioning the MSX message sent from RUC Headquarters the previous night, indicating military primacy in the matter. He was also asking questions of the Army lieutenant as to why the helicopter had opened up on the man. The officer from the Royal Regiment of Fusiliers was non-committal; he was following orders precisely.

The meeting commenced at 10 a.m. sharp. The Chief Constable was sitting at the table when they all were shown into the ground-floor conference room. Once they had settled, he started. 'Gentlemen. We have all had a relatively sleepless night, and not without good reason. The incident at the Omagh farmhouse has been confirmed. It would now appear that our man has abducted a leading member of the Provisionals, now presumed deceased – I say deceased, due to the location of a body within the last hour. Initial reports from Tyrone are that we tracked down Somerville at a place called Davagh Forest – it's in the hills west of Magherafelt. At least two explosions have occurred there, one wrecking a workman's hut and the other a blue Rover car, the one we've been looking for. In the wreckage of the hut a single body was located, badly burnt but believed to be Magee, the missing Provo. The scene has not yet been examined by forensic and the ATO is still working with the debris.' He rose from the table and walked towards the VDU which showed the latest minute-by-minute update from the ICP at Davagh Forest. 'I will now pass you to Mr Grange.'

Frank Grange took his cue. 'It has now been revealed that an MI carbine and fifteen full magazines of ammunition have been taken from the inspector's armoury, along with some other night-vision equipment. Somerville – we have to presume it was him – also took a first-aid box including a thermal blanket, and, from our search of his home, it is clear that he has taken his legally held shotgun and personal issue revolver that he has kept under licence since his suspension. Our people reckon he is totally unconcerned about capture or facing charges of murder. Personally, I feel he's prepared for war!'

The Assistant Chief Constable from Crime Branch stepped in. 'I just do not accept that a man of his principles and calibre could actually react in such a fashion. We can only conclude that his family's killings were too much for him to bear. Perhaps we, sitting at this table, should have concerned ourselves with his well-being rather than let this bloody thing develop right in front of us!'

The Chief Constable stirred slightly at the accusation.

Frank Grange erupted, banging his fist on the table-top. 'Principles! The man hasn't got any! He was suspended for having his fingers in the till and I would like to remind you, sir, that he was in your department at the time!'

'That's quite enough!' rebuked the Chief Constable. 'We are not whining school-children fighting over who burst the ball! I should remind you all of the purpose of this meeting and what we have yet to achieve, but I won't!' The silence in the room was total. 'Let us again examine our problem and decide how best to deal with it, shall we?' The question begged no reply and no one dared speak. 'Mr Grange, please continue.'

The Chief Constable left the table as Frank Grange took his lead in a more measured tone. 'It is my view, and that of Special Branch, that he will not let himself be taken alive . . . although of course every effort will be made to arrest him. I have already issued directions for the whole Davagh Forest area to be sealed off. No entry. No exit. Specialist agencies have been seconded from Military HQ, Northern Ireland, and are on their way from Aldergrove to the forest at this present time. Back-up will be given by additional Army teams, and all police are now being withdrawn from the forest except from the scene of the explosions, which has itself been cordoned off as a separate pocket within the forest. By 12 noon we estimate a completely sterile area and the deployment of the agencies. The Assistant Chief Constable for the area is going to the scene to take personal control along with the military.'

At this point the Chief Constable returned to the table carrying a fresh cup of coffee. 'That's it, gentlemen. He's in there, he can't get out. Our major concern is that no one else gets hurt and that we bring the whole thing to a conclusion today. The press blackout will continue indefinitely. As far as our own force is concerned, they will continue to believe that we are looking for a mentally disturbed, possibly suicidal, individual. We will meet again at 8 p.m. tonight, irrespective of today's outcome. That will be all.'

Only Frank Grange remained as the staff officer escorted the group from the conference room.

'Well, Frank, what do you think?' enquired the Chief Constable.

'I think he can't be taken alive, and we can't afford the embarrassment of a court case.'

'You've just asked me to condone murder!' the Chief Constable replied.

'No sir, not murder. As I said and you agreed, he is now without conscience and will kill anyone who gets in his way, including our own people and perhaps members of the public.'

'Have you given precise instructions to the SAS?'

'Yes . . . they know their actions will be determined by "Code Red" being transmitted from you. This would permit them to take the gloves off officially.'

'No, I cannot agree to that! They must only use force if they are met with such. He must be challenged and given the opportunity to surrender in safety.'

The telephone buzzed on the side table and the Chief Constable answered.

'Yes, speaking.' He listened for a few moments. 'Yes,

yes, I understand. Have his relatives been notified yet?'
He paused again. 'Thank you, John. I'll come to the
Control Centre presently.' He replaced the receiver
sharply and looked straight past Grange. 'Another one
dead . . . a young policeman this time . . . caught by
one of the explosions.' He stood up, clenching his fists.
' "Code Red" . . . I will consider it after all!' Before
Grange could reply he had left the room, slamming the
leather-padded door behind him. Frank Grange picked
up his papers from the table and smiled as he began
to light his pipe for the second time. 'Code Red' had
been signalled to the SAS operations staff ten hours
earlier . . .

By 4 p.m. Somerville had met the main river course
that meandered through the forest. He was already
quite wet from crawling through the swollen drainage
ditches. The main obstacle now before him was the
river, probably five feet in depth and fifteen feet wide
at this point, slightly swollen by the night's rainfall.
The trees on each bank had been cleared about ten
yards back from the river, forming the main fire-breaks
for the forest. Somerville had taken twenty minutes to
cross the last few yards to his vantage point, moving
like a shadow. He viewed the terrain more closely from
behind the camouflage net that draped his face and
head, but could spot no activity on the other side,
though that meant nothing. He decided to move back
into the forest until dark.

The initial SAS team had landed by Lynx helicopter
near the scene of the explosions, but away from prying
eyes. The team consisted of four men from the 22nd
Squadron of the SAS based at Aldergrove. These men
from 'D' Troop were experts in much more than
soldiery. The team leader, Staff-Sergeant Ian Lawrence, was the medical wizard; the other three were also
specialists – one in explosives and demolition, another

in linguistics and the third in communications. So it was that the team began to track their prey, quickly finding his trail heading into the main forest. Only a small detachment of 22nd Squadron had been retained from active service in the Falklands. Ian Lawrence and his men had been furious at the selection, but now they felt a sense of purpose again although it was still no compensation. They followed the trail for half a mile, using standard operating procedure; the team leader remained on point while the remainder were spread at intervals behind him. All the soldiers carried Armalite automatic rifles and standard light pack, consisting of a webbed belt and pouches containing a high-powered radio transmitter-receiver to maintain contact with the Incident Control Point.

The team leader crawled into the drainage ditch on his belly. The water was stagnant and cold, and the vile smell almost made him retch as he slithered on to the other side of the clearing, following the fresh marks on the dry forest floor. Alert for any tell-tale broken leaves, branches or even a leaf unnaturally bent, he inched towards the young fir trees planted in line ahead. He passed the first conifers slowly, feeling the ground with his left hand as he eased out again on his stomach, then took up position and awaited the arrival of the second team member. It was then that he saw it – the catgut fishing-line stretched across his path between the next two trees; it was taut, fixed about three inches above the ground. He signalled with his right hand, halting any further advance. It took Staff-Sergeant Lawrence another ten minutes' circling round to find the Mills grenade bound to the tree with fine wire. The fishing-line was tied to the grenade pin and attached to a nail embedded in an adjacent tree. He snipped the line and removed the grenade, after clipping away the attaching wire. Trooper Tom Grey, the explosives expert, was waved over to examine the find.

He whispered to his leader, 'It's probably dud.' He pointed out the red and brown marking on the base of the grenade: 'Drill ammo'. Producing a knife from his trouser pocket, he dug into the screwed cap at the bottom of the grenade, turning it slowly anti-clockwise. He had finished removing the cap by hand and was about to look in to confirm his statement when the wire fixed to the underside of the cap triggered the micro switch, detonating the grenade in his face. Ian Lawrence was shielded from the direct blast by the tree line, having assumed a defensive position while his colleague worked at the grenade. They did their best to save 'Winky' Grey, but it was no use. He had lost most of his upper chest area; his chin and left cheek lay open beyond the bone and his face was grossly pitted with shrapnel. Shortly afterwards the team received instructions to consolidate their position and await the second team. They did so reluctantly.

Darkness fell slowly that evening and Somerville took the opportunity to rest, anticipating the reluctance of those in authority to proceed after hearing of the booby-trap. He had given no thought for the victim as he heard the blast echo across the forest; the soldier was irrelevant and was paid to die.

Somerville was safe in his present position, for he had backtracked laboriously after planting the grenade. It would take a long time to trace him. Even the dogs would be confused by his constant use of the drainage ditches. It was cold, wet work but worth the effort . . . he dozed in the cover of the trees.

The Number Two team arrived at the rendezvous at 5 p.m. It didn't take them long to realise that their prey was undoubtedly as good as they were, and had given them the run-around. Night was falling swiftly on the gloomy forest floor and they had no choice but to abort all further efforts until daybreak.

The ICP was a large mobile trailer, now parked on the siding which led to the forest entrance. The Assistant Chief Constable for the region, Harry Williamson, was not surprised to learn of the SAS team's lack of success. In some respects, he admired his fellow Paddy for rubbing the faces of the best of the British Army in the mud, but he was also going to do his utmost to ensure the man was apprehended. He knew nothing about 'Code Red', but then he did not need to, for the specialist units remained under the control of an SAS Troop Commander – a Captain who had even failed to introduce himself before he left the ICP. There was also a Lieutenant-Colonel Jones from Army Headquarters at Lisburn who, much to Williamson's annoyance, never left his side. The two men rarely spoke as they sat in the trailer, lit by the mobile generator and manned by two radio operators in the end compartment.

'I suppose we've lost him until morning.' The ACC looked at the Colonel.

'Perhaps, perhaps not. We have considerable manpower along the banking of the main river course.' He pointed to a wall-map depicting the area in detail. 'We have equipment arriving shortly which will help our line to detect any approach made from the main forest area.' He glanced at the police officer. 'You see, he was trained by us. We do have an ability therefore to assess his actions, an ability that perhaps you don't possess.'

The statement smelt of contempt to Williamson and his reaction showed on his face.

Colonel Jones continued, 'I don't mean to be offensive, but he is very good, you see.'

'So, what do you presume he will do?'

'I think he will attempt to break out tonight, especially with hill fog being forecast.'

'But how? How will he break out if we've placed such a tight ring around the forest?' ACC Williamson was becoming annoyed at the soldier's arrogance.

'By following this river line here.' Jones pointed to the meandering blue line on the map. 'Right out of the forest. That is why we are putting such a large concentration on the banks, to lure him into following the river course right into our hands, here.' He moved his finger along the blue line to the edge of the dark green mass that represented the forest.

'Has he any alternative?'

'Yes, indeed. He can sit it out and take on our teams in the forest when they close in tomorrow, and that would be his downfall.'

'But what if he gets across your line on the river bank?' the ACC persisted.

'Not possible, believe me,' snapped Colonel Jones, annoyed at having to explain himself. 'Our Hawkeye equipment is already on its way from Belfast. It's a thermal imager system containing a scanner device, something our boffins have been using to great advantage on the border recently. If we station three Hawkeyes along the river course, with their 92-percent scan efficiency, we can detect the presence of the subject if he approaches anywhere near. So I can assure you, Mr Williamson, once we have them operational – by 2330 hours, I estimate – your man will find it absolutely impossible to pass us.'

'I sincerely hope you're right, Colonel, for all our sakes!'

The Chief Constable called a third meeting in his office. It recorded one more person dead – a soldier this time – and he was starting to doubt the advice of his senior officers.

The Superintendent from the Information and Control Centre spoke up. 'The newspapers are becoming curious, and since this morning our press office has been inundated with questions. We cannot keep this thing under wraps for much longer.'

'Can I be assured that everything that can be done *has* been done, gentlemen?' interrupted the Chief Constable.

The newcomer to the meeting spoke for the first time. He was Brigadier Baxter, sent from Lisburn Army Headquarters as liaison officer since the deployment of the SAS. A small squat man, he stood out from the others, dressed in a dark shirt, tweed tie and almost matching jacket, grey flannels and brown suede shoes. He reminded Frank Grange of a gamekeeper fresh from the meadow who had stumbled into a meeting of merchant bankers.

'May I interrupt please, Chief Constable?' His sharp, high-pitched Home-Counties' accent cut through the dull burble of conversation and the Chief Constable nodded for him to continue. 'We have taken very stringent measures to deal with a difficult situation, much of which I cannot disclose at this meeting. There is no such thing as 100-per-cent security. It could be possible for us to lose him. What I am saying is that you should not underestimate Somerville, and frankly until now you have all done just that.'

'Is there anything else we can do, Brigadier?' asked Grange icily.

'Yes . . . you can all pray we get him before he gets us!'

Frank Grange echoed the sentiments. 'The man's a psychopath. It's imperative he doesn't escape from that forest. If he does, nobody's safe, believe me.'

The Chief Constable nodded. 'Very good, we will terminate this meeting. Please reassemble here at 10 a.m. tomorrow. That is all, thank you.' He turned to the Army officer. 'Perhaps, Brigadier, you would stay for a few moments.' He silently signalled for Grange to keep his seat.

The Committee members filed out towards the Control Centre to examine the fresh facts from the ICP as they appeared on the computer's VDU.

When they had all gone, the Chief Constable turned to Baxter. 'Brigadier, can you elaborate on your comments on Somerville? Was he that good a student?'

'He passed out top of the course you sent him on, if that's what you mean. But I doubt if that's what you are getting at.'

'It concerns me that he had access to explosives, knows how to make a bomb, booby-trap a hand grenade and give your SAS people the slip! Have you an answer for that?' He was not hiding his irritation.

'You are both aware that Somerville was in the Armed Forces prior to joining the police, but you don't know the details.' Brigadier Baxter pulled a folder from his attaché case. 'I am not at liberty to give even Special Branch the full facts of Somerville's career, but I will try to help you as much as I may.' He broke the seal on the folder's cover and read from the top page:

Name:	Edward Robert Somerville
Born:	1 February 1945, at Belfast
Educated:	State primary, and to senior standard at Methodist College, Belfast
	Passed with distinction in all subjects
Career:	Turned down offers to University and had several office jobs, insurance mainly.
	Joined British Army 1965. Sandhurst training, Commissioned into 2nd Battalion Parachute Regiment, his first choice. As 2nd Lieutenant he was based at Aldershot until he got his second pip.

Then he went to Senalager, West Germany, on secondment to the Unit Warfare School, specialising in tactics and covert operations, including field reconnaissance operations. He had an apparent gift for getting in and out of difficult situations and returned again to England for further specialist training. He later served in an advisory capacity with the Kuwait Armed Forces in the Gulf. Then, in 1971, just after his promotion to Captain, he was involved in a rather unsavoury incident with a member of the ruling government in that country. He was recalled to UK and resigned his commission, after which he returned to Ulster to join the RUC in the same year.

The Brigadier looked up from the file. 'I should add that there was no blot on his record. The incident was unfortunate, but embarrassing enough for Her Majesty's Government to require his removal from the Armed Forces.'

'What sort of specialist training did the man have?' asked Grange.

'I'm afraid I cannot answer that question, Chief Superintendent. Even I am not privy to the full details.'

'Why precisely was he removed from the Gulf?' enquired the Chief Constable.

'All I can tell you is that there was an incident at an illegal drinking session involving officers of the Kuwaiti and British forces. Some young prince, nephew to the ruler, got himself drunk and decided to show some of the officers how to fight in hand-to-hand combat. He finally picked on a British officer; after being floored by the fellow, he produced a knife and sank the thing into the poor chap's shoulder. Somerville stepped in to break it up, and the prince tried to stab him too. Having removed the knife, Somerville proceeded to break the fellow's arm at the elbow and dislocate his wrist. As if that wasn't enough, the fool drew his pistol and tried to shoot Somerville in the back. It was the last mistake he made; he was killed by a kick to the throat.

'As you can imagine, there was a considerable diplomatic furore behind the scenes. It was accepted to be self-defence, but much was made of the inebriation of those concerned. Because of the obvious embarrassment the Kuwaitis waived the legal aspect completely, but still demanded their pound of flesh.'

'But Somerville was quite justified,' said Grange.

'Absolutely, but not in the eyes of our political masters. Arms deals and oil supplies mean money and stability for both sides. I'm afraid our gallant Captain didn't have too many friends in court. At the end of it all he simply walked out, after breaking the jaw of his own Para Adjutant when the man insisted he do the honourable thing and resign his commission. A pity, really. He was about to receive a high award for distinguished service in the Middle East. Damned lucky he wasn't cashiered!' The Brigadier frowned.

'And then he joined the RUC,' continued Grange.

'Yes, he returned home, got married and joined your lot around the same time, I think . . . Quite an asset for you – well, at least, until now!' The Brigadier appeared slightly flustered by this last remark and changed the conversation. 'Tell me, I know he was involved in your anti-terrorist squad, but was there any other specific reason why the terrorists singled him out?'

Grange spoke up. 'No, not really, but there is one thing . . . our sources in Tyrone indicate that at the time Somerville's murder was being set up, a number of other hits were arranged apparently to cover up. It seems that PIRA singled him out, but sent in some outsider to do the job. We don't know yet what the implications are, but we'll find out.'

'Very good. I'll leave you both to your work, gentlemen.' The Chief Constable stood up. 'Frank, make sure I'm kept abreast of the slightest development.' With a wave he left the office. Something was nagging at him, but his thoughts remained out of focus.

Through his night-sight Somerville could see clearly the positions of the soldiers. Probably RRF – he knew them to be serving in the area, and there were far too many to be SAS. The positions, approximately fifty metres apart, indicated two things to him. One was the intention to keep him where he was, and the second was to lure him to a probable birthday party at the edge of the forest. He decided he must cross that night, but some kind of diversion was necessary.

By 11.30 p.m. the mist had begun to thicken into fog and Barney smiled at his good fortune. Not all the soldiers would have night-vision equipment and it was not as infallible as most people thought. Quickly he put his plan into action. Taping three Shermulley flares together at the base of a fir tree, he pinned a fluorescent strip of tape on the middle flare, then moved another 150 yards downstream – which took thirty minutes. At midnight exactly he trained the sights of the MI carbine on to the fluorescent marker. It would be a difficult shot. He could not nullify the noise or the muzzle flash, but the onus would be on the man on the other side of the river. He readjusted his aim and eased the safety catch forward. He thought of the energy he was to expend within the next 60 seconds and held his breath as he gently squeezed the trigger.

The flares ignited almost simultaneously with the rifle shot. The ground around the fir tree exploded into a sea of light, and the surrounding trees caught fire as the flares strained to reach the sky only to be caught by the outspread branches. Somerville had no time to spare. He rolled over the banking and into the icy, rushing water, following the flow downstream away from the surprise firework display. It was slow going. As he reached the other side at the bend where the river twisted to the right, the flares were still burning and much of the surrounding foliage and trees was well alight. The fog swirled around him as he pulled himself up from the muddy bank. Crawling on his stomach, Somerville made for the first trees between the soldier's positions. He saw a sudden movement to his left and froze. The soldier stirred, not sure if he had seen something or not.

'Is that you, Tel?'

'Whatd'ya say?' A voice replied from Somerville's right.

'Did ya hear somfink?' asked the first voice. Somerville estimated the soldier to be thirty feet away, he lay still in the undergrowth.

'Naw. What the hell's going on up the river?'

'Don't know, mate. Looks like some sod's let off a thunderflash or summat!'

A third voice interrupted; it came from directly ahead, about fifteen yards away. 'Shut it, you two, or you're both on a fucking charge!'

There was no reply.

Somerville continued to lie still, trying to determine if he could make a detour round this rearguard position. After a few minutes, he edged slowly forward through the thick ferns and grass in the direction of the third voice. As he moved nearer, he could hear a faint whispering; then he spotted the tops of two Bergen packs sitting proud of the thick undergrowth beneath the lines of trees. Two SLRs were propped against the packs, and from the glow of a cigarette he could make out the outline of two fusiliers stretched out and obviously resting.

It took him some time to manoeuvre around this latest obstacle and he had just slipped into another drainage ditch when he heard the sound of approaching feet. They passed within inches of him as he lay almost submerged in the stagnant water. When he raised his head, he could see clearly that each of the men carried pieces of equipment, the last two holding a large covered box-like shape. One of the soldiers almost fell into the water and on top of Somerville.

'All right, men, get a move on. We should have had this stuff in position at 2300 hours!'

Another voice muttered, 'All right, Sarge. Keep yer hair on. I can hear the river now.'

Someone else croaked, 'Christ, are we sappers or suckers?' and there was a muffled snort of laughter.

Within a few seconds the soldiers were gone and Somerville rose to his knees, checking his position by the compass. He kept constantly on the move, always making the fullest use of available cover, never travelling in one direction for more than three hundred yards and avoiding any open area. He had to cross three tracks and more drainage ditches than he cared to remember before finally reaching the perimeter fence and main road.

It was now 4 a.m. The road was clear except for the vehicle checkpoint 500 yards away. This was his most dangerous manoeuvre. He jumped the wire fence and dropped silently into the small roadside ditch. There was no visible movement from the figures gathered at the VCP. The main road was only fourteen feet wide and Barney estimated it would take three strides to clear it. He ran the risk of them spotting him, even in the fog which had now reverted to a steady hill mist, and the terrain on the other side was open hill land as far as the eye could see. If he was seen he would have nowhere to hide, and would be forced to take on whatever they had at the checkpoint. Casting fate aside, he belted across the road, somersaulting over the fence. He stopped still, listening for any sound apart from his own breath. Nothing moved. Somerville began to run, keeping his torso away from the skyline until he was over the first hills. He ran without stopping for five miles; when he was above the forest area and over the open peat bogs, he rested in the cover of some woodland beside Lough Fea. He could still see the helicopter and its belly searchlight emitting one million candle watts in the distance, high over Davagh Forest.

Filling his lungs with fresh hill air, Somerville ran again for another six miles overland, taking only the shortest breaks to recover his strength. His body ached and his brain pounded as he forced himself on, trying desperately to put as much distance as possible between himself and the forest. It was almost 6 a.m. when he found the tiny farmhouse and outbuildings. There was a steady drizzle which cleared away the remnants of the mist, so he could see the corrugated iron roofs shimmering wetly in the murky dawn light. No dog barked. Parked beside the gable of the farmhouse was an old Vauxhall Viva saloon. Somerville gave it a quick examination; it seemed drivable.

The wooden door to the outhouse had long since perished, and he walked straight into the building which was covered with old straw. He settled quickly in the corner behind an ancient wooden trailer, avoiding the water dripping down through holes and cracks in the old roof. After dressing in the camouflage wet suit, he made himself comfortable. Sleep came quickly.

Staff-Sergeant Lawrence was the first to reach the river and find Somerville's firing point, recovering the spent case from the thick grass; alongside he found the discarded IWS sight. The double team followed fast across the river, eventually locating the footmarks in the muddy bank further downstream. The soldiers ran past the fusiliers without word or acknowledgement, following the broken undergrowth and intermittent tracks until finally they reached the edge of the forest and perimeter road.

'He's beaten us, the bastard!' Ian Lawrence kicked the barbed-wire fence. 'He's fucking beaten us!'

Captain Niall Scott, who had joined Lawrence and the others during the night, stepped forward and surveyed the peat bogland and distant bleak hills. He turned to Lawrence. 'Ian, call up the Lynx. We'll track him down yet!'

The Staff-Sergeant passed the word back to the radio operator and then followed the SAS Troop Commander across the road. 'If anybody's going to get him, it'll be me.' Lawrence spoke quietly and no one heard his words. He spoke as if taking an oath, an oath he was determined to keep.

5

Tuesday 8 June – Drumard Townland, County Londonderry
Somerville awoke to the sharp noise and checked his
watch. It was 8 a.m. and the banging came from
outside the small courtyard of the farmhouse. He shook
himself wide awake, crept to the broken window and
peered out. An old man was struggling to haul a large
toolbox from the boot of the Viva car.

'Good morning.'

The old man jumped as he looked round at the
camouflaged figure standing in the doorway. He saw
the blackened face and woollen hat, and took in the
folded MI carbine in Somerville's right hand.

'Ya took me by surprise, stranger!' he said. 'Ya gave
me a fright, so you did.'

'Sorry if I startled you, but I'm afraid I'm lost,'
Somerville continued. 'I'm in the UDR. We were on
exercise up in the hills there and being a new boy to
it all, I got split up from the rest of the boys.'

'Ya look sort af wet, son. C'mon on in an we'll get
ya a cup af tay,' replied the old man, still staring at
the rifle.

As they crossed the yard, Somerville's eyes searched
for the telephone line, but to no avail. They entered
the tiny house and the old man introduced his wife,
Sarah. She appeared more suspicious than her
husband, but Somerville kept up the charade. They let
him wash before he tackled the mug of strong tea and
buttered soda bread with home-made raspberry jam.
Conversation was difficult for Somerville, and he was
only too aware of the submerged tension.

'Do you have a telephone I could use by any chance?' he asked.

'Naw. We're not that newfangled here, son,' replied the old woman.

'We only got the electric in last spring.' The old man came to her side.

'Sorry, I'm very rude. I haven't introduced myself. The name's . . . Somerville.'

'Oh aye. Ours is Morgan,' said the old man, who was examining the rucksack covered in netting, and the MI carbine on the floor beside it. 'That's not an SLR you've got there, is it?'

The question surprised Somerville. 'No. You're quite correct, it isn't.'

'You don't wear a beret either?' He sucked at his unlit clay pipe.

'No, we were on an exercise, you see.'

'What regiment did ya say you was with?' The questions were becoming rapid and searching.

'The UDR, the local battalion.' Somerville tried to change the course of the conversation. 'This is very comfortable here, Mr Morgan. Where exactly are we, then?'

'You're between Draperstown and Desertmartin.'

'Is it not quite isolated for you both here?'

'Oh aye.'

Somerville caught the glint in Morgan's eye as he glanced up at the single-barrelled shotgun over the fireplace. The old man shuffled over to the open fire, and tapped his pipe into the hearth.

'Leave the shotgun, Mr Morgan. I mean you no harm,' Somerville said quietly.

'What are ya then, the IRA?'

'No, quite the opposite. I am on the run from the Security Forces, if that's what you mean.'

Mrs Morgan had been standing at the large table and sat down suddenly, shaking with fear.

'Please, Mrs Morgan, relax. I mean neither of you any harm, believe me.'

'Who the hell are ya?' growled the old man.

'My name is Somerville, as I told you. I am a policeman, or was until recently!'

'I don't believe ya . . . What are ya doin' here? We've naw money, ya know!' Mr Morgan tried to hide his fear.

'Eleven days ago the IRA killed my family. Now I'm going to kill those who were responsible – and if need be, anyone who gets in the way.'

The couple listened in silence. The old woman was the first to stir. 'I remember somethin' on the radio 'bout a man who the police were lookin' fer, but he was called Magee, I think.'

'He was one of those who butchered my wife and children . . . he's dead.' Somerville stared into the fire.

'Now that we know who ya really are, I'm goin' ta put the kettle on,' she replied.

He had made two allies for the moment and he knew it. The old woman rose from the table and lit the stove, which ran off a bottled gas cylinder standing to one side.

'I'm going to have to ask you for your car,' said Somerville.

'The keys are in her.' The old man seemed keen to help.

'Our son Fred – he's in the part-time UDR, ya know. Well, he doesn't get home till six o'clock like. Course we'll have ta tell him, an' knowing him he'll go hot-foot ta the police!'

'Thank you,' said Somerville. 'I'll skip the tea, if you don't mind.' He stood up and lifted his gear from the floor.

'There's no point in askin' ya ta give yerself up, I suppose, mister?' Mrs Morgan looked through him as if knowing his answer.

'No point missus, no point at all.' Somerville walked to the Viva, followed by the old man.

'She's half full of juice.' Morgan patted the rusty yellow body with his hand.

'Thanks. I'll leave her in the same order I got her.'

'I know ya will, son,' said Morgan. 'I know ya will. But do us a favour . . . give them one from us, will ya?'

Barney looked into the old man's eyes, which had filled with tears. 'I'll remember that, Mr Morgan.'

He peeled off the camouflage jacket and trousers, and tossed them into the open boot. Throwing the rucksack on top, he closed the lid gently. He looked a mess, his shirt and trousers wet and wrinkled.

The old man waved his hand. 'Ya wait there, will ya?' Seconds later he re-emerged from the little house carrying a jacket, cap, pullover and trousers. 'Get these on ye before ya catch a chill.'

Somerville took the clothes gladly and quickly stripped down to his underpants. The chill of the morning air surprised him. He quickly climbed into the brown corduroy trousers and grey crew-neck sweater. Both had seen better days, but their warmth was a comfort. He kept on the water-sodden boots, and shrugged off the old man's explanation that they hadn't a pair to fit him. The jacket was a Barbour; it smelled of oil and appeared to be covered in horse-hair, but it was an expensive gift and Somerville felt embarrassed. 'I shouldn't really accept this,' he said.

'Course you will – now git the hell out of here before I changes ma mind!'

Somerville touched the old man briefly on the shoulder, then threw the road map and MI carbine on to the passenger seat. The car started first time; apart from needing a new exhaust pipe, she was fine. He reversed out of the courtyard and towards the stony lane. When he looked back for a moment, the old man just stood in the middle of the yard staring after the car.

He decided the best method of getting to Pomeroy was through Desertmartin into Cookstown and straight towards the village, keeping well clear of the Davagh area. He looked at his watch; it was now 8.45 a.m. He had only travelled along the Desertmartin Road some two miles when he saw the distant shape of the helicopter to the south-west. It was perhaps half a mile off and closing fast. He decided to continue travelling at 40 m.p.h. and stick to the main road.

The Lynx roared overhead and circled round the moving vehicle. They were checking the Viva's number plate, he imagined, and probably trying to sneak a view of the driver at the same time. He didn't disappoint them, and waved through the open window as he passed underneath. The craft's observer reciprocated, waving back.

'Well, what does it come back as?' shouted Captain Scott above the noise of the Lynx's engine.

The observer handed over the plastic covered pad and chinograph scribble.

'Well?' shouted Lawrence.

'Local car . . . clean.'

'We're too far north! Let's circle over the hillside again!'

Somerville glanced up as the helicopter blades beat into the wind, and the Lynx disappeared from view over the high hedgerows. He quickly looked at the OS map, estimating how long the detour would take. The lack of checkpoints was no surprise. Most of the available manpower had been concentrated at the Forest, but Somerville took no chances and bypassed the town centres, keeping to the side roads where possible. He followed the precise instructions given by Magee. Having passed through Pomeroy village, he continued on the Carrickmore Road until he came to the old red signpost on the right-hand side. There it was, in bold letters.

BRADY'S FARM

SPUDS FOR SALE

53 p PER 7 LBS

According to his information, the farm had been derelict for at least two years. Somerville pulled into the open lane leading to the buildings clustered on the hillside before him. The old septic tank was not hard to locate, but was well grown over. He removed the weeds and dirt from the timber planking and tossed them aside. Although unused, the tank smelt vile. Then, as Magee had said, he found the wire to the side of the tank wall and with a hard yank, the bottom came up to reveal another hole underneath. The hide had been well constructed, and could easily have hidden a man as well as weapons and explosives. Somerville slid himself carefully on to the brick projection surrounding the hide. The tank was six feet deep and he had some difficulty in easing himself down the slimy sides. He switched on the torch. The second hole was another four to five feet deep, very dry and lined with thick sheets of polythene. In the bottom lay two rifles wrapped partly in blankets; one appeared to be an Armalite and the other a Garand. Somerville treated the boxes he found with great care. The hide was like an Aladdin's cave of terrorists' treasure. He quickly set to work, for he had little time left.

It was now 11 a.m. The lunchtime delivery van was due at Pomeroy Post Office, and judging by the coming and going the place was still functioning ... The money hadn't arrived yet, the robbery hadn't taken place.

He sat there for twenty minutes. Nothing happened ... nothing until a green Toyota Cressida drove past, with three men inside. It circled the village square twice. The occupants peered at the Post Office as they went by, but they were also looking at something else: the derelict houses at the corner of the Diamond, only twenty yards from the Post Office. In a split second he saw it: some grubby net curtains moved, only slightly, and they moved just once.

Somerville waited until the Cressida pulled away in the direction of the Main Street. It would be gone for a few minutes, or perhaps until the arrival of the Post Office van and police escort. He eased the Viva out of the Diamond and into the road for Dunamore, pulling into the yard behind the derelict houses. He was well concealed, and no one could see him remove the Spas 12 from the car boot. He found the forced rear door ajar, a fresh foot-mark beside the door-jamb. Tiptoeing into the kitchen, he moved towards the doorway which led to the living room fronting on to the Diamond.

Somerville could see the youth standing in the mottled light that filtered through the net curtains; he estimated him to be about 5′ 7″ and around 10 stone in weight. He was wearing a balaclava pulled over his face, and an outsize donkey jacket. In his right gloved hand he clutched a large revolver. Somerville moved silently to the centre of the room directly behind the youth, to within eight feet of him.

'Put yer fuckin' hands up, mister!' screamed a voice from behind him. He eased the grip on the Spas 12 and dropped it to the broken concrete floor. 'I said put yer hands up!' The voice was almost hysterical and Somerville raised both arms in the air. 'That's better, now turn round slow like,' continued the young and trembling voice.

The youth at the window had already jerked round in startlement and fear, as he took in Somerville's proximity and the shotgun on the floor. Somerville turned slowly to face the voice, calmly appraising the second youth standing in the light filtering in from the kitchen doorway. He was dressed like his comrade and appeared to be about nineteen, smaller – about 5′ 6″, Somerville estimated. He was holding a sawn-off double-barrelled shotgun, pointed straight at Somerville's belly.

'Who the fuck are ya?'

'My name's Somerville. What's yours?'

'Somerville . . . you're the fucker they're out ta git . . . hear that, Pat – he's the cunt we were told ta look for. Ha! You're no big deal, are ya? Cunt!' Somerville failed to reply as the first youth moved away from the window and came up beside him.

'Not so big now . . . is he?' The first youth laughed as he pulled back the hammer of the .38 Webley revolver. Clasping the gun in both hands, he pointed the barrel at Somerville's head. It was his first and only mistake. In a single fluid movement, Somerville side-stepped, grasping the gun and the youth's hands and pulling him across his own body. The second youth reacted quickly, but not quickly enough. He let go with both barrels of the shotgun and Somerville's opponent took the full force of the blast, sending both men crashing to the floor. Before they landed Somerville recovered the Webley and fired two shots, the first in the youth's chest followed by another in his forehead as he fell backwards into the disused kitchen.

Somerville had been lucky – the shotgun had contained only buckshot, with no penetration. But he cursed his own stupidity, which he blamed on general fatigue. He knelt down, and turned over the young man on the floor. The pellets had peppered his face and shoulders, but the main concentration was in his stomach, which was now producing a steady flow of blood.

Somerville supported him in his arms. 'Pat! Pat! Can you hear me?' He pulled off the youth's balaclava.

'Oh, help me, God!' cried the boy. Somerville guessed he could not be more than fifteen or sixteen.

'Who's the boys in the Cressida?' asked Somerville.

'Oh, God!' The boy winced with pain and arched his body upwards.

'I said, who are they?' Somerville shook the boy hard. 'Tully? Is Tully with them?'

The boy nodded. 'Get us a priest, will ya?'

Barney released his grip, letting the boy fall to land with a sickening thud as his head hit the concrete. He cried, the fear of the soul temporarily surmounting the pain of the body before the loss of blood blessed him into unconsciousness.

When the green Cressida came into the Diamond again, the driver got a real shock.

'Holy Mary! What's that fool doin'?'

A tall figure was walking from the front door of the derelict house carrying what appeared to be an M60 machine-gun.

'That stupid bastard! Brendan, I thought they was supposed ta wait until the GPO van arrives!' yelled the front seat passenger. 'They've fuckin' blown it!'

Brendan Tully glared from the rear seat. 'He's not one of ours! Run him over!'

The driver accelerated towards the advancing figure. The Spas 12 exploded moments before the animal cunning of Brendan Tully had caused him to throw himself flat on the back seat. The first blast was directed at the engine of the car and the metal-piercing projectile penetrated the engine block with ease. The car shuddered. The second blast was from a magnum load and shattered the windscreen. The third and fourth finished the driver as the car careered off course and into the wall of the derelict house. The front-seat passenger, wounded by flying glass and the suddenness of the impact, tried to scramble out of the car as the engine exploded. But his door was jammed and the other was blocked by the driver's body. Before he could climb into the rear of the compartment, a second explosion ripped the front of the car, rendering him unconscious and half on fire. In blind panic, Tully prised open the rear door behind the driver and crawled out, leaving his Armalite behind in the increasing inferno. He managed to stumble about forty feet from the car and close to the corner junction, before the final explosion from the petrol tank threw him flat to the ground.

Shopkeepers and shoppers alike came running to the Diamond. Just as Tully staggered to his feet, the red Post Office van pulled into the square followed closely by the armoured Cortina containing two policemen. The policemen jumped out and rushed to Tully's aid, recognizing him immediately as a local terrorist suspect. One of the policemen drew his revolver, anticipating a trap, but before they could speak Somerville stepped around the corner to face them. The flames from the burning Cressida burned in the background.

'Drop your guns, boys!' shouted Somerville, brandishing the Spas 12 in his right hand.

The two policemen stared. They didn't recognize him, and presumed from his shabby dress and stance that he was also a terrorist. The younger policeman hesitated and raised the revolver and Somerville fired his fifth cartridge into the air above their heads. The men crouched in fear. Both Rugers were thrown on the ground in front of Tully.

'Right boys, start walking . . . If you run, you should make Pomeroy Station in under five minutes, and in case you're thinking of using the radio in your police car, forget it . . .' Somerville pointed the shotgun at them and they began stepping backwards away from Tully, who was still crouched on the road. 'You Tully?'

'Yes!' He could only manage a croak.

Somerville stared coldly at the man. The two police-men stopped, only twenty paces away. 'You're very slow, boys,' said Somerville. 'May as well stay and watch our local INLA hero here! He's a big man, y'know . . . he was going to kill you both . . . weren't you, Brendan, old son?'

Tully made no reply.

'Well, boys, I'm going to give Brendan here a chance . . . a chance he never gave to anyone else. All he has to do is pick up one of your guns there and shoot me!' Somerville smiled at Tully. 'It's that simple, Brendan!'

Tully glanced back at the policemen. 'For fuck's sake, help us! He's crazy! . . . He's crazy!'

The two men watched Somerville set the shotgun on the road beside him. 'All you have to do is lift the gun . . . if you've got the guts, that is. After all, you're only used to shooting people in the back or off-duty unarmed policemen and soldiers!' He raised his voice. 'Just how many has he been credited with now, boy? Is it ten, twelve? Don't you keep a count, Brendan?'

Tully never moved.

'Well, what else do I have to do for you, Brendan? . . . Do I need to turn my back?'

Beads of sweat appeared on Tully's face. His eyes flickered to the policemen and back to Somerville standing there, hands in the deep pockets of the Barbour. Suddenly he lurched forward on his belly, grabbed the nearest Ruger and aimed it upwards at the still stationary figure. A single shot boomed loudly across the Diamond and the policemen threw them-selves flat, not knowing what would happen next. There was no sign of a single spectator.

Brendan Tully lay dead – a single hole in place of his left eye, the back of his head ripped asunder by the force of the exploding brain. His cranium resembled a misshapen half-cut turnip. Smoke filtered out of the burned hole in the left pocket of Somerville's Barbour. He bent slowly to pick up the Spas 12 in his right hand and walked towards the two policemen still crouching on the ground.

'I assume you two don't recognize me?' said Somerville, stepping over Tully's body. He pivoted to his left and fired the sixth and seventh magnum loads into the rear tyres of the police car.

'I'm Somerville,' he said. 'Can you take messages?'

Neither man spoke.

'Tell the Chief Constable that if anybody else gets in my way I'll personally blow the legs off the Chief Constable himself! Tell him that! Now get the hell out of here!' Somerville fired the eighth cartridge into the air. The pair ran off almost as though they were starting for a 100-metres sprint.

Within seconds the Viva roared out of the yard and spun left. Somerville had much to do. He couldn't afford encounters like this; a lucky shot, a simple mistake like the one in the derelict house, and it would be all over. He had set himself a target. He wondered about Doyle, where he would be hiding and what he looked like.

By the time he arrived at the Ballyronan Marina on the west shore of Lough Neagh, it was 2.30 p.m. After looking at all the assembled craft, Somerville quickly earmarked the one he needed and approached a 16-foot Shetland cruiser moored at the end of the pier. Initially he had thought it was empty, but as he approached the boat a face appeared out of the small cabin door.

'It's cleared up well, hasn't it?' As the man emerged from the cabin, Somerville noted the denims and white tee-shirt which did nothing to conceal a soft paunch. Obviously the weekend sailor type.

'I'm just admiring your craft. Is she new?'

The man took in Somerville's scruffy appearance as he stood there in a floppy old sweater and cord trousers. Barney had discarded the Barbour and had concealed the .357 Magnum at his back, stuffed into the waistband of his trousers.

'Yes, yes, she's one of the Shetland range. Only bought her last year.'

'Was she cheap?'

'Well, I wouldn't know for sure. She's second-hand, although quite new. But there's a lot of equipment and extras I got included in the price . . . she cost me three grand.'

Somerville feigned shock. 'Have you had her out far in the Lough?'

'Sure, I've had her all over the place. To tell you the truth, I'm getting sort of tired of it; the open sea's the thing!'

'Too much wear and tear. You're better off here for the moment, especially if you're not used to boats.'

'What do you mean?' The man looked puzzled.

'The knot you used here is no better than a "granny."' Somerville pointed to the rear mooring point and the limp nylon rope.

The man laughed. 'Come aboard and I'll show you round.'

Somerville did not hesitate.

'My name's Tom Davidson.' They shook hands.

'Mine's Barney, Barney Somers.'

'Pleased to meet you, Barney. C'mon, I'll take you round.'

It emerged during the tour that Davidson was a shopkeeper from Magherafelt, in the drapery business. This was his excuse to break away from the monotony of the shop and a nagging wife. Somerville was surprised to find himself quite taken by the middle-aged little man with the pot-belly, and felt guilty about his real intentions. After fifteen minutes Davidson finished the tour with his pride and joy, the latest sonar equipment complete with monitoring television.

'Fancy a spin around the shoreline, then?' he asked.

'I'd love it!' Somerville grinned.

When they reached the pier's limits, Davidson gave the boat full throttle. Somerville soon had all the technical information he required, especially the fuel capacity and consumption. He was glad to see that the tanks were kept topped up. They set a steady course south along the shoreline and very quickly Barney took advantage of the situation.

'What's that island over there?' he shouted above the noise of the engines and pounding waves.

'Kinturk Flat. I think it's a bird or wildlife sanctuary.'

The man was spun to the side of the boat as Somerville suddenly pulled the wheel to the left. He lay in a daze of disbelief and shock which quickly turned to fear as he saw the revolver. The boat slowed and Somerville issued his instructions clearly.

'Get in the cabin and shut the door.'

Davidson paused.

'Move it!' Somerville cocked the gun and the man scurried inside and closed the door. It took Somerville another six minutes to make the island and he brought the boat to rest as close as he could. They were just rubbing into the soft sandy bottom and reeds when he threw the engine into idle.

'All right, friend, come on out!' he shouted into the cabin.

The part-time mariner could see their position from his view through the small porthole. He hesitated.

'Look, you either come out and get your feet wet, or I may have to start shooting!'

The door opened.

'Please don't kill me,' stuttered Davidson. 'You can

have the boat and my money . . . here.' He offered a brown leather wallet.

'Keep it, I only want to borrow your boat.'

Davidson slipped it back into his hip pocket.

'Now climb into the water and wade to the island.'

The man looked down into the murky water, judging it to be three or four feet deep. He climbed over the side oblivious to the cold, only too glad to escape from this devil. As he waded ashore through the thick reeds, he heard Somerville shout after him: 'Fishermen often use this island to lay out their nets. You'll be spotted within the day, but if you really want to, it's a short swim to shore from the other side!'

The engine immediately roared and the boat reversed from the sandbank and quickly out of sight. Somerville headed straight for the inlet near Ballydonnell just a short distance north of the island. This small inlet was used by the local fishing community, but was deserted except for four old wooden hulls lying upturned on the grass, disused fishing boats from a once profitable fishing fleet.

Somerville jumped on to the grass bank, wetting his feet in the lapping water as he landed. He ran fast to the Viva and unlocked the boot, pulling out the rucksack and shotgun. Pushing back to the Shetland, he heard a distant bang and saw a bright orange light arch high into the sky to the south. It came from the small island. When he checked the emergency box in the cabin, the flare gun was missing. He half smiled at Davidson's enterprise.

As he manoeuvred the cruiser away from the inlet and into the Lough, Somerville saw the two small fishing boats moving steadily towards the castaway's island. He checked the fuel gauge and calculated he had enough to reach the other side of the Lough.

Somerville kept strictly to the chart he found in the cabin and surprised himself by accurately arriving at

Antrim Marina. Having waited almost until dark before coasting up the river inlet away from the normal tourist mooring, he tied the boat up to a tree that bent out from the river's bank. He searched the seat storage and found a pair of blue jeans and white running shoes. The jeans were slightly large around the waist and he found that he had to cut the hems on the legs before they looked even half normal. But the white running shoes fitted him perfectly and dry woollen football socks were tucked inside each one. The old grey pullover given him by Mr Morgan was quickly covered by an orange nylon waterproof top he found rolled up under the small folding table. The camouflage cover of the rucksack discarded, Somerville looked at himself in the small wall-mounted mirror. Unshaven and rugged, he looked like any hitch-hiker – perhaps a little down on his luck, but reasonably authentic. For a moment, he thought of those early days of their marriage, but he stamped out the memory and concentrated on the map. It was now 7.30 p.m. and he had to find a place for the night. He left the Shetland cruiser, turning off the crackle from the VHF radio transmitter. The bus station in Antrim was about three miles away, he estimated.

RUC Headquarters, Brooklyn, Belfast
The Chief Constable looked tired as he convened the 8 o'clock security meeting of his Chief Officers' Group.

'Gentlemen, our up-date is simply that the bird has flown again. I have been on the telephone with ACC Williamson, who is still in South Derry. I'm afraid our worst fears have materialised.' He looked at Grange. 'Frank, give the committee a résumé, please.'

'As you are all aware, the SAS tracked Somerville's trail out of the forest, right through the line of soldiers placed beside the river. We lost his trail some two miles from the forest. He was heading in a north-westerly direction, and the SAS followed quickly in a helicopter. VCP operations were stepped up throughout the area to the north, but he slipped through.

'This afternoon, five terrorists were killed at Pomeroy when they attempted to rob a Post Office delivery van and presumably kill the police escort. The two constables identified the perpetrator as Somerville. There is no doubt that he saved police lives, but he murdered the terrorists in cold blood. Again he made good his escape in a Viva car which he had hijacked from a smallholding near to Draperstown. Thankfully the owners, two pensioners, were unhurt.' Frank Grange stood up from the table. 'We acted accordingly and increased our VCPs in the area. The west of the Province was effectively sealed in every direction . . . all except one. Later this afternoon we received a report from Magherafelt police that a small cruiser had been hijacked from Ballyronan, the owner left on a deserted island just off the west shoreline. We were lucky. The man had kept a distress flare gun and was picked up quickly by some local fishermen from Ardboe. Before anyone asks, the description of the thief fits Somerville. We are presently scouring the entire area, especially to the Antrim side, and have already found the Viva car a couple of miles south of Ballyronan. ATO is clearing the vehicle at the moment.'

The Chief Constable interrupted. 'We are now faced with exactly what we did not want: a Province-wide hunt and the news media demanding a full story. I have made contact with the Secretary of State, who has requested an urgent meeting. He has agreed that there should be absolutely no press release for the moment on the death of the soldier in Davagh. The young constable's death has been explained as an unfortunate mishap in the clearance of dangerous explosives located during a planned search operation. 'The charred remains have been verified as those of the terrorist Magee. No private or public statement will be made on the matter and his "disappearance" will be allowed to continue in the media. ACC Williamson is being recalled to these headquarters and will take personal charge of all coordinated action, along with Detective Chief Superintendent Grange. That will be all. The next meeting is scheduled for 10 a.m. sharp. Thank you.' He looked across the floor at Frank Grange, who was examining a wall map of Ulster. 'I want to see you later, Frank. Meet me at my office at ten-thirty. We have to go to Stormont Castle.' He continued, 'Somerville's stirred up a real hornets' nest, and the repercussions are by no means confined to the public relations aspect.'

Grange returned to the table and sat down.

'I want to stop this man immediately,' emphasised the Chief Constable. 'If we can achieve his detention and a quick appearance in court, we may just head off the inevitable political reaction – the 64,000-dollar question is, can we get him?'

Frank Grange patted the table. 'I see no reason why not, sir. To date he has left us plenty of clues. I think he wants to be caught, perhaps wants to mess us about a bit, but at the end of it I think he's done his worst.'

'Let us hope you're right in your assumption, Mr Grange.'

'Assumption is nine-tenths of police work, sir.' Grange smiled.

'Just make sure you don't mix up presumption with assumption.'

The smile disappeared from Grange's face. 'Yes, sir,' he said.

The blue single-decker Ulsterbus pulled into Glengall Street depot beside the Europa Hotel in Belfast at 10.45 p.m. Somerville joined the throng of people scurrying towards the city centre, eyeing one of the taxis at the rank in the old Great Northern Railway Station.

As a schoolboy at Methodist College, he had come to this great architectural delight and sketched the ironwork for hours on end. At first he had criticised his art teacher's choice of venue, but after studying the intricate detail he had begun to appreciate the place – so much so, that he returned on days off to continue his study. It had won him top grade in his senior exams. Now the station had been bastardised by development, development enhanced or perhaps shoved along by continual terrorist bombs and indifferent government departments.

The Botanic Hotel could hardly have been described as one-star, but its anonymity was ideal. The door was opened by a security man who seemed half inebriated; he looked about fifty, and although quite nattily dressed, Somerville sensed he was probably happier in the back room of some dingy pub collecting empty glasses in exchange for the odd free drink.

'C'mon in, son. Are ya by yerself then?' The man had a broad Belfast accent.

'Aye, just hiking. I need a room for the night if you've got one?'

'Got one – we've git more rooms than the City Hall, son. Go on over ta the desk there. That wee girl'll fix ya up all right.'

The receptionist surveyed Somerville's scruffy appearance with obvious displeasure. 'I'm afraid it's in advance . . . cash only, unless you've got a cash card?'

Somerville ignored the obvious insult. 'How much for a single room and bath?'

'No baths, I'm afraid; just showers. And then it's three-fifty extra.' She flicked through the hotel register with her brightly-painted fingers.

'What's the price overall then, with shower?' Somerville kept a rein on his rising irritation.

'Eighteen pounds fifty pence, and that includes continental breakfast. Cooked will be extra, another two-pounds-fifty.'

'Basic price is fine.' He handed her a twenty-pound note and signed the registration card under the name of 'Peter Dunn from Coleraine'. He made up the rest of the address and hoped no one would check it out. He was handed the key, and change from a small petty-cash box the girl kept in a drawer beneath the desk.

'The room's on the first floor, at the back of the hotel. Jimmy will show you to your room, all right?' To Somerville's surprise she actually smiled. He imagined she must have been practising for receptionist of the year with the 'Antarctic Tourist Board'.

'Thank you very much, but I'm sure I can find my own way.'

The room was small, but clean and pleasant. The divan bed was soft and felt invitingly comfortable under the pressure of his hand. The single-sash cord window looked on to an open yard and the backs of other Victorian town houses. He pulled closed the flowery-patterned curtains and switched on the light to the shower room. It was tiny, with a little corner shower, wash-hand-basin and toilet. He stared at himself in the large mirror over the basin; from his appearance he couldn't blame the receptionist for her attitude.

Peeling off the nylon top and grey pullover, he stripped down to his underwear. The shower took several minutes to warm up, but it was relaxing and eased the pain and aches in his tired muscles. He remained under the steady stream until it began to run cold. Once dried with the white bath towel, he washed out the socks, underpants and crumpled shirt he produced from the damp pocket of the rucksack. When finished, they were left to dry over the double radiator in the bedroom. The jeans, pullover and nylon jacket he placed in the wardrobe alongside the running shoes, and then wrapped a fresh towel around his waist.

After unpacking the rucksack he checked the MI carbine and magazines of ammunition and laid aside the additional cartridges for the Spas 12; they were now superfluous to his requirements. The Zycon was checked and found to be still in working order; he questioned the practicality of hanging on to it – he had never used it as planned – but kept it anyway. Finally he removed the Ruger's holster, repacked the rucksack and placed it in the tiny wardrobe. Ruger and holster went under the mattress, and he picked up the commando knife and scabbard, once a present from his course controller at Hereford. How ironic that he had probably killed one of their people.

He ordered some food by telephone. It took forty minutes to arrive and consisted of minute steak and chips garnished with lettuce, tomato and peas, all floating in grease. He paid for the meal immediately and the waitress had the exact change ready. She was a young girl of about seventeen, well-proportioned, with dyed blonde hair which still remained black at the roots.

'If there's anything ya like, just ring them ones downstairs.' She smiled at him from the doorway.

'There is.' The girl came slowly back into the room. 'My electric razor is broken. I wonder could I borrow or purchase a razor from the hotel?'

'I don't see why not . . . I'll get you one before I finish at twelve.'

'Could you perhaps also bring me a bottle of whisky and some soda?'

'I don't drink whisky,' she said, 'but I like vodka!' Her eyes were bright.

'I doubt if I could stay awake for a party. Whisky and a razor will do just fine.' He feigned a smile.

The girl shrugged her shoulders. 'We've been told that it's strictly cash with ya . . . must have been somethin' ta do with yer appearance when ya arrived.'

He locked the door behind her. Switching on the black and white television, he heard about the killings of the terrorists near Omagh and media opinion that it was probably the result of internal feuding. He also heard a report on the young constable caught in a blast during a planned search operation to locate an explosives cache. The next item was on the killing of five men, believed to be terrorists, at Pomeroy. Once again the presenter indicated police opinion that this was retaliation for the murders of the two members of the Provisional IRA near Omagh and the earlier killing of Kevin and Moira McNamara. There was no mention of the hijacked Viva or the boat. There was no mention of him whatsoever. But it didn't surprise Somerville; they were playing it down, and the next extended bulletin dealt with the Falklands.

The girl returned sooner than expected. Her knock on the door awakened Somerville from an unintended slumber on top of the narrow divan bed.

'Did ya enjoy yer meal, then?' She hurried across the room to put the tray down on the dressing table and could see that nothing had been left on his plate.

'Yes, thank you . . . What do I owe you for the drink?'

She examined the tariff. 'I got ya Powers. I hope it's all right . . . and of course the soda water. Oh yeah, the razor. I got ya some disposables from the wee shop across the street. Are they OK, then?'

'Fine. What do I owe you?'

'Comes ta twelve pounds forty-eight. It's extra for the whisky in here – bar prices, ya know.' She handed him the bill.

Somerville removed three five-pound notes from the bedside table and handed them to the girl, telling her to keep the change. To his surprise she sat down beside him on the bed. 'As ya can see,' she said, 'I brought two glasses.'

'Are you not going to be missed by the bar manager if you stay here?'

'There's a disco on tonight. He'll be too busy ta notice.'

She was a pretty girl, but Somerville could not risk any undue attention by hotel staff and possibly the local police if things got out of hand. 'Young lady,' he said, 'I'm a married man. I don't think you should stay here any longer.'

'You're a snobby bastard, that's what ya are, a snob!' She stood up, fixing her skirt into position. 'I'm not used to that sort of suggestion, ya know!' She slammed the door as she went out.

Somerville hadn't wanted to hurt her feelings. She had been keen to help, but he couldn't risk any kind of relationship, however brief. He poured a large drink and sat down to examine the map. He had reached Belfast and Doyle was probably here, but for the moment he might as well have been in Australia.

The two men passed through the new annexe adjoining Stormont Castle. Security restrictions were not lifted even for Chief Constables, and they had to go through three separate checks before being shown along the panelled corridor to some double mahogany doors by a grey-suited civil servant, who knocked just once and entered.

'The Chief Constable, sir.' The man spoke in a soft English accent.

'Thank you, Charles,' replied a voice from within.

The two police officers were ushered into the dimly lit room. The Secretary of State for Northern Ireland arose from behind a large teak-veneer executive desk. He didn't much like the furniture, which was a legacy from the old Labour regime when all the original furnishings had been replaced with what his wife described as 'modern laminate'.

'David, how nice to see you. Thank you for coming at such short notice. I can appreciate you have much on your hands at present.' He strode towards the Chief Constable and they shook hands. 'Hello, sir, may I introduce Detective Chief Superintendent Grange from Special Branch?'

The Secretary of State shook Frank Grange's hand loosely and beckoned them both to sit down on the large four-seater leather sofa, something he was proud of having had returned to the office on his appointment to Northern Ireland. They made themselves comfortable beside the unlit fire, piled high with logs and surrounded by a large brass fireguard. The Secretary sat on one of the adjacent high-backed library chairs. 'David, I appreciate you calling at this unearthly hour.' The Secretary rubbed his hands together. 'I really should have had that fire lit. It's freezing in here.'

The door opened and another man entered the room.

'You know Cecil Rose, David. He's a Permanent Secretary here, under the auspices of the Political Affairs Division.'

'Yes, we have met on a number of occasions.' replied the Chief Constable. He stood up and shook the hand of Ulster's master of MI5.

Cecil Rose spoke with a languid English drawl. 'Chief Constable, nice to meet you again.' He turned to Frank Grange. 'Hello, Frank.'

Grange nodded in response. He knew the local head of 'Five' only too well. Cecil Rose was fifty-two years old, Winchester, Oxford and an Army veteran of considerable experience. It was while serving in Aden with his detachment alongside the Irish Guards that he had single-handedly caused the collapse of a main pocket of unrest by planting 'volunteers' from his unit in the rebel areas, and by extracting vital information from captured suspects. He employed a number of techniques – specifically one which required the use of a wet towel placed tightly over the suspect's head, then regularly doused with water. It induced the effect of drowning, before the individual was revived at the very last moment. Rose never admitted where he developed his unsavoury interview methods but by the time his superiors discovered his private declaration of war he had obtained significant results and ensured his own professional safety. Questions had been raised at the United Nations security conference in New York, but floundered under political pressure. It had been his callous, calculating but innovative action which had brought him to the attention of Britain's master spy-catchers. And so it was that Major Rose, MM, traded in his light field dress, pistol and webbing for lounge suit and club lunches at Whitehall.

He had found the first few years rather boring, but he was a fast learner and was soon switching sections with increasing regularity. After an eventful secondment to the British Embassy in Washington, he was brought back to England as section leader dealing with Russian affairs. His insight and ability to get results were much appreciated by his masters and – with the change in governing political parties – this led to his being asked to take the Northern Irish post. To many this posting would have seemed a dangerous demotion, but Cecil Rose – a dedicated bachelor – undertook the job with relish. He introduced many of the new covert hard-line tactics. Opponents and politicians alike had criticised Rose's 'shoot to kill' policy, but most knew very little about the other major developments created by MI5. Northern Ireland had become the testing ground for more than military tactics and hardware. Frank Grange was wary of Rose's intellect and the clinical way in which he analysed everything. He knew him from the weekly Northern Ireland Intelligence Co-Ordinating Group meetings. The man had an uncanny knack of assessing problems and producing solutions well in advance of everyone else. And Frank Grange didn't like to be upstaged by anyone.

'Cecil, perhaps you could organise coffee for our guests?' the Secretary of State continued.

Rose pressed the intercom set on the Secretary's desk. 'Charles, coffee for four, please.' The response was immediate and he flicked off the set.

The Secretary of State then turned to the Chief Constable. 'To the point, David. Give me the present situation regarding this man Somerville.'

The Chief Constable cleared his throat. 'To date he has accounted for twelve people . . . Nine terrorists, the wife of a terrorist leader, a young policeman and a soldier. He has gone to ground on the Antrim side, we suspect, but to date we haven't been able to locate the Shetland cruiser he hijacked from Ballyronan – that's a small village on the Ardboe shoreline.'

The Secretary of State interrupted irritably. 'Yes, I know where it is. Are you saying we've no trace at all on his whereabouts?'

'We've lost track of him for the moment, but Chief Superintendent Grange now feels we should concentrate on Belfast.'

'What sort of capability has he got? I believe some firearms are missing?'

The Chief Constable handed over a sheet of paper showing the outstanding items believed taken by Somerville. 'The search operation is now under my direct control and I have placed an Assistant Chief to stay on the case along with the Chief Superintendent here.'

'Who's that?' replied the Secretary.

'ACC Williamson.'

'Wasn't he the man in charge of the muck-up at

Davagh? David, I hardly think he's the man for the job. Is he your first choice?'

'He's the best choice, the operation at Davagh –'

The Chief Constable was interrupted before he could explain in greater detail. 'Where will Somerville go next? You mentioned Belfast, what's the significance of the city?'

Grange sat up sharply on the sofa. 'A PIRA operative by the name of Seamus Doyle. I believe Somerville now knows him to have been responsible for his family's murders. We think he comes from Andersonstown and should know more within a few hours.'

'Do you intend to arrest this man Doyle?'

'No, he's the bait,' replied Grange.

'What if Somerville gets to him first and beats your trap?' Cecil Rose interceded.

Frank Grange smiled. 'I'll be in charge this time. Anyway, Doyle is our only viable option if the normal security operation fails.'

The coffee arrived and there was a brief pause while it was handed round. The Secretary of State then continued to question every detail put forward by the Chief Constable and Chief Superintendent. Cecil Rose remained silent.

'This Somerville is an embarrassment to us all,' said the Secretary. 'David, I want it made perfectly clear that it would not be in this government's interests for the matter to be placed before the open courts.' The statement came as no surprise to the Chief Constable; he had quietly accepted 'Code Red' as the only alternative.

The Secretary looked at Grange. 'Well, Chief Superintendent, it's all on your shoulders, then . . . Cecil here could probably re-route some of his resources for your assistance.'

'Thank you, sir,' said Grange. 'We already have SAS

teams working with my people on the investigation; I should be glad of Mr Rose's assistance.'

The last part was meant to indicate Rose's subservience and, although Frank Grange knew he wouldn't be able to get away with it, he was pleased to fire one across the bows of the Security Service.

'I think it proper at this juncture to make it plain, gentlemen, that it is the Prime Minister's view that henceforth MI5 approves all actions on this matter. This is an extremely delicate situation, especially with the proposed talks with Dublin on the slips. A rogue policeman killing all and sundry and perhaps inducing the IRA to escalate their campaign, especially on the mainland, is just not on. After the hunger strikes last year, the level of violence has decreased to an almost acceptable level. Now it could become uncontrollable.'

When Grange and Rose left, the attitude of the Supremo changed.

'You drink gin and tonic with no lemon and just a little ice, right, David?'

The Chief Constable relaxed for the first time that day. 'Yes, sir, thank you.' He was glad of the drink.

'Well, tell me, old friend, just what is this man Somerville like? By the way, I have read his personal police file.'

'May I ask you how, sir?'

'Let's say my hands can dig deeply into your pockets. Don't be offended, I had no choice.' He raised his glass, and both men drank. 'Do you realise, David, that since killing this man McNamara, all PIRA and INLA activity north of the border has ceased! They're on the defensive now, and searching desperately for him, just as we are. For once in their miserable existence they are being terrorised . . . and frankly, we like the sound of that.'

The Chief Constable nodded. 'But what if the IRA leak the story?'

'They won't – and that's Rose's judgement too. Can you imagine them spreading the news that one of their botched-up operations has resulted in one ordinary man taking them on and making them run for it?'

'Somerville's no ordinary man, sir,' replied the Chief Constable.

'I agree, but to the public he is. There is another aspect that you don't know about, and what I have to tell you is for your ears only . . . Somerville was framed regarding his alleged appropriations.'

'But I saw his bank statement myself!'

'I know you did. And quite rightly you had him suspended from duty. But I can assure you it was a put-up job.'

'How do you know for sure? And why was I not told before?' The Chief Constable could not hide his anger.

'It's quite simple. He was set up by your own people! That's all I can tell you for now, but trust me and make sure your man Grange takes no action on Somerville unless Rose approves.'

'Very well, but I must protest . . .'

'No!' interrupted the Secretary. 'You've no one to protest to. David, understand me, there are bigger fish at stake and we're going to get them, you and me. And you will not repeat this conversation to anyone!'

Wednesday 9 June – Belfast

It was 6 a.m. when Barney Somerville awoke. He had only managed one drink before exhaustion overwhelmed him. He washed and shaved quickly before checking the socks and pants he had placed over the radiator; they were still damp, but would have to do. Hurriedly he put on his old shirt and strapped the knife to his left forearm, under the pullover.

Then he pulled back the curtains. It was beginning to brighten up and for a change it was dry. Before leaving the room, he stuffed the nylon top and Ruger into the rucksack. The night porter – the same man he had met on the way in – sat behind the receptionist's desk with his feet up on the desk-top.

'Good mornin' . . . Yer up early, aren't ya? Afraid breakfast isn't served till about seven.'

'It's all right, I've a train to catch. Tell me, are the buses on yet?' asked Somerville.

'Oh aye.'

'Well, I'm off then . . . I settled the bill in advance and the key's in the room, number twenty-six.'

'Oh, that's fine, Mr —' – he checked the tariff tables – 'Mr Dunn, thank you very much indeed, sir.'

The air was cool and fresh as he walked to the telephone kiosk at Shaftesbury Square. He remembered the Belfast number and dialled, but it rang for almost one and a half minutes before the receiver was lifted.

'Hello, yes?' The woman's voice was thick with sleep.

'Margaret, it's me.'

'Barney, Barney!' Her tone changed immediately. 'Where are you!'

'I can't tell you. But listen, I need some money, clothes and a car – and quickly . . . Can you meet me at Whitehead this afternoon at two o'clock?'

'Whitehead . . . Why Whitehead? Look, Barney, the police have been to the house. The Chief Inspector told Dick and me you were missing and weren't well . . . You need help. Let me collect you now and take you back there, and then perhaps you can talk to them – please?'

'Margaret, I can't. You'll just have to trust me for the moment, I'll explain when I see you. Will you do it?'

'If it's what you want, OK. I'll get some of Dick's old things and bring them in my car.'

'Is that the Mini?'

'Yes. But where will you be; where will we meet?'

'Along the front, near the old swimming-pool, remember?'

'Yes, I remember.'

'Margaret, you must promise me – not a word to anyone, including that husband of yours.'

'I promise.'

'By the way, who was the Chief Inspector who called?'

'I think his name was Black.'

'That's fine. Just you park at the sea-front and I'll find you. Please be there at two.'

'Don't worry.' The telephone clicked at the other end and he was gone. Before she replaced the receiver Margaret Cunningham heard another click, but thought no more about it. She was already working out who she could leave the children with that afternoon, and what clothes she could pinch from her husband, without creating too much suspicion.

The Gazelle helicopter combed the shoreline on the Antrim side of Lough Neagh. The pilot and observer, both from 655 Squadron based at Aldergrove, had been given their coordinates, excluding Antrim Marina, which had been checked from the ground the previous evening. The members of the aircrew were becoming bored with the constant circling of the various inlets. The observer kept singing 'The Yellow Rose of Texas' into the aircraft's internal communications system, much to the annoyance of the pilot as he skilfully manipulated the craft's controls against a strong side wind blowing across the Lough.

'Ken, just shut it, will ya? You're supposed to talk to me through this fucking flight and that includes reading the blasted map on your knee. Do ya know you've missed telling me about the last two sets of pylons and haven't given me a direction for the last ten minutes!'

The observer stopped his lyrics momentarily. 'Aw, c'mon mate, this here's a fucking bore. You've got two eyes, you can see where we're going. There's good visibility all round, so what's there to worry about? Just follow the shoreline like we're supposed to. The sooner we get the job done, the sooner we can get back to the mess for a proper breakfast.'

To another chorus of 'The Yellow Rose of Texas', the pilot made a final swoop across the Marina, following the river's course inland. It was on the eighth or ninth repeat of the song that the observer spotted the Shetland moored from the river bank beneath the outstretched trees, well away from the normal tourist haunts of the Marina. 'There it is, mate . . . at five o'clock under those ruddy trees. We've struck gold!'

It took twenty minutes for police and Army back-up to arrive at the boat. They found the Spas 12 shotgun, discarded clothing and a message drawn in crayon on the small mirror. The police inspector scratched his forehead, as he turned to the constable. 'Better get photography to take a snap of that while they're it.'

A transcript of the telephone message was on Grange's desk before he arrived at the office that morning, still tired after the late-night deliberations with MI5. Rose infuriated him; he never tired, or so it seemed – not only questioning every action, but supplying possible solutions in his usual impeccable manner. Frank Grange called in his assistant, Detective Chief Inspector Black, also directly responsible for the operations of E4A – the Branch's Surveillance Section.

'You say they've found the blasted boat then, Winston?'

'Yes, sir, in the river up from the Antrim Marina. Our boys must have missed it yesterday; it's almost impossible to trace from the ground.'

'For God's sake!' Grange ached with impotent fury.

'As well as having to tolerate our people's pathetic incompetence, I have to kow-tow to the Security Service and convince them about our every move.'

'You'll feel happier after you read this transcript.'

Grange quickly scanned the paper. 'So he's finally surfaced!' His eyes glittered. 'Is there any more coffee going around this place?'

Black nipped out of the office to try to scrounge two cups from the canteen, still not officially open. Frank Grange lifted his private line, which bypassed the main switchboard and inquisitive ears.

Five minutes later, Black returned with two piping-hot mugs of Nescafé.

'Somerville left a message in the boat, scribbled it on a mirror,' said the Chief Inspector.

'Very fond of giving out messages, our friend. Well, at least he's given us our first lead with this phone call.'

'Sir, the message he left . . . it was for you.'

'For me! What the hell did he say?' Grange almost spat out the coffee and wiped his mouth with the back of his hand.

Black handed Grange a 6-inch by 9-inch black and white photograph. It depicted a mirror with a clearly printed statement in what appeared to be lipstick or crayon: *TELL GRANGE CODE RED'S FOR HIM TOO!*

'How the hell did he know . . .' He grabbed the paper again. 'You say it was a local call from Belfast, eh?'

'Yes, sir, from a public kiosk. Not long enough for us to get a trace.'

Grange studied the transcript again. 'So the bastard contacted his sister. Seems we backed the right horse.' He looked up at his assistant. 'Has anyone else seen this?'

'No, sir. Just the audio typist.'

'No copy to the Chief Constable or ACC Williamson?'

'Not yet, sir.'

'Leave it with me, then. I'll give him a copy.'

'Yes, sir,' replied the Chief Inspector.

'I want a meeting with the following people by 10.30 a.m.: Chief Inspector Marshall from the SSU ... and Colonel Jones from Thiepval Barracks. Have them in this office as top priority.'

The meeting of the emergency committee, now including Assistant Chief Constable Williamson, went on as normal that day. Grange avoided revealing the latest information; he rushed through the meeting and didn't stay for the coffee and repetitious chat afterwards.

Two men were waiting in his office when he arrived.

'Gentlemen!' As he slammed the door shut he turned, beaming widely. 'Sorry for keeping you.' He sat down behind the large desk at the far side of the office. 'We need an operation mounted for this afternoon. Our man has surfaced!'

The train journey to Whitehead reminded Somerville of his youth, when he and Margaret often went there to the open-air salt-water swimming pool. Seeing the closed and dilapidated building, he was decidedly against the idea now. He walked into the small town and stopped for tea and scones at the cake-shop. The tea was too milky and the scones didn't taste too fresh, but he was hungry.

At 11.30 a.m. Somerville strode up to the road junction above the town. It was the only road leading into the place: one way in and one way out. He decided to stop Margaret near here. He knew she would travel along the A2 in the brown Mini Clubman Estate car from the direction of Carrickfergus. He picked his vantage point and crossed the barbed-wire fence some

250 yards down the road, cutting back out of sight, to a predetermined position overlooking the junction.

He lay still among the bushes until 12.30 p.m., when he saw the red Triumph Dolomite pass. It was not unlike dozens of other cars he had seen, except that the sole occupant was Chief Inspector Marshall from the Special Support Unit based at RUC Headquarters. Somerville recognised him instantly, even with the black wig, and smiled at the amateurism of the man. It was a trap; Margaret had set him up. He wondered what lies they had told her. They must have spun her some story for her to sound so convincing on the telephone, unless of course the bastards had tapped her line? But then that was what he had expected.

Twenty minutes later he saw the grey Sherpa van, with the words 'Isobel's Florists' painted on the side in bold yellow letters. That thin disguise didn't fool him either – SAS or SSU, he reckoned.

At exactly two o'clock he saw the brown Mini Clubman Estate turn into the junction and down the sloping road to the town. It was followed discreetly by a blue Fiat 127 which stopped at the junction only to continue on the road towards Larne.

After half an hour Somerville broke cover and darted across the road. He had to get to her somehow. At 3.15 p.m. he saw the Mini drive slowly up the winding road below. He could see the Sherpa in the distance and estimated a 15-second gap at their present rate of travel. When Margaret accelerated the little Clubman to the hill-top junction, she came to a halt. Somerville immediately leapt over the fence and pulled at the passenger door. Thankfully it was open and he climbed in.

Margaret was visibly startled. 'Where the hell have you been?' she shouted, more from shock than annoyance.

'Just put your foot down and turn right!' Barney looked behind for the Sherpa.

'But that's to Larne!'

'Go right!' he ordered, easing the rucksack on to the back seat.

Behind them, the Sherpa van crawled up the steep hill.

Margaret threw the car into first gear and raced off in the direction of Larne. The change in direction was noted by the Sherpa's driver and relayed quickly to the blue Fiat parked in the lay-by along the same road. The transmission was only received when the two policemen saw the Mini pass and, on detecting an additional passenger, they were swift to follow. They in turn transmitted the information to the red Dolomite, and instantly the combined resources of E4A, the SSU and SAS went into full action.

Somerville had seen the Fiat and realised that they were being followed, but he hadn't predicted the quick and effective VCP established ahead by the uniformed members of the SSU. Margaret slowed as they approached the Cortina with the flashing hazard lights.

'Stop!' said Somerville.

'What did you say?'

'Stop the bloody car now!'

Margaret brought the Mini to a sudden halt, almost stalling the engine. The car came to rest just seventy yards from the VCP.

'What! Are you crazy? Oh, I didn't mean that, Barney!'

'Get out, Margaret, and for God's sake do as you're told!'

She climbed out and ran to the other side of the road. Somerville eased himself into the driver's seat and shouted through the open door. 'Now lie down, damn it!' She didn't; she was standing crying. Somerville saw the blue Fiat 127 come round the corner behind him and stop; he estimated it to be two hundred yards away. The police at the checkpoint were well positioned – at least four of them, he thought. Suddenly, Somerville shoved the little car into first and then second gear, getting to about 30 m.p.h. The police thought he was going to ram them, but instead he threw the front-wheel-drive Mini into a spin, turning the car 180 degrees within its own width. He hurled a grenade from the car as he raced towards the waiting Fiat. The two detectives jumped out brandishing Ingram sub-machine guns; the driver took careful aim at the Mini, but was forced to realign because of the screaming woman still standing at the roadside. The detective's hesitation cost him his life. As the Mini approached, he caught a glimpse of the .357 Magnum pointing from the driver's open window.

The explosion from the Mills grenade took everyone by surprise. The police at the road-block were thrown to the ground, Margaret was tossed like a rag doll into the ditch and the young detective with the Ingram glanced around in complete surprise for just a fraction of a second. The single bullet hit him squarely on the head just above the right eye, and traversed through his brain exploding his skull at the other side. As he was thrown backwards, the nervous reaction of his fingers squeezed the light trigger of the deadly little gun and the Mini was sprayed momentarily before the gun shot crazily into the sky. Five bullets struck the bodywork, one penetrating the driver's door and striking Somerville in the upper right arm. The force dislocated his shoulder and the Magnum revolver was jerked from his hand on to the tarmacadam road surface.

The other detective from the Fiat rolled over beside the body of his comrade and emptied his magazine at the disappearing car, but he was too late – only succeeding in hitting the rear window, but on the wrong side. Somehow, Somerville controlled the steering wheel with his knees as he changed gear into third with his left hand. His right arm was wrapped around his neck and as he yanked it on to his lap he heard the bone crack back into its socket. The arm was completely numb.

A side road loomed ahead and Somerville would see the grey Sherpa tailing along behind an articulated lorry heading towards him. Just as he was almost parallel with the right-hand junction he swerved into the path of the lorry, catching the frenzied look on the face of its driver. He screeched into the junction with inches to spare and the articulated lorry, braking furiously, jack-knifed across the junction blocking his escape route. The driver of the Sherpa tried in vain to avoid the collision. His brakes locked and the van smashed into the side of the lorry, sending the van's occupants crashing in every direction.

Somerville checked his rear-view mirror as he accelerated away from the snare. He hoped Margaret was all right; obviously she had known nothing about the trap, which could only confirm that her telephone was being tapped. It took all of fifteen minutes before the numbing shock of the gunshot wound abated and he felt the terrible pain in his arm. He drove on, determined to stay alive.

The side roads to Larne were difficult enough to drive along even in the ordinary way. Somerville thought he must have urinated until he realised he was sitting in a pool of blood. He pulled into the entrance to what appeared to be the municipal dumping grounds. Quickly removing his trouser belt and strapping it round his arm, he tightened it with his teeth. Through the gaping hole in his pullover, he could see that the oozing wound was beginning to dry up. Somerville sat still for a moment, resting his pain-racked body. It was hard to concentrate; only his hatred for Doyle burnt deeper than the gunshot wound.

Driving on to the coast road, six miles north of the portal town of Larne, he pushed on towards Glenarm. It was now 6 p.m. and he had already passed out once with the increasing agony of his arm injury, but thankfully he had managed to pull up in time and they had not discovered him. He passed through the sleepy village of Glenarm at twenty minutes past six, and was relieved to find no checkpoint outside the village's police station. They hadn't anticipated he would circumnavigate Larne and head for the Antrim coast.

As he rounded the bend into a bay outside the village of Carnlough, just past what the locals called 'the Black Rock' – a small outcrop of rock lying yards from the shore – pain overwhelmed him. The Mini swerved across the road, striking the low stone wall; Barney managed to swing the car round before directly colliding with the wall, but it wasn't enough. One side was smashed and scraped as he skidded against the sharp stone. With all the remaining strength in his left arm, he just managed to steer the car back on to the left-hand side of the road. Miraculously, no passing motorist had seen the incident.

Revitalised by the surge of adrenalin, Somerville pushed the car around the sweeping bay and through the village. The last leg of the coast road seemed to go on for ever, but eventually he reached the village of Cushendall. Then he saw the old house loom ahead on the left beside the Methodist Church: a Victorian country house fronting on to the sea and road. It was old and dilapidated, but probably still the finest building in the village. It had once served in part as the only general provisions store for the area, but had since fallen into a general state of disuse.

Good fortune favoured Somerville again. No one saw him drive up the side road past the gable of the massive nine-bedroomed house, past the large double wooden gates, stopping almost at the top of the hill by a small wrought-iron gate and archway cut into the thick stone wall. The gate led to an enclosed orchard and Somerville staggered to the steps and struggled up to the door of the converted cottage and stables. It was impossible for him to break in here without drawing attention to himself. He stumbled out on to the road again and reversed the Mini downhill to stop right up against the wooden gates; they were seven feet high to the timber cross-beam. Forcing himself on to the roof of the car, he vaulted over the gate, landing badly on the other side. The impact stunned him as he lay for a moment on the rough gravel trying desperately to get to his feet. He recalled that the right gate always stuck. It took all his remaining strength to free the fixing bolt from its bed in the gravel and intermingling weeds. The Mini was driven into the open courtyard and he turned off the lights. Having pulled the gates together again, he realised that someone had oiled them recently.

The small yard was subdivided from the main house by a high brick wall, and the Mini was well hidden except from the air. The old stables and attached cottage had been well converted by their new absentee owners, whose name he could not begin to remember. The little door into the downstairs dining room was still the same and the light glass panel beside the Yale lock did not present any problems, unlike the new front door he had tried. With one measured blow from his left elbow, the pane disintegrated on to the tiled floor. Only one lock held the door now, and from what he could see there was no burglar alarm system. The noise was unavoidable, but he had to risk it; he was desperate for a rest.

Having gained access, he returned to the Mini and removed the rucksack with difficulty, bumping his injured arm on the driver's door in the process. On entering the house, he carefully avoided the broken glass and groped his way through the darkened interior. The unresponsive light switch indicated the power supply had been switched off. He found the meter box, still located under the staircase. Throwing the switch, he hoped no lights had been left on. It was another chance he had to take and, to his utter relief, it paid off.

The wooden staircase leading to the main floor of the house creaked, but to his amazement the first floor had been transformed into a modern abode of excellent taste. Even in the semi-darkness the interior design was clear evidence of the opulent lifestyle of the new owners. Thank goodness they preferred to be absentee landlords, he thought. Somerville could make out the furniture in the lounge quite clearly as the fading sunlight drifted through the curtained picture window which stretched the full length of the room. From the lounge he moved to the bedrooms, finally selecting the suite because it was the room furthest from the road and faced the high-walled orchard, away from idle prying eyes.

Back downstairs, Somerville re-secured the bottom door as best he could, and returned to place a chain and additional bolt on the main entrance before lying down. The pain continued unabated and he was now undoubtedly feverish. He had already closed the velvet curtains to the bedroom and switched on the bedside lamp; now he forced himself up and removed his bloody top clothing. It was agonising in the extreme and he had to release the tourniquet before pulling off his pullover. The wound was red raw and swollen and began to bleed again. He cut the sleeve from his shirt with the commando knife before stumbling into the adjoining bathroom; from the light of the table lamp he could see it had no windows and only a single roof light. Having pulled on the cord and illuminated the room in bright fluorescent light, Somerville looked back at himself in the smoked-glass mirror. Worn, ashen features indicated his pathetic condition and extreme fatigue. Moving closer, he examined the bullet hole on the back of his upper arm.

The medical cabinet on the wall above the basin was full of the usual barbiturates and other mild narcotics for the modern hypochondriac. He saw the name on a bottle, *M. Russell*. The address was in Belfast – the home address, he imagined. Somerville took his first-aid kit from the rucksack and set about cleaning the wound. It took some time. No bones were broken and, amazingly, the head of the bullet protruded from the skin at the partial exit wound on the other side of his arm. Despite his trembling hand, he managed to use tweezers to ease the foreign object from his flesh and tossed the bullet into the basin. The exit wound began to bleed and he poured Savlon lotion directly on it and also on the gaping entrance hole. Clumsily applying a sterile field dressing, Somerville bandaged the arm as tightly as he could. It throbbed fiercely, disinfectant and blood oozing out from beneath the bandage. He wrapped two more elastic bandages around the dressing to help clot the flow. It would have to do. Then he took a total of six tablets, three penicillin and three DF 118s. The dislocation of his shoulder had left its mark in the form of bruising around the chest and armpit, and made any movement almost impossible.

Somerville lay down on the double bed. He couldn't decide whether it was the pain or his present desperate situation which kept him awake. Thoughts came in bursts. For the first time he felt regret for his actions and gave thought to those of his ex-comrades he had destroyed. He wondered about the young policeman in the forest and how exactly he had died. He thought of the explosion he had heard and of the soldier or soldiers possibly injured – but, as he concluded before, a soldier should expect to die as a logical progression of his craft. He thought of the policeman at the checkpoint . . . the man had tried to kill him.

Obliterating the victims from his mind was not easy, as he lay sweating under heavy blankets and a quilt. He had accepted his own fate – his limited lifespan when he commenced this campaign – but he had never anticipated his importance to the Provos. They had sent a man from Belfast just to eliminate him. It was certainly a departure from the norm. The killings coincided too closely with his suspension for the two matters to be unrelated. The thoughts nagged him as he drifted off to sleep and so did two names, Seamus Doyle and Geddis, the bank manager who had appended his signature to the allegations. How could two persons so different have a common desire to destroy him, and why? Sleep claimed him on that thought. He was grateful for the release.

The meeting at 10 p.m. was in the Chief Constable's office. Only two people had been invited, Colonel Jones and Frank Grange. The Chief Constable came quickly to the point.

'Between the two of you, every rule in the book has been broken!'

Neither dared reply.

'The Secretary of State gave specific instructions that MI5 were to be in complete charge of the investigation and the apprehension of this man. The clandestine operation you two mounted is tantamount to disobedience of orders . . . I should have you both destroyed for this, but you can thank your lucky stars that that decision is no longer my responsibility!'

The men looked at each other, trying to establish what the Chief Constable was getting at.

'You are both to report immediately to Mr Rose at Stormont Castle. You will take your directions personally from him and he will debrief you on the operation. It is no thanks to either of you that another policeman lies dead, two more are injured and Somerville's sister has been admitted to hospital. Now I have to attend another funeral, and I can tell you both that if I have to do it again not only will your jobs be at risk, but your pensions will go as well!' The Chief Constable slammed shut the file on his desk. 'Now get out of my sight!'

They left the office like two schoolboys reprimanded by their headmaster.

'If it had worked, you and I would have been heralded as heroes,' muttered Jones.

Grange was slow to respond to the SAS officer's remark. As they walked along the corridor towards the waiting car, he said, 'Heroes are born, not made . . . I wonder what category Somerville thinks he fits into?'

The reception at Stormont Castle was in stark contrast to their reprimand from the Chief Constable. Or so it seemed to begin with.

Cecil Rose invited them into the library and all three sat in a semi-circle around a low oval table, neatly laid out with cups and saucers. Rose spoke first. 'Coffee's on the way. Perhaps, Frank, you can give me a rundown on what happened.'

Frank Grange gave a resumé in detail, hinting at the inadequacy of the police on the ground as the reason for Somerville's escape. The loss of his trail was more difficult to explain, but the unfortunate accident involving the lorry was a crucial contributory factor. 'Somerville's gone to ground now,' he said, 'and we have no indication where at the present. He was observed going through a small village only two miles from the scene which would have pointed him in the direction of Larne, but we have the town sealed fast.

My guess is that he's hightailed it back towards Belfast.'

'What about his sister? Does she know anything?' asked Rose.

'She hasn't been questioned in detail. At present she's in hospital suffering from shock. The bastard threw a grenade from the car after he pushed her out!'

'But is she supportive of our efforts to track him down? Can she indicate anything in the pattern of her brother's behaviour to suggest where he may have gone to?' Cecil Rose spoke too quietly for Grange's liking.

'No, sir, not at all.'

'You haven't answered the question, Frank. Is she telling us everything she really knows, consciously or unconsciously?'

Frank Grange's temper exploded. He was obliged to take rebukes from his chief but not from this English twat. 'Look! I've been a peeler for twenty-five bloody years and I don't need you, or anyone else for that matter, to tell me how to do my job. The bloody woman knows nothing, nothing at all!'

Rose's expression did not flicker. 'I've seen the transcript of the telephone conversation. Tell me who gave you permission to tap the line? You are aware of the Home Office guidelines, I assume?'

'Yes, yes, but we didn't have time! You do want this man, don't you?' Grange had climbed to his feet and was jabbing his finger at the intelligence officer.

Cecil Rose ignored him and looked round at the Army officer. 'Colonel, I think it would be best if you missed the coffee. Brigadier Baxter wants you to call on him at his house in Thiepval.'

Colonel Jones stood up, relieved to avoid confrontation. He forced a smile as he spoke. 'Good night, gentlemen.'

As the door closed behind Jones, Frank Grange remained standing, eyes fixed on the rows of leather-bound books and journals covering the entire wall area except for the fireplace and a large painting of Sir Edward Carson. Frank Grange didn't think much of Carson either. Bloody man ran off and died in England somewhere. Couldn't even stay in the mess he'd created!

'Frank, perhaps you should sit down. We've much to discuss.'

Grange spun round. 'Sit down! How the hell can I do that when the bastard's still at large? There he is running around blowing people up, shooting the place to blazes and avoiding capture every time! Here we are and we can't even establish where he got the grenades and explosives from!'

'It's time for a few home-truths, Frank. ACC Williamson has borne the brunt of the Secretary's wrath after today's fiasco, and has been removed from this investigation. You were totally out of line in what you did today, but I'm not necessarily disagreeing with your actions; I would probably have done something similar in your position. But if we're to continue working together, there must be positively no more clandestine operations. Do you understand?' Cecil Rose had raised his voice. For the first time, his anger showed.

Seamus Doyle had not slept well or remained patient as he waited day after day for a decision on his fate. His return meeting with Paddy was cool, to say the least. Clearly he had lost the confidence and therefore the protection of the Brigade Commandant.

'Ya have ta lie low for the meantime. We'll be in touch. Don't contact anybody and keep yerself available. OK?'

'What's to happen to me, then?' he asked, not knowing if he really wanted to hear the answer.

'There's to be a meetin' . . . yer fouled-up operation cost us dearly.'

'Look,' said Doyle, 'ya've always been fair with me and I've got results for ya. Are they goin' ta cripple me or fuck me off for one mistake?'

'I don't know, lad. But what I do know is the effect on the organisation. Since this bastard went looking for revenge he's killed a hell of a lot of us, that's what I know. Our mid-Ulster operation's come to a halt. In fact, the way it's goin', the whole of the six counties could end up affected, all thanks to you!'

'Ya think he'll come for me, don't ya?' said Doyle. 'Ya think the bastard has it in 'im ta get me. Eh?'

Paddy hesitated, then nodded. 'Yes, lad, I do, and so do a lot of others. At the moment we don't know for sure he knows ya, so go home and stay put for the time bein'.'

Seamus Doyle was certainly not going to let a committee of has-been Republicans decide his fate, and he had every intention of swaying the decision in his favour.

Geoffrey Williams was by now a nervous wreck, and it was beginning to show. He had already panicked on the day he was fed back the information from Murray on what the Provisionals knew. He was linked to murder – the murder of a woman and children – and that mad dog was now on the loose, hunting down his prey. Murray had found it hard to appear confident when explaining the Provos' actions, which did nothing to alleviate Geoffrey's increasing neurosis.

He had to talk to someone – but not to Ralph Hawthorne – for reassurance. Shortly after 9 o'clock, Geoffrey was joined at the Union Club by two other members – Roland Briggs and Mark Taylor. He was annoyed that his old partner had not come alone as requested, but then he was not really surprised by his

150

sidekick and founder member of their group. Roland was forty years old, a quantity surveyor by training, who had drifted into an estate agency and valuation business. His business acumen was exceptional and soon he had joined the boards of several of the Williams' companies. The two had met initially during boardroom discussion and their friendship had blossomed quickly. After the slump in the building trade during the mid-seventies, work was hard to find, and Geoffrey soon realized that Roland Briggs had salvaged many contracts with his keen tendering. At the suggestion of Sir Ralph, the two men had joined forces and amalgamated resources. They had become an unbeatable team and now controlled not only all the major private and public building projects in Ulster, but had expanded into the Republic of Ireland with a franchise in Dublin. All had been organised by Sir Ralph.

At twenty-six years of age, Mark Taylor was the baby of the group who had joined the circle at the instigation of Roland Briggs. Mark had finished his education at Oxford, obtaining a first-class honours degree in economics. He had failed to live up to his father's expectations and follow the family tradition by getting a commission in the Irish Guards. His father had stayed longer than intended in the regiment, rising to the rank of major before taking up the reins of the family linen business after Mark's grandfather had died from tuberculosis. However, the Ulster linen business had undergone a drastic decline and very quickly the Taylor family had found themselves more and more dependent on their farm. So it was that the family sold up their Belfast interests and substantial Antrim Road mansion and moved to the five-hundred-acre inheritance in County Armagh.

Mark had been only four when they moved, and relished the new-found freedom of farm life. He and his three older brothers played furiously during the next few years, but his pleasure was short-lived. At the age of seven he had followed in his brothers' footsteps and gone to boarding school. Private education and severe restrictions on the homesick seven-year-old were to exert a profound influence on him. He discovered that in exchange for certain personal favours rendered to the senior boys, his life began to improve. His homosexual lifestyle had nevertheless remained quite secret and Oxford had only given him more opportunity to indulge discreetly. The age gap between Mark and his brothers was considerable and his 'sexual deviance', as described by his brother Thomas, remained unnoticed until the family discovered that Mark had been living in the Oxford home of a well-known writer. They had tried to halt the affair and every effort had been made to flush away Mark's 'perversion', but all had failed and the family had chosen to disown the young man.

He had met Roland Briggs during one of the latter's frequent business trips to London. Mark had secured a job in Fleet Street, where his flair for languages gave him the edge required in foreign reporting. He had specialised in the political-economic field, and his knowledge of the European Parliament intrigued Roland Briggs; but Roland had found much more – he had found a kindred spirit and companion. Ralph Hawthorne had also been interested in the young Ulster Protestant with the financial background and a talent for languages; he knew Taylor's breed, seed and generation. It had not taken much to convince the banker to have the young man join their group.

Only after the attentive waiter had deposited their drinks and left the readers' lounge did the trio begin their conversation at the dimly-lit corner table. Geoffrey explained what had happened and his conviction that Somerville or the police would be on to him as a matter of course. Both men tried to convince him otherwise, but it soon became clear that this would not be easy. After some thirty minutes Roland Briggs excused himself, but instead of going to the washroom he used the foyer pay-phone; he knew the number of Eastleigh House by heart.

'Yes?'

'Ralph, this is Roland. Can you speak?'

'Why, of course, old boy. What can I do for you?' Sir Ralph sounded almost affable – a dangerous sign, Roland thought.

'It's Geoffrey. I think he's about to flip.'

'Flip? What exactly do you mean by flip?'

Roland Briggs could imagine Geoffrey confessing all to some Sunday newspaper in part penance for his crimes, imaginary or otherwise.

'He can't be trusted any more.'

'Who's he been talking to?'

'Murray. I don't think he inspired much confidence. It appears our friends are in a bit of a tizzy.'

'All right, this is what you do . . .'

The trio left the club quite late that night. Geoffrey was in no fit state to know it, but he now had two 'minders'.

Thursday 10 June, 1 a.m. – Lisburn Army HQ, Northern Ireland

Cecil Rose pondered over the latest developments. He went to MI5's operational HQ set deep within the guarded confines of Army HQNI at Thiepval Barracks, Lisburn, some ten miles from Belfast. Then he sent for Major Lewis McCabe, the canny little Scotsman who was a late entrant into MI5, but who was assured of clear career prospects under Rose's umbrella. McCabe had impressed Rose from the moment they had met, and his ability to react and decide on matters well above his station was vital to Rose.

Some thought freelancing dangerous, but Rose was reminded of the SAS motto, 'Who Dares Wins', as well as his mother's advice to him when he joined his father's old regiment: 'You get nowhere in life without taking chances, but remember always to take measured chances, never hopeless ones.'

His thoughts were interrupted by the arrival of McCabe at the signal room for MI5's operation. 'Lewis, give me an update.'

McCabe had to clear his dry throat first. 'Well, our surveillance on Hawthorne is proving difficult. He keeps flitting in and out of the country with the regularity of an airline pilot. Over the last fortnight it's been Switzerland once, France twice, and America to New York. He uses his private jet for the short "yomps" and without involving GCHQ and satellite surveillance – including bringing Six into it – that is, if they haven't cottoned on already – we just aren't going to be able to keep up with him.'

'I see,' replied Rose thoughtfully. 'Let's go to your office, shall we?'

They passed down the gloomy corridor running centrally through the self-contained modern office block, and McCabe unlocked a fire door at one end marked simply 'Blue Permit Holders Only'. Once inside the atmosphere changed, revealing another smaller corridor which was thickly carpeted and well-lit. McCabe's office looked like any other normal office except that it had no windows. None of the offices in the 'Blue Area' had windows, and large air-conditioning units worked silently above the false ceiling construction and grilles.

'Lewis, I want a temporary operations room set up for this thing. I want it well away from here, at Stormont Castle. From now on, only you and I will know what's happening.'

'Why Stormont?'

'I can't tell you now, but I want a separate signals system set up. Fly someone unknown, someone you can borrow without people asking questions. All surveillance on Doyle and his chummies will be supervised by you. There is to be no more SAS action on Somerville, if he surfaces. Set up an independent team for standby. Use Keating's mob – fly them across today. I'll explain it all to Keating when he gets here.' Rose pulled out an envelope from his inside pocket. 'I've been carrying this around for some days in anticipation. See Keating personally; give this to him – it's the authorisation he'll require. The contact address is on the envelope cover. They think they're being organized for another operation, so expect Keating to be more than annoyed!' Rose smiled.

'Right, boss, I'll get on it straight away.'

'One more thing. Get some camp-beds for yourself and the signaller, and another for my Stormont office. From now on we live, eat and sleep with this situation. When Keating's people come across, put them in a safe house away from all of this.'

6

Thursday 10 June – Cushendall, County Antrim Coast

Somerville roused himself just after 3 a.m. He was cold, although sweating, and the pain had intensified. He felt like screaming, but was too weak. A change of bandages, more ointment, disinfectant and medicine were necessary, but he doubted his competence to do it. It took him twenty minutes to get himself up from the blood-stained bed and into the bathroom, where he persevered with a replacement bandage. Reeling from door-jamb to wall was not the ideal way to travel, but the only one for Somerville just now.

He finally made it back to the large bed and pulled the blankets around himself. He slept soundly with the help of the whisky and awoke briefly some ten hours later. His temperature had subsided somewhat and on examination he found the gauze had stuck firmly to the gaping entrance hole. The bleeding wasn't too bad; it surprised him that he had any blood left to come out. He was still in agony, and the re-dressing of the wounds took some time. He took a further four tablets from the bottle marked 'DF 118', counting only seven more remaining; they would not be enough to keep the pain away. But for the first time he could move his fingers slightly, although without feeling. He wondered whether he would be able to complete his task. There was no answer from his conscious mind. He prayed for help, but he was closer to hell than heaven. He reckoned the local Presbyterian minister at Omagh would object strongly to his interment with Janet and the kids. He thought of the good days and how remote from them he was now.

The television news that evening showed his photograph clearly. It was a copy of the snap in his warrant card, but he looked a hundred years older now. The story about a mentally disturbed policeman was delivered with some conviction and Somerville almost believed it himself. He thought of countering their lies with a press statement of his own; the idea was ludicrous and he put it down to exhaustion, but the main points echoed in his mind.

'The public are at risk.'

'A danger to himself and others.'

'Do not approach.'

'Highly dangerous.'

The announcer put it over very clearly.

That evening he sat quietly in the large corner chair, drifting in and out of sleep. Suddenly, a noise triggered all his senses alert: there was someone at the iron gate. The television was switched off as fast as he could manage, and the electric light extinguished. Somerville moved quickly through the house to the top of the hall, facing the mahogany door. Through the small glazed panel he saw the blurred shape of a woman's head as she reached forward to ring the bell. When there was no reply, she moved away towards the lounge window. He followed, until he could see her through the uncurtained glass; she was quite tall, about mid-thirties, with thick black shoulder-length hair. He continued to watch her as she returned to the door, his heart lurching when he heard a key being inserted into the latch as she attempted to open it and shoved hopelessly against the bolt he had placed in position. Then the woman began knocking; the letter-box was pushed open and she peered into the black hallway.

'Look, I know you're in there. Open this door immediately, or I'm going to the police.' The accent was local, he knew that from his summer holidays spent in the place year after year. 'I mean it . . . You'd better open up now, I'm not messing about!'

Somerville froze. The MI was no use; he couldn't afford the noise. He still had the knife on his left forearm as he approached the door. He eased back the bolt and, disconnecting the chain, opening the door slowly.

The woman was still standing there. When he glanced to her right there was no one in sight, but that meant nothing. He grabbed her by the loose scarf around her neck and pulled her into the hall. She went sailing past, falling face-first on the plush carpet. He jumped back inside the house, slamming the door shut.

'Get up and into the lounge, first on the right!' he hissed.

But she was shocked and failed to move.

'Move it!'

Slowly, she got to her feet and Somerville found himself having to help her the rest of the way, as she seemed to have hurt her leg in the fall. Once in the lounge, he closed the door and pulled the curtains. After putting on the lights, he gazed into the pale face of the frightened woman.

'It's me, Mary O'Sullivan. Don't you remember me?'

He stared deep into her eyes, but the memory failed to crystallise.

'We used to play down on the rocks when we were kiddies.'

'What do you want?' Somerville felt unsteady. The intense effort of the last few moments was beginning to tell.

'You're Eddie Somerville and, by the looks of it, I think you need some help.'

Somerville staggered slightly, trying to keep a fix on her face. 'It's a bit much to expect me to believe you . . .' He winced at the swift rush of pain, and his focus blurred slightly.

'I want to help you.' She smiled. 'Now why don't you sit down?'

Somerville collapsed on to the floor, still clutching the weapon. He had to trust her; there was no other choice.

Friday 11 June – Castle Street, Belfast

Desmond Murray was going through some papers in his windowless office, a converted store-room at the rear of the shabby snooker hall. The door swung open without warning and Seamus Doyle stood grimly in the opening.

'Seamus . . . ya gave us a start. C'mon on in and sit yourself down.' Murray made a feeble attempt at smiling.

Doyle closed the door behind him and sidled over to the paper-cluttered knee-hole desk. 'Two hundred quids worth,' he said.

'What d'ya mean? Ya need some money, is that it?' replied Murray.

'No, not money. I'm here to collect an old debt, Desi. I want a favour returned.'

'What d'ya want then?'

'There's to be a meetin' to decide my fate. Ya heard about the Omagh job?'

'I heard. I heard a lotta people are smarting.' Murray shook his head.

'You could be a part of the meetin'. You've got pull with them, I know ya have. Simply, I don't want ta be left out ta grass. I've places ta go yet!' Doyle's agitation was clear.

'I don't think I could do anythin' . . . have ya spoken to Paddy?'

'Paddy! Paddy can do so much! Look what I've done for ya. You owe me. Ya could be at that meetin' if ya wanted, and with yer Dublin contacts the rest could be fixed and ya know it!'

Desmond Murray was not a man who responded to threats. He had held the strings of power in the movement for too long to be browbeaten by some youngster.

'Listen, ya wee boy! Don't try and put the screws on me or it'll be a hood ya'll be facing!'

'Ye'll do better than say that!' said Doyle. 'There's a lot of people at that meetin' who'd be interested ta know af yer nephew's punishment and what ya offered me! Just remember I've nothin' ta lose!'

Murray recognised the truth of the last part of Doyle's statement. Desperate men do desperate things, and the last thing he needed at that moment was the finger pointed from any direction. He stood up and walked around the table, smiling. 'Take it easy, take it easy, young fella. Y'know the meetin's not my scene; in fact ya haven't even a clue what my scene is, have ya?' Doyle didn't reply. 'All right, all right, I'll see what I can do.'

'You'd better, or I swear ta God, I'll – ' Doyle's words were cut short as the little man grabbed him by the arm.

'Look! I said I'd see ya all right! I will, but don't ya threaten me son – don't ya ever threaten me again. See!' Doyle had never seen Murray so angry and upset. 'I was shooting up RUC stations when ya weren't even a dirty thought in yer ma's head!'

Doyle thought of hitting him. The closeness of the man, his bad breath and the spittle splashing from his lips as he shouted was enough to push Doyle over the edge. Then, as suddenly as the little man's anger had arisen, it disappeared and he released his grip.

'Ye'll be OK. Trust me, son.' Murray patted Doyle on the shoulder.

The young man shrugged the hand away. 'Thanks, but I trust nobody!' He went to the door and, without looking behind him, spoke again. 'Just ya see me all right, it's all I'm askin'.'

As Seamus Doyle left the Castle Street pool-room, he was immediately followed by a man with a collie dog who had been standing at the taxi rank on the opposite side of the busy street. Doyle went through the security barriers at Castle Street, past the civilian searchers and the UDR soldiers on static point duty, through Donegall Place and the pedestrian zones of Cornmarket and Ann Street. It was not until he was out of the city centre and approaching Laganbank Road from Oxford Street that the man and dog left his trail, walking on across the Kings Bridge. By then pursuit had already been taken up by a young woman pushing a pram. Before Doyle arrived at his girl-friend's house just off the Short Strand, his tail had been changed once more, this time to a window cleaner equipped with bucket, chamois and small ladder over one shoulder as he cycled merrily along the side-streets of Mountpottinger, whistling as he rode.

Evening, Friday 11 June – Andersonstown, Belfast
The meeting was convened in the front room of a little house in Gartree Place, in the middle of Andersonstown. The talking had gone on for half an hour, and smoke from continuous rounds of cigarettes clung thickly under the low ceiling.

The five men were deep in discussion when there was a knock on the kitchen door and in walked Desmond Murray. He had approached the house from the rear garden to avoid attracting suspicion.

'Sorry I'm late . . . got held up at a VCP on the Falls for forty bloody minutes while the Brits pulled the Cortina apart. I'll have to get rid of the fuckin' car. They even sent for the peelers after one of them decided ma driving licence was a forgery!'

Paddy grinned. 'Don't tell me the grandkids pulled yer photo off it an' stuck on Des O'Connor's!' Everyone laughed and Paddy continued, 'Maybe they just scribbled some hair on that billiard ball af yours.' The laughter increased and the two men on the sofa moved up to let Murray sit down. The only man who failed to even smile was Joe McNulty; he disapproved of humour during business, especially when an outsider had gained entry to their circle only to turn up late.

Paddy raised his hands to restore order. 'Desi . . . We've been talkin' over our strategy for the next three weeks. We're goin' ta have a big push against the economic targets, especially in the city centre, but there's problems that Dublin doesn't understand.'

'What problems would those be, Paddy?' asked Murray.

'Dublin's sent us this ultimatum. All Brigades to be on the look-out for this bastard peeler.'

'I don't see what the problem is? I brought ya that message meself.'

'The problem is, I've also now been told that we've ta drop everythin' just to get this bastard and give attention to Doyle. We have a photo of Somerville. Joe got it from the *Irish News* this morning.' Paddy tossed the grubby copy over to Murray. 'It's better than the one they put on the TV. It was taken at the funeral.'

Murray looked at the photograph and handed it back again. 'I don't understand the other part. What did Dublin say to you about young Doyle?'

Paddy flashed a glance around the room. 'I'm comin' ta that. The boys here feel he has to be disciplined. We can't let him aff with this thing . . .'

'But what does Dublin say? Ya did say they mentioned him?' continued Murray.

'Oh, aye. But they left it fer us ta sort out.'

'Well, I've given the matter some thought.' Murray sat forward on the settee. 'If we "punish" him, it'll draw attention to him. After all, he's quite unknown outside this room. The other thing is this: what if Somerville tries to get at him? It'd be a handy trap,

162

but again we could be barkin' up the wrong tree and wastin' our time . . . if ya want to, why not send him away for a bit?'

Joe McNulty was the first to reply. 'Looks like ya thought it all out before ya got here!'

Murray could see the man's anger compounding his initial annoyance at Murray's presence, but he pressed on. 'Sure Dublin's annoyed about his botched-up job, but they also appreciate that he's a damned good operator. What happened to Doyle could have happened to anybody.'

'I say he gets punished good and proper. There's others lookin' to us ta see just what we do,' said McNulty.

'Look, why not send him off to England or somewhere, where he's still of use to the movement? We could even use him with the ASUs across the water. I can tell ya he'll know it's a punishment by the time he's through.'

Paddy clapped his hands together. 'Desi's got a point. Just because he's taken away from the area means nothin'. He'll be given shit, shitty jobs. We'll see to that.'

'And when this Somerville is taken care of, ye can bring him back if ya want,' Murray replied, taking his cue from Paddy's tacit approval. 'Pack him off ta England, and you've got a good soldier, for that's what he is. He'd be available for use in steppin' up the campaign over there. If he fucks up in the same way in England, the consequences are all to our favour!'

'OK, Desi, leave it with us. We'll let ya know.' Paddy could read the unrest in the faces of the others present.

After Murray was shown the door, the young girl brought in a tray of tea and biscuits. The meeting was going to be a long one.

Seamus Doyle had his own ideas about his future, and

it would be under his control. Accordingly, he'd taken the stolen police Walther PPK and magazine containing seven rounds of 9mm-short from the hide in the old lady's house just off the Glen Road.

'Don't worry, missus, I'll only be a minute,' he explained as he passed her in the cramped hallway of the terraced house. In fact, it took him almost ten minutes to unscrew the hardboard panel with the knife-blade, and remove the small paper parcel from its makeshift shelf of six pieces of wire welded to the bottom of the cast-iron bath. The old woman was waiting for him in the hall.

'Mrs Reilly, I've tided up again. The bathroom's in the state I found it.'

The old woman never spoke; she just opened the door and let him past. Doyle went back quickly to Kenard Avenue.

No RUC bastard was going to have him. He was in such a hurry that he failed to see the young couple kissing in the Vauxhall Chevette parked opposite the old woman's house. He failed to notice the car again as it passed him at the Kennedy Way roundabout. His return to his mother's house was observed from behind the net curtains of the first-floor window of the terraced house opposite.

Doyle had decided not to go out that night with his girl-friend from the Short Strand, but later in the evening he succumbed to the invitation of his younger brother Kieran. He left the Walther in his bedroom, tucked under the divan's light mattress.

They walked the short distance to the CESA Social Club on the Glen Road. It was a dingy place, but had been brightly decorated for the weekly Friday-night dance. Extra disco lighting had been borrowed and installed. The group – five young men brought up from Newry – were already tuning up their instruments and the Club was packed. The two brothers had to struggle through the chattering crowd to get to the bar counter, which was slick with spilled drink. They drank steadily for almost two hours, ordering doubles each time to avoid the persistent queue. Doyle was beginning to unwind, forgetting the past week's events and his future prospects. Kieran was well on his way, getting off with one of the local girls. But Seamus just could not stir up any interest – at least not until, half-heartedly watching the small dance floor and sea of bobbing figures, he saw long black hair and a face he recognized. It was Susan White, the school-teacher who had accompanied him to Omagh. He watched her for a few minutes. She knew how to use her body to the best advantage, most of the men in the club had their eyes firmly fixed on her sensual movements. By club standards she was smartly dressed. Her partner was a tall, skinny fellow with long, curly fair hair, who couldn't take his eyes off Susan and periodically pulled her close to him and spoke into her ear. She laughed in response.

Doyle moved closer to the side of the dance floor and Susan White caught his stare several times before realising who he was, but decided to ignore him for the moment. When the group finished playing and took a short break, Susan's partner led her to a table before joining the shoving mass around the tiny bar. Doyle watched as she began to check her hair in a small mirror produced from a black shoulder-bag, then he moved through the milling crowd until he stood in front of her.

'Hi ya! What's your name?' He smiled down at her.

'Hello, Seamus, you took long enough to come over.' Her smile was radiant.

'What's a nice girl like you doing in a place like this, then?' replied Doyle, encouraged by the cordial greeting.

'I assume those were your two best starting lines for chatting up the local girls?' She flirted with her eyes, but she had no need to. He felt she was a kindred spirit, intelligent, unlike the rest of the scrubbers who came to this place. Doyle pulled up a chair.

'I really meant it. This isn't a place for the likes of you.'

'I was born and reared on the Falls, just the same as you, Seamus. Too bad we never met before now.'

'Yeah, suppose so.' he agreed. 'So how's the teachin', then?'

'OK, I'm at St Louisa's now. It's nice to be full-time, instead of taking on relief work all over the place. What about you? Ever thought of getting up and out of all this?'

'Many times. But I still come up with the same thing – like you I'm part of this area, no matter where I go.'

'Even to Omagh?'

Doyle's smile was wiped from his face. 'That's enough! If ya know what's good for ya, ye'll not repeat that! Understand?'

'All right! All right! Keep your beard on! I'm only kidding. Forget it, just forget it.' She snatched for her drink.

Doyle leaned over and held her wrist, preventing the glass from reaching her lips which now quivered. 'There's some things ya don't kid about!' he said.

'I said OK! Now let go of my arm!' At that moment, her dancing companion returned to the table in time to see Doyle release his grip and Susan shakily replace the glass on the table.

'Is he annoying you, Susan?' He spoke with quiet authority and Doyle immediately took him for another school-teacher. He stood facing Doyle, clutching two large tumblers of Vodka and a bottle of coca-cola.

'You're in my seat there!' he said. 'Why don't you clear off, before you get hurt!'

Doyle did not hesitate. He lunged forward and punched the man on the right side of the face and he fell backwards on to the empty dance floor, glasses and bottles smashing around him. Startled, he pulled himself to his feet as Doyle's second blow landed. This time it was a kick to the shoulder and he fell back again in agony, face contorted, mouth open, with no breath left to yell. Susan White was screaming amidst the mounting hysteria of the other semi-inebriated women present. Before Doyle could strike another blow, he was pounced upon by three of the Club's stewards. To everyone's astonishment, he beat them off for almost a minute, until Kieran Doyle and a couple of his mates intervened, acting like UN peace troops. At the bar manager's insistence Doyle was shown out unceremoniously to avoid any more trouble. Two stewards lay unconscious on the dance floor and Susan White was bent over her boy-friend, nursing his head on her lap.

Once outside, Doyle quickly forgot about the girl as he examined his torn shirt and ripped leather jacket. The shirt collar was badly bloodstained from the deep cut on his left ear where he had been struck with an empty bottle. Even with his belly full of drink and reactions slowed, the stewards had been no match for him. Shrugging off Kieran's attempts to guide him home, he walked away from the Club grounds. He thought what a fool he had been and of the attention he had drawn to himself. He decided to walk up to the Glen Road and down Shaws Road rather than go directly home, and let the cold night air do its work.

Morning, Saturday 12 June – Andersonstown, Belfast
Returning home with the morning papers, Seamus Doyle noticed the red Cortina parked outside his house and found Desmond Murray waiting for him in the living room.

'Yer all mine from now on, Seamus.'

'What the fuck d'ya mean?'

'Simple. I got ya off, but there's a catch. Ye've got ta go ta England!'

'England! What the fuck for?'

'The furtherance of the Republican cause, Seamus lad. I'll tell ya better tomorrow. I've a mind to introduce you to where the real power lies – all this here isn't for you, is it?'

It was a fact that Doyle could not dispute. 'OK, then. So you've got me off. Now what?'

'Tomorrow you begin yer education proper. You come and see me at the pool-hall, then we'll talk shop.'

Doyle saw him to the front door and walked with him to the Cortina. 'Thanks, Desi,' he said. 'I really mean it.' Doyle put out his hand and Murray took it, winking to him as he stooped into the car.

The Nikon camera clicked continuously as the zoom lens focused sharply on both men. In those few seconds, thirty-six shots had been taken from behind the net curtains opposite.

The meeting with Murray next morning was more interesting than Doyle had imagined.

'Don't misunderstand me lad,' said Murray. 'My job is a wee one in the affair. But you could rise, you could be a star if ya wanted. I've already set ya up in a job in London. It's with a firm of stockbrokers. We have a contact there, and they do a lot of business for us. Ye'll get the hang of it in no time.'

'What's yer angle, Desi?' Doyle was curious.

'Angle? I don't understand ya?' Murray pretended to look puzzled.

'Yer not doin' me any favours. What's in it for you?'

'If ya must know, it'd benefit me – I mean the organisation – to have somebody on the inside, that's all. I might ask ya for the odd piece of information on top of whatever else you're required to do. You ask too many questions for yer own good, son. Take a bit of advice from an older man and walk before ya can run. Let's say it does to have a man with yer other talents in a place like that.' Murray was smiling again. 'Yer being taken into the confidence of those who control the real power, don't ya ever forget that, cause if yer mouth becomes loose you'll be dead before ya utter one other word!'

'You can depend on me, ya know that,' said Doyle.

'Yer movin' next week. It's the earliest I can get it set up. You've to stay in yer house; there's ta be no more goin' out ta the Club, like ya did last night.'

'Yer well informed, Desi.'

'It's how I stay alive, son, remember that.'

Wednesday, 16 June – Cushendall, County Antrim Coast
Somerville awoke with a start. The fever had abated. His arm still hurt, but fresh bandages indicated the wounds had been treated and he could move both hand and arm reasonably freely. Remembering the woman, he sat up slowly and pulled back the bedclothes, finding he was dressed in a pair of blue pyjamas. He got up and crossed the room slowly; his legs felt weak, his head light and his vision was unclear. As he put on the newly laundered shirt and fresh trousers which had been left draped over a chair, he peered out between the heavily-curtained windows. The orchard seemed to come alive in the brilliant sunshine. He walked barefoot to the kitchen. She stood with her back to him, tending pots on the small cooker, but she had heard him come downstairs.

'Good afternoon, Eddie. Did you sleep well?' As she turned to face him, he realised for the first time how attractive she was. He nodded once.

'Well, ya slept long enough anyway,' she said. 'Like some coffee? It's just ready.'

'Yes, yes, I would. Thank you,' Somerville replied through a dry throat, continuing to stare intensely at her thick black hair and sculptured features. She was tall, he reckoned at least 5′ 9″ or 5′ 10″, slim, with penetrating hazel eyes which scrutinised him sharply through metal-rimmed spectacles.

'Now what would ya be standing there for? Go into the lounge and sit yerself down, will you?' She waved with her hand as if chasing away some child. 'Go on. Shoo, will ya!' Almost against his will, Somerville found himself smiling.

Relaxed in the lounge armchair and sipping coffee, he felt quite at home. 'I see you've tidied up a bit.'

'Yes, but I'm afraid I couldn't get them bloodstains out of the carpet there; I do hope the Russells won't be too upset,' she paused, 'especially since they pay me to keep up the place for them.'

Barney was not surprised. 'Have they owned it long?'

'Going on ten years now.'

'So you had a key. You could have opened the door and just walked in! Why didn't you?' He set the coffee aside, remembering the bolt on the door.

'Because I knew you were here . . . God knows! The way you greeted me, if I'd just sauntered in, you might have done me in for sure!'

'How long have I been asleep?' Somerville asked.

'Six whole days. I've been here most of the time. Ya ought ta have heard the excuses I made to me father.'

'What?' Barney screwed up his face, not in pain, but with a shock of disbelief at the length of time he had been unconscious.

'You had a hell of a fever and I had to work on you night and day. Yer a lucky man, the infection in that arm had spread badly but I got the swelling down with some drugs from the hospital. I had to swab out and stitch the wound. Ya lost a lot of blood.'

'What date is it?' interrupted Barney.

'The sixteenth, Wednesday the sixteenth.'

'How the blazes did I manage to sleep for six whole days?'

'Fever, combined with the drugs I got hold of. By the way, be careful for a while; you're full of xynocaine. It's working fine now, but it will wear off quickly.'

'What hospital?' asked Somerville, his mind racing.

'I was an auxiliary nurse in Larne Hospital until recently. I got yer stuff from a doctor friend – he fancies me, ya know, him a married man and all!'

'Did he not suspect?'

'Oh Lord, no! I told him it was for my brother, who'd hurt himself in a fishing accident while he was poaching the salmon nets down the coast in Carnlough Bay!' She laughed loudly. 'All he wanted in return was to bed me in the Ballygally Castle Hotel.'

Somerville's embarrassment showed on his face.

'Don't worry,' said Mary. 'He got that drunk he fell asleep on us!' They both laughed.

That afternoon, for the first time since the bomb, he felt at ease. They talked over childhood memories, comparing recollections and updating each other on what had happened since. Somerville learned she had spent most of her adolescent life nursing a sick mother and rearing her younger brothers and sisters, with hardly any time for much else. Romance had eluded her in later years, while she continued to give her commitment to the family after her mother died. Her only love, Tommy O'Neill, could wait no longer and finally ended up putting another local girl, Eileen Sweeney, in the family way. It had been the scandal of the village and when the Sweeney brothers had started regular street brawls with the O'Neill clan in the time leading up to the 'quickie' wedding, gossip had spread. Mary had been hurt initially by the exposure of Tommy's additional relationship, but hurt gave way to sadness and disappointment. She honestly could not blame him; after all, she had called off so many dates with him to stay at home with her ailing father.

Curiously, if it had not been for Mary's suggestion that he do the decent thing by Eileen, Tommy would have been away to his cousin Damian in Hull and the deep-sea fishing fleet. She couldn't help chuckling, reminiscing about the wedding day, when the two families turned up with the four Sweeney boys and six O'Neills all sporting bruises and black eyes. One or two even had their arms in slings, and the youngest of the Sweeney clan hobbled along on crutches with a broken ankle – the result of his tumble from the first floor of a public house on to the street below.

The wedding photographs had created uproarious mirth when first presented in the local pub by Tommy's father, Dan O'Neill. The local parish priest, Father McNamara, stood in the front row, face emanating stern disapproval at the array of injured bodies on either side of him. Good humour soon turned sour when old Dan and his best drinking pals wrecked what remained of the village's only public house, the fact that it was owned by an uncle of the Sweeneys only adding fuel to his fury.

And so the afternoon continued, Mary helping Somerville to forget his problems. After a dinner of boiled fish, parsley sauce, jacket potatoes and vegetables, they sat again over coffee at the small oval dining-table.

'That was very nice, Mary,' said Somerville, 'but I can't help feeling guilty sitting here in someone else's house!'

'Forget the guilt, ya need building up! Them pyjamas almost swamped you!' She frowned. 'Can I ask you a question, Eddie?'

'Look, call me Barney. Everybody else does,' he told her.

172

'I've always known you as Eddie, and Eddie it is!' She paused. 'Who is Doyle?'

Barney was immediately on his guard. 'Where did you hear that name?'

'From you. You were full of fever, ranting and yelling at the top of yer voice. I had to stay with you the whole time, except for the wee while it took me to get the medicines from the doctor and avoid his groping hands. It took me all of three hours – not a bad record, eh?'

'He was the one who planted the bomb.' Somerville stared her straight in the face.

For a while they remained silent, just drinking their coffee.

'Ya know, yer becoming quite a folk hero,' said Mary. 'The press releases make you out to be mental, suffering from depression and so on, but public interest seems to have gone full circle. To some, yer only doing what many of them wanted to do themselves, but never had the fortitude – well, that's how the papers describe it.' She stood up, took a copy of the *Belfast Telegraph* from the sideboard and began reading from the leader column. 'This paper even describes yer actions as – where is it now . . . oh, yes! Here it is: "The physical manifestation of the frustrations facing the law-abiding citizen living in an unlawful society, where criminals and terrorists walk freely amongst us without fear of apprehension. Somerville's actions, although drastic and against God's law, are nevertheless a reflection of this state of limbo, induced by successive governments who have accepted unequivocally the philosophy of 'An acceptable level of violence'. We, society, must take full responsibility for Inspector Somerville's actions and the outcome, because of our apathetic approach over countless years. Perhaps if we realigned our thoughts to a previous doctrine of letting the punishment fit the crime and unchaining the leash of conscience that binds the actions of our security forces so intolerably, then and only then could we avoid the Somervilles of this world taking matters into their own hands." It goes on a bit more, but I'm sure ya get the drift.'

She handed the paper to him and he examined the other front-page headlines. 'How did the papers tie in my name to all the killings?'

'I don't know.'

'Does the telephone here work?' he asked, still staring at the newspaper.

'Yes.'

'I may need some things. If I give you a list and some money, can you get them?'

'I'll do what you want, within reason.' She smiled again.

Somerville did not respond, but eased back in the chair turning his face to the ceiling as if seeking some heavenly inspiration . . . or was it solace?

Friday, 18 June – Omagh, County Tyrone

Billy Martin answered the ringing telephone with some reluctance at 2 a.m. that morning. He had tried to nudge his wife into stretching over him to the receiver at the bedside, but it had been no use – she remained fast asleep. With some degree of discomfort, he pulled the receiver off the hook. Finally, after another few seconds of fumbling, he managed to get it to his ear.

'Yes?' he croaked.

'Billy . . . it's me.' Recognition of the voice made him wake up with a jolt.

'Barney. Jesus! Where the hell are you?'

'It doesn't matter, Billy, better if you don't know. Look, I need your help, old son.'

Billy glanced down at his wife; she hadn't stirred. 'Shoot!' he said.

'Firstly, how is my sister?'

174

'She's all right. She had a bit of a shock, but she's well on the mend now.'

'Listen, Billy, I need to know about a man called Doyle. He's from Belfast, I think Andersonstown. His full name is Seamus Doyle. Have you got that?'

'Yes, yes,' said Billy, keeping his voice low. 'Seamus Doyle, Andersonstown. What do you want to know about him?'

'His address and if he's working, his place of employment – and a good description too. He's bound to be on record.'

'Need I ask why?' whispered Billy.

'He killed them and maybe he also knows why.'

Billy gritted his teeth. 'Where can I contact you?'

'You can't. I'll ring you, same time again tomorrow morning. Good night, chum.'

The line went dead and Billy Martin carefully replaced the receiver and lay back on his pillows. Sleep would not come to him again that night.

Friday 18 June – RUC Headquarters, Belfast

Even with Williamson out of the way, Frank Grange was becoming disenchanted with playing second fiddle to Cecil Rose and his department. He had heard since that Colonel Jones had been severely reprimanded; the Army did not tolerate broken rules, or 'SOP' as the Colonel had explained to him. On enquiring further, he found the letters stood for 'Standard Operating Procedure', but he had a procedure of his own and it was about time that he showed the half-baked policemen of MI5 just what he was capable of.

He summoned the local branch inspector responsible for West Belfast; it took the man over an hour to reach his office, having to extricate himself from an interview with a difficult suspect at Castlereagh Holding Centre. Detective Inspector Sam Mooney was shown into the office by Chief Inspector Black, who remained during the meeting.

'Sam, so good of you to come at such short notice,' Grange took the man's hand and beckoned him to a chair. Mooney made no reply.

'There's something going down in your area, Sam, and up to now you've been kept in the dark. I think it's high time you knew.'

'I don't know what you mean, sir,' said the unsettled policeman.

'Ever heard of a runner called Seamus Doyle, Kenard Avenue?'

'Nothing much. A student activist, from the old reports I got from our man at the University.'

'Not true . . . Now listen carefully to what I'm about to tell you.'

Saturday 19 June – Omagh, County Tyrone
Billy Martin sat in the kitchen resting a cup of warm cocoa in his hands. He was staring at the telephone on the middle of the kitchen table. At 2 a.m. precisely it burred into life, but he hesitated before answering.

'Hello.'

'It's me again, Billy.'

'Barney . . . I did what you asked.'

'Well, spit it out, man!'

'He's in the Holding Centre at Castlereagh Police Station. Arrested yesterday under Section 12.'

'He's what! What the hell happened?'

'Easy. It appears his house was searched by the Army – just a normal search, except that Doyle cut up a squaddie pretty badly when he went into his bedroom: pulled a flick-knife or something and cut the fella in the arm and face.'

'Hell's gates! He'll go down for six months for that.'

'More like five to ten years,' replied Billy. 'When they searched his room after the assault, they found a stolen police issue pistol and ammo. They're pushing for possession with intent after the assault on the soldier.'

'Damn it!' Somerville snapped.

'Sorry, Barney, looks like you're wasting your time. Listen, why don't you give yourself up? There's a lot of people would be very sympathetic to your plight, especially if they heard the truth for a change.'

'Sympathetic? Billy, I'd have thought you'd have had more sense . . . Tell me, were you able to get the information discreetly?'

'Yeah, I spoke to a girl I know in the CID at Andersonstown. She was able to check with Criminal Intelligence and get an update on him. The strange thing is, he doesn't have a lot of form. He's only mentioned in a source report by the Branch some years ago, and all that related to was his association in left-wing student politics when he was deputy chairman of the Students' Union at Queen's University.'

'Did you get a description?'

'No, I didn't see any point, although he'd be noticed in a crowd by the broken nose he got when the Brits took exception to him cutting one of their mates.' Billy laughed; there was no reply. 'I'm sorry Barney, real sorry. If there was anything I could do . . .'

The telephone went dead in mid-sentence. Billy Martin shook his head and hung up the receiver.

Sunday 20 June – Cushendall, County Antrim Coast
At Somerville's request, Mary had tried to vary her routine, calling less frequently at the cottage and spending more time with her father and brothers.

When she turned up late that morning, she found him in the lounge. He had covered the dining-table in newspaper and spread out his wares. The MI carbine was stripped and being cleaned; to the other side lay

177

the Zyconn radio, a pile of ammunition and Somerville's other utensils of combat.

'Good morning, are ya planning on starting a war?'

'No, finishing one.' His face was pale as he rose from the table clutching a tennis ball in his right hand and began squeezing. She could see from his face that the exertion hurt him, but there was no point in making any comment.

'Listen.' He pulled a piece of paper from his left pocket and handed it to her. 'This is the list I mentioned. You can buy most of the items from any chemist's shop. Can you get them today?'

Mary unfolded the paper, which contained £50, and examined the list. 'I think I can find a chemist's open in Cushendun or Carnlough this afternoon. I'll use the da's car.' She read the list aloud: 'Hair dye, white rinse, electric razor, cotton-wool wads like the dentist uses. What do you mean by that?'

'The wads a dentist would put into your mouth to dry up saliva – you know.'

'Oh, yes.' She continued looking at the sheet, more confused than ever. 'Make-up powder! Now what do ya mean exactly?'

'Powder to give a person a pale complexion.'

'So yer going away again?' she asked.

'I have to, Mary, the choice is not mine.'

'Not yours? Then who the hell's choice is it?' She threw the list and money on to the table.

'Circumstances have forced me to take certain actions, which I must complete. It's all I live for, if you can call this living!' He was annoyed at having to explain, and folded the list back into her open hands. 'Please help me.'

'Ya mean, give ya a better chance to kill somebody else!' Tears filled her eyes.

'Give me a better chance to stay alive.'

'I'll get your stuff, may God forgive me.' Her cheeks were wet now.

He kissed her on the forehead. 'Thank you,' he said.

She rushed from the house crying and in that moment realized how foolishly she had deluded herself. 'God curse him!' she cried as she ran from the orchard gateway.

The items were delivered as requested. Somerville noted a change in her attitude, an aloofness, but he did not question her. It was pointless.

'There, everything as you asked. I hope the old clothes fit you, they're clean, but a bit scruffy-looking.'

'Thank you, Mary. I don't know how to repay you.'

'I don't want yer thanks. I'm going now . . . will you be here if I call tomorrow?'

There was no reply, but he gazed at her with genuine affection.

'Well, I suppose this is good-bye then. What should I say to make you change yer mind? Tell me!' Tears filled her eyes as Somerville turned away towards the lounge window. He heard the door slam for the second time that day.

Monday 21 June – Cushendall, County Antrim Coast
It was 5 a.m. when the bedside alarm went off. Somerville showered and dressed. He had already shaved the crown of his head and brought a chair into the bathroom. The make-up and other bits and pieces from the chemist were intermingled with the things he had removed from the medicine cabinet.

The preparation took a full hour, but the result was astounding. When Somerville finally looked into the mirror his own eyes met him, but that was where any resemblance ended. His appearance was now that of a man in his fifties, his face bloated by the insertion of some cotton wads along the outer line of his back teeth. Pale colouring was induced by the make-up which also

179

covered his freshly shaven skull, hiding the hurried shaving job from the night before.

By 6.30 a.m. he was off, carrying a small battered brown case just large enough to hold the MI carbine and other necessary items. The knife was now strapped to his right arm. Although reasonable power had returned to his hand, he was taking no chances on weakness letting him down. He walked towards Cush-endun until the first morning bus came along at 7.10 a.m. The journey into Larne was slow and tedious, but after the confinement of the cottage, the early-morning view was invigorating.

Mary O'Sullivan arrived at the cottage early the same morning, with renewed determination to try to prevent him from carrying out his plans. As she let herself in by the front door, the grandfather clock at the end of the hallway struck half-past seven. She found the note on the oval dining table, it read simply, 'Thank you. Eddie.' She bent over the table holding on to it for support; there was so much she wanted to say to him and would never be able to tell him now.

Somerville arrived in Belfast at York Street Railway Station. He walked the distance into the city centre in his practised shuffle, and, avoiding the security barriers, went to the Salvation Army Hostel in Corpor-ation Street. After assessing its potential, he continued on his way across the Queen's Bridge and East Belfast. He would return to the hostel in the evening when his other work was complete.

7

Tuesday 22 June – Castlereagh RUC Station, Belfast
The perimeter walls and fence-line of the Castlereagh
police complex encompassed not only a functional
police station but many other branches and departments. Amongst the array of outbuildings that house
the RUC's traffic pool, maintenance and office accommodation, exists an unobtrusive series of blocks known
simply as the Holding Centre. It was established to
house the longer term prisoners held under the Emergency Powers legislation, and to establish some continuity in the handling of such prisoners. Containing
interview rooms, medical rooms, and accommodation
for over thirty prisoners, it is under constant monitor
and guard by remote cameras and there is an abun-
dance of police on security duty.

Barney Somerville applied his mind and soul to the
task of entering the place. He adopted the attitude that
the Holding Centre meant exactly what it was called
and to break in might perhaps be something else
entirely.

Cregagh Dairies began to come alive at around 5
a.m. that morning when the delivery men started
wheeling their daily service into operation. Fred
Harvey rumbled out of the yard gates in his Bedford
van; his run was to the village of Ballygowan, some
distance across the Castlereagh Hills. He delivered to
shops and premises as well as carrying out the domestic
delivery, and the purpose-made van was laden with
boxes of ice cream and frozen products in the large
refrigeration compartment to the rear. The other half

of the van carried crates of milk, bags of potatoes and boxes of farm eggs.

He had reached the roundabout at the junction of Castlereagh Road and Knock dual carriageway when a solitary figure waved to him from the roadside. Harvey stopped and leaned over to the passenger door, opening the handle at the same time, to speak to the middle-aged man.

'Good morning,' said the stranger.

'What can I do for you?' asked Fred. Before he could settle back into his seat the stranger had jumped in on the passenger side, slamming the door behind him. Fred could feel the point of the commando knife prick into his side, even through his overcoat and pullover. At fifty-seven years of age, he was not about to take any chances.

'Look, mister, I don't have any money, if that's what you're after?'

'You've nothing to fear from me. Just drive around that roundabout and back down the Castlereagh Road.'

Fred hesitated and Somerville raised his voice. 'Look, I don't want to hurt you. Just do it!'

After ten minutes, Somerville directed Fred to drive into the open gates of the disused factory in East Belfast. The van came to a halt at the rear service bay of the abandoned engineering plant.

'The door's open. Just wheel the van in.' Somerville pointed to the open shutters beside the concrete ramp. When the van finally stopped Fred Harvey found himself in the middle of the mammoth covered area, segmented only by the rows and rows of steel stanchions and hanging wires once connected to heavy machinery; this had long since been sold off to a developing country in Africa by auditors desperate to recover every penny from the stricken business. The concrete floor was covered in pools of murky water, gathered over months of dereliction.

'What's your name?' asked Somerville.

'Fred Harvey,' the terrified man replied.

'Well, Fred, I mean you no harm. So here's what we're going to do . . .'

At a quarter to six, the dairy van pulled up at the barrier and entrance to the Castlereagh complex. Beside the four-foot-thick blast walls stood a young Reserve constable, SMG at the ready. The van was approached by the other policeman who was much older – old enough to be the younger man's father, thought Somerville as he stepped down from the driver's cab. 'Morning, boys . . . what about ye?' He exaggerated the Belfast accent and hoped he was not overdoing his part.

The older officer looked at Somerville's balding head and the grey hair around his temples; the sallow complexion seemed almost peculiar on the tall, fit-looking figure.

'We aren't expecting a delivery van this morning.'

'Don't know anything about that. This here is Castlereagh Police Station, isn't it?'

'It is, aye.'

'Well, I'm just told to deliver the stuff.' Somerville handed the man a scribbled invoice.

'Look, I can't let you in . . .' The policeman turned to the younger man. 'Sammy, ring the enquiry office – see if Cregagh Dairies are supposed ta deliver here, will ya?'

'I wouldn't bother with that,' said Somerville. One telephone call and he would have to fight his way out. 'You'd be wasting yer time and mine – the dairy offices don't open until nine. But if ya ring yer kitchen they'd probably know.' He forced a smile.

'Sure the kitchen ain't open yet either – at least their office isn't, and those wee girls in there wouldn't know their arses from their elbows!' shouted the officer from

183

the wooden hut, as he tried to ring the kitchen on the internal line. After a few moments, he came back. 'Told ya so! They haven't got a clue in there, but Sadie says to bring the stuff in and she'll sort it out later.'

'Well, boys, all I know is that I've got to unload this delivery, otherwise you don't get yer breakfast,' said Barney as he pulled out the crumpled piece of paper again from the breast pocket of his white overall. 'There's six hundred farm eggs, two hundred pints, twenty pounds of butter, and there's ice cream and – '

He was interrupted by the older policeman. 'OK! OK! Have ya any ID?'

'ID?' queried Somerville, pausing as if puzzled.

'Identification,' said the policeman, rolling his eyes to heaven.

'Oh! Aye!' Somerville pulled out a driving licence and handed it to the policeman. The light was poor and Somerville had banked on it; the policeman wouldn't be able to detect the hurried replacement photograph in Fred Harvey's licence. 'All right,' he said. 'Let's see the back of the van.' He handed Barney back the licence. The complete search was swift but precise. The younger Reserve constable paced about, obviously annoyed by his senior's ponderous adherence to procedure.

The policeman finally closed the bonnet of the Bedford's engine and turned to Barney. 'All right. D'ya know where ta go?'

'Aye.' Somerville tried to look fed-up.

'Sammy, ye go with him to the kitchen and stay until he's finished.' He looked at Somerville. 'He'll go in the van with ya, and travel out again to the other gate there when you've finished.' He pointed towards the exit which lay on the other side of the brick wall.

'Thanks,' replied Somerville.

The two men travelled in silence to the rear doors of the kitchen delivery area. Somerville could not take his eyes off the Holding Centre, only thirty feet away across the empty yard.

The girls in the kitchen exclaimed in horror as he carried in the mountain of supplies. Their main store-room was locked, the keys kept by the manageress who never started before 8.30 a.m., which meant that later they would have to move all the supplies themselves, and Sadie, in particular let him know she wasn't too pleased about it; but he continued, ignoring their complaints. All the same he kept an eye on Sammy, who was more interested in scrounging a cup of tea from Sadie's pretty assistant and concentrating on her wiggle as she busied herself round the bain-marie.

Somerville took his chance. 'Look, son, I wouldn't ask ya this, but it's me arthritis, ya see.' Somerville rubbed at his right upper arm – the pain did not need to be feigned. 'Could ya help us carry in them remaining boxes of ice-cream?'

'Lead the way, mister,' said Sammy, placing his half-finished cup on the worktop. 'See ya later on, Maggie,' he shouted to the young girl serving up the first fry of the morning to a hungry-looking detective. The girl made no reply, but turned her head back towards him, smiling.

Sammy was right inside the refrigerator compart-ment and trying to lift the top stacked box when the blow from Somerville's taut left hand crunched into the nape of his neck. The single chop left him unconscious and lying in a heap amidst the remaining cartons. Having removed the boy's SMG and Walther pistol, Somerville jumped out of the compartment, slamming the door shut. After hiding the SMG behind the driver's seat, he lifted the wooden tray from the back of the van and began loading it with eggs and milk. On crossing the yard he hit the buzzer beside the door with his left elbow and the remote camera overhead flicked him into focus. The observer could see nothing except the presence of the milkman at the door. The intercom above the buzzer crackled in Somerville's ear.

'Yes?'

He leant over and spoke into the tiny grille. 'I had extra on board. The kitchen says ya can have it, if ya want.'

'The kitchen says *what?*' The voice sounded astonished at the offer.

'They're closing down for a while – some fault in the electric supply. It's the only way yer customers may get their breakfast.'

'I'm not too worried about *them*. Feed the boys first!' The voice sounded elated. 'Well, it's the first I've heard of it, but we'll take the stuff all right. Wait a tick.' The intercom went dead.

Those were the worst moments Barney spent as he thought of all the things that could go wrong. Then suddenly the heavy door opened and a middle-aged police guard took the tray from him. 'Thanks, mate.'

Somerville stepped towards him, just out of sight of the camera. As the man grasped the tray, his eyes took in the Walther pointed at his stomach. 'Move backwards. Now!' commanded Somerville and the man complied. Once inside, the green light switched off in the Centre's control room: this indicated the entrance to be re-sealed and the controller settled back to watch 'TV a.m.' on a portable black and white set.

The police guard stood speechless, almost dropping the tray and its contents on the floor.

'Move back into the control room – and don't mess me about. I know where it is!' snapped Somerville.

The guard obeyed without hesitation. The corridor turned to the right and then left; after climbing three steps, they were inside the police accommodation block. An open door on the left led into the control room and Barney unceremoniously shoved the man into it. He stumbled into the disconnected control panel

186

on the far wall, tray and contents crashing to the floor. Before the controller could fully swivel around in his chair, he received a sharp crack on the right temple from the barrel of the Walther. The first man tried to regain his balance, but unarmed he was no match for his opponent. As he lunged towards Somerville he was met by a kick to the stomach and crumpled to the floor. Before he regained his breath, Barney's knee crashed into his face and he fell backwards, unconscious.

Somerville surveyed the bank of VDUs and the board on the wall beside the row of screens. Thirty boxes for thirty cells. He ran down the list quickly:

'No. 26 – "B" BLOCK – DOYLE, SEAMUS (SECTION 12)'

There it was, chalked up on the board. Slipping out into the complex of portacabins and more solid structures that made up the ground floor, he quickly found the stairs with the arrow and sign displaying 'B BLOCK'. Ascending the metal open-tread staircase, he stopped at the door which was hung to the right-hand side and opened on to the staircase. Only one policeman was in sight and he was sitting at the far end of the corridor reading a magazine. Somerville rang the doorbell, then climbed up over the open balustrade, balancing in mid-air twelve feet from the floor below.

The policeman walked the length of the corridor and peered out through the panel of reinforced glass. He could see no one on the small landing but he opened the door anyway, letting curiosity – mixed with a natural apathy for his job – take control of his better judgement. With one foot inside the doorway he called, 'Anyone there?'

There was no reply and he took a step forward. 'Phil, is that you?' It was just enough to put him within Barney's reach. Somerville swung round the door, the Walther muzzle smacked the policeman in the mouth and he fell back into the corridor. Somerville was on him immediately, a strong hand on his throat, the gun digging into the man's chest.

'Open up twenty-six, and make it quick!' Somerville yanked him to his feet.

The man could not reply, but self-preservation helped him to pull out the bunch of keys from the clip on his waist. Somerville released his grip and pushed the man along the corridor until they reached cell twenty-six.

'Open it!' said Barney.

The man fumbled with the keys and then the lock before pulling back the heavy latch and swinging open the grey metal door. The room was quite small and well-lit; a figure lay on the single bed with a blanket pulled over his head. Somerville shoved the policeman ahead of him into the cell and kicked the legs of the sleeping prisoner. The blankets moved slightly and a head of black curly hair and bearded face appeared.

'Get up!' snapped Somerville.

'What . . . what the fuck's going on?' Doyle yawned.

Somerville grabbed him by the thick curls with such force that the young man hit the floor. 'Get up!' Doyle was slow to move, so Somerville acted. Wearing only a grubby vest and underpants, Doyle was tugged into the corridor and Somerville slammed the cell door shut in the face of the policeman who was still clutching his mouth.

As he turned, Doyle reacted as best he could and made a dive at Somerville from his crouched position on the floor, but Somerville swiftly side-stepped and cracked him on the back of the head with the Walther. Ignoring the blow, Doyle struggled to his feet, but Somerville kicked him hard in the kidneys and continued kicking as Doyle crawled towards the exit. At the open door, as he pulled himself up using the steel balustrade, Somerville's left hand crashed into his shoulder and sent him toppling down the metal staircase.

While he lay groaning at the bottom of the twelve-foot drop, Somerville caught hold of his left wrist with demonic force. He tried to resist and began shouting, 'Stop it! What's goin' on? Jasus!' The last word made something snap inside Somerville. What did this snake know about Jesus, about anything? Somerville knew his own soul was forfeit – that was the price. Christ knew the provocation – but this scum had no principles, no soul to barter. He turned and kicked Doyle in the chest, breaking two ribs. The young man screamed, then fainted. Somerville dragged the body out of the Holding Centre and into the yard. His luck held. Opening the refrigerator door, he found Sammy still unconscious amidst the boxes. He dragged Doyle in and slammed the door tightly behind him as he hurried to the driver's cab. The diesel engine spluttered into life and, with the Walther sitting on his lap, he cornered slowly to the exit gate.

The policeman leaned out from beside the barrier. 'Where's the young lad, then?' He was shouting over the noise of the spluttering engine.

Somehow, Barney smiled back. 'He's drinking tea in yer canteen . . . I think he's trying to score with the wee lassie there.' He kept smiling.

'I'll kill him!' shouted the policeman. 'I'll bloody kill him! Leaving me here while he cavorts around . . . the wee bastard! I'll have his guts!' He was still fuming as he flicked open the electrically controlled barrier arm and Barney drove out. He failed to hear the thumping at the refrigeration door as Sammy tried to open the safety handle. The young man was wasting his time; the mechanism had been rendered useless by a mixture of superglue and chewing gum.

The journey to the factory took only five minutes. At the Holding Centre, the alarm had been raised by the awakened residue of the night duty guard. Confusion reigned.

The exact words used by Detective Chief Superintendent Grange were unrepeatable. He was informed by telephone shortly after the 'escape', as the duty inspector described it. He was not completely surprised; they had all underestimated Somerville. It had to be him. The job bore his trade marks, if not his physical description.

On arrival at the disused factory, Somerville stopped the Bedford just inside the gateway. He closed the gates, locking them at the centre with the new Chubb lock he had obtained as a replacement for the original.

It took a bucket of ice-cold water to revive Doyle and initially he was not able to focus on the tall figure that stood before him.

'Well, Doyle, we meet at last!'

Doyle ached from head to toe and was aware of a jagging pain in his left side where the broken ribs were digging into his skin and tissue. He could now see his captor. He did not recognise the middle-aged man at first, but quickly realized the horror of his situation. He strained at the ropes that held his arms behind him and around the rusty stanchion.

'I know you,' he croaked.

Somerville straddled the wooden chair he had salvaged from one of the old offices, where he had safely tucked Sammy away alongside Fred. Both men had been tied up and left in an office store-room beside the main office block.

'What do ya want?' Doyle was regaining his senses quickly.

'Once upon a time . . . when I was a young constable, I was sent on a search operation to South Armagh. We were looking for a UDR part-time soldier; actually he was a farmer. Anyway, this chap was abducted by your lot and according to the press statement he had been interrogated regarding military matters and crimes against the Irish people and had been tried by an IRA court. He was sentenced to death and summarily executed. Your people even told us where his body was, or thereabouts . . .'

'Look! Just get to the fuckin' point, ya bastard!' Doyle struggled hopelessly against his bonds.

'Give me time, sonny. The best part is yet to come.' Somerville paused to light a small cigar. He was unused to the smoke, which irritated his eyes, lungs and throat. 'I found him. He was lying in a ditch, hooded and face down, hands bound tightly behind him and both feet also tied up. As first policeman at the scene, I had to remain there once the area was cleared for booby-traps. You boys so enjoy providing them for us, don't you?' Doyle said nothing. 'I was one of the first to see his tortured face. His eyes had been burnt clean out – probably by a red-hot poker, according to the pathologist. His left ear had been severed. He had still gone on living even after that. Then they worked on his hands; they tore out all his fingernails and broke three of his fingers. After that they worked on his feet with another red-hot poker and thrust it into his stomach for good measure, and according to the doc he *still* kept on going. They can tell by the way the wounds bleed and congeal, you know.'

'If you think yer scarin' me, forget it! Bastard!'

'That's the second time you've called me that, sonny. You really should take more care with your language.' Somerville's tone was quiet and icily controlled. 'Well, as I was saying . . . all that was nothing to what they did to him next. We found it in his mouth.' He stopped for a moment and looked hard at Doyle. 'They had cut off his penis and stuffed it into his mouth; actually it wedged in his throat. You know what else? He must have been alive when it was done, for the poor bastard actually choked to death. Oh yes! He was shot in the

191

head for good measure, but he was already dead.' Somerville puffed again at the cigar, savouring Doyle's obvious fear. 'Tell me, Seamus. Just how long do you reckon you can live when yours is cut off? I suppose it would depend on how resilient you are to the bleeding, but you know, those minutes will seem like for ever!'

Somerville stood up, throwing the chair aside and removing the commando knife from its arm-sheath. He crossed the nine steps to Doyle, the black six-inch double-edged blade plainly visible. As Somerville knelt beside Doyle he saw him flinch and turn his head away, tears streaming from his eyes. Somerville stubbed out the cigar on Doyle's leg. He screamed loudly but quickly stopped as his tormentor tugged at his underpants, cutting the thin cloth with one movement of the sharp blade.

'For God's sake! What do ya want from me?' Doyle was screaming again, and trying to wriggle away.

'I want you to imagine how a five-year-old boy, a seven-year-old girl and a young woman look after you did your handiwork!'

'For God's sake, tell me what you want!' sobbed Doyle.

'Very well. You can save yourself from this.' Somerville waved the knife close to Doyle's face. 'You can save yourself by giving me answers.' He stood back. 'Who sent you to Omagh?'

'It was ordered.'

'By whom?' Somerville's raised voice was enough for Doyle to speed up his answers.

'A man by the name of Patrick Hagan. He runs a bookshop at the "Busy Bee" – that's a shopping centre in Andytown.'

'And just who the hell is Patrick Hagan?'

'He's the OC of the Provisionals in Belfast.'

'Why me? What reason?'

'A man called Murray, Desi Murray. He came to

see us at the shop; he said you were a threat to the organisation's finances – something to do with gambling.' Doyle hesitated again – he had already signed his death warrant with the organisation for revealing so much. 'Can I have a drink?'

'After you're finished and not before,' snapped Somerville.

'Murray runs a pool-room and bingo hall down Castle Street; it's called "The Golden Nugget" '. Doyle began to cough and Barney relented with his questioning. He removed the flask from the haversack, poured out some warm chicken soup and held a plastic cup to Doyle's lips. This act of consideration for the man sickened him, but he needed the information.

'Well, what else?'

'That's it. I don't know any more,' said Doyle.

'Oh yes you do, sonny! What rank are you in the Provos?'

'Staff Officer.'

'Well, Staff Officer Doyle, tell me more about this meeting with Hagan and Murray. What else was said?'

'Murray mentioned that you were being taken care of. He was telling us that they were goin' ta suspend ya or somethin'.'

'How the hell did he know that?'

'I don't know. He said somethin' about benefactors takin' a personal interest in ya.'

'What benefactors?' Somerville was becoming more and more puzzled by the replies.

'Don't know. But Murray has big pull in the money circles, I know that for sure.'

'And how the hell do you know that?'

'Sure, he fixed me up with a job in London . . . in some broker's office.' The pain of Doyle's injury was easing and the shock of Barney's initial questioning had abated.

'So why try to kill me after fixing me up with the phoney allegations?'

'It was a Brigade decision, sanctioned by Dublin. As far as I know, Murray's action had been overruled, but it was too late to stop it.'

'How did they know so much about me? I haven't been involved in any investigations for some time.'

'They knew you kept askin' questions. As far as they were concerned, the thing had been buried with your move to Omagh in the first place.'

'You mean they got me transferred to Omagh because of the gaming enquiries? They had that much influence?'

Doyle didn't answer; he had said far too much already.

'You're lying, boy! And definitely not playing the game!' But he knew it was there – something in Doyle's face betrayed him. Somerville bent over him and put the knife to his face for the second time.

'I heard Paddy mention something in passing! Builders called Williams and Briggs – Williams himself I think.'

Somerville could not hide his shock. 'Why?'

'Money of course . . . money for the cause.'

Somerville had heard enough. 'What cause would that be then, eh?' Doyle looked up at him. 'You've just no idea, have you, sonny? Your sort of anarchist's been walking the earth ever since time began, and where has it got any of you?'

'This is our country,' Doyle retorted. 'Taken from us by the British, and kept from us by people like you!'

Somerville bent down, cutting the ropes round Doyle's legs. With another movement of the knife the bonds fastening his outstretched arms parted and Doyle fell on his side. As he sprawled on the damp concrete, Somerville walked back to the haversack.

'Would ya have cut me? Would ya?' Doyle shouted to him.

'Sonny, you killed my wife and kids. When they died, you killed me too.'

Somerville's words stuck in Doyle's head. He did not fully understand the man and was beginning to feel more confident about his future. 'They should never have been caught up in it . . . I watched every mornin' for a week. Ya always took the car out yerself. Never yer woman!'

Somerville heard a noise at the far end of the massive building and crossed swiftly to the small window at the side of the service entrance. There were three men at the side gates, one of whom appeared to be snipping the new lock with a pair of bolt cutters. They were either terrorists or security forces – either way, it made little difference to him now. He estimated it would take only a couple of minutes before they made their way through the complex, found the van and his position.

He turned to Doyle. 'Our time has run out,' he said as he crossed the floor and knelt beside the man.

'No!' squealed Doyle, but Somerville grabbed the terrorist's gaping mouth and slit his throat with the sharp edge of the blade. The carotid artery was severed and blood spurted profusely from the wound. Somerville stood up and Doyle tried to scream, but nothing emitted from the open mouth except more brightly coloured blood. His body convulsed on the floor as Somerville removed his last Mills grenade from the bag.

The three soldiers moved silently through the old factory complex, following the puddles of water left by the tyre-marks in the broken asphalt surface outside. Each man carried a Heckler and Koch machine gun. A fourth waited at the side gate with the Renault 20 Saloon, engine idling, while he transmitted information via the field radio set on the back seat.

They were good and it took them less time to find Doyle's body in the dull light than Somerville had anticipated. The first man kicked the side door open and the second somersaulted into the shadows beside the old transformer. He surveyed the area from behind the Heckler and Koch's sights. The second reacted to a numbered signal, and darted. He was the first to locate Doyle, lying face down in a pool of blood. He knelt beside the body and checked for a pulse. There was none. Looking round, he gave the second signal. 'Seven-three!'

The other man responded immediately. 'Seven' meant seven o'clock. He looked and saw the metal staircase running up the side of the office accommodation block. 'Three' meant stage three – fire on manoeuvre. He rushed towards the bottom of the staircase and fired several short automatic bursts aimed at the open door at the top of the steps. He was halfway up the stairs when the soldier by Doyle's body gave an incoherent yell; glancing down, he saw him dive away just as the grenade – so delicately placed under Doyle's chest – exploded, hurling both corpse and fleeing soldier into the air.

Suddenly Somerville appeared at the top of the staircase beside the open fire door. The surviving soldier's highly trained reflexes were not fast enough and as Somerville's MI carbine was emptied down the staircase he was thrown back and died immediately with two bullets through his skull. As he crashed to the floor, the third soldier arrived on the scene and began firing automatically in Somerville's direction, but their quarry had vanished . . . and two more members of Staff-Sergeant Ian Lawrence's original team lay dead.

It took Somerville only seconds to climb on to the flat felt roof and run towards the roof top of the adjacent workshop block. The roof was surrounded by a small parapet with concrete coping stones around the top brick line. Somerville judged the distance between the two flat roofs to be about ten feet and he ran hard, pacing himself to hit the parapet's coping with his right foot. He had almost reached the edge of the roof when he realised the distance was further than he had imagined but undaunted, he leaped into space and landed jarringly on the other side. He was just picking himself up when Ian Lawrence opened up with the Heckler and Koch from the other roof. Bullets smashed into the water tanks beside Somerville as he jumped for cover; he responded immediately with several bursts from the MI but Lawrence was experienced and held off his advance for several moments. It was enough time for Somerville to reach the edge and jump on to the lower roof beneath. The jump was eight feet, but he had made much worse in the Regiment. He landed in true Para style, making sure he favoured his left shoulder and rolling half over to cushion the impact. He had reached ground level by the time Lawrence followed him over the gap between the two buildings.

The driver of the Renault had heard the explosion and gunfire. Instinctively he was out of the vehicle, 9mm Browning pistol at the ready. He identified the figure crossing the forecourt as the probable target, but he hesitated and called out. He had neither the training nor the experience of the SAS men, having been dispatched from the Military Intelligence driving pool at the last minute. As Somerville emptied a fresh magazine into the Renault, the flying glass caught the young RCT driver in the face and eyes. He dived to the ground still clutching the pistol, but unable to use it as Somerville passed into the main road and out of sight.

Lawrence reached the Renault within seconds, but was too late; Somerville had disappeared into the back streets surrounding Connswater. The soldier reached the Newtownards Road, still brandishing the machine gun, before realising the futility of following him through the morning rush-hour traffic.

It was the nineteenth meeting of the Chief Officers' Group. Although they had ceased to gather as regularly as before, the Chief Constable had continued to insist on a daily meeting chaired by himself or a senior Assistant Chief Constable. The Chief Constable joined the group ten minutes after the scheduled start at 10 a.m. He was not alone, and Grange was surprised to see him accompanied by Cecil Rose.

Grange had his own daily deliberations with the head of MI5 and had grown to hate the man profoundly. Even his detestation of Somerville was overshadowed by the resentment he felt at having his every action approved or disapproved by Rose. Bitterly, he recalled the rebuke he had received from Rose the morning after Doyle had been arrested; he remembered the exact words of the conversation.

'What is going on, Chief Superintendent?' Rose had asked.

Frank Grange had feigned surprise.

'Seamus Doyle had his house searched by the local Army regiment in West Belfast. During the search they discovered a firearm in his bedroom. He now lies in Castlereagh Holding Centre, probably facing many years behind bars. Can you tell me how and why this operation was interrupted by such an action?' Cecil Rose remained as cool and calm as ever. It seemed to Grange that he was monitoring every response, looking for any sign of weakness; he was determined to give Rose no satisfaction.

'I'm not responsible for military intervention!'

'No? Every military search is approved by your local Special Branch office. Does it not seem appropriate to you that you should be fully aware of their actions, especially in this extremely sensitive field?'

'Of course I should. But if the stupid bastard hadn't had the bloody gun, he would never have been nicked!' Grange was on his feet again, trembling with anger. 'It was a simple search op – nothing more. Normally, it would never have affected our plans and you know it!'

Cecil Rose's reply had astonished Grange, who was finally expecting a showdown. 'That will be all, Chief Superintendent. You may go for now.'

Grange had been devastated to find he was being dismissed like some naughty child, and couldn't leave the room without saying something. 'You'd better believe that will be all! It's all the talking I'll ever have with you. In future, if you want to speak to me, you can forget it! Send one of your lapdogs with any questions in writing!' He had stalked out of the library without shutting the door . . .

Now the Chief Constable's words brought Frank Grange out of his trance.

'Can I have your fullest attention, please? For those of you who do not know him, may I introduce to you Mr Cecil Rose, from the NIO.' He stopped, ensuring the fullest attention of everyone there. 'It has been decided to bring this committee's action to an end . . . in short, we now believe Somerville to be outside our jurisdiction.'

Frank Grange was the first to interject. 'Sir, that is nonsense! Only a few hours ago Somerville broke into Castlereagh and escaped with a prisoner. He can't have got too far.'

'Chief Superintendent, perhaps I could finish what I have to say first!' The Chief Constable glared at Grange, and the deputy head of Special Branch knew exactly what it meant. 'Gentlemen, we have fresh information from the Security Services that Somerville is now out of the Province and possibly out of Ireland.

199

The hunt will be continued on a different level. On the point made by Mr Grange, the man involved in the breakout this morning is described as being much older than Somerville, and is believed to be a confederate of Doyle's. Now, I would like to take this opportunity to thank you for the sterling work you have all put into the search coordination. I must again remind every person here of the continued blanket of secrecy on this matter. All department files relating to this committee must be submitted to my office forthwith under the grading "Secret". Thank you all very much.' The Chief Constable left the room accompanied by Cecil Rose. Outside he turned to the MI5 officer and smiled. 'Well, how was I?'

'Let's say you may never win an Oscar, but the local rep. would be greatly enhanced by your presence.' Both men laughed as they strolled towards the Chief's offices.

Frank Grange was bemused, to say the least, as he turned to his assistant, Detective Chief Inspector Winston Black. 'Tie up the necessary details and call off the hounds. Contact Colonel Jones' assistant – that Captain, whatever his name is. Get him to meet me at some suitable venue away from here.' He left the room without waiting for a reply.

Castle Street, Belfast
Somerville sat in the café area of the bingo hall. The pool-rooms at the 'Golden Nugget' were on the first floor, along with rows and rows of gaming machines. He had a full view of the bingo area through the glass doors and partition subdividing the ground floor of the old grocery store, which had been acquired by Murray Developments Limited four years before. Somerville was well aware that Murray Developments stood for the Provisional IRA, like many other businesses and companies which had flourished since the mid-

seventies, when the paramilitaries had begun to make full use of the loopholes in company laws. The Inland Revenue could make no headway, especially in the field of tax exemption certificates used by sub-contractors in the building trade. It was nauseating for officials to be aware that the government's 33 per cent share was going directly into the hands of the organizations, and to be unable to put a stop to the matter. Somerville heartily concurred with their sentiments, but in trying to rectify the situation the organization had shoved him aside. However, he was never going to be pushed around again.

He caught sight of Desmond Murray, walking up to an employee beside the bingo caller's stand. Somerville had seen the type before, acting as doormen to various Belfast clubs, or as bouncers in the city's discotheques. He stood easily six feet three inches tall and weighed around seventeen stone. He looked like an out-of-work wrestler – no doubt a PIRA volunteer of the lower echelons. Both men cast the odd glance towards him during their conversation, before they disappeared into the rear of the building.

Somerville wasn't worried about losing them; there was only one entrance to the front. He sat for almost an hour over two cups of foul-tasting coffee, a gristly hamburger and chips. He watched and waited until at 12.30 p.m. the two men emerged again. Murray carried a black briefcase and was now sporting a grey trilby. Somerville followed them at a discreet distance, still carrying the old brown case; apart from having removed the cotton wads, he still looked like a middle-aged man. They walked along Castle Street and across the traffic lights in the direction of Divis Street. Somerville waited at the King Street traffic lights and watched as the pair entered a car park on the right-hand side of the road. He crossed, much to the annoyance of a black taxi driver who, ignoring the stop signal, had pushed on across the junction already blocking the traffic coming from Smithfield. Somerville ignored the driver's insults and carried on to the car park entrance where he saw the two men walk over to a red Cortina.

Neither man heard his approach until he was behind them. The heavyweight turned in time to meet a vicious left hook and staggered back, but as he attempted to focus on his assailant Barney sidestepped and kicked him right in the face. He fell to the gravel, but gamely tried to get to his feet, only to be kneed under the chin. This time he lay still. Murray was already cowering away in terror, but before he rounded the front of the car Barney caught him by the arm and he turned to see the black blade of a knife pointing at his ribs. He froze instantly. 'Take it!' He raised the black briefcase in his free hand. 'Take it! The money's inside.'

'I want you to drive slowly out of this place,' said Somerville. 'Don't make any stupid moves, understand?'

'Yes! All right!'

They left Murray's henchman lying beside a fully laden rubbish skip. 'They'll probably think he fell out of that,' said Somerville; Murray failed to smile.

Under instructions, the car sped towards the Malone Road. 'Where are ya takin' me?' asked Murray, but there was no reply except an order to change direction. At the Old Shaws Bridge Murray was told to take the road to Edenderry village.

Eventually they drew to a halt at a secluded picnic area. The place was completely deserted.

'Now get out,' Somerville instructed. Murray did so, leaving the car keys in the ignition as ordered.

'All right. You've been very wise, so far. Now walk down towards the river and keep to the path.'

'Why? For God's sake, ye have the last two days' takings and the car!'

'Move it!' said Barney, digging the knife into Murray's back. 'Move, or I'll stick you!'

The little man did what he was told.

'What are ya going to do?' he muttered as he walked. 'I'll not tell the peelers, if that's what yer worried about.' There was no reply, just a brutal shove in the back.

The riverside picnic area was shielded by high banking which was now lined with wooden planks holding in the soil. Above the banking, tall coniferous trees shaded the spot from the midday sun.

Murray stopped and turned. He did not like the coldness in Somerville's eyes. 'Look, ye have what ya want. What else is there?'

'You.'

'What d'ya mean, me?' Murray's face drained of blood.

'Tell me about your benefactors, as you call them . . . that is what you said to Doyle and Hagan, isn't it?'

'I . . . I don't know what ya mean. I don't know them names . . .' Murray could hear his heart thump into his brain as he backed towards the high wooden retaining wall. He had nowhere else to run.

Frank Grange met Captain Niall Scott for lunch in the basement grill-room of the Stormont Hotel. Grange could not muster any interest in the menu, but the SAS Troop Commander had just arrived and was enjoying his first gin and tonic of the day. 'Thanks. I needed that. Apologies for being late, but we had a bit of a flap on.'

'Nothing serious, I hope?'

'It's always serious in this place!' The Army officer swilled back the remainder of his drink. 'God! I think I could do with another of those.'

Grange was surprised at the man's state, since he knew him well as one of the most unflappable operators

Lisburn could field. Fresh drinks arrived and he passed over the menu.

'I'm not exactly hungry at the moment,' said Scott. 'Perhaps a sandwich shortly – if that's OK with you, Frank?'

'Sure. I'm not too hungry myself.'

The SAS man continued, 'Well, what's it been like down at Castlereagh? I suppose the purge has started?'

'Oh, aye! There'll be skulls to crush after that bloody fiasco.' Grange gulped his drink.

'I thought you'd be hot on the trail of our man by now. Frankly, I was surprised you asked me to lunch with so much happening.'

'You obviously haven't heard, Niall. According to the latest, Somerville's out of the Province and has been for some time. Although I felt the breakout this morning was exactly his style.'

'Out of what?' The SAS man had to look about him, making sure his raised voice had not attracted the attention of the other customers standing at the bar. 'Obviously you haven't heard yet!'

'Heard what?' asked Grange, setting his glass aside.

'It was him all right. He killed Doyle and two of my men in the process!'

'He did what?' It was Frank Grange's turn to curb his excitement and the young woman at the bar gave them a disapproving glance. Re-crossing her long legs, she adjusted her position on the stool and continued chatting to the older man in the dark business suit. 'So I was right! It *was* him! What happened? How did your men get on to him?'

'Easy. We had been watching Castlereagh for something like this to happen.'

'Who the hell told you to watch Castlereagh?'

'No one. That's the problem! After he took out one of our men at the forest, I let myself be convinced by one of our senior NCOs that we should try to nab

Somerville before anything else went wrong. We got lucky. Our men on watch thought something was not right with a delivery van leaving the station, so they followed it to a disused factory complex in East Belfast.'

'Go on!'

'Well, the signal was received by the very same NCO, who had a personal vendetta against Somerville after losing a team member in the forest. Without waiting for back-up, he rushed to the factory with the guts of a team and set about things. But he lost out again, and Somerville escaped.' The SAS officer emptied his second glass.

Frank Grange reflected for a moment. 'You said Doyle was killed. Is that right?'

'Yep! Throat cut and blown up for good measure. Somerville had stuffed a grenade under the body and it triggered when Doyle was moved.'

'So that's the end of our bait, eh?' Grange's gaze remained fixed.

'I suppose so.'

'Would Somerville have had much time alone with Doyle before your boys arrived?'

'About half an hour, outside.'

'A lot can happen in thirty minutes,' Grange said.

Detective Chief Inspector Black was summoned to Grange's office immediately on his return.

'Come in and close that door!' Grange could not conceal his agitation. 'We're being fed false information by the NIO and the Chief. Sit down and listen to this.'

For the next hour the two men exchanged views and ideas on the morning's events. Finally Grange brought the discussion to an end. 'Look, I want you to find out why the branch is being kept in the bloody dark on this thing. OK, it may be that my recent disagreements with Rose have done a great deal to dampen our relationship with MI5, but I think there may be more to it and I want to know. Use whoever the hell you need to, but find out – and find out quickly!'

By 7 p.m. that evening, Grange had secured a meeting at Stormont Castle with Cecil Rose. He had also asked the Chief Constable to join them and advised Rose's office to secure the presence of the Secretary of State. He expressed profound concern on a matter of state security.

Rose had deliberately failed to mention the request to the Secretary, but word had reached the Supremo's office from the Chief Constable, who was becoming more and more concerned by the obvious rift between Rose and Grange and was trying to avoid any further embarrassment for the RUC.

Rose was irritated but not surprised as Grange unravelled the details of the fouled-up SAS operation, mixed with his own inimitable innuendo. The professionalism of Her Majesty's Security Service was under question and Colonel Jones, who had also been asked to attend by Grange, could sense a grudge match in session.

The Secretary of State took his leave at the earliest opportunity, not wanting to hear any more stories of mistakes and alleged incompetence. He made his parting gesture with conviction: 'Look – I do not want a post mortem, we've had enough already. What I do want to know is precisely why our best resources are totally incapable of completing what appears to be a relatively straightforward task!' He looked at the Colonel. 'I wanted Somerville and you gave me, to quote the Chief Superintendent here, "another clandestine operation". A failed one at that!' He left the library followed by his personal secretary, but as he opened the door he looked back at Rose. 'It's all yours, Cecil. Just sort it out!' And then he was gone.

Rose continued his official response. 'The Security

Services are in charge of this one, Colonel, and I need not remind you of the existing offer from your superiors to effect your replacement immediately'.

The Colonel was annoyed by the remark, but hardly concerned that Grange had heard the words. It was an open secret between the two of them that the Colonel had received an official reprimand from Brigadier Baxter.

Rose turned his attention to the Chief Constable and Frank Grange, who were sitting on the leather sofa. 'Chief Constable, I cannot even begin to apologise for the ineptitude of our SAS colleagues. However, the Colonel was not aware of this morning's operation; had he been, I feel sure that the matter would have been handled properly. As for the Chief Superintendent's comments, I have to concur that there has been a failure of communication. On that point, I must stress that I personally accept a degree of fault on my side, and I earnestly hope that we can work together in future.'

Frank Grange waved his hand in the air; he had made his point. 'Forget it! I didn't come here to get at you or anyone else. I want this job done as much as you do. There's no need to apologise – I'm known to be a stubborn bastard meself, you know!' There was general laughter, and very quickly the cold atmosphere was dissipated by the continued discussion.

'As I said, Frank, I'm sorry we had to dupe you into believing Somerville had gone south, but it was necessary to reduce this case's profile. I do hope you understand?' Grange nodded as Cecil Rose began to pour out the coffee. 'Let's examine what we now have here. Where might he have gone?'

Grange was keen to be in on the hunt again. 'A red Cortina was stolen and the owner believed abducted too. It happened early this afternoon in Castle Street.'

'Yes, I got a report on it,' replied Rose.

'The owner is Desmond Patrick Murray, from Lenadoon Avenue, Belfast – last seen driving out of a DOE car park at Castle Street. Some shoppers returning to their cars found another man by the name of Sean Devlin, traced PIRA, lying unconscious in the car park. Both these men had left the "Golden Nugget" pool-rooms and bingo hall a short time before. Now it may be robbery or it may be coincidence, but the car-park attendant says there was a man fitting Somerville's disguise – according to the description given by the police interviewed at Castlereagh – sitting in the front passenger seat. Murray had a briefcase with him containing about £4000 to £5000 in used bank-notes, so it may be just a robbery we're dealing with.'

'Could Murray have any connection with Somerville?' Rose paced around the room.

'Well, he's traced as being on the periphery of the Republican movement, but not on the military side. His exact role is very hazy. Way back in the fifties he was involved in the old IRA, and at one stage was a candidate for internment. However, he was one of the people who made allegations against Somerville.'

'I assume that his car has been circulated to all our people?' Rose enquired.

'That was done within five minutes of it coming to our notice.'

'Good. It may be a little far-fetched, but as our only real possibility I think we should bet on it.'

The meeting terminated at 7.30 p.m. and the Chief Constable excused himself and hurried to his car. He was already late for another appointment.

The bookshop and video library at the 'Busy Bee' shops was empty by nine o'clock, when Paddy Hagan put up the shutter on the front door and secured it with four padlocks. He lit a cigarette and tucked a brown-paper parcel under his arm as he walked across the car-park area to his orange Allegro Estate. He then drove off along the Andersonstown Road, turning right past the traffic lights up Shaws Road and stopping beside a black taxi halted on the opposite side. After a brief discussion through the open window he drove on, turning left into Lenadoon Estate where he pulled up outside Desmond Murray's house and carried the small parcel to the front door. He spoke for a short time to the woman who answered his rings before leaving the parcel and returning to the Allegro.

After turning the car round, he moved off past a light blue Escort van and took a left turn towards the Glen Road junction. The Escort was quick to follow, maintaining a discreet distance behind as Hagan drove straight to the Social Club in Ballymurphy Estate. The forecourt was surrounded by oil-drums filled with concrete and interjoined by a single line of hollow metal poles. This was a popular way to evade would-be car bombers in Northern Ireland. Somerville watched Hagan enter the club through the wire cage built around the front entrance, which was controlled automatically from inside. He could not see any cameras, and decided that if a check was made it would be done from a small side window. The door was lined on the outside with what appeared to be mild sheet steel; it was always left ajar, and the only real security at the entrance was the single electronically controlled lock on the wire-mesh gate. The wire cage surrounded the entrance to a height of seven feet, the top sealed in by corrugated iron panels angled up towards the gutter line.

The building itself was a temporary construction: a number of sectional prefabricated units slotted together at intervals. Somerville examined the windows; again they were covered by wire grilles and not readily accessible. The only way in would be the most direct. He gave it another twenty minutes before deciding to approach the building. Taking the MI carbine from behind the front passenger seat he cocked the mechanism, wrapping the folded weapon and double-taped magazines inside an old anorak he had found on the front seat when stealing the van from a Finaghy builder's yard that same evening. Then he took his chance. Seeing a Ford Transit van drive into the car park, he followed, tagging in behind two men and a woman as they approached the entrance. The buzzer sounded before the woman pressed the button on the wire gate and the trio made their way inside. Somerville had the gate held open for him by the last of the three, a young man in his early twenties.

'Thanks, mate,' said Barney as he pushed the gate open further against the strong retaining spring. The young man never answered and pushed his way inside.

As Somerville entered the vestibule, his path was abruptly halted by two youths dressed in combat jackets and jeans, the uniform of the area. Both had shaved heads.

'What d'ya want, mister?' questioned the first youth. He was obviously the elder of the pair, and with their similar appearance Barney imagined them to be brothers.

'Paddy Hagan sent for me . . . where is he?'

'What's yer name, then?' responded the other youth.

'None of yer business, son!' The youth seemed to melt under Somerville's glare and stood aside, but his brother had not backed down yet.

'What are ya carryin'?' He moved forward as if to touch the rolled-up anorak.

'Touch that an' yer dead! Wee lad!' said Somerville.

The confrontation was interrupted by the noise of the bell. Another customer was waiting inside.

'All right, mister. Keep yer fuckin' hair on!' responded the first youth. Both brothers laughed at the remark as they eyed Somerville's bald scalp.

210

He pushed past them. The one light in the bar came from behind the counter. The room – including the small stage at the far end – was empty. The only people standing at the bar were the three from the transit van. Just as he ordered a half-pint of Guinness from the elderly barman, another man came in and Somerville watched him carefully in the smoked-glass mirror behind the row of optics on the bar wall. The man stood talking for a few moments to the two youths as they pointed out Somerville. He still held the wrapped gun at his side and pretended not to notice the sidelong glance from Joe McNulty as he strode across the dance floor towards a door to one side of the stage. Somerville turned to his Guinness which had just been served up.

'Haven't seen ya before, mister. Do ya come from round here, then?' the barman asked. He had noted the interest displayed by McNulty.

'Naw, I don't.'

'Are ya meetin' somebody, then?'

'Aye, I am. He said for me ta meet him here at the bar.' Somerville's attention was drawn once more to the door beside the stage. Two men came out, but he recognised neither. Both belonged to the same family as the ape he had silenced in the car park that morning and they lounged beside the door with their eyes fixed on him.

'Can I ask ya who yer ta meet?' prompted the barman as he wiped a pint glass for the umpteenth time.

'Paddy Hagan.'

'Paddy . . .' replied the barman. 'Ye'll have ta wait a wee while longer.' He turned away and moved down to the end of the long bar where he was immediately approached by one of the two heavies. After a short discussion the man made a telephone call from the wall-mounted coin-box at the end of the bar. The front door slammed shut and Somerville whipped round to see that the two youths had been joined by another ape, who was busy bolting the door. Then he swaggered over to Barney.

Mousey Reilly carried a hurling stick in one hand. The other man had since finished his telephone conversation and Somerville observed his thumbs-up sign to the man with the stick. He reckoned it would be a matter of minutes before reinforcements arrived. The barman had already had a few words with the other customers and they moved away from the bar towards the tables and chairs on the opposite side of the large room.

'Visitors aren't welcome here unless invited, see?' said Mousey. 'Ya gave the boys at the door a bit of lip there. Just who the fuck are ya?' He stopped five feet away.

'What's it to you?' replied Somerville, no longer feigning a Belfast accent.

'Smart cunt, are we? Eh!' Mousey was in his element and swung at Somerville's head with the hurling stick, but he was not fast enough to connect; his target ducked and side-kicked him in the chest with the left foot. Reilly fell back winded, crashing into a table and chairs. Somerville chucked the anorak aside and walked towards the two men at the end of the bar. As he came level with the barman, he saw the man's right arm come up brandishing a baseball bat. Somerville trained the MI carbine at him and the barman dropped the bat and stood back. He no longer wanted any part of this fight.

The two men stood their ground and Somerville was within twenty feet when the one on the right pulled a revolver from inside an old Army surplus jacket. Somerville fired the MI from the hip, using his left hand. The short burst ripped into the man's stomach and he doubled over as he was tossed backwards into the wall. The second man dived to one side, but Somerville showed him no mercy. Another burst and he lay still on the stage floor, wounded in the side.

The gunfire outside the room immediately alerted Hagan and his associates. However, they had no time to escape through the fire exit for the bar door was kicked open and Somerville stood there staring blankly at the four men. Two attempted to run towards the exit after seeing the rifle, but both were cut down from behind well before they reached the door.

The first magazine was empty and was quickly replaced by the second, taped underneath. Somerville continued his progress into the snooker room and around the table where his sentence of death had been unanimously carried. Paddy Hagan and Joe McNulty looked in horror at their two comrades lying splattered all over the floor.

'Yer Somerville! Aren't ya!' shouted McNulty as he partly shielded himself behind Paddy. Both were visibly trembling.

Somerville stared at the pair for a couple of seconds. He re-cocked the MI. 'And you're dead!' The clatter of the MI filled the air as the magazine was emptied into the men and their bullet-riddled bodies were thrown back, blood splashing on to the ceiling and wall. After the smoke had settled, Somerville walked round the snooker table to examine his work. Four single shots rang out, the *coup-de-grace*.

The group in the bar remained in their places, all except the barman who had picked up the dead IRA man's .38 Special Colt Python. Unchallenged, Somerville walked towards the front door. He noticed the barman now standing well away from the body and eyed him carefully; there was something besides fear in the man's eyes.

He was half-way across the room when a movement from the two youths at the door alerted him to something behind. He ducked and twisted round, swinging the MI as he moved. The barman fired once but the shot missed, burying itself in the wall beside the youths; the MI cracked twice and both bullets found their target, one hitting the barman in the left thigh and the second in his stomach. Somerville continued on to the door past Mousey Reilly, still unconscious from the impact of the table edge on his skull. The animal instincts of the remaining customers warned them not to become involved.

The two youths had left their post at the door and Somerville ordered the eldest one back again.

'Open up!' he ordered and the youth pulled frantically at the bolts and lock until the door swung open once more. Somerville could smell the skinhead's fear as he slipped out into the night. He moved more quickly now; it was time to find another hiding place and decide on his next move. He had completed far more than he ever intended, but could feel no remorse for any of the dead or injured. They were simply casualties of a lost cause – and most of them a cancer which had fed on hate and fear for too long. Somerville hoped Janet and the children would rest more easily now. He found himself thinking how he would never touch her again . . . play with the children . . . even the family dog.

He got in the van like an automaton, switched on the ignition, put the vehicle into gear and swung the van into the road past a gathering crowd, heading towards the sanctuary of the urbanised Black Mountains.

He stopped at a lay-by on the barren countryside road. Even from this distance, the echo of sirens rose above the toy-town shapes of Belfast's street lights. As Barney stared blindly at the scene an overwhelming tiredness consumed him. His muscles felt slack, but not relaxed, the adrenalin slowly ebbing away. It was done – but there was no satisfaction. The hate that had driven him on had also been a protection against the fears, the hurt, the overwhelming loneliness and the memories. But now they returned with a vengeance, saturating his mind with love, wife, home, the birth of babies, the first days at school, the pride in passed exams and triumph at school sports days, the smiles, the tears, the plans they had – dreams of peace on some desert island, the children successful, married, grandchildren . . . Wiped out by death, theirs and his in one horrifying bloody split-second in time. Gone. A lifetime finished. For the first time since those awful moments after their murder he cried, aloud and alone.

The Chief Constable was interrupted abruptly that night, just after enjoying a late dinner with his wife and a few guests. He left the dining room and took the telephone call in his study.

'Yes?' he said irritably.

'Sir, this is Grange. We've just received reports of a multiple killing at Ballymurphy. Looks like our man again!'

'He didn't waste much time, did he?' The Chief Constable allowed no opportunity for reply. 'Any trace on him?'

'Our friends, under Mr Jones, are now in the area. Nothing yet, I'm afraid.'

'Who exactly did he get?'

'Four of the very top runners in Belfast, and two other well-traced members. It happened at a club. Two more are in hospital. The barman's in theatre, pretty badly shot up, and there's another well-known runner has got concussion.'

'My God!' whispered the Chief Constable.

'Sir, you don't understand. He's taken out the complete Belfast Brigade staff structure in one fell swoop!' Frank Grange could not hold back the delight in his voice, for these were men he had toiled to put away for years.

'Don't give him credit, Grange! The repercussions could be damaging in the extreme! I want an update within the hour. You may contact me here. Also send my staff officer to my house immediately. Thank you, Frank.'

The line went dead and Frank Grange sat back basking in the light from the anglepoise lamp. He smiled again. Everything suddenly seemed very clear.

Geoffrey Williams had demanded a meeting of the entire group that night. It was dangerous, but Sir Ralph had reluctantly agreed in the hope that the man's obvious panic could be dampened. When Roland Briggs arrived at the club, Geoffrey was already there with Mark Taylor who had remained close to his side the entire day.

'Geoffrey, what on earth's the matter? Why get us here at such short notice?' Briggs spoke softly.

'That little worm Murray's disappeared, that's what's the matter!'

'And you think it's connected with this rogue elephant we have on the loose?'

'Of course I bloody do! Wouldn't you?' Williams began to raise his voice. 'He's got him, I'm bloody telling you! He's got him, and God knows what he's told him about us!'

'Keep calm! Look, I assume you've asked Ralph to join us?' Briggs knew the answer already.

'Yes, yes. But as usual, he appeared quite unconcerned. It may be all right for him, but not for me! I'm the bastard who's going to fall, not him, or you!'

'No one's going to fall, old chum. That's why we're here.' Briggs patted him on the knee.

'That's right,' said Taylor. 'If we close ranks on this matter, we've nothing to fear. When you think about it, Murray knows as much about us as the ordinary man in the street.'

'He knows *me!*' exclaimed Williams.

'And so does half the adult population of Ulster; you're a well-known figure. You're hardly to blame if some little moron like Murray spills some story about you – a story he can't prove.' Mark Taylor smiled.

'Can't he? I'm not so sure.' Williams needed more than platitudes to convince him.

The conversation was interrupted by the arrival of Sir Ralph Hawthorne. He was dressed in black tie and dinner jacket, and also wearing one of his most unmistakable frowns. Quickly dismissing the head waiter, he sat in the fourth leather-bound chair.

'Well, Geoffrey,' he said, 'I don't know what you've done, but it would appear that you could be in a very exposed position if this thing continues to explode.'

'Explode! I'll tell you exactly, shall I? These thick paramilitaries decide to develop their sphere of operations and ignore our insurance policies, then overnight wreck our prospects of continuing in this game!'

'For God's sake,' said Briggs. 'Make sense, man! The paramilitaries have nothing to do with it; they want this thing tidied up as much as we do.'

'It's all right for all of you, but I'm the link man. I'm the only real name that can be directly linked with these people. I'm telling you – the game's over.'

'Hardly, Geoffrey,' said Briggs. 'We've all become very rich playing the game, as you put it. I'm damned if one vigilante policeman is going to mess things up for us.'

'Oh, gentlemen, gentlemen!' Sir Ralph had heard enough. 'Let us examine the salient facts. Fact Number One: A policeman suspects some large-scale financial manipulation from the use of illegal gaming establishments in the Province, but this is purely a paramilitary affair. Fact Number Two: He, the policeman, is investigated thoroughly and suspended from duty. Meanwhile the terrorists unwittingly kill his family and the poor man goes berserk, killing everyone in sight. Some could call it "Summary Justice". Fact Number Three: He's now a marked man, with an extremely limited lifespan. In the time remaining to him he can do absolutely nothing of consequence to threaten anyone in this room.' He paused, rubbing his chin. 'The only pointer to Geoffrey here is the suspension aspect. He must know by now that there is an outside influence in the entire matter. The suspension and planting of evidence on this Somerville individual was a mistake – a mistake made in conjunction with the stupid, bungling murder attempt by the Provisional IRA. We now know from the news bulletins that Geoffrey's contact, Murray, is missing. I presume, after the news flash about the multiple murders at West Belfast, that Somerville had extracted some information from the unfortunate Mr Murray.' He looked directly at Williams. 'But think, Geoffrey, how much could he honestly tell him? Or for that matter, dishonestly?'

'Murray was our only contact, he dealt solely with me. I knew he told Hagan and someone in Dublin. Dublin had to approve the arrangement all those years ago, and Hagan was responsible for the security,' replied Williams. 'Then there was the meeting we all had in 1980 in Dublin. I would assume Murray had knowledge of it, but of course he wasn't present.'

'Very good, Geoffrey. As you say, Murray could only tell so much, namely your identity. Even then, there was precious little else he could have known since our dealings are at another level altogether. All that Murray could say, apart from revealing your name, was that money was transferred via a London city broker, the same broker that your main company uses. And that, my dear boy, is it.' Sir Ralph smiled the condescending smile that so irritated Williams, yet the man demanded respect. He continued, taking advantage of Geoffrey's slightly more relaxed state. 'The only two avenues that Somerville may have are quite clear. You, dear Geoffrey, are the first. And our friendly little alcoholic bank manager, Mr Geddis, is the second. I would place bets on Somerville opting for Geddis rather than you.' He took a gulp of brandy, emptying his large glass. 'You, Geoffrey, are in dire need of a holiday. Why not take that gorgeous wife of yours and have a flutter for, say, three or four weeks? By then this thing will have blown over.'

Geoffrey Williams considered the suggestion. 'I suppose it wouldn't do any harm,' he said.

'Of course it wouldn't. Pick somewhere hot and relaxing. Perhaps you might consider my villa in Tenerife?' Sir Ralph smiled again. 'I wouldn't waste any time. Fly out tomorrow. Tell that pretty lady you want a second honeymoon!'

Shortly afterwards Sir Ralph Hawthorne excused himself and left the lounge for the Committee members' private rooms. Once alone, he picked up the ebony and silver receiver of the antique telephone and dialled a Dublin number direct. The receiver was lifted at the other end, but no one answered.

'Good evening. This is Father Mulally; may I speak to David please?' Sir Ralph spoke precisely.

'Right ya are, Father. He's been expectin' yer call. I'll get him fer ya now,' replied a youthful-sounding male voice.

Sir Ralph rejoined the group after another couple of minutes. They were ready now to go their separate ways.

'What about this bank manager?' Williams asked Sir Ralph as they put on their coats.

'Leave that to your elders, my boy. Just enjoy a well-earned rest. By the way, if you do want the villa, ring my personal secretary first thing in the morning; she has all the details. It's important to go tomorrow.'

'Thank you, Ralph. It's very considerate of you. I'll take it.'

Ralph Hawthorne patted him on the shoulder. 'You'll love it there. Just remember to avoid the local plonk!'

They walked into the cool night air and Ralph was ushered into his Rolls-Royce by the liveried chauffeur. He sat back and pressed the central panel; the rear window began to unwind and Mark Taylor looked in, but did not speak. 'Well, Mark, it looks to me as if you were right. Poor Geoffrey can't take the pace. I think you and Roland should continue to keep an eye on him. Make sure he takes that flight. I want to know where he goes to and all that . . . What I failed to say in there is that Hagan is one of those dead tonight.' Mark Taylor did not seem unduly surprised and Sir Ralph continued, 'Of course Hagan's name will not be released until tomorrow morning at the earliest, so young Williams will not have too long to panic. Oh yes! The other point I would stress is this snivelling assistant bank manager, Geddis. Contact our other associates; see if they can get one job right – that is, if they have enough men left! An attempted robbery or abduction gone wrong would do very nicely. As long as they don't botch that too!' He looked at the younger man knowingly. 'It must be done early tomorrow. Set it up and ring me on my private line at Eastleigh House, not before 1.30 a.m. and not later than 3 a.m.' Taylor nodded and Sir Ralph laughed dryly. 'When the going gets rough, they say, the rough get going! Remember that, dear boy.' He patted Taylor on the arm, and tapped the glass panel between the rear compartment and the driver. As the car purred smoothly away, he closed the window again and lit a Havana cigar, thinking idly of the ghastly dinner party his wife had agreed to organise the following month in reciprocation for the Chief Constable's invitation that evening. He looked at the clock on the lower dividing panel; he would be just in time for coffee and liqueurs and a tolerable amount of boring after-dinner chat.

Taylor and Briggs sat in the Lotus, discussing the evening's revelations.

'He wants me to arrange for Geddis to be sorted out.' Mark Taylor was clearly not overjoyed with his mission.

'I thought as much. He doesn't seem too happy with our Geoffrey, does he?'

'No. He wants us to continue keeping an eye on him – see him off and all that.'

'Quite right. There's no doubt that if Geoffrey was pushed he'd crack wide open at the seams.' Briggs slapped the steering wheel.

'And he thinks he's the only bugger to have contact with these scum! If he only bloody knew! To listen to Geoffrey – '

'Oh, stop acting the bitch, Mark!' said Briggs. 'If it hadn't been for Geoffrey, neither of us would be sitting here today. So just shut up! He's the one who's taken the risks in contacting Murray, on a very regular basis.'

'OK! OK! Take it easy, will you! I'll see you later.' Taylor climbed out of the low sports car. Before shutting the door, he laughed. 'Don't wait up.'

Roland Briggs continued to sit there behind the wheel. He was worried. He would make sure Geoffrey caught his flight and much more besides.

Meanwhile Williams raced his Mercedes convertible the twelve miles to his residence at Helen's Bay, which was set in three acres of the most prestigious property in North Down. Overlooking Belfast Lough and thick woodland, the Tudor-style house had an indoor swimming pool and squash court and was immaculately placed amongst trees, with a panoramic view of the County Antrim coastline towards Larne.

Geoffrey's first action when he got in was to check his Beretta 9mm-pistol, which he always kept in a locked drawer of the large bookcase in his private study. Then he poured himself another gin and tonic from the Japanese cabinet he had purchased on one of his round-the-world trips. The room had been designed around the antique cabinet, and so it should have been, considering the thing had cost him £48,000 excluding transportation. To the left he had designed himself a built-in drinks dispenser and refrigerator, incorporating computerised hi-fi control panel programmed for his every whim. The speakers were concealed in the ornate ceiling, behind meticulously detailed grilles and wood designs also in Eastern style. One complete wall was made of toughened glass, forty feet long and ten feet high. When he flicked at the controls, the heavy curtaining slid aside to reveal the brightly-lit indoor pool. The study was situated well below the surface of the water so as to look out on it, and through the bouncing shades and reflections in its pale blue depths he could make out the beautiful naked form of his wife, Julia. She had noticed the movement behind the glass and dived down to greet him. He was aroused by her body as she kept moving to stay under water. She motioned him to join her and he smiled back, saluting with the glass. Julia liked to flaunt herself and it would have been just the same if he had returned home with some business associate; she had no scruples, especially when it came to showing off her body. In a way it excited him too, and she knew it . . . she knew it only too well.

Julia waved and pushed off from the panel up towards the surface. He brought her a glass of chilled Chablis to the poolside, where he found her drying her hair with a large bath-towel. He handed her the towelling robe which had been draped over the lounger. 'You know, my dear, you really shouldn't keep swimming in the altogether; I might have brought home a guest.'

'I didn't know you were coming home at this time, darling. Anyway, I might have made somebody's night if you had!' She laughed aloud and kissed him on the cheek.

'Fancy some time away from this place?' he asked in as offhand a manner as he could manage.

'Some what?' She looked at him impishly. 'Just what are you suggesting?'

'Oh, for goodness' sake, Julia! Be serious for one moment, will you?'

She recoiled, almost as though she had been slapped in the face. 'What is it, darling? What's wrong?'

'Nothing's wrong. I . . . I just felt we should get away to the sun for a few weeks.' Geoffrey desperately tried to hide his all-consuming fear.

'Get away? Now? Geoffrey, there's something wrong. What is it?' She had started drying her hair, almost absentmindedly.

'There is absolutely nothing wrong!' His temper flared up. 'I have a few quiet weeks ahead and Roland has agreed to stand in for me, that's all. I thought we might go to Tenerife, Ralph's old place.'

'You're becoming very considerate all of a sudden, aren't you?'

'Look, we haven't had a break on our own since before last Christmas. You can't blame me for wanting to have you all to myself, can you?'

She smiled radiantly and put her arms around his neck. The bath-robe fell open and he stared down at her full breasts.

'Shall we go then?' he whispered into her ear.

'How could I refuse . . . but there's just one thing.'

He looked at her anxiously. 'What might that be?'

'If we go to Tenerife, Spanish law says I have to keep my bikini bottom on!'

The telephone call to Anthony Campbell, the manager of the Red Hand public house on the Ormeau Road, was quite unremarkable.

'Hello. Is that you, Mr Campbell?'

'Who's calling?'

'Taylor.'

'I've been expecting yer call for some time.'

'I must talk with you urgently regarding an important sale.'

'OK, mister. Come round about 11.30. Take the side entrance. I'll be clearing up; the door'll be open.'

The line went dead and Campbell replaced the receiver, returning to the shouts from his thirsty customers.

The Rolls-Royce pulled up on the gravel drive outside the Chief Constable's Victorian country house. The police guard at the front gate had immediately recognised Sir Ralph. 'I'm afraid I've missed the pudding,' he joked as the guard waved him through.

He had timed his return perfectly. The men had gone into the main lounge and he joined them for a brandy, giving coffee a miss.

'Well, Ralph, get the job done, eh?' The Chief Constable emerged from the main group gathered round the fireplace.

'Yes, thank you. David, I must apologise again for my rudeness, but those blasted Americans will wait for no one. Not even me!' He laughed.

'Ralph, let me introduce you to Cecil Rose. Cecil, this is Sir Ralph Hawthorne, one of our leading lights in industry, banking, law, finance and God knows what else!'

Ralph shook the newcomer's hand lightly. He did

not like strangers in this world. 'In business yourself, Mr Rose?'

'No, I'm with the Political Affairs Division of the Northern Ireland Office.' Rose smiled blandly.

'I know most of the people at the Castle. I don't think we've met before, have we?'

'I don't think so. I'm usually office-bound, and only met our good host during one of the Secretary of State's dinner parties.' Rose rolled the brandy around his glass before raising it to his lips.

'I haven't seen the Secretary for some weeks now. How is he?'

'Looking forward to the summer recess, I think.' Rose was watching the man's reaction with interest.

'Tell him I asked after him, won't you?'

'Of course.'

'Good.' Sir Ralph turned to another of the guests standing by the bay window. 'William! We must have a word.' Sir Ralph nodded to Rose and walked over to the beaming businessman. 'I hear you're interested in buying a certain city centre department store. Is it true?' The other man's smile turned to a sudden flush at his words. As the evening wore on, Cecil Rose continued to watch Sir Ralph operate. He had a remarkable gift for knocking people off balance.

It was 11.30 p.m. precisely when Mark Taylor parked his Toyota Celica unobtrusively at the side entrance to the Red Hand bar, in the lower Ormeau Road district of Belfast. He locked the car in the darkened street, and entered as directed through the open door normally reserved for late-night drinkers who needed to evade the notice of the local constabulary. But after-hours drinking had been curtailed for once, and Tony Campbell was not the most popular man on the Ormeau Road that night.

As Taylor closed the door behind him, he failed to

notice the grey Citroen Estate which pulled up on the opposite side of the street.

He entered the main bar and found Campbell supervising the washing-up and cleaning. He left the two girls drying glasses and beckoned for Taylor to follow him into the smaller snug bar. Once they were alone, Taylor rounded on him. 'I thought you'd be alone!'

'Oh, they're all right. C'mon, what are ya having, then?' Campbell reached out two glasses from under the small bar and turned to the row of optics on the wall.

'A large Scotch, please,' replied Taylor as he perched on a high bar stool on the other side of the counter.

Campbell handed over the whisky. 'Neat, if I remember right?'

'You remember correctly, thank you.'

Campbell took his first drink of the night, a vodka with a dash of orange which he sipped slowly. 'I haven't seen ya for some time, Mr Taylor.' He stressed the 'mister' part.

Mark Taylor savoured his whisky. 'No. I've been quite busy lately, and our other avenues of contact were sufficient until now.'

'Of course. An awful deed there in West Belfast . . . and I believe Desi Murray's also disappeared. Terrible thing. Terrible thing, that.'

Taylor knew perfectly well that there was no love lost between Murray and Campbell. 'You've heard that young Doyle from Andersonstown is also dead?' he asked.

'Aye . . . news travels fast, even if it isn't on Downtown Radio. All they said was that he'd been busted out of Castlereagh. Just what the hell's it all coming to? First Doyle is missing and then the radio tell ya a pack of stinkin' lies. Eh?'

'Your organisation . . . our association . . . are threatened by just one man.' Taylor tried to hide his dislike of this uppity working-class Fenian.

'Naw, Mr Taylor, yer dead wrong. We'll never be threatened, we can always re-build. But once yer down yerself, that's fuckin' it.' Campbell smirked.

'Without us your organisation has only a very limited access to supplies – in fact, none of the right quality. Just remember that!'

'You've somethin' ya want, so come to the point, will ya?' Campbell thumped his empty glass on the counter.

'There's a policeman, an inspector called Somerville, who's on a witch-hunt after your people killed his family . . .'

Campbell interrupted him. 'Aye, aye. Everybody knows that. If ya want him, ye'll have to join the queue . . . that is, if he ever features again – which I doubt!'

'He isn't the immediate target. It's a man called Geddis, a bank manager. This is his address. He must be silenced before Somerville gets to him.' Taylor handed over the folded white sheet and Campbell examined it:

29 EDENCOURT GARDENS,
SAINTFIELD ROAD,
BELFAST.

'Why not stake the place out and wait for Somerville to show?' asked Campbell.

'Too long and too risky. Wherever he goes the police will not be far behind.'

'OK, I'll see to it,' said Campbell.

'Tonight?'

'Ya must be fuckin' jokin'!'

'It *has* to be tonight!'

'This requires more plannin' than just sendin' the

boys to a house, ya know!' Campbell stood back from the counter.

'It's urgent and it's very important,' said Taylor. 'I'm sure that my confederates will reward your organisation substantially for swift and effective action.' He smiled. 'All you have to do is ask your price.'

'If it's ta be – and I'm not saying it is, mind – it'll not be until late mornin'. But I'll see.' Campbell was trying to determine just how important Geddis really was.

'Thank you.' Taylor rose to leave.

'Yer quite right. It'll cost ya a bomb! I'll be in touch – ye'll be at the usual number?'

'Yes, ring me as soon as you can. You'll find us very generous, Mr Campbell.'

Mark Taylor was too engrossed in his thoughts and the Celica's stereo tape system to notice the Citroen following him back to his Malone Road apartment.

The telephone rang at Sir Ralph Hawthorne's luxurious mansion at Hillsborough. As he picked up the receiver in the library, he checked his watch. It was 3.25 a.m.

'Yes?'

'It's Mark.'

'You're late!' said Sir Ralph.

'I'm sorry, but I only just found out. It's set up for the morning; they couldn't do it any earlier.' The tension in Mark Taylor's voice was clear.

'See me for lunch at one, will you, dear boy?' Sir Ralph's tone softened.

'Yes, of course! See you then. Oh! Before I forget, Roland is seeing Geoffrey off.'

'Thank you. Good night.'

Mark breathed a sigh of relief as he put down the phone and returned to the drinks cabinet. He had never really appreciated the tightrope he had walked until now, and his shoulders felt strangely heavy.

Cecil Rose joined Major Lewis McCabe in the conference room at Stormont Castle. This room was now off limits to all personnel except MI5, and a permanent guard from the Military Police was positioned in the entrance corridor.

'Well, Lewis, it had better be good at this unearthly hour!' Cecil Rose stood in the centre of the large room, dressed in pyjamas and silk dressing-gown. He had been summoned hurriedly from his temporary sleeping quarters at the Castle by an armed MP only five minutes earlier.

'I believe it may well be worthwhile, sir.' Lewis McCabe handed Rose a hot cup of coffee and beckoned him to a nearby armchair. Rose noted that he seemed tired, but pushed on by some nervous energy.

'At 11.30 p.m. the subject, Taylor, went to the Red Hand pub. It's on the Ormeau Road. There he appears to have spoken to one Anthony Campbell; he's the manager and also heavily traced as a runner in the Provisionals, very much an organiser.' He passed Rose a sheet of paper.

Rose examined the transcript of the telephone call between Taylor and Campbell. 'Go on,' he said.

'Beforehand, Taylor had been at the Union Club. After the meeting he returned to his flat on the Malone Road and at 3.21 a.m. he had a phone-call from Campbell.' He handed over another sheet of paper. 'This is the transcript of a further call made by Taylor at 3.25 a.m. We're working on the voice identification of the recipient.'

Rose sipped some coffee and studied the transcripts for a full minute. He did not need any confirmation by voice identification. Then he spoke slowly. 'A job . . . they're going to hit someone. But who?'

'How do you deduce that, sir?'

Cecil Rose looked up. 'Don't clutter your mind with facts like our Special Branch colleagues, Lewis. We have to think ahead. It's no use relying on Intelligence source reports.'

'I still don't understand.' McCabe was out of his depth.

'The "gang of four" is clearly panicking and they're going for self-preservation rather than making a run for it.' Rose stood up and pulled out a mobile display board from behind the temporary screen placed across part of the room. With a black marker he began to write.

'Number one: We've known for some time that the "gang of four" were deeply involved with terrorists in Ulster. Terrorists from both sides, I might add; they simply buy and sell to the highest bidder.' He scribbled the four names on the board. 'Number two: They must have contacts with both terrorists and security forces alike, and I'll tell you about that in a minute. Now, I ask myself one more question, Lewis. Somerville was nearly caught by the unofficial actions of the SAS and Special Branch – namely Colonel Jones and Chief Superintendent Grange. Why did they do it?'

'Well,' McCabe thought aloud, 'the Colonel has a personal vendetta after the killing of his men. As for Grange, he's a complicated man; it's hard to say.'

'Hard to say? Lewis, tell me who organized Somerville's suspension?'

'Well . . . Murray, wherever the hell he is, and I suppose Williams. And he would have discussed it with the other three.'

'Do you not think they needed inside help? After all, how did they know Somerville wanted to renew investigations? Investigations into the money rackets he had exposed in Belfast? And why was he promoted so quickly away from the city?' He turned from the display board and looked hard at McCabe. 'What do you think?'

'I suppose you're right. They had to have influence of some kind.'

'Lewis, we need answers quickly, very quickly, and as far as I can see the main key to this whole mess lies in the RUC.'

'So you believe somebody high up may be implicated, sir?'

'We've known that for a while. That's why MI5 kept away from the "gang of four" – or "three" as it was a few years ago – in the hope that this person would reveal himself. But now it appears there may be more than one individual.'

They both stood back and studied the display board.

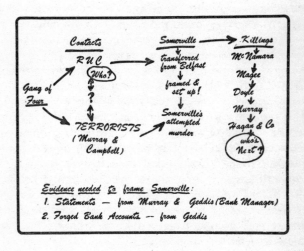

'There is something else we should consider, Lewis,' said Rose. 'Grange either lied to me or he's been suckered. When the Army went to search Doyle's house, they were accompanied by a policeman who already had authority to arrest Doyle under Section 12. Now why? Why get Doyle out of the way and ruin our surveillance operation? You know, Lewis, the more I think of Grange's reaction, the more I'm convinced. Research the authority for that arrest again. I want to know everything.'

McCabe nodded.

'You mentioned before the trips which Hawthorne made recently. I want to know the dates and the exact places he went to, plus names of everyone he met. I also want to speak to Carl Wheeler from the CIA office in London. I must have him on the line tonight.'

McCabe hesitated before leaving the room. 'Who's to benefit from Hawthorne and his little group meddling in this affair?'

Rose was examining the board again and didn't bother to turn round. 'Who knows? For monetary gain, perhaps. Some of them may even be politically motivated towards the terrorists.' He circled Somerville's name. 'One thing is for certain: the only way we're going to find out the truth is by allowing Somerville to go full term.' He looked at McCabe, who was now standing at his side. 'You know, of course, that before your requisition to Ulster we had toyed with triggering an individual like Somerville?' He paced down the room while McCabe remained staring at the board. 'Single-handed, Lewis, this man has devastated the IRA offensive . . you know, even though it has cost us dearly, I would honestly like to see the chap survive.'

'You make it sound like a game,' said McCabe. 'Mind you, if one triggered a "Somerville" a year, there'd be no terrorist problem!'

'It *is* a game,' replied Rose, turning towards him. 'Aren't you glad you're not on the chess-board?' Without waiting for a reply, he was once again busy studying the board. 'Now to work! Who and where? We know when roughly?'

'It's an impossible task, sir,' said McCabe.

'If you thought it impossible, then why wake me up at four o'clock in the bloody morning!'

McCabe held his tongue.

'Somerville must have extracted information from Doyle and of course Murray, whom we've yet to locate. Now, that obviously led to the multiple killings in Ballymurphy. Could these persons have put the finger on our four main players? I would think only one. Hawthorne's not stupid. Now, Lewis, how did these people decide to stop our man in the first place?'

'They simply had him framed.'

'Not so simple! They had to fabricate the evidence, using a bank – a bank controlled by our friend Sir Ralph Hawthorne. Now that required, if I recall our information, the precise evidence of an assistant manager called Geddis. He's worth watching, I think . . . If Somerville knows about the bank manager, he also knows about Williams as Murray's main contact. The manager's survival is crucial to both them and us and we can use that to our advantage. Now listen, this is what I have in mind . . .'

It was 6 a.m. before Lewis McCabe had finalised the arrangements and got what he wanted. He stared at the copy of the arrest authorisation form on his desk: it was signed, 'F. Grange, DC Supt.' There was no mistaking the handwriting.

8

Wednesday 23 June – Saintfield Road, Belfast
It was 7 a.m. when the red Escort Van drove along
Edencourt Gardens for the second time in fifteen
minutes. The front-seat passenger lifted a microphone
and spoke: 'It's all clear. Go in now.'

A navy blue Ford Cortina entered the road from the
lower end and stopped outside No. 29. One policeman
stepped out while his colleague switched off the engine
and followed him up the tarmac pathway to the front
door. Olive Geddis opened the door quickly when she
saw the dark green uniforms.

'Good morning. Would Mr Geddis be in, please?'
The first policeman touched the peak of his cap.

'Why yes, constable. What appears to be the matter?'

'It's the alarm at your husband's bank, madam: the
normal keyholder isn't available. Could you get him,
please?' As Olive Geddis turned to walk down the
hallway, she was followed by the two policemen. She
was about to turn and ask them to wait in the living
room when she was pushed roughly to the floor by the
first man just as the second slammed the door shut.
She screamed out loud, and her husband raced into
the hall to face the .38 Smith and Wesson revolver.

'You! Ya bastard!' shouted the gunman. 'Get inta
the kitchen there and nobody's going ta get hurt!'

Barry Geddis hesitated for a split second, then moved
back into the kitchen followed by the gunman. The
second man lifted Olive Geddis to her feet and elbowed
her into the rear dining room where their petrified six-
year-old boy was cowering in a corner by a standard
lamp.

'Come on, missus, we just want the keys to the bank, nothing else. Now stay here and no funny business.'

He shut the door and crossed to the French windows; making sure they were locked, he removed the key. As he checked the windows he stared at the mature garden, which stretched at least a hundred yards from the house. The lawn was flat and freshly cut, the garden's borders festooned with thick lines of trees and shrubs which gave a very secluded aspect to the place. He turned and looked blankly at the woman, who was holding the boy to her at the dining-table.

Barry Geddis stood trembling in his shirt-sleeves and braces. 'This is a robbery, isn't it?' he blurted, his stomach churning with fear. 'You know of course that I carry no money and the safe at the bank is on a time clock!'

'Aye, we know all that, but yer goin' ta lift it for us and yer wife and kid will be returned safe when ya do. Understand?' Taylor's proposal had been amended; Campbell had decided to take what he could from the bank before killing the manager.

'Yes! Yes! Don't shoot! How much?' cried Geddis.

'We want £50,000, all in small bills, or they get it!'

The gunman waved his gun towards the dining room. Pitifully, Barry Geddis made an attempt to dissuade him from the gross amount and the nature of the demand. It was a ploy all bank officials were instructed to attempt.

Suddenly, the front-door bell rang. The second gunman left the woman and child in the dining room and looked down the hall towards the net-curtained front door. Through the large single glass panel he could see a man in a peaked cap with a parcel under his arm, who seemed to be leafing through a small notebook. The kitchen door opened slightly. 'Who the hell is it?' hissed the first gunman.

'A postman ... with a parcel.' The other's voice quavered. 'I'll have to let her answer the door!'

'Fuck off! Ye'll do it yerself, and fuckin' hurry up!'

The second gunman went back into the dining room and pointed his gun at the woman. 'Stay there with that brat or yer dead.'

Olive Geddis did not respond, except to lower her head over her son's body and hold him tighter against her. The man holstered his weapon as he closed the door behind him. He studied the little postman standing outside, but was too preoccupied with his rapid preparation for conversation to notice the 9mm Walther PPK with silencer, carefully concealed under the brown-paper package now held in the postman's hands. As the outer glass door opened, the postman smiled and a single puff from the gun spelt death as the small 9mm-round crashed through the gunman's chest. A second bullet split the soft skin under his chin, obliterating any cry as it became embedded in the unregistering brain. The terrorist was hurled backwards, crashing through the inner doorway.

As the remaining terrorist came out of the kitchen, he caught a glimpse of the green-uniformed body slumped against the single-panelled radiator and blue carpet, and then slammed the lightweight door closed as if to shut out the inevitable.

Outside the kitchen window there was a movement. The single pane of glass was shattered with a short burst from a 9mm Mini UZI sub-machine gun, extended by a bulbous seven-inch French silencer. The shots threw the gunman across the hall and he was dead by the time he hit the tiled floor. Barry Geddis stood aghast, awaiting salvation from the nightmare.

Simultaneously the French windows in the dining room were smashed by a single kick and another man sprang into the room. UZI at the ready, he reported the situation through a throat microphone. Olive Geddis screamed hysterically. The long-haired young man in jeans and navy combat-style jacket touched her on the right shoulder with his free hand. He spoke clearly as if to himself.

'Entry to dining room gained. Woman and child OK. No terrorists here.' She reacted immediately to the sound of his Newcastle accent and began to cry.

McCabe entered the house following clearance from the scene controller, some four minutes after the six-second storming operation. He spoke to a small fair-haired man in post-office uniform now standing in the hallway. 'Where are they, George?'

'In the dining room.'

'All OK?'

'No problem.' George nodded towards the sprawled body of the gunman in the hallway, now handcuffed with plastic strips snapped tightly around the wrists bound behind the body. It was an amendment to the rule book by the controller, a fundamental safety measure gleaned from his invaluable experience in the jungles of South Vietnam and Cambodia while serving under the auspices of the Australian Armed Forces.

McCabe met the controller in the kitchen. He had a radio in one hand. Captain David Keating, late of the SAS, was five years younger than McCabe and also small in stature, but he exuded a restless vigour that was the mark of an officer in peak condition for action.

McCabe smiled. 'Congratulations, David. A job well done!'

'Of course, old man,' replied Keating. 'I'm pulling out now. Arrangements are in hand for the local branch men to control the police action for the interim, until the CID are let in on this.'

McCabe glanced at the second uniformed body lying face down, hands strapped tightly behind the back with white plastic handcuffs.

'I'll see the man Geddis in here. The sight of Johnny Provo here should encourage the right response.'

Keating went to fetch the bank manager from the dining room, where he was trying to console his family. Meanwhile, McCabe turned the bloodstained body over.

The sight of the dead terrorist made Geddis turn very pale.

'I trust you're unharmed after your ordeal?' McCabe was charm itself.

'Yes, thanks . . . but who are you? How – '

'I'll ask the questions, Mr Geddis,' replied McCabe. 'Now, you see this unfortunate fellow down here? Well, you were to die in a similar fashion.'

'But. . . . Why?' Geddis was shaking with a new fear, and began to rub his arms as if against the cold when he looked into the staring eyes of the terrorist.

'Do the names Williams, Briggs, Taylor or Hawthorne mean much to you?' asked McCabe. David Keating shut the kitchen door and stood against it.

Barry Geddis stiffened. 'You mean they wanted me dead!'

'Precisely. And frankly it's of little concern to us, except that the streets of Ulster have been bloody enough recently.' McCabe let his eyes stray down to the body on the floor once more. 'We want to know everything about the group and you're going to tell us, or else we'll leave you like this.'

'What do you want me to do?' Geddis sobbed into his hands.

'That's better, Barry,' said McCabe. 'Get your family together, along with some clothing for a few days. We'll look after the rest.'

'We can't simply leave like that!' cried Geddis. 'Just who are you people?'

'We're in the policing business, and the gentleman behind you hates to be held up, so be a good fellow.'

The Geddis family left the house within ten minutes and only David Keating remained to hand over to the local police and Special Branch. The incident came as much a surprise to the police as to the neighbours, who had been attracted to their bay windows by the noisy comings and goings at No. 29.

The official version was announced at 11 a.m. that morning on all the local radio stations, but Anthony Campbell had already heard the news from his own sources and his ears were warm. His godfathers would have their inquisition; they did not tolerate fools or bunglers. But before the back-street post mortem and kangaroo court in some pub or smelly social club, he proposed to set things right with Mr Mark Taylor.

In his Belfast office, Geoffrey Williams had finished making arrangements for an indefinite vacation in Tenerife. He had already telephoned Ralph Hawthorne's private secretary; Miss Carruthers had received her instructions and reserved two tickets on the two o'clock flight from Belfast. The tickets could be collected at the airport. He would be met at Tenerife by the houseman, Ramon Fernandez.

Julia was going to pick him up within the hour in her Mazda sports car. They would leave the Mercedes in the firm's car park and travel together to the airport.

He opened the drinks cabinet and poured a cognac, tuning the built-in radio to catch the latest news headlines. With a start, he recognized the house-owner's name as the details unfolded. The desk telephone rang before the bulletin had finished and he recognized Roland Briggs immediately.

'Geoffrey! You've heard the news! Have you heard the news?'

Geoffrey's heart pounded. 'Yes, just now.'

'I don't like it, Geoffrey. I've tried to get Ralph for the last half hour, but he's unavailable. I can't get anything out of that damned Miss Carruthers of his! Where the hell is he?'

'How would I know?' said Williams. 'Look, Roland, I'm going away today and I'm busy. You might get him through the Bar Library at the Royal Courts of Justice.' Although Geoffrey Williams was frightened, he was also wary and did not want this conversation to develop on an open telephone line.

'Yes, yes, all right! I'll try that. Cheerio.' Williams was relieved the man had hung up. He had much to do and this latest news – obviously orchestrated by the group, without his knowledge – concerned him greatly. He wondered if he would ever return from Tenerife.

The opening session of the murder trial of Declan Coyle in Crumlin Road's No. 4 Court commenced slowly. The case revolved around the murder of a part-time RUC Reservist who had been gunned down at his grocery shop in the Waterside area of Londonderry. The preamble by the prosecution took over thirty minutes, followed by the submission of police photographic and mapping evidence. The judge, Mr Justice McIntyre-Scott, took much time to determine the position of photographs depicting the murder scene, marking them meticulously on the maps produced by the police. Sir Ralph Hawthorne, on one of his increasingly rare appearances at Belfast's Crown Court, left the minor interjections to his junior counsels.

The first few witnesses were given a minimal cross-examination, but the fourth provided Sir Ralph with his stage. An elderly woman entered the witness box and was duly sworn in, referred to only as 'Witness B'. Sir Ralph was aroused by the emphasis the prosecution placed on withholding the old woman's identity; he immediately signalled to his nearest junior and the younger man reacted swiftly.

'If your lordship pleases . . . the defence strongly

objects to the procedure adopted by my learned friend for the prosecution. It is my submission that the defence counsel should know this witness's identity.' Charles Callaghan was in his element.

The judge looked over the top of his gold-rimmed glasses, pushing the desk-top lamp to one side to avoid the glare.

'A salient point, Mr Callaghan.' He looked towards the prosecution counsel seated beside Sir Ralph on the front bench. 'Mr Lynch, have you any objection to the request? This witness will of course be required to submit her name and address on a piece of paper to myself and the court officers for inclusion on the official court records.'

Raymond Lynch had anticipated the submission and he stood up, turning slightly towards Sir Ralph who sat expressionless on the seat next to him. 'No, my lord, I have no objection whatsoever.' He turned to the witness box and handed the sixty-eight-year-old woman a notepad and pencil. 'Mrs B, will you please put your name and address on that notepad for the information of the court and counsel only.'

She fumbled for her glasses, dropping the pencil and pad in the process. Sir Ralph's scheme was working, for his target was becoming more and more nervous by the minute. Finally she completed the details and handed the pad back to Lynch, who in turn passed it to the judge via the court officer. The judge grunted, nodding his approval as he handed it back. Sir Ralph eagerly examined the old lady's details before passing the pad to his assistants. Finally it was returned to the clerk of the court, who tore out the top page and placed it in a sealed envelope, much to the relief of 'Witness B'.

As her evidence continued to unfold, it was apparent that she was quite certain of her facts. Much to everyone's surprise, she proved an excellent and coherent witness. Then came the crunch, when she was asked to point out the young man running from the shop and carrying the sawn-off shotgun. She looked nervously around the court. In the packed confines of the room, the dock was almost obscured by four prison officers and the close proximity of the packed gallery. The old woman adjusted her glasses and pointed. 'That's him there, that's the man I saw.'

Sir Ralph looked around as the judge asked the man to stand up and a half-smile appeared on his face when the youth in the public gallery rose. He was the defendant's brother; only one year divided them. He was dressed in a green combat jacket and yellow scarf, similar to those worn by his brother when he had murdered the part-time Reservist eighteen months before. His hair was long and unkempt, just as Sir Ralph had suggested six months earlier when he had sought an adjournment and compared the appearance of his client with a photograph taken around the time of the murder.

The old lady realised her mistake when the beaming prisoner's brother hopped to his feet to the laughter and cat-calls of other relatives and IRA sympathisers in the gallery. It was then that she focused on the short-cropped head of the murderer in the dock. 'No! No! Yer worship, that's him there, in that there box there!' But it was too late; the laughter heightened; the damage had been done.

Although the prosecuting cousel tried to minimize the damage, Lynch's reiteration of the witness's earlier positive identification at an identity parade two days after the murder, and the submission as to how the prosecution would later show that the defendant's appearance had changed since that time, were greeted with obvious scepticism by the elderly judge.

'I think, Mr Lynch, that if you are now finished with the witness, we can leave the cross-examination until the afternoon. Is that agreeable to both counsels?' He sat forward in his red chair.

'I have no objection, your honour. This witness has now completed her direct evidence,' blurted an irate prosecution counsel. Raymond Lynch had no heart to add 'and made a positive identification of the defendant'. The judge peered over towards Sir Ralph, who rose slightly in his seat. 'I have no objection, my lord.'

'Very well then.' He turned towards the witness. 'Mrs B. You understand that you are not to communicate with anyone on the matter of your evidence or this trial in general, and furthermore you will be required to return here this afternoon for cross-examination?' The old woman nodded her head in agreement as the court was adjourned until 2 p.m.

After the judge left the court and the old lady had been escorted away by two prison officers, Sir Ralph was approached by Raymond Lynch. 'You old dog! I think you've got us in a corner.'

Sir Ralph smiled back as he peered over the seat at Callaghan. 'I think an application may be made this afternoon, Charles. I really cannot see much point in continuing with this charade.'

The young assistant was laughing back as he left to speak to the defendant, and followed Coyle when he was removed to the cells below.

'You orchestrated that demonstration. I should have anticipated as much, after you began to intimidate the witness,' continued Lynch.

'Ah!' said Sir Ralph. 'But you didn't. And that's the secret!'

Both men left for lunch together. It seemed peculiar to onlookers that the two opposing counsels should be so friendly. Little did they know! As they descended the staircase, Raymond Lynch continued the conversation. 'I'll fight you on the basis of the positive identification she made just after the shooting, and of course there's the forensic evidence yet to come.'

'You have to put on your show, Raymond, that's your prerogative,' replied Sir Ralph, confident that his case was won.

Deep beneath the courts, Charles Callaghan was counselling his client on the implications of mistaken identity.

'Yes, Declan, I think we may be able to swing this one.'

The young Derry man could not touch his lunch for excitement. 'Thanks, Mr Callaghan. The brother did a good job up there.'

Callaghan smiled and stood up.

'Tell us – that auld woman, what's her name?'

Callaghan glanced over at the cell door and small heavily glazed panel; the prison guard was sitting on the far side of the corridor. He looked back again at the prisoner, adjusting his robes and wig. 'Betty Rodgers, she lives in Rossdowney Street in the Waterside.'

'I know it. Thank ya, Mr Callaghan.' Declan smiled.

'But you've nothing to fear from her now.'

'It doesn't do any harm, Mr Callaghan. Ye can call it insurance if ya like.' Declan went back to picking at his food.

Drinking some ghastly coffee in the communal foyer which divides the two main courts at Crumlin Road, Sir Ralph Hawthorne was shaken by a conversation he overheard between two policemen. The deaths of the terrorists at Geddis's house meant there had been a tip-off, and it did not require his legal genius to predict what would happen next. The group was now at serious risk and he was powerless for the moment to do anything about it.

He quickly dismissed himself from the case after consulting with a surprised Raymond Lynch. Then he spoke to Charles Callaghan, who had returned from consultation with Coyle. A deal had been struck, and the juniors would see it through. Unknown to the young man in the cells below, he was about to have his plea changed to guilty on the murder charge. The change in plea would be explained to him as being in his own best interests, with the agreed intercession of the prosecution counsel to minimise the more damaging evidence.

Charles Callaghan protested, stating his determination to fight on with an application to have the case dismissed, but he was easily dissuaded by Sir Ralph. Callaghan returned to the cells and told Coyle the shocking news, advising him that with the right presentation the trial judge would go leniently on the young Derry IRA volunteer.

Coyle would know no better as he went off to face a minimum ten years sentence, but then the practice of law was a game to Ralph Hawthorne and many colleagues shared his view. The innocent could suffer and the guilty walk free. As Coyle walked to the prison van which was waiting to take him to H. M. Prison, the Maze, he would even thank his lawyers for their 'efforts'. They would console him with assurances that he had made the right choice in throwing himself on the mercy of the court, and dangle the prospect of an early appeal.

What they failed to tell the twenty-year-old was that his senior counsel had not the time to fight his case – a case which, although his client was guilty, he could have certainly won!

The car trip from the City Centre to Belfast Airport took Julia Williams' Mazda a mere twenty minutes, even in heavy traffic. She passed through the only public entrance to the airport, the static police check-point, about one mile along the sealed road from the terminal buildings. All vehicles entering the zone of the airport were logged and checked through the police computer, which was linked to the Vehicle Licensing Office for Northern Ireland based at Coleraine. Only an occasional search or physical check was made and by the time a vehicle passed the initial checkpoint to the vehicle search bay – a distance of 100 yards – the computer check was complete and suspect vehicles were directed off the road for a further examination.

The Ford Escort van was no exception to the computer check and, although stolen the previous night, was now fitted with a new registration plate matching a similar vehicle. This was an old terrorist ploy, but for no apparent reason the van was directed into the search bay. Somerville drove in reluctantly, watching the red Mazda speed off into the distance. He stopped and rolled down the window.

'Hello, sir, can I see your driving licence please?' requested the young Reserve policeman. Somerville kept calm and smiled back. 'Would you believe, I've left it in the house, constable. I'm afraid I was in a bit of a hurry to collect the wife off the London shuttle.'

'Have you any other identification?' The policeman was looking past Somerville into the rear of the van.

'I'm sorry, nothing except my banker's card.' He reached into his inside jacket pocket and produced a plastic wallet containing several credit cards and a bank card.

The young policeman studied the name: 'Desmond Francis Murray.' 'Do you know the registration number of this van?' he continued.

'I do, but before you go any further, she's the firm's van – belongs to H. T. Beggs and Partners, Wholesalers on the Shore Road. I'm the manager there.' Somerville tried to avoid showing his rising impatience.

The policeman toyed with a further examination of the van and insisted that 'Mr Murray' produce his driving licence, Road Fund Licence and insurance documents at his nearest police station without delay. Then his radio crackled: 'Romeo Two from Romeo One, you have a Volvo Estate entering the bay. Over.'

He glanced behind the Escort to see a blue Volvo stopping at the other end of the search bay and lifted the radio microphone to his mouth. 'Romeo One from Romeo Two. Roger, I have it in sight. Out.'

'All right Sir,' he said to Somerville. 'Go on ahead. Thank you very much.' He handed back the wallet.

'You're welcome, son.' Somerville managed another smile as he revved up the engine and pulled out of the search bay. Quickly he sped away towards the terminal buildings.

The car park was a sea of colour and he estimated at least a couple of thousand vehicles. Somerville parked without locking the driver's door, and rushed towards the main complex. After passing through the security check and electronic sensors, he walked to the main floor and soon located his man in the lounge bar.

The call over the Tannoy system startled Geoffrey Williams, and he excused himself from Julia's pre-holiday rambling and headed for the nearest courtesy telephone where he dialled the airport reception number. The telephonist was not amused by the silence of the caller when Williams froze with shock as a voice sounded in his right ear.

'You can hang up the phone now.' The man took the receiver from Geoffrey's left hand. 'Please excuse this dramatic approach to locate you, Mr Williams. I do hope you weren't too alarmed.'

'No ... But just who are you?' asked Williams, trying to regain his self-control.

'I'm glad I caught you before you left. My name is Kessel and I'm with the Ministry of Defence, Buildings and Finance, Procurement Branch. We need your help.'

'Help?' exclaimed Williams.

David Keating produced an identity card indicating his name as Kessel, David Arthur, Principal Officer with the Ministry of Defence. 'Your building methods, specifically the erection of fast and efficient multi-span housing construction, are well known to all British designers.'

'I'm afraid I'm at a loss, Mr. Kessel. Just how did you find me?'

'Your office told me.'

'I don't get the point, Mr Kessel.' Williams looked at his watch nervously. 'I'm just about to take a short trip. Perhaps you should contact my office again and discuss the details with my partner, Mr Briggs.'

The Tannoy crackled and a female voice boomed in their ears. 'Announcing the departure of Flight BA 7320 to Tenerife, now boarding at gate number 4. I repeat, the departure . . .'

The second part of the announcement was ignored by Williams.

'Look, Mr . . . Kessel, I'll have to go; my wife is waiting. If you contact my office, they will do all they can to help you. Good day.' He turned to leave, but was restrained by a powerful grip on his right forearm.

'This is of national importance, Mr Williams. I should not really say here, but it's to do with the Falklands. A contract worth perhaps forty to fifty million – and it's now or never.' Keating glimpsed the excitement stirring in Williams' eyes.

'Fifty *what?*' said Williams.

'A contract for building worth fifty million pounds. Your personal profit margin could amount to, say, twenty per cent. We pay well for speed and efficiency.' Keating released his grip.

'That sounds like loose bribery, Mr Kessel.'

'We need action now, and Her Majesty's Government is prepared to pay for it – through the nose if necessary.' Keating guided him away from the telephone.

'You say I need to go somewhere now?' asked Williams.

'Yes. Immediately, I'm afraid. Our chief engineer is flying into Ulster this evening, specifically to see you.'

'You put up a very convincing proposal, if that's what it is!' Faced with the prospect of a quick killing, Williams' fears for his personal safety evaporated. 'Well, I suppose I ought to have a word with my wife. Exactly how long will these initial discussions take?'

'Oh, no more than two or three days. Then when the design team's finalized you could continue with your holiday. Although you may be required to fly on to Ascension, but don't worry, we can take care of all that.'

'Why my firm, when you have the Royal Engineers and the Pioneer Corps?' Geoffrey Williams was now playing with the man.

'Politics, Mr Williams, politics.'

At Keating's request the couple followed him towards an empty area of the departure building, past a further security checkpoint. Julia was dismayed at the sight of the two tough-looking men who now accompanied her husband and this stranger from London, but she knew enough of high-level business dealings not to argue.

In the seclusion of the unused lounge, but still within earshot of Keating and his assistants, Geoffrey Williams tried to placate his now distraught wife. 'Darling, listen to me. We haven't much time. Something has come up. These men are from the government; it's to do with the Falklands thing. They want my advice in Whitehall on a rebuilding programme for the island.'

'Why you?' Julia was red with anger. 'Why an

Ulsterman, just about to fly away on a holiday? Haven't they got any builders in bloody Whitehall?'

'I don't know. All I can say is that they want to see me. Some of our firm's ideas have revolutionized cheap multiple building and they will probably need to house a lot of people quickly and in bad weather conditions. In that sphere, your dull little husband here is an innovator.' Geoffrey Williams forced a grin. 'It's not just me; I imagine they are calling engineers from all over.'

'Well, I want you too! Doesn't that matter?'

'It will only be for one or two days, they say. Then I'll join you, I promise.' He took her hand.

Julia pulled away, tears in her eyes. 'Your promises don't mean a bloody thing, Geoffrey . . . Well, I suppose I'm lucky I've still got a separate passport.'

He grasped her hand tightly. 'Look – it will all mean a great deal more business. More money for us. Think of the opportunity!' Geoffrey Williams could not hide his excitement and this was the final insult to Julia.

'To hell with your bloody opportunities! If you decide to fly from London or wherever, you may *just* catch me. On the other hand, you may not. Frankly, it's of no consequence to me either way!' Pulling away from him, she snatched her large brown leather Gucci shoulder-bag, threw down his ticket and boarding card and stomped off towards the departure gate. She never looked back.

Geoffrey Williams stood motionless. There was no point in shouting after her. She was gone – her moods could last for ever. He picked up the ticket. It would make no difference what he said; he would still have to face the inevitable deluge of abuse, the torrent of rebuke and river of tears. It was his penalty for marrying one of England's 'fairest flowers'.

Sitting in the back of the Granada saloon with Keating, he asked, 'Just how did you manage to find me here?' He lit another cigarette and puffed nervously, his initial enthusiasm fading fast.

'As I said, Mr Williams, your office told us. I telephoned via the NIO. As you can imagine, we are trying to keep a low profile on the Falklands build-up. I do hope, sir, that you said nothing to your wife about it?' Keating had overheard the conversation, but he was amusing himself with Williams and wanted to see him squirm.

'Of course not. Mind you, it was damned hard under the circumstances.'

Keating changed the subject. 'I do hope you don't mind, but we've selected your house as the most suitable meeting place.'

'You've what?' Williams was thrown. 'You seem to know a great deal about me, Mr Kessel! What time is the meeting scheduled for?'

'Around six o'clock this evening. I'm sorry, but we had to run a security clearance on you first, which is why we know so much. Nothing to be alarmed about. Tell me, how long do you think it should take us to get to your house? An hour?'

'I suppose so.' Geoffrey Williams sat back, becoming more and more suspicious by the minute.

Somerville had recognized the two heavies accompanying Keating even before he saw Williams approach the telephone. As he stood at the bookstall, pretending to browse through the fiction section, he had watched the four men go up to the woman whom he assumed to be Julia Williams.

After the group went through the security barrier, Somerville hung about for a few moments. There were at least two more heavies mingling with the bustling queues of holidaymakers. Unobtrusively, he stole away. He no longer felt safe in his disguise; Williams would have to wait for now.

Outside, the weather had begun to worsen and dark clouds hovered ominously over the airport. Somerville quickened his step as the first drops of rain fell, but by the time he had crossed to the car park he was drenched. He was running through the rows of parked cars, not waiting a second to check for traffic on the one-way system, when the Volvo Estate swerved and struck him. He tumbled across the bonnet, smashing into the windscreen.

The Volvo had only been travelling at 20 m.p.h. and quickly came to rest. Somerville slid off the bonnet on to the wet ground and the driver and front-seat passenger quickly jumped out, the driver checking his pulse.

'Unconscious, but all right . . . he's got a strong pulse.' He spoke with a gentle Scottish accent.

The passenger nodded. 'Better get him into the back; he may need attention. Here, give us a hand.' The older man's broad Belfast accent was clear and unmistakable.

Quickly they bundled Somerville into the rear seat, where the passenger joined him and as they drove off, he began a detailed search. 'He's clean,' he said.

'Good,' replied the driver. 'You'd better cuff him before he wakes up.'

'Ya had better let control know "Chummy" here's safe,' continued the passenger as he eased Somerville on to his side. After they had passed through the police checkpoint, he produced a syringe from a small black box.

'I'm going to give him a jab, just in case.' He winked at the driver, who smiled back into the rear-view mirror as they drove quickly towards the motorway.

While the two men waited outside in the car, Williams showed Keating into the poolside lounge. At Keating's suggestion he gave Maureen, the daily housemaid, the rest of the day off. She was bemused by Williams' unexpected return and wanted to know if 'madam' was all right, but she had no real objections to leaving early.

'Mr Kessel,' said Williams, after failing to get one satisfactory answer in five minutes, 'I'd like to bring my junior partner in on this. His name is Roland Briggs – but then you probably know that. Excuse me while I ring him.' Williams stood up, setting a half-finished gin and tonic on the glass table-top.

'I don't think that would be wise at this stage, Mr Williams. It is imperative we have complete secrecy on this matter until the deal is firmly set. Our chief engineer should not be very long now; he'll have all the maps, plans and proposals with him.' Keating examined his watch.

Williams exploded. 'Look here, I'm making no deal until my junior partner agrees with me on the matter! He is completely trustworthy. I honestly can't see how his presence is likely to have any detrimental effect on our discussions.' He picked up the phone.

'I wouldn't do that, if I were you,' advised Keating.

Geoffrey Williams' mouth dried up as he saw the muzzle of the 9mm Parabellum Steyr GB pointing directly at his head.

'Please! Put it down.'

Williams almost dropped the telephone off the bar counter. 'Are you . . . ?' He found the words impossible to pronounce; his heart raced.

'Somerville, you mean? Oh no. You're lucky, I could have been. He was pretty close at the airport. In a manner of speaking, you can thank me for saving your life.'

'I can look after myself, thank you very much. Just who are you, anyway?' Williams shouted, trying to control himself and stop shaking.

'Sit down, Mr Williams. Sit down here.' David Keating pointed with the pistol to the long white leather seating which curved all the way round the pool.

Williams complied without hesitation. 'Put the gun away, will you?' he asked.

Keating dropped his aim, but still cradled the pistol in his right hand. 'Just sit quietly, and all will be revealed in good time,' he responded.

Twenty minutes later, Lewis McCabe arrived. He entered unannounced from the raised lounge area, carrying a brown briefcase in one hand.

'This is quite a spread you have here.' He spoke directly to Williams, acknowledging Keating's raised salute with the Steyr. 'You don't know me, but I know an awful lot about you.' As Williams turned towards him, McCabe noticed a cut just above his right temple. The bleeding had congealed but was obviously fresh.

'So you gave our Mr Kessel here a little trouble? That was a bit silly, don't you think? Especially since the gentleman saved your neck!'

Williams broke his self-imposed silence. 'Who the hell are you? For God's sake, what do you want?'

McCabe rested the briefcase on the glass-topped table directly in front of the frightened man. 'Open it,' he said.

Williams looked at the case and then at the two men in turn.

'Open it!' repeated McCabe. 'It's not going to blow up in your face. Things like that only happen in James Bond films!'

Williams slowly unlocked the single clasp and lifted out a green folder. When he opened it, he saw that the first page was a photocopy of an old newspaper cutting, dated 11 April 1972, concerning a sailing accident at the mouth of Strangford Lough. The headlines bore the title 'YACHTING TRAGEDY' and the first paragraph read:

Sir Frederick Williams, MP and architect, was lost overboard when his thirty-foot yacht *Blue Diamond* foundered at the mouth of Strangford Lough early yesterday morning. Rescue services spent ten hours combing the area before calling off the search owing to darkness and deteriorating weather conditions. The other crew member, believed to be a close friend of the deceased, was pulled from the water by coastguard officials. He was suffering from exposure, but is now recovering well in Newtownards Hospital. His condition is reported as 'comfortable'. The full circumstances of the accident will not be known for several days, according to a police spokesman.

The remainder of the article read as an obituary. Geoffrey Williams flicked over to the next pages in the file; he was suddenly struck dumb.

Barney Somerville awoke to find himself lying on a divan bed, a single sheet and blanket pulled up tightly under his chin. His head pounded and made it difficult for him to focus on the strange environment. It was only after he had blinked away from the bright ceiling light that he realized he was not alone.

'How do you feel, Mr Somerville?'

He stirred, recognizing the voice to be English, but still failing to focus on the speaker.

'You will feel groggy – that's the thiopentone. And of course you will be sore in parts, but the MO says you're OK otherwise. The arm wound seems to be clearing up nicely; you've obviously had some expert medical attention.'

Somerville made no reply, but began raising himself from the bed using his left arm. He discovered he was naked apart from his underpants. His throat hurt and his mouth was dry, and it was hard to speak but his captor saved him the trouble. 'My name is McCabe, and you are in a place of safety.'

'Place of what!?' croaked Barney. For the first time he was able to see the man properly. 'Oh, forget it . . . suppose I'm surprised to be still alive.'

'Yes, indeed . . . Barney, isn't it?' McCabe did not await a reply. 'Yes, there are plenty of people who long to see you dead and buried. I suppose I can understand why.'

'You haven't told me who you are and what you want,' said Somerville.

'All in good time. You'll get some food shortly, then you can freshen up.' McCabe looked at his watch. 'I'll see you in two hours.' He left the room by a Georgian-style mahogany door.

It was only when he heard the key turn in the lock that Somerville began to fully appreciate the neglected splendour of the bedroom. Ornate moulding decorated the ceiling, from which hung a dusty chandelier. Full-length deep red velvet curtains stretched right along one wall – he estimated the full width to be approximately twenty feet. The wallpaper was of a fine white pattern, now yellowed with age and damp. The floor, however, was covered with dark green linoleum and was not the only thing which seemed inappropriate. The small divan bed he sat on would have fitted better in a squaddie's billet; the only other piece of furniture in the elegantly spacious room was a crude metal chair.

A single hand-basin was located in the opposite corner of the room, encased in a white melamine cabinet with a storage cupboard underneath. Somerville crossed the floor slowly, feeling as if he'd been through the mangle. Opening the cupboard, he found a thin blue bath-towel. As he lifted out the folded towel, a bar of soap dropped to the chilly linoleum. He picked it up and ran the water taps. The soap was unperfumed and yellow in appearance – typical MOD supply.

Somerville splashed the sleep from his eyes, rubbing arms and chest with wet soapy hands, until he found the pinhole surrounded by deep bruising on his right forearm. He wondered just how long he had been under sedation, and for the first time, why he was still alive.

Suddenly, the door swung open and two men entered. The younger one, who appeared to be in his twenties, had a large hand-gun protruding from his waistband but concealed under a floppy grey sweater. The older man watched Somerville like a hawk. He was balding, about forty, dressed casually in faded blue jeans and a maroon polo-neck jumper. He made no attempt to conceal the 9mm Browning pistol worn high in a leather holster on his left hip. The pistol grips had been removed to reduce the bulk of the weapon – a favourite Army trick adopted in covert operations during the late sixties. Somerville imagined the man to be a veteran of a number of wars, known and unknown.

The older man carried some clothing which he dumped unceremoniously on the bed. 'They should fit you. Food will be up shortly.' The broad Belfast accent betrayed no emotion and his expression was equally bland. Somerville had seen the look before. He was a killer all right. The two men left the room and the door was locked again.

Somerville gazed into the mottled wall mirror above the white corner unit, examining the worn unshaven face closely. This too was the face of a killer . . . he did not like what he saw.

He put on the loose-fitting trousers and thick wool shirt which had a loud blue and red check pattern. The footwear was the correct size – white trainers, quite comfortable without socks. He moved to the curtains and pulled them back, but to his astonishment his eyes met only the cold face of recently cemented breeze-blocks. The view had been obliterated completely.

The food was hot and simple: a stew of tinned meat and potatoes. The hot sweet tea tasted of tinned milk, but he drank gratefully. The door reopened some time later and the same two men stood on the threshold.

'You've to come with us,' snapped the younger man.

When Somerville stood up the oversize navy cords sagged slightly, but obviously he was not going to be given a belt. The younger man led the way along the wide panelled corridor and across a minstrel's gallery which gave a commanding view of a long banqueting hall. Somerville was then shown into a room which must once have been a library, only now the shelves were empty. The two men took up positions on either side of the door.

'Sit down, Barney.' Lewis McCabe indicated an easy chair in the centre of the room facing his large leather-topped desk. Somerville obeyed. 'Well, how are you feeling?'

Somerville studied his sharp features, which were enhanced by a dark brown Harris tweed three-piece suit.

'Come to the point. What do you want?' he asked wearily.

'Want? We've got what we want . . . well, almost.' McCabe leaned back in his chair.

'Who are you, McCabe? I assume you're connected in some way to the security forces?'

'Let's say we operate under the umbrella of MI5. When there's trouble of a particular kind, we are called in.'

'A dirty tricks department?'

'Very.' McCabe permitted himself a smile.

On a low coffee table set against a wall Somerville noticed his Zyconn radio, MI carbine, ammunition, knife and other items lying scattered across the surface. 'I see you found the van,' he said.

'Can you tell me why the radio was tuned into an

exclusive frequency used by the "muppets" and our own people? Also, GCHQ would be keen to know where you obtained the extra crystals for it. Any comment?'

Somerville remained silent.

'Barney, we are not here to fight. We can help each other. However, I should warn you that these two gentlemen have clear instructions to kill, if you get out of hand.'

Somerville shrugged his shoulders. 'I decided to die the day the remaining pieces of my family were buried. You can't kill me.'

'Spare me the melodrama, Barney.' McCabe lit a cigarette. 'I thought you might like to know the identity of the other parties involved in the deaths of your wife and kids.'

'Murder! The name is *Murder!* Death is for people who die in their sleep or get hit by a bus when crossing the road, not when they are torn limb from limb – a head missing, never found, a stomach ripped open to reveal the fully-formed foetus of your third child. So don't patronise me, you little bastard!' Somerville lunged forward across the desk and grabbed McCabe's throat, knocking his cigarette to the floor. McCabe's face became distorted as he felt the vice-like grip tighten. All his training could not get him out of it; he was wedged tightly against the desk and could not move. Fortunately for him, however, he was not alone in the room.

It took their combined efforts to stop Somerville and it was only after the fourth sharp blow to his kidneys that he crumpled to the floor in agony. He lay there for a few moments assessing his chances of retaliation and escape, but the odds were too high. These men were professionals.

'Set him . . . back in the . . . chair,' croaked McCabe, as he fought for breath and rubbed his neck.

Somerville was dumped roughly into the easy chair and given a punch in the stomach for good measure by the younger man. As he sat nursing his new injuries, the 22-inch TV screen in the corner sprang into life with a still colour photograph of Seamus Doyle standing at the front door of his house.

Lewis McCabe sipped a glass of water and coughed. In the light of the desk-top lamp, he and Somerville looked like worn-out street fighters. 'May I continue? If you please.' McCabe had recovered his composure. 'Seamus Doyle, deceased, a staff officer with the 2nd Battalion of the Provisional IRA.'

There was no reaction from Somerville.

The picture lasted another ten seconds and then into focus came a second; it was Desmond Murray.

'The RUC found his body in the River Lagan this afternoon – near to where you dumped it.'

The next photograph Somerville did not recognise.

'His name is Barry Geddis . . . you never caught up with him. He's the bank manager who framed you – on instructions, of course. We have him in "protective custody"; our Irish friends tried to take him out this morning.'

The next photograph made Somerville stir in his seat and the two men moved close, but were waved away by McCabe. 'Detective Chief Superintendent Francis Robert Grange, Queen's Police Medal, second-in-command of Special Branch. You never got him either. In fact, I'd be surprised if any of the gents you interrogated could have even told you his name.'

Somerville glared at McCabe. 'How does he fit into all this?'

'Don't be so impatient, old boy.' McCabe was enjoying Somerville's rekindled interest Another face appeared on the screen. 'Recognise him? Of course you do. He's Sir Ralph Hawthorne, entrepreneur, million-aire, legal genius, a senior Q.C. and also a close associate of your Chief Constable and the Secretary of State. I've even heard he's in line for a government appointment.' McCabe flicked the control unit on the trolley at his side. 'This was taken in March last year.' The television clicked again and a video film began.

The scene was Shannon Airport and into the foreground strutted Hawthorne accompanied by Williams. Both men were boarding an Aer Lingus Trident jet. 'Now,' continued McCabe, 'this was taken two days later – after a lot of amazing cat and mouse, I might add.' The camera zoomed in from its distant position to show the same pair sitting under the shade of a giant striped umbrella.

The sun shone brilliantly on palm trees and bright bougainvillea beside a large circular swimming-pool. Seated next to Geoffrey Williams was a dark-skinned man in a military uniform consisting of an olive-green bush shirt, trousers and high brown paratrooper boots. He also sported a sidearm in a covered leather holster on his right side. 'The man in the uniform is the head of a Middle East terrorist group,' said McCabe. 'Now look carefully.' The camera panned to the edge of the pool and into frame walked a party of six people.

Somerville sat forward again in his chair, unable to believe what he was witnessing. With his curly black hair and flowing white robes, the central figure in the group was unmistakable. He smiled and embraced Hawthorne warmly, then turned to Williams and they shook hands. There was a brief exchange between all three, after which Hawthorne presented the Libyan leader with a green attaché case which Colonel Gadaffi passed to one of his heavily-armed aides. Chatting animatedly, the two main actors left the stage followed by Williams and the other minor players.

The film cut to Williams and Murray; they were sitting in Murray's car deep in conversation. After a few more seconds, McCabe turned the television off.

'Now, that last scene took place immediately on Williams' return to Ulster. We have a tape of the conversation; it relates to the delivery of supplies to the Provisionals, direct from Libya.' McCabe leaned across the desk, still rubbing his throat and readjusting his collar and tie. 'What do you think of all that, Barney?'

'Nothing. But then nothing surprises me, except the fact that you showed it to me and that you still let me live. I assume you have a precise reason?' Somerville sat back in his chair and waited.

'We'll come to that. You see, we knew all about your being framed by Murray and company from the very start.'

'You mean I was placed on suspension, fixed for corruption, humiliated . . . and you could have stopped it?'

'We would have, believe me, but unknown to us you were being set up by Doyle. It appears that the Belfast Brigade were not satisfied with Murray's efforts and decided to put paid to you for ever – '

'I don't believe you, McCabe! If you know so much, how come you didn't know about the plot to kill me?'

'We weren't involved on the scale you imagine. Our source simply indicated that you would be suspended. You would have been reinstated after we had cracked Hawthorne and his group – we weren't really bothered about you.'

'Bastard!' muttered Somerville.

'Yes, indeed. You've given us quite a run. In fact, you were doing such a good job that we *let* you run. I knew you were something special after you gave the SAS the slip at Davagh Forest. We also did our bit along the way to keep certain people out of your hair. What you have done, apart from removing some very prominent terrorists, is to fracture the Provisionals' effectiveness irrevocably for the next twelve months at least.' McCabe lit another cigarette. 'To come to the point, we want you to finish the job you started.'

'And kill Hawthorne?'

'Oh, no! We want you to kill a policeman . . . one Detective Chief Superintendent Grange.' McCabe exhaled a long plume of smoke.

'What's his involvement in all this?'

'Hawthorne and his cronies set up an arms delivery service for the up-and-coming terrorists in Ulster. They also include Great Britain and the Republic in their market area.' McCabe flicked on the television again to show Mark Taylor and Ralph Hawthorne ascending the steps of the Union Club. Taylor carried a small briefcase. 'They needed a man on the inside.' McCabe supplied the commentary. 'An early warning system if you like. Grange – we think he was recruited at least ten years ago.'

Somerville continued to watch in silence. Another man was getting out of his Lotus beside the club entrance. 'That's Roland Briggs, by the way. Well, as I was saying, you inadvertently stumbled on some unofficial cash books kept by the Murray syndicate, which disclosed the numbers of two accounts used in direct transactions on arms and drugs.'

'So Grange set me up for suspension?' Somerville stared at the floor.

'At Hawthorne's instigation. He also orchestrated the Provisionals' assassination attempt.'

'Why don't you kill him yourselves?' asked Barney. 'What's to stop you killing me afterwards? Dead men can't talk. I'd be a security risk.'

'Quite. It's a chance you will have to take, but I imagine there may be some satisfaction in killing Grange. As things stand now, you could be dead in seconds. On the other hand, you may continue to be of use to us.'

Somerville went back to the video, which showed

two more men emerging from the Union Club's entrance. One was Ralph Hawthorne. He didn't recognise the other, but there was something about his walk that triggered a memory.

'Hold it there!' shouted Somerville. 'Can you wind it back?'

Frame by frame, McCabe pressed the remote control until both men moved back into fuller focus. 'There!' Somerville slapped his hand on the leather-topped desk.

'Can you enlarge that shot?' he said.

'I think so, wait a second.' McCabe fiddled with the controls of the specialized unit. The frozen, slightly blurred image began to swell the screen. 'Any particular face you want, or the whole thing?' asked McCabe.

Somerville's reply surprised him. 'The briefcase: it's the same one Hawthorne's associate carried in. Enlarge it! Enlarge the briefcase!'

'Right. By the way, the associate is Mark Taylor.' McCabe typed a code into the control panel on the trolley. Somerville was not listening; he watched carefully as the frame began to change, zooming in on the man's hand and the briefcase.

'Well? What is it?' exclaimed McCabe.

'Get me Rose,' Somerville said.

'Who?' McCabe stared at him incredulously.

'I said, get me Rose . . . get me your superior. I want to speak to him.'

Thursday 24 June – Stormont Castle, Belfast
Lewis McCabe was shown into the first-floor apartment suite of the Secretary of State at 1.10 a.m. Cecil Rose was already there sitting on the adjacent couch to the Secretary. McCabe noticed that the latter appeared tired and anxious.

Rose gestured to the seat next to him and McCabe

nodded to Ulster's 'Supremo', who returned his greeting. 'How are you, Lewis?'

'Fine, thank you, sir.'

'We have just been talking over what you have achieved. Again my profound congratulations on our man's capture.'

McCabe remained silent, remembering his boss's earlier advice to say very little during the meeting. Rose stood up and began to pace the room.

'I have explained to the Secretary just how we propose to handle this situation. Did Somerville accept the scenario we proposed?'

'Yes, sir.'

'Good!' McCabe sensed that the Secretary of State did not like what he had been drawn into one bit, and that Rose was relishing the role of master puppeteer.

'Where is Grange now, Lewis?' Rose did not look at McCabe, but kept staring at the Secretary.

'At his office, working late – third night in a row.'

'And Hawthorne?'

'At home. Having a dinner party, which includes the Chief Constable.'

The Secretary of State interrupted. 'I don't have much of a stomach for all this. Democracy does have a price, but we can't afford to keep increasing the stakes!'

Cecil Rose pretended to look surprised. 'Sir, it is my opinion, and the opinion of my department, that this matter should be resolved as cleanly as possible. I give you my assurance that it will be.'

'Cecil, I do not want this to continue and I intend to advise the Prime Minister accordingly.'

'Lewis, would you please leave us for a moment and wait outside?' asked Rose.

Once the doors had closed, Cecil Rose picked up the red telephone, the direct line to Number 10 Downing Street. It was answered immediately.

'Prime Minister. I have the Secretary of State; he wishes to speak with you.' Rose handed over the receiver.

'Prime Minister . . . good morning.' The Secretary tried to hide his surprise and nervous tone. He listened intently for several minutes, interjecting with an occasional 'Yes, I understand', 'Indeed', and 'Of course I do', and terminated with a courteous farewell. Replacing the receiver, he sat back in the high chair and smoothed his hair. 'Well,' he said, distaste etched clearly on his face, 'It would appear the ball is in your court Mr Rose.'

Thursday 24 June – RUC Headquarters, Belfast

Frank Grange sat quietly in his second-floor office next to the Special Branch registry. He checked the small electric wall clock – it had just turned 2.15 a.m. He toyed with the prospect of spending yet another night on the camp-bed which was made up in the far corner of the large office.

During the last few weeks, frantic activity had taken its toll on Grange's normally immaculate routine. Files were piled high across his 'In' trays and desk-top. Step by step, he forced himself to re-examine the latest intelligence assessment from Londonderry and did not hear the door click shut.

But something made him look up, though for a moment he could not believe the evidence of his eyesight. Although Grange felt tired and light-headed, there was still no mistaking his adversary – or the .357 Magnum revolver in Somerville's right hand.

'We meet once more.'

Grange remained silent: amidst rising panic he rummaged in his mind to recall how far into the top drawer he had stuck his Walther PP.

'Heard you've been looking for me,' said Somerville.

'I got your message,' answered Grange. 'How did

you know it was me in charge of the hunt?' He knew that somehow he had to catch Somerville off guard in order to stand the remotest chance of staying alive. So he had to keep talking.

'I don't know how you got in here, but I suppose I shouldn't really be surprised. You've done a hell of a lot.' Grange's right hand stole slowly towards the drawer where his pistol was hidden.

'This is not a social call or surrender,' said Barney. 'And keep both your hands on the desk.'

Grange complied. 'I didn't think it was. But I am very curious to know how you managed to keep one step ahead of us every time? And that message – it really confused me for quite a while.'

Somerville lowered the Magnum revolver to his side. 'I think it's time for plain talking, Grange. I have something you want, evidence that can blow the lid off this province. Interested?'

'Now what evidence would that be?' Grange sat back in the swivel chair, his finger-tips still resting on the desk-top.

'Cash books, ledgers, books that implicate Hawthorne. Not forgetting your own sizable bank accounts – the ones nobody knows about.'

'And where are these books exactly?'

'Safe for the moment.'

'You're bluffing.'

'Call your assistant, Black; I know he's still somewhere in this building. Get him on the phone now.' Somerville pulled out a piece of paper from his coat pocket and tossed it on to Grange's desk. 'Tell him to retrieve that file from your registry.'

Grange examined the paper. It bore a single reference number 'SB 10735/82/P'.

'It's a sealed file in your "P" section; you'll find it marked "No Future Action". Have Black bring it here now, unopened.' Somerville raised the gun again. 'No wrong moves!'

'No wrong moves,' replied Grange, having already lifted the telephone receiver. It was answered immediately.

'Listen, I want you to go into the registry and bring me file number "10735/82/P".' Grange hung up instantly. 'So now we wait, eh?' He stared at Somerville, who had moved to a side armchair away from the door.

'Now we wait,' Somerville agreed.

It took Detective Chief Inspector Black ten minutes to arrive. He knocked, and was about to enter when Frank Grange met him at the door and took the file without letting the head of E4A into the room. 'Thanks. I'll ring you at your office if I need you. Stay around for a while, will you?'

Black gave a brief nod. 'Whatever you say.'

Grange closed the door and returned to his desk with the folder, which he proceeded to open. Inside he found four pages of a bank statement – a bank statement in his name, although he had never seen it before. 'I think you should explain, Somerville!'

'I will, on the way to Carrickmore where you will see the rest of what I have. By the way, don't forget your Walther in the top drawer and don't get any ideas. If anything happens to me, full copies of everything go to the national newspapers.'

Grange pulled on his overcoat and removed the Walther. He was tempted but shoved the gun inside his deep coat pocket.

Somerville stood up. 'Before we leave, ring Black and tell him you have to go out – and make it convincing.'

'Whatever you say, Somerville.' Grange rang the extension again. 'Look there's been a change in plans and I have to go out, urgently. I think you had better get some sleep. I'll be out most of the night.'

'Right, sir. Is there nothing you need help with?' questioned Black.

Grange hung up without reply. Black cursed his ignorance and moved to the window of his office. He was still watching as the two men crossed the well-lit car park and climbed into Grange's silver BMW. He knew the stride of his boss's companion; he would have recognized that walk anywhere.

The journey to Tyrone took about fifty minutes. Somerville never spoke, taking the opportunity to doze in the passenger seat. At the main Cookstown to Dungannon Road, Frank Grange gave him a nudge: 'Here's the signpost for Pomeroy – which way now?'

'Turn left.'

'How much farther?'

Somerville rubbed his eyes. 'Straight through the village and keep going.' They drove past the police station and into the village square.

'They call this "The Diamond",' said Somerville. 'God knows why.'

'Why did you pick this place to hide the books?' Grange was keeping an eye on the road, but he had the policeman's constant underlying curiosity – and strangely, for the first time he was beginning to admire his former quarry.

'It's out of the way and has easy access. It was used by a friend of mine called Magee,' answered Somerville. Grange did not reply.

They travelled another three miles, during which time Barney began to expand on the situation. Finally, a very confused Frank Grange was told to turn right at a sign indicating potatoes for sale. The BMW bumped along a small track until it arrived in the clearing with the disused farmhouse and dilapidated outbuildings. They talked for a few minutes before Somerville finally stepped out of the car.

'I hope you've got a torch.' Grange pulled one out

of the glove compartment. The rain was pelting down and it was slippery underfoot as Grange shone the torch after Somerville, slithering behind him.

'The house is derelict,' shouted Somerville over his shoulder, 'But the outbuildings are used to store hay and stuff.'

'I can do without the guided tour!' grunted Grange. 'Just get to it, will you?'

Pushing through overgrown gardens at the side of the farmhouse, Somerville halted beside the septic tank. 'It's under this lot,' he said as he bent down and felt for a few seconds with his hands. The cover was difficult to manipulate in the dark, but eventually he forced it open to reveal the empty pit. With the aid of the torch handed down by Grange, he found the wire and with one single pull the trap-door came up. 'It's down there, in the blue plastic bag.'

Grange took the torch from him and flashed it into the hide. The small bag was lying beside an old Garand rifle and a folded Armalite.

'Whose are the guns?' he asked.

'A dead man's. He never did put them to good use,' Barney replied.

Grange reached into his pocket. 'You certainly gave us the run-around.' Barney remained kneeling beside the hide and did not look up.

'I loved them. When they died, I died too,' he said. Grange pointed the Walther at his skull; there was a single crack from the small 9mm-cartridge as it exploded in the chamber and Somerville slumped over, motionless. Grange followed up quickly, running the torch's beam over the body.

'That's far enough!' A voice sounded from the bushes. 'Drop that gun!'

Grange whipped the torch round in the direction of the voice but the next moment he was blown off his feet as a bullet ripped into his left side. He landed on the wet grass, face down. His grip relaxed and both torch and pistol were tossed into the darkness. He rolled over slowly on to his back and raised his head as the lone figure approached in the gloom.

'You!' cried Grange.

Detective Chief Inspector Winston Black stood over him, legs astride.

'Sorry it had to come to this. It was the devil's own job keeping up with you on the way here. Where are the rest of the books, then?'

Grange spat at him. 'You bastard!'

Black laughed, picked up the torch and began searching until he found the Walther. He walked to the open hide and flashed the light towards Somerville's body. Then he saw the blue plastic bag; he had to ease himself into the hole to reach it.

A moment later the explosion occurred. Four pounds of commercial, a detonating device and pressure pad had been activated and Black was blown into pieces.

It took several seconds for the debris to settle. Covered in mud and dirt, Frank Grange struggled painfully to his knees and crawled over to Barney's body, which had lain much closer to the source of the explosion than he had. Then slowly Somerville clambered to his feet. The air was still clouded with smoke and dust which intermingled with the steady rain and Somerville appeared to Grange like a risen corpse, covered completely in a layer of dirt.

'Are you all right?' Grange winced.

'Except for a powder burn on my head, I'm still in one piece.'

Grange tried to smile, but the pain of his wound had overcome him.

'I think I'd better get you to a hospital. Come on.' Barney helped the Detective Chief Superintendent to his feet, supporting him on his left shoulder. Grange stared at Somerville with tears in his eyes – a mixture

of pain and admiration for the quarry he had so relentlessly hunted.

'I owe you,' grunted Grange as he was hobbled
towards the BMW.

As Barney raced the car to the South Tyrone
Hospital in Dungannon, Grange tried to keep up a
conversation as he lay sprawled in the rear seat.
'Omagh would have been quicker!'

'Too risky. The noise of the explosion would have
carried. By now the local police will have been alerted
and the Omagh station will be on notice to keep tabs on
the casualty department at their local hospital. Don't
worry, you'll make it OK to Dungannon.'

Grange grunted again, fighting against the burning
pain. 'You know . . . at one point I thought of re-
loading my gun with the live magazine instead of the
one you gave me.' His face contorted as the pain
increased. 'just one more thing. How did you keep one
step ahead of me all the time?'

Somerville grinned into the driver's mirror. 'By
radio. I was in constant contact with your mate, Rose.'

'That son of a bitch!' Grange spat up some blood,
but his temper fused his pain wracked body for a time.
'It's a damned pity all the evidence was blown up with
that bastard back there!'

Somerville was slow to answer as he pushed the
BMW along the winding country road. 'What
evidence? There never was any in the first place – at
least, nothing that could amount to much in a court.
Black's Provo friends panicked; they couldn't see the
grass for the bloody trees! Any half-decent lawyer could
have destroyed any prospect of a prosecution. The only
question remaining unanswered was whether you were
in with the Hawthorne mob or not. And that's what
we had to determine. As it turned out, Black was
planting more evidence against you than me.'

Grange was shattered. 'Well I'll be damned!' he exclaimed.

The BMW screeched to a halt outside the casualty department of the South Tyrone Hospital and Somerville helped Grange out. He could just stand and no more. His shirt, coat and trousers were saturated in blood.

'You'd think I'd peed meself!' laughed Grange as he spat more blood from his mouth.

'By the way,' said Somerville, 'don't say a word about this until you've seen Rose. You're on your own now.'

'What about you?' cried Grange as he hung on to the locked swing doors of the entrance to casualty. But Somerville merely waved goodbye.

The BMW was gone before Grange hit the emergency door-bell. Within moments he was being wheeled towards the casualty room, surrounded by three nurses who were quickly joined by a young junior houseman abruptly roused from a comfortable sofa in the staff common-room.

Frank Grange was still giving orders, even before his examination.

'Sister – or whoever the hell you are – get on to Dungannon RUC. I want the duty inspector here immediately!'

The staff nurse crossed to the wall-mounted telephone and dialled '999'. She looked at the young nurse nearest her. 'Cheeky bugger, isn't he?'

'I heard that, young lady! I damned well heard that!' Grange coughed. The staff nurse raised her eyes heavenwards, then cut the shirt from his body.

9

Thursday 24 June – Hillsborough, County Down
It was 11 p.m. when the Lotus Esprit braked abruptly
outside Eastleigh House, scattering gravel into the
manicured flower-beds. Mark Taylor had always
admired the majesty of the place; it was not so much
a home as a status symbol. But then Ralph Hawthorne
was an establishment, and part of the right-wing infra-
structure that kept Tory governments in power.

The main façade was constructed of granite stone
blocks. Commenced in 1790, the building had taken
fourteen years to complete, along with the ornate
formal gardens. The house had been converted and
modernised in the 1960's, but, except for extensive re-
wiring and plumbing, it had kept its old charm. And,
on precise instructions, the architect had meticulously
ensured that none of the ornate mouldings and panel-
ling was damaged in any way.

The twenty-bedroomed mansion was situated in one
hundred acres of the most exclusive countryside around
Hillsborough. Apart from the Governor's old residence,
Eastleigh House was the finest house in the area, being
one of the main listed buildings in the province.

Mark Taylor did not bother to lock Roland Briggs's
car before striding to the front porch; it was well-lit by
unobtrusive security lights positioned in the ceiling of
the portico. He pressed the brass buzzer to the left of
the great walnut double doors.

'Speak.' The voice sounded clipped and tinny over
the intercom.

'It's Mark.'

The right-hand door clicked ajar and Taylor stepped

into the vestibule. He had only been to Ralph Hawthorne's house once before, when he was still at school, on the occasion when his mother and father had been invited to a garden party held in honour of the late Governor upon his departure from Hillsborough House. It had been a defiant gesture as the Stormont Parliament closed its doors for the last time; it all seemed a long time ago now.

Mark Taylor was greeted by Roland Briggs. 'Thank God you've made it . . . come into the library.'

Hawthorne stood by a drinks cabinet built into the book-covered shelving. Without turning around, he continued to pour from the old bottle of malt whisky. 'Vodka and white . . . isn't it?'

'Yes, thank you,' said Taylor.

'Sit down, will you both?'

The pair sat like schoolboys in the headmaster's study, on a leather four-seater sofa. Drinks were served in silence and only when Ralph Hawthorne had himself sat down in a high-backed winged chair did conversation begin.

'Cheers, gentlemen!' Hawthorne raised his half-filled Waterford tumbler. Taylor could not help but note a certain grimness about the great man, as he smoothed out the paisley patterned silk dressing-gown he wore over a dark red cravat, open-necked shirt and trousers. 'You both know about the Geddis thing. He's disappeared; even the police don't know his whereabouts.'

'Oh, my God!' Taylor muttered.

'It appears that our Mr Somerville, or someone else, has put paid to Geoffrey. I have ascertained that his wife left for Tenerife alone. Mark, did I not ask you to see him off safely?'

'I . . . I was too busy trying to contact you after what happened at that drunken bank manager's house!' replied Taylor, irked by the unfair criticism.

'Well, whatever . . .' continued Sir Ralph. 'The authorities are on to us. Today I received a telex from our Zurich bankers. It would appear that the Swiss are carrying out an investigation and our account has been frozen. Further, I am reliably informed that we three may be indicted shortly for our recent ventures.'

Briggs shook his head. 'Even if they do freeze the account, they can't keep it frozen for ever. It's part of the free-standing of Swiss banking. Also, no one has any concrete proof of our involvement. Geddis can say so much, but there is nothing they can pin on us officially. Anyway, we've always got the Dublin accounts along with our proletarian "freedom fighters", if the worst comes to the worst.'

'Have we? I'm not so sure that the Dublin government will not resort to similar action.' He went over to the eighteenth-century French desk and picked up some photographs. 'These arrived in my private mail today, delivered by hand.'

Taylor and Briggs flicked through six photographs. The first two depicted Hawthorne and Williams meeting Gadaffi. The other four were more startling; they showed Williams, Taylor and Briggs around a large table in conversation with identifiable members of the Provisionals' Army Council, in a Dublin hotel suite.

Briggs spoke first. 'Our only full meeting and someone . . . How on earth? It's unbelievable!'

'Unfortunately, it's quite believable,' said Sir Ralph languidly. 'We, gentlemen, are dead – if not by our own government, by our co-conspirators.'

'Aren't you jumping to conclusions, Ralph?' asked Taylor.

'Am I?' Sir Ralph raised an eyebrow. 'This afternoon I tried to contact some of my friends in government. None was available. I left messages for over a dozen people and not one responded. I also spoke with our bankers in Dublin and asked them to begin the transfer of monies to their German counterparts. They refused – ever so politely, and with an impenetrable series of excuses.'

Briggs spoke up again. 'Ralph, excuse me, but even if these photographs are made public or whatever, we still have time to get away. I can see considerable legal problems in trying to present them to a court.'

'Who's talking about courts, you stupid boy!' Sir Ralph actually raised his voice. 'We are finished! Now, I have called you here to give you some serious advice. One, we are all under surveillance and have been for some time. Two, the government cannot afford the embarrassment of our trial. And three, as I said, if they do not remove us there are those who will.'

'There must be a way out of this!' Taylor emptied his glass and set it on a side table.

'There is. That is why I called you both here. I have made you both into millionaires and I know what I'm talking about. It is time to consolidate, to cut losses and remaining investments.'

'Just what are you saying? That we should run?' cried Taylor.

'It's every man for himself. We can no longer meet together. I have here all details of your apportionments of the Dublin and Swiss accounts. I imagine that in time they will in fact be released to you.' He handed over two white envelopes. 'With this I wish you "Bon Voyage"'. Sir Ralph smiled and stood up, pressing a silver button on the side of the marble fireplace. 'There will be absolutely no further contact from this date. My personal advice to you young men is quite simple: get out of this country as fast as you can.'

There was a knock at the door and an elderly butler entered.

'Franklyn, will you please show these gentlemen out.'

They left the room in silence. Taylor turned for a

277

moment in the doorway to say 'Goodbye', but Ralph Hawthorne had his back to them, watching six photographs burn on the roaring fire.

Outside, both men shivered in the chill night air.

'What do you make of all that?' asked Briggs.

'Panic.' Taylor handed him the car keys. 'You drive.'

'Do you really believe that?'

'No, but it was a nice idea!' Taylor laughed mirthlessly. 'He's right; we have to get out of here.'

'I hear it's nice in South Africa at this time of year,' said Briggs.

Taylor was in the process of clearing out the wall safe in the main lounge of their luxurious first-floor Malone Road apartment when the doorbell rang.

Briggs ran out of the bedroom and joined his friend in the hallway. 'Expecting anyone?' Taylor was still clutching the papers he had removed from the safe.

'Don't answer it, douse the lights,' whispered Briggs.

Taylor dashed into the lounge, hitting the master switch which extinguished the room's wall and ceiling lights. Through a chink in the heavy curtains he had a limited view into the forecourt below, where he could see the Lotus but nothing else.

The doorbell rang again.

Briggs was at the doorway, silhouetted by the hall light. 'What shall we do?' cried Taylor.

'Shut up, will you! Be quiet!' hissed Briggs. He moved stealthily towards the solid reinforced front door and paused. After a few seconds he heard heavy footsteps receding down the corridor outside.

Taylor was still standing at the break in the curtains when he saw Anthony Campbell cross the parking area. Campbell stopped beside the Lotus and looked up suddenly towards the window, Taylor moved back sharply, but he knew he had been spotted.

They waited until after 7 a.m. that morning before

executing their evacuation plan. The Lotus was ruled out in case of a booby-trap. Instead, they chose to sneak along the rear fire escape; this led into a secluded garden which they crossed with all haste. Unobserved, they slipped into the tree-lined grounds of the largest house in the area. It was constructed in red brick, the empty offices of a veterinary surgeon; Taylor had picked it because it was easily distinguishable amongst the rows of large detached houses on the Avenue, and he knew the place to be vacant until 8.30 a.m. each day.

As arranged, they found the silver Ford Escort Ghia in the secluded side parking area of the surgery. Taylor had persuaded his secretary, Amanda Jamieson, to leave her car there. She had reacted eagerly to the idea of helping her boss, even though the phone call to her Lisburn Road flat had come at the unearthly hour of 4.45 a.m. She had always been pleased to lend her assistance and although well aware of his homosexual tendencies, she had nevertheless struck up a strong relationship with him. She was a strikingly beautiful girl, whose initial nervousness had been overcome by his obvious sincerity and frankness. For the first time since adolescence, she had met a man who was not preoccupied with bedding her.

Amanda had been astonished by Taylor's bizarre request that morning and the nervous tension in his voice concerned her, but she complied with his instructions, writing down every detail to avoid mistakes. She didn't notice the telephone line click twice after her boss had replaced his receiver.

Taylor found the ignition and door-key concealed on top of the rear off-side wheel. Unlocking the car quickly, they sped away towards Newtownards on the shore of Strangford Lough. The Escort pulled into the

Flying Club off the Greyabbey Road. It was a fine morning. 'Good flying weather,' commented Briggs.

'The way I feel, I'd take off in a Force 10 gale,' said Taylor grimly.

The twin-engined red and white Cessna was standing on the side of the main runway apron. A small white lorry was parked beside the aircraft and a lone figure in brown overalls stood beside it.

The Escort came to a halt alongside the aeroplane and the two men alighted. While Taylor removed the cases from the boot, Briggs strode over to greet the little man.

'Morning, Jimmy.'

'Morning, Mr Briggs, sir. The baby's all tanked up as ya asked me.' He touched his cap as he spoke.

Briggs removed a plain brown envelope from his pocket. 'A small token of my appreciation, Jimmy. Sorry I got you up so early.'

'Thank you very much, sir.' The man took the envelope nervously, hands shaking. 'Well, then,' he said, 'I'll be off now.'

'You made no mention of this to anyone, Jimmy, did you?' asked Briggs.

'Oh no, sir! Not me. I just done as ya told me on the phone, charging the fuel and service check to your Club account as ya ordered.'

Roland Briggs patted him on the shoulder. 'You had better be off now, Jimmy, thank you.'

'Oh, right! Right ya are, then.' Jimmy fiddled with the envelope before hurriedly driving the tanker towards the cluster of club buildings which lined the airfield apron.

Pre-flight checks complete, Roland Briggs steered the aircraft to the tip of the runway. Within thirty seconds, they were fully airborne, climbing high above Strangford Lough and circling left across the Ards Peninsula. He had decided to fly southwards, using the Irish Sea route and keeping to within four to five miles of the coastline before turning inland south of Dublin. He began to calculate their flying time to Shannon Flying Club and its private airstrip.

They had reached the half-way stage when the explosion occurred. The little aircraft plunged towards the white rolling waves and disappeared beneath the swelling surface.

Geoffrey Williams heard the announcement of the aircraft crash on the 10 a.m. news. It was his second dismal day of house arrest. The man from British Intelligence had given him two options, one of which he could not refuse. The collated Intelligence presentation on the subject of his father's death had been designed for impact, and it worked. Williams was devastated.

They had left the file with him, but had not discussed the matter further. Maureen, the housekeeper, had been given the week off on full pay, his telephone calls were intercepted and his house line was dead to him. He was pacing the plush study when David Keating came in.

'What the hell's happening?' asked Williams. 'That air crash. The news said a private flight from Newtownards. Two businessmen missing. It's Briggs and Taylor, isn't it?'

'Yes,' replied Keating coolly.

'Why?' shouted Williams. 'Who did it?'

'You people made a lot of enemies,' said Keating. 'Your Provo friends don't want you any more.'

'You promised me protection! An opportunity to even a family score. My heritage! My rightful heritage!'

'Our proposal is terminated. Plans have changed.'

Williams continued to shout abuse at Keating as he went to the bookcase beside the Japanese cabinet and pulled open the drawer.

'Looking for this?'

Williams turned to see David Keating pointing the Beretta pistol at his head.

ITN's 'News at Ten' programme gave further details of the air crash off the eastern coastline of Ireland. The male announcer continued: 'It has now been revealed that three persons are believed to have been aboard the Cessna twin-engined aircraft.' A map depicting the crash location flashed up behind him. 'Two bodies have been recovered by Irish Air and Sea Rescue, and Coastguard agencies. The Royal Navy frigate *HMS Gwent* is now in the area and has joined in the search operation; it will remain there until first light tomorrow. Ulster authorities have now released the names of two persons known to have been on the aircraft. They were Roland Briggs, aged forty, a well-known builder and businessman, and his associate Mark Taylor, aged twenty-six. Both men were single and from Belfast. The third man's name has not yet been released; it is believed his next of kin have yet to be informed. Now over to Mary Edgar in Dublin for the full story.'

The screen cut to a scene at Dublin Coastguard HQ, where a young brunette with a solemn face was standing outside the entrance to the building.

'The cause of the air crash is not yet clear. Officials from the Civil Aviation Authority are now in charge of the investigation, and rescue and recovery ships have been over the crash scene all afternoon. First indications are, however, that pilot error or malfunction may have caused this, the eighth air tragedy in the British Isles this year. I have with me now Mr Niall Tomlin, an aviation official.' The camera brought a man into focus and the reporter continued: 'Mr Tomlin, just how is the recovery operation progressing?'

The man spoke with a strong Dublin accent. 'We

have located surface wreckage and the bodies of two male persons. The main wreckage lies in deep water five miles off Wicklow Head; we have established the exact location of the aircraft and from our initial findings its fuselage appears well intact.'

'Intact? What does that indicate exactly?'

'It is hard to see any particular reason why the crash occurred. There are signs that the passengers tried to get out, suggesting the aircraft's gradual descent and a possible attempted surface landing,' replied Tomlin.

'So you can't tell us what caused the crash?' she persisted.

'It's early days yet. Our experts are on the scene and as you know, we are still trying to locate the body of the third man.' Tomlin was solemn.

'He was definitely known to be on board?'

'Yes, we have that confirmation from the Northern authorities.' He was becoming agitated by the questioning. 'The aircraft was on a private flight from Newtownards, just outside Belfast.'

'Mr Tomlin, thank you.' The reporter turned to the camera. 'This is Mary Edgar, News at Ten, Dublin.'

The scene switched back to the studio in London where the presenter continued: 'We have just received news of the third missing man. He has been named as Geoffrey Williams, an architect and businessman, also from Belfast and a senior associate of the two men named. And now on to Lebanon, where renewed fighting has broken out again between – '

Ralph Hawthorne switched off the television set in his study, then returned to the French desk and sat down heavily in the ornate Italian high-backed chair. His eyes were closed as if he were trying desperately to shut out the world.

At 11.40 p.m. Cecil Rose was shown into the library by Franklyn, the elderly butler.

'I knew you'd come eventually.' Sir Ralph stayed where he was at the desk.

'It's all over. Your cover is blown,' said Rose.

'How dramatic. What do you intend to do?' asked Sir Ralph wearily.

'When you killed Fred Williams back in 1972, he had discovered how his partner and old friend had been swindling him for years. But he was a decent man and he wouldn't just shop you to the police; he confronted you with the facts instead. Perhaps he actually believed you might pay the money back, but instead you arranged a sailing accident off the County Down coastline. Miraculously you survived, or so it was reported in the press. A perfect alibi. But your plan went wrong. The young policeman in charge of the investigation did his job well and he assembled enough evidence to make you face charges. That's when you first met Detective Chief Inspector Black, then a local CID Sergeant in Newtownards. He had a price and you paid it. You've been paying it ever since, except that the initial bribe developed into a business relationship from which you both profited. Then your greed really took hold and you entered the arms trade. We were on to you after your 1980 exploit, when your chums tried to obtain SAM systems from the Libyans. You got too big for your boots, didn't you?'

'Do please go on. Your imagination astounds me, Rose.' Hawthorne smiled sardonically.

'Through your banking contacts, you knew of the impending proposal for an Anglo-Irish settlement. By manipulating your financial empire and terrorist puppets, you were in a position to ensure its failure, which in turn would be very much to your benefit. It's probably the main reason you kept your hand in, supplying the terrorists as and when required, sometimes for money but more often for services rendered – business rivals destroyed and obstacles in your path removed. Of course, Black was always three moves ahead of everyone around you.'

'Your hypothesis amazes me, Rose. If I am who you say I am, then why have I permitted you to discover all this? Why have I permitted you to live?'

'You could have removed me easily, I have no doubt, had it not been for a terrible mistake by your fumbling terrorist friends. They messed up the assassination of a police inspector who had apparently discovered a low-level chink in the terrorist organisation's armour. They killed his family instead, and you had never envisaged a scenario where an ordinary man would turn on the terrorists. He had training, he had contacts and one of them was me. I played him just as you played Williams, except for one thing: Somerville knew when he started that he was a dead man; it didn't matter to him.

'I used him because we knew someone high up in the RUC was connected with you and therefore the IRA. My initial briefing on coming to Ulster was to collect all the information I could on you, but the main part was to nail that man. And we had our suspicions – you saw to that. Enough innuendo and a clever trail pointed the finger well and truly at Frank Grange. He was the perfect fall guy – obtuse, aggressive, a policeman who went by the book. But once again, you got too greedy. As you saw from the photographs I sent, you were tracked down in Libya and on return your RUC contact had to collect his cut. The exchange at the Union Club, like all your other exchanges, would have gone undetected except for a distinctive ring on your contact's right index finger. The policeman whom you failed to kill recognized the ring and the disguise could no longer hide the man who had once been his friend. You had him well placed – an ideal early warning system, with automatic promotion on the removal of Grange.

'It nearly worked, except that Black failed to understand the significance of Somerville's message to Grange. It was a simple little message left on a mirror, but it made Grange think. That was our final test on him, and he failed to bite. But your man did! He panicked.

'Grange arranged for the arrest of a suspect called Doyle, but he never ordered the house to be searched. He only wanted Doyle kept safe for a while. A silly move, but then caution was never his strong point. However, your man did more; he knew about the gun just as Grange did, so he went to the Military Intelligence officer for that area and told him to make sure the soldiers accompanying the arresting officer undertook a full search of the place. He too wanted Doyle out of the way, but unlike Grange – whose intention was to keep him locked up for only a few days and then release him after reorganizing his plans to capture Somerville – he wanted Doyle offside for some years, just as you told him.

'Black finally followed Grange and Somerville in the early hours of Thursday morning. Like you, he still thought Somerville had evidence that could link you and your friends to the terrorists. It was a chance we took. Your man was killed when an explosion occurred, but before he died he admitted your part. So now you see, even if you decide to kill me and make it past the front door, that's as far as you'd get.'

'You underestimate me, dear boy.'

Rose had to give his adversary full marks for composure and tried another tack. 'As you told Briggs and Taylor, the IRA won't be happy. They've already put paid to your friends and their scorpion's tail is still high in the air!' Rose moved towards the fire and warmed his hands.

Hawthorne's mind was racing, analysing the options

that remained to him. He was extremely annoyed at failing to anticipate the bugging of his own study.

'To quote your terrorist associates, they do not accept failure well. Too many of their own have perished for the matter to rest there. Moves are already afoot by the Garda to track down the ill-gotten gains in their Dublin accounts, and that really is going to sting!' He turned from the fire. 'No, Sir Ralph – you have, as they say, had it. Especially when they hear you've been working for British Intelligence all along!'

Sir Ralph pulled absent-mindedly at his left ear.

'The last lot of arms you supplied to them was "spiked". Our people intercepted the shipment and doctored all the weapons, rendering them useless and booby-trapping several more so as to explode in their faces when examined. Also, some of the money you passed to Gadaffi was replaced with counterfeit notes, and you know what they are capable of!'

'I'm sure this is all very amusing,' said Hawthorne, but his face looked grey and strained.

'You made one colossal mistake which overshadows everything else and it assisted me in obtaining Cabinet approval to take the gloves off. You knew from your contacts inside Latin America what the Argentines were planning. You even went to New York and met a certain General Jorge Manzano in March; he also happens to be the Argentine Military Attaché in Washington. You calculated that Galtieri would invade the Malvinas, and you also correctly anticipated the reaction of a British government with a bloody nose. But you failed to assess your contact. Manzano was not the lackey of the Junta, and had no desire to help precipitate a war which in time could engulf his country, already threatened by Chile on her doorstep. He spoke to his American counterparts and you eventually became part of Reagan's "material aid". In turn London was informed; it was the confirmation we

needed. And when you cancelled your French nego-
tiations for the Exocets, you had fallen right into the
net.' Rose walked over to the door. 'In the morning
the police will be calling to arrest you. The holding
charge will be arms smuggling, but it won't stick. You
will be released eventually, and I have no doubt your
IRA friends will be waiting to escort you home!'

There was no reply. Sir Ralph Hawthorne sat with
his head in his hands.

'Goodbye, Sir Ralph.' Rose turned and walked out.

After several minutes Hawthorne telephoned his
Dublin contact. 'This is Father Mulally. Let me speak
to David.'

An old lady's voice answered. 'There's no one here of
that name, Father. Ya must have the wrong number.'

'Listen, you idiot! This is Father Mulally, do you
understand?'

'There's no need to shout, Father. Ya have the wrong
number. Perhaps ya should try again. Good evenin',
Father, I'm sorry now.' She hung up.

10

The blue Volvo Estate car turned towards the hangar on the edge of the RAF complex at Aldergrove. Used mainly for long-term storage, it sat almost unnoticed, except that night the immediate area and ten foot-high wire fencing was ringed by RAF police and dog patrols. The mammoth fifty-foot-high hangar doors were ajar and a ray of yellow light shone out, casting ghostly shadows beyond the waiting giant C-130 Hercules Transport aircraft outlined in the patchy fog.

As the Volvo came to a halt, a black-clad figure silently crossed the tarmac, undetected and inside the temporary security cordon.

Somerville alighted from the car and shook hands with McCabe, who had been waiting at the hangar.

'If I'd known you were with us, I'd have given you an easier time back there at the house,' said McCabe.

'If you'd known, it would have made no difference. You had a job to do.'

'The boss has arranged for you to have a quick transfer to RAF Brize Norton. I'm afraid they haven't told me what's happening to you after that,' McCabe smiled.

Somerville turned his head towards the aircraft when the four 4,508-hp Allison T56-A-15 turbo-props began a deafening rev-up as the pilot maintained the engine temperature.

'You'd better get on board,' said McCabe, seeing the pilot wave frantically from the cockpit window. 'He's only got limited clearance to the Civil Airport's runway and this bloody fog's closing in fast!'

Somerville glanced briefly towards the open belly door of the aircraft.

'So, goodbye then!' McCabe was almost consolatory. 'If it means anything, you're one of the best . . . I'm glad you were on our side after all!'

Somerville glared back. 'You really don't understand, do you? I never took any side except my own.' He squeezed McCabe's arm to emphasise the words. 'Just like you, I was used – expendable right up to the end!'

McCabe regretted having opened the conversation and he seized the moment to shake hands again, but Somerville had turned away and was jogging towards the aircraft. With the roar of the engines the crack from the Browning pistol failed to register with anyone. Somerville was spun sideways by the impact of the 9mm-slug as it ripped into his right shoulder.

McCabe tugged at the spring-loaded holster dangling under his left armpit, withdrawing the Colt .45 pistol from its upturned position at lightning speed. The black-clad gunman had already reached Somerville, now sprawled on the wet tarmac over 200 feet away from McCabe's position. McCabe could just make out the outline of a tall balaclava-veiled figure as he aimed towards the still form.

McCabe yelled and began to run forward and, alerted by the sudden movement, the gunman dropped into a crouch and spun round. McCabe was closing fast as the Browning fired and two bullets tore into his left thigh and kneecap. He crumpled to the ground, losing grip of the Colt, and could only stare in defiance as the gunman took a steadied aim.

The man's finger had just begun to tighten on the trigger when a stiffened leg jabbed, heel first, into his right side. He gave a squeal, as the sharp pain shot through his body, and struggled to regain his balance, but before he could get up Somerville was upon him like a wild-cat, ignoring the wound to his shoulder. Before the gunman could counter-attack, another high kick struck him squarely on the chest and he reeled backwards, choking desperately for air but still firmly clutching the Browning in his right hand, punching it towards Somerville as he fought to regain his balance. Somerville expertly parried the weapon with the outward swing of his left forearm. The gun cracked again, but the bullet had whistled past Barney's ear as he swung a left hook into the side of the gunman's face.

'Get down!' screamed McCabe, who had recovered his gun and was now trying desperately to get in a clear shot, but the constant thundering of the aircraft's engines obliterated his words.

Instantly, Somerville was again at close quarters with his attacker, who had recovered sufficiently to crash his right knee upwards into Barney's groin. Somerville gritted his teeth against the pain and the sickness welling in his stomach and before the gunman could topple him, grabbed for his throat – but he missed, only ripping the nylon balaclava from the man's head. He fought desperately to stay on his feet, but with his fresh wound he was no match for a fit assailant. Nevertheless, he managed two jolting jabs to head and rib-cage before the Browning came crashing down on his neck. It was the deciding blow and Somerville collapsed at the gunman's feet. As he struggled to get up, a boot lashed into his shattered shoulder and he reeled backwards once more.

McCabe forced himself on to both elbows, instinctively discharging his gun. Within a split second the adapted mechanism automatically discharged eight tracer rounds towards the gunman, but the elusive target had already changed position, diving and rolling to one side, and avoiding the phosphorous slugs. As McCabe fumed and fumbled to reload, the gunman was already lining the night sights on his head.

'No! For God's sake! No!' screamed Somerville as he attempted to rise and stagger towards the gunman. The tall black-clad figure pivoted sharply and grinned as he took aim.

Somerville glanced towards McCabe but it was no use. McCabe's gun would not be reloaded in time.

'Go on! Shoot, you bastard! Shoot!' he urged, looking steadily into the gunman's eyes.

The man kept smiling as he fired once more into Somerville's chest. The 9mm-bullet crashed into him like a pile-driver, hurling him violently off his feet and on to his back.

Immediately an RAF policeman armed with an SMG appeared, ducking the aircraft fuselage, but before he could assimilate the situation a bullet had hit him squarely in the forehead.

Somerville was lying face up, but still conscious. Slowly he forced himself on to his right side to try to prevent the blood from filling his lungs and throat. He spat the bright orange-red froth from his mouth as he lay there, helplessly watching the assassin disappear across the runway and through the gap in the perimeter fencing. He squeezed his eyes tight shut against the burning pain. Seconds passed like minutes as the pain began to give way to a coldness that seemed to freeze his very thoughts. He opened his eyes to see McCabe hobbling to his side assisted by an RAF Corporal. McCabe eased down uncomfortably on the wet tarmac beside him.

'Took your time . . . getting here,' whispered Barney.

McCabe could just make out the words as he moved closer to exclude the aircraft engine noise. 'You saved my life back there. He would have killed me, if you hadn't intervened. You fool! You bloody idiot!' Tears began to trickle down McCabe's rugged features.

Somerville forced a smile. 'They say . . . if you look a man in the face he'll find it harder to kill you. Looks like they were wrong . . . doesn't it?' He coughed again violently, vomiting more bright blood on to the ground. McCabe placed an arm around him until the retching stopped. Two aircrew from the Hercules ran forward, one carrying a medical bag.

'Look after him!' McCabe said to the RAF Corporal. 'Don't just stand there, man. Help me up!'

The fouled-up attack had delayed the gunman, and the perimeter patrols he had so easily eluded earlier were now on full alert and converging on the scene. He was feeling more confident, having slipped through the perimeter fence without another confrontation, when suddenly a flare shot high into the fog above the airfield. Before it exploded he had sought painful refuge in the cover of some gorse bushes. The flare exploded, illuminating the entire area as it began to fall earthwards suspended from a tiny parachute. He glanced back toward the aircraft to see RAF police and soldiers running in every direction and at least four Land-rovers converging on the Hercules, now lavishly bathed in a surreal brightness in the mist.

He began crawling forward again and had only advanced several feet when his left leg became hopelessly entangled in some barbed wire; he tried to kick himself free for several seconds before accepting the futility of his actions. Then he worked steadily, pulling at the rusty wire until he was almost clear when the first Alsatian found him. As the young bitch tried to close her jaws on his neck, he violently yanked the animal's front legs apart. The bitch yelped as she fell on one side, but before she could turn on him in a renewed attack, the gunman forced the animal's head upwards, snapping the neck. A second Alsatian pounced before he could retrieve the Browning and began tearing at his free leg, but he found the gun and beat the larger dog with the metal butt until it whimpered into unconsciousness.

He had just managed to free his badly torn left leg when the first RAF police dog-handler caught up with him. The policeman was no match, and as he reached toward him the gunman delivered a single crushing death blow to his throat. The second policeman cocked his 7.62mm self-loading rifle. Having witnessed the fate of his colleague he took no chances, emptying the magazine towards the fleeing figure. He was a novice at night shooting, especially at a moving target. Only one of the powerful rounds connected, smashing into the gunman's right thigh and tearing bone and sinew apart. Assisted by the RAF Corporal, McCabe caught up with the gunman who was now lying face down, just twenty yards outside the fenceline and through the opening cut in the wire mesh.

'Cease fire! Cease fire!' he shouted. The prostrate form was suddenly bathed in the headlamps of an RAF Land-rover driving over the bumpy ground towards him. As McCabe was almost on top of him the black-clad torso rolled to one side. The gunman began to yell, pointing the pistol towards McCabe who had no time to recognize the blackened and distorted face of Staff-Sergeant Ian Lawrence before he emptied a fresh magazine from the .45, hitting him point-blank in the stomach and chest. The eight phosphorescent tracer rounds turned Lawrence's black pullover into flame. Smoke was still rising from the wounds, and Lawrence's hands and fingers twitched spasmodically as life ebbed from his body.

'You OK, sir?' asked a frightened-looking RAF Sergeant, but McCabe failed to reply. He bent down and lifted the Browning from the dead man's limp hand. The slide was set to the rear, showing an empty magazine.

'Bloody Norah!' cried one of the other two policemen who had just caught up. 'He never had any ammo left!

God! You were lucky, sir, he definitely was turning over to shoot you. He must have thought he had you.'

'He knew it was empty,' replied McCabe, but the reply was lost on the policeman as they examined the still shape.

'Know him, do you, sir?' asked the Corporal.

McCabe hesitated. 'No.'

'IRA bastard!' snorted the Sergeant, spitting on the ground beside the body. 'Just how the fuck did he get in here?'

'There'll be hell to pay, that's for sure!' replied the third man, looking towards the dead Alsatian guard-dogs and dog-handler.

To their amazement nothing ever came of the incident . . .

All RAF personnel were throughly debriefed and lectured on the severity of breaching the Official Secrets Act. All were then posted away from Ulster immediately, never to meet or work together again. The death of the dog-handler was explained as an accident during routine training . . .

On his return to the Hercules, assisted again by the young RAF Corporal, McCabe found Somerville in the arms of two aircrew and being gently eased on to a stretcher.

'How bad is he?' asked McCabe, looking at the unconscious man.

'Bad,' responded a Flying Officer who was standing over the stretcher, holding a bottle of plasma and a plastic feeder tube connected intravenously to Somerville's bared right forearm. 'Took two in the chest, only just missed his heart. He's lost a great deal of blood.'

'OK. Get him on board and get clearance for take-off,' ordered McCabe reluctantly.

'What?' retorted the Flying Officer. 'I've already contacted RAF ground control to send a field ambulance.'

'Cancel it! And get the hell out of here!' bellowed McCabe over the engine noise.

'But he'll die! He'll die before we get to Brize Norton!' the Flying Officer shouted back.

'That's an order!' McCabe grabbed the man by the shoulder. 'Get out of here immediately. It's a matter of state security and that's final!'

The officer reacted sharply. 'I don't know who the hell you are – ' he began, but before he could finish McCabe shouted at the RAF Corporal still supporting him. 'Corporal! You will arrest this man if he fails to take off now!'

The Flying Officer gazed at Somerville, now deathly pale from loss of blood.

'Lift him! Get him on board, and be quick about it.' He ran alongside the stretcher until it was eased through the open hatch. His final glare at McCabe did not go unnoticed as he pulled the door closed. The giant Hercules slowly moved into the fog, the Allison engines resonating to a new pitch. Lewis McCabe was helped to the Volvo, only then becoming aware of the pain in his left knee-cap. The Hercules roared down the main runway and disappeared into the fog. 'Tell me, Corporal, just how long does it take to fly to Brize Norton?'

'By Herc, sir? Oh, I should say about fifty-five minutes, but probably more in this weather.' The RAF policeman raised McCabe's injured leg gently on to the seat. 'Try to keep it up sir, it'll stop the blood loss.' He removed his tie, strapped it around McCabe's thigh and tightened it with a biro pen stuck into the knot. 'Keep it tight, sir, I'll tell you when to ease the pressure every few minutes.'

As the Volvo arrived at the military wing of Belfast's Musgrave Park Hospital, McCabe was immediately wheeled inside to the operating theatre. He asked the

Army major who was preparing him for surgery only one question.

'Could a man, a fit man, survive for over an hour with gunshot wounds to the chest?'

He failed to get his answer, and drifted into unconsciousness as the general anaesthetic was fed into the back of his right hand.

Franklyn was up early as usual and at 6 a.m. he began his morning routine – preparing the kitchen for the arrival of the daily cook and housekeeper, Mrs Reid, from Hillsborough village. After stoking the gigantic Aga cooker, he began his rounds of Eastleigh House, firstly to set the breakfast room and then to see to the main lounge. His final pre-breakfast chore was to clear out the fire in the master's library; the room was often kept locked and only cleaned by Mrs Reid under his personal supervision. He tested the door, found it open and entered into the darkness of the room. As he went over to the large bay window and the thick curtains, the morning sunrise filled the large room with a pink glow.

The old butler cried out in horror as he saw his master in his favourite fireside chair. Sir Ralph was white and lifeless, his eyes staring from his head. A little blood was congealed around his mouth and nose, and only a small hole was apparent at his left temple. His ex-service .45 Webley revolver lay on the floor beneath his outstretched arm.

Sunday 27 June – Ward 2, Musgrave Park military wing, Belfast

Lewis McCabe lay in a private room away from the other members of the armed services resident in the military wing.

He was entered in the hospital register as Captain Ford, Royal Corps of Transport, Thiepval Barracks,

Lisburn. He had no difficulty in remembering the name, since he had used it many times before.

Cecil Rose walked into the first-floor room unannounced and shut the door behind him, pulling the cover across the door's viewing panel. 'I hear you will soon be out of here,' he smiled.

'The sooner the better,' replied McCabe. His distinguished visitor set a small basket of fruit on a side trolley before sitting down.

'How are things?' asked McCabe.

'Fine,' replied Rose as he picked at one of the grapes. 'My favourite, you know.'

'No, I didn't,' said McCabe. He paused. 'You never told me how Somerville knew to contact you in the first place.'

'He always knew I was in the Province. When he was fitted up he contacted me, but then the terrorists murdered his family. Later I agreed to help point him in the right direction, that's all.'

'So that's how he had access to the explosives.'

'And information . . . when necessary,' replied Rose as he picked another grape.

'It was a set-up all along!' McCabe was annoyed at not having been privy to all the facts.

'No, he was on his own. He ran the risks and he knew the outcome.' Rose popped a grape into his mouth.

'Poor bastard!'

Rose gazed out of the window.

'Just as well I put him on that bloody plane when I did.' McCabe read something in Rose's eyes. 'He *is* dead, isn't he?'

Rose looked at him. 'Could a man with two 9mm-parabellums lodged in his body survive an arduous air trip of an hour, followed by another journey to some out-of-the-way hospital?'

McCabe stared closely at his inscrutable MI5 master, but he could not gauge the truth. 'I suppose it was a stupid question to ask. What happens now? What about his killer?'

'Under a "John Doe" as the Americans say.'

'I knew him.' McCabe pulled himself up in bed. 'From the debriefing after the Castlereagh thing. I recognized the face after I killed him. The poor bastard, he actually wanted me to do it; he pointed an empty pistol at my head!'

'It was his only way out, Lewis.' Rose stood up and replaced his chair at the bottom of the bed.

'But why did he do it?'

'Somerville had wiped out most of his original team. What better motive is there than revenge?'

'How the hell did Lawrence know Somerville would be there at that time?'

'Who knows?' replied Rose. Seeing the same look again, McCabe now knew the truth – or at least part of it.

'It was you, wasn't it?'

Cecil Rose opened the door. 'Lewis, national security is a very dirty game, sometimes requiring dirty decisions.' Then he was gone, the door left open against the wall. As he walked down the empty corridor he could hear the shouting.

'You're a bastard! Son of a bitch! I resign! Do you hear me?'

He would forgive Lewis McCabe. In fact, he had no doubt that his aide would apologize upon his return to Lisburn. He smiled gently as he began to descend the staircase, past the duty nurse now rushing towards the noisy patient in Room 3.

Epilogue

Wednesday 28 June
Sir Ralph Hawthorne's funeral was one of Ulster's grand affairs, attended by representatives from the Northern Ireland Office and Her Majesty's Government. They were joined by many local dignitaries and representatives. The manner of his death, explained by a police spokesman as 'suicide', was puzzling to many gathered at Belfast's St Anne's Cathedral. Later, a pathologist's report was submitted at the Coroner's inquest which revealed Sir Ralph to be suffering from an incurable disease. This was corroborated by the submission of further medical evidence from a police investigator, which showed the deceased to have been receiving private treatment for the same terminal diagnosis.

Thursday 29 June
Detective Chief Inspector Black's remains were buried informally and without police honours, at his family's specific request. The funeral was well attended and the press release from RUC Headquarters indicated the police officer to have died while examining a terrorist arms cache in the course of his duty. The details were minimal, the explanation was for 'security reasons'. Present at the funeral was Detective Chief Superintendent Frank Grange in a wheelchair; he attended against his doctor's wishes and stayed at the widow's side throughout the service.

When the bodies of Williams, Briggs and Taylor were released by the Dublin authorities, they were in sealed coffins. If any inquisitive person had been suspicious enough to investigate, there would have been no evidence of any gunshot wound on the body of Geoffrey Williams. His remains were mutilated and headless, which was put down to the nature of the crash and the time spent in the sea. On 1 July 1982 a cavalcade of three hearses passed unimpeded over the Newry border crossing. The services and burials were separate affairs, and in the troubled times of Ulster went ahead unnoticed. Julia Williams inherited the mammoth business and returned to live in England with her parents the following month. She placed the running of the business in the hands of Geoffrey's mother and the remaining board of directors, who were joined by Sir Ralph's only son and heir. She wanted nothing more to do with Ulster. The later award of a sizeable building contract in the Falklands did little to impress her; she would never return to Ireland.

The family of Ian Lawrence had to wait almost a month to hear of his death. The Staff-Sergeant was buried with full military honours at a Wiltshire cemetery, his death officially recorded on 24 July 1982 as the result of a military action in South Armagh. The country parish church was filled with the usual representatives of government, the military and police. The official explanation simply stated 'Killed on active service in Northern Ireland'. There was much speculation in military circles with regard to an award of some kind, but Ian Lawrence's widow never received his posthumous George Cross. To his young family it made little difference. He lived on in their memory as a quiet unassuming father and husband.

Glossary

ASU	Active Service Unit (IRA)
Black bastard	Slang term for member of the Royal Ulster Constabulary
'Chummy'	Term given to surveillance subject (MI5/MI6 slang)
DSO	Distinguished Service Order
E4A	Special Branch Surveillance (RUC)
COG	Chief Officers' Group (RUC)
CESA	Catholic Ex-Servicemen's Association
GCHQ	Government Communications Headquarters
HMSU	Headquarters Mobile Support Unit (RUC)
ICP	Incident Control Point
INLA	Irish National Liberation Army
MI5	British Security Service
MI6	British Secret Intelligence Service
MIO	Military Intelligence Officer
MM	Military Medal
MO	Medical Officer (British Army)
MOD	Ministry of Defence
'Muppets'	Term given to covert operatives (Army slang)
NIO	Northern Ireland Office
OOB	Out of bounds
PIRA	Provisional Irish Republican Army
RUC	Royal Ulster Constabulary
SAS	Special Air Service
SB	Special Branch
SOP	Standard Operating Procedure
SSU	Special Support Unit (RUC uniformed back-up to E4A)

Sunray	Commanding Officer (British Army – radio call sign)
TPU	Timer Power Unit (initiating device in home-made explosive device)
UVF	Ulster Volunteer Force (Protestant paramilitary)
VCP	Vehicle Checkpoint
VDU	Visual Display Unit

Jack Higgins
Confessional £2.99

'Do I presume that you gentlemen believe that the man Kelly, or Cuchulain to give him his codename, is actually active in Ireland . . .?'

Mikhail Kelly's credentials were impeccable. Russian mother, Irish father hanged by the British. He could split an apple – or a head – across a large room with a handgun. And his special talent was acting. The KGB gave him the perfect part . . . assassin.

For more than twenty years Cuchulain has created chaos, fear and disorder in Ireland by hitting counter-productive targets on both sides of the border, making fools of British Intelligence and the IRA. But Cuchulain is a man whose time is nearly up.

The one person who can identify him is the beautiful Tanya Voroninova, daughter of a KGB general. And the one person who can persuade her to defect is Liam Devlin, poet, scholar, IRA gunman retired.

Hunted by the combined forces of British Intelligence, the IRA and the KGB who now regard him as an expendable embarrassment, Cuchulain prepares to hit the most counter-productive target of all time . . . Pope John Paul . . .

A Prayer for the Dying £2.99

Now a major film starring Mickey Rourke, Bob Hoskins and Alan Bates

'What do I have to do? Kill somebody?'

Fallon was the best you could get with a gun in his hand. His track record went back a long and shady way.

This time the bidding came from Dandy Jack Meehan, an underworld baron with a thin varnish of respectability. Not exactly the type you'd want to meet up a dark alley.

The job Dandy Jack wanted doing was up North, but when Fallon got there he soon found himself changing sides. Which put him in opposition to Meehan. A place where life expectancy suddenly gets very short indeed.

Jonathan Havard
The Stockholm Syndrome £2.95

In the global war of the terrorist, the bizarre bond of affinity between the hostage and the hostage-taker through days of nightmare tension has become known as . .

The Stockholm Syndrome

Rhys Wyn Owen is a consultant surgeon in a state-of-the-art transplant unit in a South Wales hospital.

He's a man with four women on his mind . . . Alex, the haughty, faithless wife; Nansi, the warm-hearted, warm-bodied lover; and Hannah, the lovely teenager turned star patient, who raises the ghost of Helen, the first love who died in a night of blood and horror with Owen's son in her womb.

Suddenly, the surgeon of the troubled heart and healing hands is thrust into a vortex of terror . . .

Torn between the impossible demands of conflicting loyalties, he must take up the scalpel for life or death surgery in the ominous shadow of a loaded Armalite rifle . . .

Blood and Judgment £2.95

Consultant surgeon Michael Brookes has existed in comfortable solitude since his wife's death. His work and his teenage son absorb him totally. Only his neighbour's wife Alison disturbs the calm of his celibate, dedicated life.

Alison's husband Larry is an alcoholic teetering on the verge of self-destruction. His marriage is on the rocks, and his company's vital contract with Teflo, the giant chemical complex that dominates Dunbridge, is about to be cancelled.

Teflo itself has problems. Pushed to the limits by the demands of a multi-million takeover battle, chairman Sir John Anderson makes a decision that will haunt him for the rest of his life – and have catastrophic consequences for Dunbridge, for Michael and Larry, and for the woman they both love . . .

Sweeping relentlessly from tension in the operating theatre to cynicism in the boardroom, from drama in the courtroom to tenderness in the bedroom, *Blood and Judgment* is a thrilling and irresistible novel from a gifted new storyteller.

Ira Levin
This Perfect Day £3.50

By the author of *Rosemary's Baby*

The terrors of *Rosemary's Baby* were the terrors out of mankind's past . . . the terrors of *This Perfect Day* are the terrors that wait in mankind's future . . .

Suspense, love and adventure break through in a horrifying computer-controlled world. A world where sex is programmed weekly, where monthly treatments keep people docile, and where everyone is scheduled to die at the age of sixty-two, for efficiency.

How LiRM35M4419 (the hero of this book) comes into conflict with the forces that control this world makes hair-raising and spell-binding reading . . .

A Kiss before Dying £2.95

Dorothy's murder had been perfect. There were no questions, no suspicion – hence no investigation. Only one thing troubled him. All his careful planning had not advanced him in the slightest. Dorothy's death was a defensive measure. Her father would have cut her off from the Kingship Copper millions once he'd learned she was pregnant.

Still, there were Dorothy's sisters, Ellen and Marion . . .

Martin Cruz Smith
Stallion Gate £2.95

Los Alamos, New Mexico, 1945. Robert Oppenheimer's team of elite
scientists race to develop the atomic bomb that will force Japan's
surrender. Captain Augustino, chief of security, is convinced
Oppenheimer and mathematician Anna Weiss are Soviet spies and
uses Sergeant Joe Pena, Oppenheimer's Indian driver, to prove it.
But Augustino cannot control Joe's mounting inner conflicts of
loyalty – to Oppenheimer himself; to Anna, who becomes his lover;
to his fellow Indians displaced by the vast test site; and to his army
comrades back in the Pacific whose lives the bomb may save . . .

Meanwhile a countdown has begun that will change destiny
itself . . .

'Remarkable . . He has taken a great theme and made the ultimate
horror intelligible. This is a novel of quality and perception and
should not be missed' *BRYAN FORBES*

Nightwing £2.95

Out of the black night in the Painted Desert a grotesque terror
descends. Has it been summoned by the old Hopi Indian, running
coloured sands through his hands into an intricate painting? Black
for death, red for blood.

'I'm going to end the world,' he tells Youngman Duran, a bemused
ex-convict the Hopis have made into a deputy sheriff. Youngman
understands the old man's rage at the humiliations which have been
inflicted upon the Hopis. But still he smiles when he asks, 'When?'

'Today . . .'

Next morning the medicine man is dead. Every night from then on
Death stirs. Its sound is a whisper, its wings are gossamer, its teeth
are razor sharp, its appetite is insatiable. As a carrier of the most
virulent disease known to man, it threatens to exterminate the entire
American Southwest.

The burden of defeating this scourge rests on Youngman, who alone
understands the significance of the painting, and on the obsessed
scientist Hayden Paine, whose life is eaten up by its pursuit . . .

Robert Littell
The Sisters £2.95

In the enclosed world of the CIA, they are known as 'the sisters Death and Night' – Francis and Carroll are a team, an odd couple. Everyone knows who they are, few know what they do.

What they do is plot. Betrayal, defection, assassination. And this latest scheme is their best, the most beautiful operation that has ever existed in the annals of intelligence work.

Two men watch the events from a distance. Because they are vaguely related, and because they direct the sabotage and assassination unit of the KGB, their subordinates refer to them as the Cousins.

Someone is bound to end up victim. But who controls who?

'A fixating read . . . A Moscow defection is arranged, a New York sleeper awakened, bureaucratic spiders weave their webs and men die' GUARDIAN

All Pan books are available at your local bookshop or newsagent, or can be ordered direct from the publisher. Indicate the number of copies required and fill in the form below.

Send to: **CS Department, Pan Books Ltd., P.O. Box 40, Basingstoke, Hants.   RG21 2YT.**

or phone: 0256 469551 (Ansaphone), quoting title, author and Credit Card number.

Please enclose a remittance* to the value of the cover price plus: 60p for the first book plus 30p per copy for each additional book ordered to a maximum charge of £2.40 to cover postage and packing.

*Payment may be made in sterling by UK personal cheque, postal order, sterling draft or international money order, made payable to Pan Books Ltd.

Alternatively by Barclaycard/Access:

Card No. ☐☐☐☐☐☐☐☐☐☐☐☐☐☐☐☐☐☐

Signature:

Applicable only in the UK and Republic of Ireland.

While every effort is made to keep prices low, it is sometimes necessary to increase prices at short notice. Pan Books reserve the right to show on covers and charge new retail prices which may differ from those advertised in the text or elsewhere.

NAME AND ADDRESS IN BLOCK LETTERS PLEASE:

....

Name ——————————————————————

Address ——————————————————————

——————————————————————————

——————————————————————————

——————————————————————————